# WHERE WE STARTED

## STONE RIDERS MC
## BOOK 1

## ASHLEY MUÑOZ

*To Kailey, my first adventure.*
*You entered this world under a star-speckled sky, bursting with colors. I'll never tire of telling you the Fourth of July was really all done in your honor. You're on the cusp of becoming an adult now and I still think back to that chaotically humid night. How I realized you were the culmination of all my fears and hopes.*
*I thought having you would be the hardest part of becoming a parent, but with a horrific realization, it's letting you go that will be my undoing.*

# WHERE WE STARTED

# ONE
## CALLIE

I couldn't recall the air feeling so thick or sticky when I was last here, but then again, I had never chosen to stand in the middle of Rose Ridge cemetery in the height of an August heatwave.

Sweat trickled down my back as the humidity curled around me while I watched the spectacle unfolding below. It was pure stubbornness that had me anchored near the tree, along with a healthy dose of resentment.

Neither the heat nor occasion had stopped the crowd around my father's casket from wearing their typical attire of black leather and denim. I was a little surprised they were listening to the preacher droning on about peace and heaven. My daddy didn't know a thing about either, and if he were alive, he'd laugh at the words and roar off into the sunset on his Harley. He probably would have preferred his body burned, tossed into an empty bottle of Jack, and placed on the mantel in his beloved club house.

He'd have wanted a huge party thrown, with naked women, loud music, and all other forms of debauchery. But because I was his only living relative, this funeral wasn't up to him. It was up to me. I chose an outdoor ceremony, with a preacher, a six-foot hole in the ground, and a gaudy headstone that boasted of his accomplishments in the war and the few years he was a husband. I left out the fact that he was a father, because in the end, he wasn't. Not to me, at least.

The only person who knew I was in attendance today was Killian, whom I had messaged regarding the funeral plans. I knew he'd share it with Red and the word would spread. However, he knew better than to look back here or tell anyone else. As it was, I wore a pair of over-sized sunglasses to conceal my hazel eyes, which were the mirror image of my father's and a dead giveaway that his only living relative was in attendance. My lips were coated with my favorite shade of pink, which seemed to be the only pop of color among the ocean of black before me. My dark dress was itchy, my heels were too tight on my feet, and all I really wanted to do was walk away from the murmur of mourners, the sea of leather, and the heat.

Goddamn it, I *really* wanted to get out of this fucking heat.

"Amen," the crowd rumbled in front of me, and suddenly heads lifted, and I realized I had skipped another prayer. Being on the edge of the ceremony meant I missed nearly every word the preacher said, but I refused to stand any closer. My father's *family* stood around his casket. The people he put above all else in his life, including his only daughter.

The men and women of the Stone Riders Motorcycle Club.

I knew if I looked closely, tears would cloud nearly every eye and a sorrow would hang around their necks, driving their faces downward. I also knew I'd recognize nearly all of them. My father's club bred loyalty, and the Stone Riders were as steadfast as they came, so the mere notion that the initial members wouldn't be in attendance was unthinkable. Which meant half the men and women responsible for raising me were in that group. I didn't want to pity them, nor did I want to mourn my father, and most of all, I didn't want to feel sorry for myself.

So, I stood behind the line. Nearby, to oversee that my money was spent properly, and well, to be honest, I wanted one last moment with my father before he was given back to the earth.

The men near the front moved, bent down to grab a handful of dirt, and then tossed it on the casket. I watched as a few women, wearing leather skirts and tight tops, did the same. My eyes locked on

Red, Hamish, Killian, and Brooks. My heart was a jagged rock, hammering against my ribs.

Once upon a time they were my family, the people who helped teach me to tie my shoes and ride a bike. Red had taught me what to do when I got my period, and how to apply mascara. Hamish taught me how to cheat in poker and the importance of keeping my thumb over my knuckles when throwing a punch. Killian was the closest thing I'd ever had to a sibling, and I knew he was hurting today like I was. All I wanted to do was be with him and mourn the man who'd raised us. He was about as much as my dad as he was Kill's, and yet I was back here, and he was down there.

My lips parted the slightest bit as my toes pressed into the tips of my shoes. The little girl inside of me wanted them today. Seven years had passed since I'd spoken with any of them, including my father. Yet, that brokenhearted little girl wished so badly that they'd look up and turn around. That they'd search for me and pull me into their arms. I gripped the tree behind me just to hold off the overwhelming urge to slip out of my shoes and run down there.

Instead, I watched as more attendees repeated the process of tossing in dirt, over and over, until there was just one person left standing in front of my father's coffin. I imagined what the warm dirt might feel like under their fingers. I pictured the discoloration now under their nails, carrying a tiny piece of my father's resting place with them. It took me back to being ten and camping on the back of the property with my dad, his smile as he took store-bought colored sand and poured it into a jar, telling me it was treasure.

That was before I was old enough to understand that the only treasure he valued was the club.

The group had all departed, gathering near their chrome-laden bikes parked in the grass along the small asphalt path cutting through the cemetery.

The remaining man near my father's casket didn't move. His jeans looked freshly washed, and there weren't any holes in them from what I could tell. His white T-shirt still had the crisp look of a brand-new one pulled from a bundle pack.

The back of his leather cut read *Stone Riders* right above the

insignia of their club—a skull with roses blooming from the eye sockets. Below the skull, sewn into the leather, was a name that caught my
eye. It shouldn't have made my heart thump as drastically as it did.
Still, my eyes narrowed and could have burned a hole in the back of
this man's shoulders as I finally processed who he was and what he'd
become.

*Wes.*

*President.*

Shock had my eyes widening, and my lips parting on a silent
breath.

My stomach churned as thoughts flitted through my mind at a
rapid pace—questions I had no right asking and confusion all swirled
in my chest like a storm cloud. My nose burned, which was usually
the only warning I got before the tears started. So, I dropped the rose
I had intended to place as an act of peace upon my father's grave,
stepped on the petals, crushing them under my heel, and left. With
every stride away from the funeral, I felt pieces of my heart tumble
around, as frail as the petals crushed beneath my feet.

I wasn't supposed to mourn my father.

I wasn't supposed to be affected at all. And I certainly wasn't
supposed to see that Wesley Ryan had decided to stay with the club
*and* had succeeded my father as president.

I blinked, pushing the hurt back. My glasses would hide my tears
if they did fall, but I had promised myself I wouldn't shed a single tear
today. Not one. I was headed right back up to DC. I just had to get
back in the car and ignore the sensation that I was bleeding out every
ounce of hope I'd ever had of the possibility of reconciliation with my
father—*or Wes.*

"Miss Stone?"

I turned quickly on my heel, a tiny yelp escaping my lungs.

"Sorry, I didn't mean to scare you, I just wasn't sure if that was
you or not." A small, thin man held his hands up with a wince.

I adjusted my posture, flicking my gaze over his shoulder to ensure
no one from the ceremony was headed in my direction.

"No, it's fine. I was just lost in my thoughts."

The man's expression stayed even but he took a step closer.

"I'm Earl Staton, your father's lawyer. I saw you rushing off and wanted to stop you before you left."

*Oh.* Lawyer meant he had legal matters to address.

"I just need a few minutes of your time tomorrow. There's a few signatures I need from you."

I tucked my arms in close as a phantom chill found its way to the back of my neck even in the sweltering heat.

"I planned on leaving this evening actually …"

Earl shifted in his suit. It was too big for him, but he still wore it with confidence.

"My office opens at eight, and the meeting won't take long. There isn't much to go over."

No, there probably wouldn't be.

I nodded my agreement. One more night wasn't going to make or break me.

Earl handed me a business card with his office info on it and sauntered off, winding his way along the headstones that littered the grass.

I gripped the edges of the card and continued toward my car. Right before I unlocked the doors and slid inside, I peered over my shoulder one last time. I hated the tug in my belly that demanded I turn around and go cry in front of my father's coffin. One last look, and I'd let him go. But it wasn't the casket that drew my gaze, it was the man standing next to it with his face upturned in my direction.

I hadn't seen Wesley Ryan in seven years, but the letters sitting in my top drawer at home suddenly came to mind. He'd started sending them about three years ago, once a month. I hadn't opened a single one, not after that first letter, nor did I return to sender. I just collected them and hated myself for caring enough to keep them.

What could he have possibly wanted to say?

The last letter he'd sent, two weeks after our breakup, was still fresh in my mind.

*I don't love you… I've only ever pitied you.*

The tight ball of emotion lodged in my throat, rekindling the burning in my nose. I had to get out of there.

I turned around, got into my car, and sped away without another glance back.

# TWO
## WES
AGE 9

IT WAS TOO HOT.

I had told Mom and Dad that there wasn't enough air up on the second floor, but they just told us to sleep downstairs or outside. My sisters kept hogging the living room, and I wasn't about to sleep on the floor.

So, I had the idea to head outside and sleep in my tree house. I wasn't sure why I hadn't thought of it before. Some nights, we'd try to sleep on the trampoline, but the bugs would always drive us back inside. In the tree house, there were sheets over the windows to keep them out, and I could light one of those bug candles to keep them away.

I tugged my blankets and pillows up over my head as I climbed the planks nailed into the bark of the tree. The moon was just a sliver in the sky, so the stars were out, bright and dotting the dark with a million glowing dots. Crickets sang loudly all along the tall grass past the yard, but the sound carrying on the wind from down the road nearly rivaled them.

It was the same thing every weekend. Distant music, the revving of engines and loud yelling. Dad said it was just a bunch of people partying and to not pay attention to it. Mom said it was a bunch of sinners who needed Jesus. My brothers said not to get caught near them because the men and women making all that noise were the most dangerous group of people in Virginia.

Once, we were driving home late one night, and I saw the group outside in the yard in front of the old Stone house. I'd seen some of them around town, and they always looked nice enough. They smiled at people, helped old ladies with groceries, and even helped build a house for the Barclays after theirs burned down. I didn't understand why them being loud on weekends meant they were dangerous, but I suppose it didn't matter much.

Not when it was so hot that I wanted to crawl out of my skin and trade with a snake or a frog. Anything that would feel cooler than this.

I lifted the latch built into the tree house and pushed up until I was crawling through the opening.

The small floor was cluttered with cards and a few board games, like always. I kicked the remnants with my foot, shoving it all to the side so I could create a space for my comforter and pillow. Once it was all ready, I laid down and pulled my arms behind my head.

There was a breeze that drifted over my body, and it felt so nice I closed my eyes and tried to fall asleep.

Right when I was about to nod off completely, I heard the distant sound of feet slapping against the earth and someone breathing hard. I sat up and scrambled to the window, but there wasn't anyone down on the ground.

I then peered over at the house, trying to see in the dark, but nothing moved.

When suddenly the hatch over the opening to the treehouse lifted, and a head popped through.

I yelled and fell backward.

"Shhh! Stop yelling." A person emerged through the hole, and suddenly there was a girl my age crawling toward me. Her dark hair hung in two long curtains on either side of her face as she moved.

"I'm sorry. I won't hurt you," she repeated, putting her hands up.

I calmed, swallowing the last scream while sizing her up. She was small, thin and scrawny looking. I was bigger than her, so there wasn't really any reason to be afraid.

"What are you doing here?"

Her big hazel eyes moved over my face until finally she plopped down on the edge of the blanket.

"I'm Callie."

I put my knees in close on the opposite end of the blanket.

"You homeless?"

Her head swung up.

"No. Just needed to get away for the night. Saturday nights are the hardest."

Something clicked in my brain...the sound from down the road. The pink bicycle I once saw on our way home outside the Stone house.

"You live down the road."

Callie stared at me, then slowly nodded.

"What's your name?" she asked, lifting her head in my direction.

"Wes."

She tucked her knees under her chin, looking off to the side of the treehouse. She wore a T-shirt that swallowed her body so I couldn't even tell if she was wearing shorts underneath. Her bare feet were dirty, but her fingernails were carefully painted a soft pink.

"Can I stay here? I'll be over here in the corner, not bothering you at all. I promise. I just need a place to stay until the sun comes out. They usually stop by then."

"What did—" I swallowed my words, unsure if I wanted to know.

She didn't look over at me, but she must have known what I wanted to ask.

"No one hurt me or anything. I just don't like being there when they open the doors for the other members from out of town. They come from all over and there's more of them than usual. It's too loud. I couldn't hear my cartoons anymore, and I was so tired. I tried to sleep in my dad's room, but he came in with someone and got mad at me."

On instinct, I looked over at my house. It was dark and quiet. Mom and Dad had us all in bed by ten, even on weekends.

Something flickered in my gut like a tiny prick from a knife. I didn't like the way it made me look at her, but I felt bad that she couldn't even sleep in her own house.

I lifted my pillow toward her.

"You can stay."

She held her hand out and carefully accepted the cushion.

"Just for tonight…"

I nodded. "Just this once."

She tucked her arms into her shirt and curled on her side, lying down against the pillow. I stayed on my side of the blanket and closed my eyes, but sleep didn't come. I found myself watching to make sure no one else came up, so she'd be safe all night.

# THREE
## CALLIE

ROSE RIDGE, VIRGINIA, WAS A TINY SCRAP OF LAND HUDDLED AGAINST a wide, long river. The town was old, with weathered brick buildings and thin panes of glass. Wood structures sported chipped paint and were in desperate need of repairs. There were only two major grocers, three gas stations, and a few banks stretched across town. Then there were the coffee huts, and a handful of cafés and clothing shops. Those little shops were the only redeeming thing about this place.

The thought blinked out as quickly as it came in as I considered how untrue that sentiment really was. I used to love this place. I loved everything that made it imperfect, but when I left, I had taken the proverbial paint brush and done a wide stroke across this whole city, painting it all in the painful colors that had shaded my life.

Sliding my jacket on, I cleared my throat to chase away any lingering emotion and pulled on the brass knob of my motel door. Outside, the sky was a gorgeous blue with a streak of hazy white clouds. The sun was blinding, making me dig for my sunglasses. Right as I dipped my face, I heard my neighbors exit their room.

"There's more of them. I'm talking to the manager about it. I heard them all night."

I smirked as I slid on my shades. The three chrome and black bikes that had been parked in the lot overnight had multiplied into ten, and yes, I could hear them partying all night too. But I had learned a long time ago to travel with noise-canceling headphones. The elderly couple in front of me obviously hadn't.

What did they expect, though? The White Knight Motel & Inn wasn't known for being quiet—or clean, for that matter. Which was why I traveled with a sleeping bag. I wasn't picky; I had grown up sleeping in worse.

One of the doors opened a few rooms down, and a figure stumbled outside. Tattooed arms were all we could see under his leather cut until he turned, and I caught sight of his fitted tank top, revealing every single defined muscle along his chest. I wasn't staring, but he caught my gaze as he straddled one of the bikes.

He froze for a second, his lips slung to the side in a sensual smile.

"Hey, Beautiful, wanna come for a ride?" he called to me while pulling on his bucket helmet.

I was frozen for an entirely different reason. Seven years removed from this life still didn't erase the red flags or gut check you obtained while surviving it. This guy was dangerous, I could feel it. I may not know if he belonged to the Stone Riders, without seeing his patch, but there was no doubt there was something dangerous about him.

The elderly couple had said something while loading up their car, but I didn't catch it. I was too busy tilting my wrist to hide my tattoo. Whoever this was didn't need to know who I was connected to.

I shook my head as a way of responding because my throat was tight. Something about him had a trail of angry goosebumps running down my arms. He lifted one of his shoulders before sliding his key in and twisting the handles on his bike. Then in a loud roar, he was speeding off, and that's when I saw his colors.

The back of his vest didn't have the Stone Riders patch.

Instead, it was the Grim Reaper sickle-cutting a skull in half. *Death Raiders.*

The air was trapped behind my breast.

*No, no, no.*

I needed to leave before any more exited the motel. I gripped my bag and sleeping bag and threw them both in the back of my car then got inside and locked the doors.

I held my keys in a death grip as I sat there staring at the steering wheel. The past was a ghost with clawed fingers, raking against my mind as I battled to control my emotions.

*Death Raiders were in Rose Ridge.* Death Raiders were sleeping here, as though they were on vacation. My mind whirled. Had Dad called a truce with them? No way. There's no way in this life he would, not after what happened.

Clenching my fists, I counted to ten and tried to collect my thoughts. A lot of time had passed; maybe there was a reasonable explanation for this, but as I wasn't currently speaking to any of the members from the club and my father, the president, had just died, that meant this little blip would have to go unchecked. I couldn't worry about it. This wasn't my life anymore.

With thirty minutes until my meeting with the lawyer started, my car pulled easily into one of the available spots outside my favorite coffee shop. The fact that The Drip was still open and bustling with people brought me some sense of joy. It was nice to see that some things hadn't changed. Once I had a medium coffee in my hands and had settled back into my car with the doors locked, I pulled my cell phone out. I had a few missed texts from my best friend, Laura, who was pet sitting for me.

> Laura: he's a monster

> Laura: or at least like a goat. I know his breed is technically Great Dane, but he eats EVERYTHING. He tried to eat my Kindle, Callie. My KINDLE.

> Laura: You owe me a thousand dollars in crypto for having to clean up that mess he just made in the street. Yes, the street.

> Laura: Why do you live like this? He's a horse. He just hit me with his tail and now I'm icing my knee. That's not normal.

I smiled, punching out a new text.

> Me: He gives the best hugs. Better than humans.

> Me: Be good to him. It's not his fault he's a giant. Besides, your finished tattoo will look so beautiful. Just think about that.

Since paying for my dad's funeral slightly cleaned me out, I was trading a tattoo for her watching Maxwell. Well, and a few other things. I'd started her mermaid scales a few months ago, and as she helped with things like pet sitting while I took on extra shifts, or went to work-mandated trainings and expos, I would work on her design. It was almost finished and looked incredible.

> Laura: I just went from a medium-sized mermaid to a fucking Loch Ness monster

I sputtered a bit of my coffee, picturing her gorgeous scales transitioning into that creature.

> Me: You're only punishing yourself.

> Laura: I feel like it might scare Maxwell when he sees it, so it'd be worth it. So, off-topic, but are you ready to hear what the lawyer has to say?

The reminder of the meeting pulled me back into the moment, making me glance at the time on my dash. I had fifteen minutes.

> Me: I'm nervous and desperate to come home. I miss my boy.

> Laura: *eyeroll* He misses you too. He keeps sniffing your pillow like a weirdo.

· · ·

Smiling, I tucked my phone away and started the car up. I'd rather sit in the law office parking lot, so I didn't risk being late. Pulling back onto Main Street, I heard the rumble of a motorcycle behind me. Gently sipping my coffee, I peeked into my rearview mirror, nervous that it might be the guy from the hotel.

Chrome gleamed under the early sun as a man straddling a black leather seat made his way down the main artery of town. His dark sunglasses shielded his face, and at this range I couldn't tell who it was, but I saw the red and white patch color for Stone Riders and immediately released a pent-up breath.

Some things would never change, and regardless of all my emotional damage, the safety I felt when I saw that patch would never waver for as long as I lived. Of that, I was positive.

Still, I wanted to get back home, away from motorcycle clubs and ex boyfriends. My life in DC wasn't glamorous or amazing. I didn't have a boyfriend, or a family, or an amazing community in which I took refuge. I had Max, Laura, my chair in the tattoo studio, and a tiny apartment. It was in one of the worst parts of the city, and the danger I was eager to escape here was likely ten times worse in my stairwell alone.

But it was a harbor for my heart.

It had held me and kept me intact seven years ago, when all I wanted to do was fall apart. The city was a rough landscape I learned through trial and error. It was the duct tape to my tattered past, and that shit was still holding. I hated that a tiny, frail piece of me felt like being back here was tugging at the seams of my proverbial patch job. Just a few signatures, and a quick document saying I could sell Dad's car or bike or whatever, and then I'd return to my comfort zone.

The engine behind me cut right, veering off down a different street, and I pushed down the gas a little harder. The sooner this meeting was over the better.

Earl's office sat near the river, with a gorgeous view of the docks and a few fishing boats. His building was freshly painted a beautiful sapphire blue with clever signage. Honestly, it looked like something you'd find in the DC metro area, not small-town Rose Ridge. It spoke to how well Earl must be doing as a lawyer in this area.

I parked, hopped out, and slammed my car door shut, tossing my cell and keys into my purse.

The glass door pushed open easily as I found my way to a neatly organized desk with two chairs positioned in front of it. Earl wore a similar suit to the one the day before, this time in gray. He waved me over, gesturing toward one of the chairs in front of his desk.

"Just finishing up a few copies, help yourself to coffee or water."

There was a cute coffee bar to the left of his desk, but I had already had my fill of caffeine, so I took a seat, kicking my leg over my knee. His office wasn't large, but the windows facing the river offered the illusion of space.

"Okay, we are just waiting for one more and we can get started," Earl murmured, staring down at the pile of papers on his desk.

My brows caved into the center of my forehead as I processed his statement.

"Who else—"

Words died on my tongue as the sound of a motorcycle cut through the office from the parking lot. I turned in my seat to look past the glass door I had come through in time to see someone park right next to my car.

The man cleared the bike and removed his sunglasses. His mouth turned down into what seemed like a natural frown as he traipsed up the few steps to the door. My confusion turned to alarm, smearing my thoughts into a jumbled mess.

*Wes.*

I briskly straightened in my seat, facing forward, as the man made his way inside and bobbed his head at Earl.

"Mr. Ryan, so nice of you to join us. Ms. Stone just arrived, so if you want to take a seat, we'll get started."

My face was suddenly warm. *Why was he here?*

Wes made his way around the chair, and his eyes pinned me down before his body claimed the seat. The intensity of his stare was like stepping into one of those murky lakes that went too deep, too fast. His elbows nearly touched mine with how close the chairs were placed; his knee nearly grazed my foot as he folded himself into the cushioned seat.

I quickly jerked my leg back.

I heard him scoff but didn't pay it any mind.

"Okay, let's get things started," Earl said cheerfully, apparently unaware of the tension between us.

My pulse quickened as two folders were placed in front of us while Earl flipped through a few pieces of paperwork.

"This is the last will and testimony of Simon Stone. Wesley Ryan and Callie Stone are the only two living beneficiaries of his estate."

I leaned forward, feeling heat creep up my neck.

"Sorry, I think there's been a mistake. Wes is not family, so he wouldn't be listed as a beneficiary."

Earl stared at me, blinking, unbothered by my outburst. I could feel Wesley's gaze on the side of my face, but I refused to glance over. I had no idea what his relationship was to my dad, but it didn't change the facts. He wasn't blood. *I was.*

"Right, well, that may be true, but Simon Stone named Wesley in his will. Let's get on with it, shall we?"

Wes stretched in his chair, forcing his knee to take up even more of my space. I was two seconds away from standing for the rest of the meeting.

"Okay, here we go," Earl began. "Simon's bike was left to you, Wesley. He put here in the notes, 'put it on your show.'" Earl looked up from his paper. "Any idea what that means?"

Wes cleared his throat and replied. "Yeah, I have a television show about restoring bikes and occasionally cars..."

His voice was still gravel deep, something that used to feel like midnight velvet against my skin. That tenor was like a rope in the middle of a raging storm. I wasn't as unaware of his life as I wish I was, or as I really should have been. I was well aware of his accomplishments with the digital streaming show. Hell, nearly everyone on planet Earth seemed to know about his freaking series.

According to his Netflix special, he was doing custom work for Hollywood movie stars and even foreign royalty. Did it cut me deeper than a hunting knife when I saw those TV producers zoom in on his chiseled jaw or well-toned body? Fuck yes, it did.

Did I torture myself for days on end, watching all the clips where he'd taken his shirt off and the people on the internet apparently went insane, stitching, duetting, and every other type of sharing to show how drool worthy Wes was? Also yes.

I hated myself for caring. I had moved on. I remember watching that special right after a hookup. I was still pulling up my jeans when Wesley's face popped into view on the television, and my heart nearly flung from my chest. The guy I was with had started telling me all about the famous Wes Ryan, and his garage, and how everyone wanted to have their cars worked on by him.

I remember just sitting there, feeling like I was having an out of body experience.

It was at that point I had kicked my hookup out and cried in the bathtub for an hour. I didn't even fill it with water; I just crawled into the empty basin and begged Max to follow me in so I could lean against his massive chest. He never did, but he placed his face next to mine with a worried look in his blue eyes.

"Wes, he also left you whatever remains in his savings and checking accounts and his investments, which were mostly made to your shop from the looks of it. He had a car—older model—that's been left to you as well."

Suddenly a swarm of insecurity fluttered behind my chest.

What was I here for? My father didn't want me. Of course he'd leave everything he ever owned to Wes, because apparently over the past seven years, he'd become the son he never had.

If all I got was his DVD collection or an old dish set, I was going to scream.

"Okay, that seems to be it for you, Mr. Ryan. Ms. Stone, there's a letter here for you from your father. He asked that you read it privately. You've also been left the property on Belvin Drive. Looks like ten acres in total and a house registered to the Stone Riders Motorcycle Club?" Earl looked up, confused.

His beady blue eyes searched my face, and then Wesley's.

"Do either of you know what that means?"

Wes looked nearly as confused as I felt. I mean, on some level it made sense—it was my childhood home. But why was it registered to the club? I dug deep for the ability to appear smug, but it didn't come, even as I watched Wesley's Adam's apple bob and his square jaw tense. This was obviously not the news he was expecting.

"That's the clubhouse. You're sure you didn't mix up the paperwork? It would have made more sense that he left that to me, or someone who could continue his legacy…it doesn't make sense he'd leave it to Callie."

Okay, that fucking hurt.

I was my father's legacy, and the only reason he wouldn't have left it to me was because he chose his club over me. Also, I hated how Wes saying my name sent butterflies erupting in my chest. Scratch that, they were moths. After all this time, the dust was being kicked up, so they were absolutely moths.

Earl went back through the papers but shook his head.

"I verified all of this myself, ensuring Simon knew exactly what he was doing. Maybe the letter Callie has will explain things better."

Our eyes all landed on the letter in question. I leaned forward to snag it before Wes got any ideas.

"Well, that's it. Wes, you've got what you need. There's bank passwords in here and a list of assets. Callie, within the next few weeks the title of the property will be signed over with new paperwork showing your name as the owner."

Wes leaned forward, leveling Earl with a severe glare.

"People live in that club. They have a right to stay there. What do I need to file to stop her from selling it out from under us?"

Earl looked over at me for help, as if I would assure them that I would never kick anyone out of their home.

I had no idea what I would do, but the idea of owning something that would just be mine was so appealing, I might just kick whoever was there out to get it. When I didn't say anything, Earl let out a long sigh.

"By the time she gets the title, and the house were to actually go up for sale, that would have been sufficient time for whoever is there to find a new place to go. Even if it wasn't, all she would have to do is give them ninety days with a certified letter to make it official. It would be futile fighting her over the sale of the home. You'd be better off just coming up with an offer yourself to buy it from her."

I saw Wes's jaw do that nerve-jumpy thing.

He was pissed by this news, and it thrilled me to no end that the man who once confessed to pitying me now required a little pity himself. He likely knew there was no way I'd sell to him, even if he offered me triple the worth.

I stood and held out my hand to Earl.

"Thank you for your time. What do you need me to sign? I need to get back to DC."

Earl handed me a file, and while Wes argued with him to find some way to work around this, I began to sign on all the tabs.

Once I was finished, he handed me an envelope with a pair of golden keys inside. Dad must have left them when he left the letter. My heart swelled with emotion. My father was a distant and emotionally negligent jerk, but he was a generous one. He'd left me his most prized possession, and I had no idea why he'd do that when there was a possibility I'd just burn it to the ground then parcel off the property and buy myself a place in DC.

I pushed through the glass door with the grace of a bull in a china shop and quickly scaled the three concrete steps outside of Earl's office. I was rounding the hood of my car when Wes barreled through the exit, his caramel eyes scanning the parking lot. His gaze went to his bike first, then swung over to me.

Did he think I would have done something to his precious motorcycle?

Maybe I should have.

With the key fob tucked away in my purse, I gave him a sugar-sweet smile and pressed my thumb to the door handle, expecting the lock to slide up just like it always did for keyless entry. Nothing happened.

I lowered my gaze to the handle under my touch and pressed my thumb again, and nothing. Panic squeezed my chest as I began rifling through my purse.

Wes didn't waste a second. His long legs ate up the space between Earl's office and my car. I glanced up and saw that his face was a fuming mass of hard lines and furious edges.

"Wes. Don't," I warned, my hand still buried in my purse, my other clutching the letter.

But he was already in front of me. His tall stature nearly swallowed me up, his broad chest and strong hands were all I could see as he closed in. Then his right hand went to my clenched fist, and I had to withhold a gasp as his fingers tugged at mine to pry them open.

I wasn't prepared for the contact.

His warmth, his scent…his touch. I hadn't even realized I closed my eyes until his rough voice scraped against the shell of my ear.

"You don't get to suddenly show up and decide to start reading his letters. Not after you've ignored them for the past three years."

Shock had my eyes flying open and my grip going slack.

"What are you talking about? My father never wrote me." He didn't call me; he didn't do anything to reach out and have a relationship with me.

Wes scoffed, and this close I could smell the delicious scent of leather and cedar, plus something else annoyingly intoxicating. His body was still nearly flush with mine as his chest heaved and his eyes searched the envelope he'd stolen from me.

His eyes roamed over the page for a brief second before they landed back on me, as if I'd stolen his attention. This close, it felt like we'd stepped back in time. He was my first love. He was once my protector, my savior…and then he ruined me.

"He sent you one once a month for the past three years. I know because I was the one who took them to the post office for him."

My brows pulled forward as I tried to make sense of what he was saying. I should have kept my thoughts to myself, but my mind was racing too fast so I mused my confusion out loud.

"The only letters I received were from you, and I haven't opened any of them."

Whiskey eyes narrowed on my face, before a sneer lifted his lips.

"You actually thought they were from me? Maybe he put my name and address, but they were from him. I had nothing to say to you."

Hurt wound through me like a poisonous vine, gripping my organs and squeezing tight. Why did it matter that they weren't from him? I wanted to snarl back about the one letter he'd sent right after we'd broken up and how he had something to say then, but considering that letter eviscerated my heart, I wasn't eager to draw attention to it.

What should matter is that I had a handful of unread letters from my dad sitting in my top drawer at home. Maybe there was a chance at some kind of reconciliation to be found in his musings.

My back was against my car, and my eyes were on the letter in his hand. *My letter.*

I snatched it as quickly as I could from his fingers and tried to slip away from him. I had no idea where I would go, but my fucking keyless entry wasn't working, and I had to get this letter away from him.

So like a mature adult, I stuffed it inside my bra.

Wes watched with narrowed eyes and a strong tick in his jaw. I hated how good his hair looked.

"You think I won't reach in between your tits to grab it?" He stalked closer, a dark glint shining in his eyes. "You must have forgotten how much I enjoyed them, Callie. It would be a fucking pleasure to frisk you."

Why was my tongue so dry? Shit, did my heart just fucking stop? He was messing with me, trying to get into my head. I took two steps back and gathered my resolve.

"This is *my* letter, and the only reason I didn't touch the others you sent was because I assumed they were from *you*. Now that I know they're not, I *will* go home and read them, just like this one." I lifted the paper and shook it slightly.

Wes's face transformed, as if the sun had suddenly broken through the graying clouds. His lips twisted to the side with a sly grin and his arms came across his chest, linking under his armpits.

"Why'd you keep them?" He stepped closer, that curl of his lips growing more sinister. "Better yet, why keep them and not read them? Why not just trash them?"

How did I get out of this?

"Just fuck off, Wes. I don't owe you shit."

His face shuttered the slightest bit, his jaw tightened, and then his eyes found the concrete at our feet.

"Callie, you can't take the club. Your dad wouldn't have wanted that."

Why did it hurt so badly to hear from him what my father would have wanted?

I needed to get out of there and collect myself, because there was a sob working its way up my throat. My father rejected me. Wes didn't choose me. Now it felt like they were both mocking me somehow.

"Why do you even care? And why did you stay in the club, anyway, much less become the president? I thought you'd have gone to college or started your own garage."

I didn't think he'd reply, but he shocked me by saying, "I did both, actually. I just also stayed in the club."

A few silent seconds slipped by, the sounds from the dock and the river echoing around us, the sun was making its way higher in the sky. His response landed in my sternum like concrete. He'd done all of it. College, a shop…he had a life, one he always talked about, but he also had the club. He chose the club and that life over me. The pain from seven years ago burned fresh as I tried to take a calming breath.

"Just let me leave, Wes. You remember how that goes, right? You simply let me walk away. I get it…it's not about me, it's about your stupid clubhouse. I don't know what I plan to do, but if you don't give me two seconds to gather myself and read this letter then I'll do something reckless, like hire a bulldozer and level the place."

He seemed to think it over, this time backing up with a small shake of his head.

My shoulders sagged with relief as I made my way back to my car, right as Wes straddled his bike.

Before he turned the engine over, I had to ask one last thing.

"Wes, why was a Death Raider at my motel this morning?"

His fingers froze, hovering over the key. Whiskey eyes tilted up, landing on me like I'd just grown a second head. I shifted uncomfortably in my boots, scraping a tiny pebble from the asphalt as I waited for his reply. I had left this place, but there were things about this place that would never leave me. I wanted to make sure Rose Ridge was still safe. There was a reason Death Raiders didn't come here. Rose Ridge was strictly Stone Rider territory…especially after what happened eight years ago.

"You saw one this morning?" Wes asked.

The fact that he didn't know made my stomach churn. If Dad was gone, that meant Wes was in charge now, which meant he oversaw keeping the town safe from them.

I nodded, gripping my key fob tightly as I watched him.

"Right as I was coming out of my room, he was exiting a few doors down."

Wes cursed, looking off to the side.

"Did he say anything to you?"

I should lie. The tremor in my stomach told me as much. I should just forget I saw anyone and leave. Take my new property and get the hell out of Dodge. But I'd dealt with the Death Raiders, and if they were fraternizing with his members, he needed to know.

"I don't think so. He asked if I wanted a ride, but I think if he'd recognized me, he wouldn't have asked."

When he didn't reply, I took a step closer to him.

"What's going on, Wes?"

Deliberating, with a jaw that looked as though he was chewing glass, my ex finally let out a ragged breath and ran a hasty hand through his hair. "You don't need to know. Just go back to DC. There was a"—his chin dipped to his chest as he let out a muttered curse—"just go back to your life."

"I will right after I get what's mine. That's my property now, and my house. I'm coming for it."

His expression hardened. He toyed with the key in his bike before leveling me with that glare again.

"If you come for the clubhouse, you'll be met with a war, Princess."

I didn't want to show that I was already afraid that I might be walking into a turf war, but like hell would I let that stop me from taking what was owed to me.

"In case you forgot, I grew up in this life, Wes. You don't scare me."

*He terrified me.*

His eyes stayed locked on mine as he started his engine, which was his form of cutting our conversation off. When he began backing his bike out of the space, I finally ducked into my car.

Then I inhaled a choppy breath and resisted the urge to scream.

# FOUR
## WES
### AGE 10

"Don't be a sore loser," Dustin teased while gathering up the pieces of our boardgame.

My brother was winning because he cheated, and while I knew he was doing it, I didn't care enough to stop him.

I was biding my time.

It was Saturday night and way past our bedtime.

I was focused on my tree house.

Last summer, Callie would sneak up into my treehouse every Saturday night. Most nights I would go out and say hi to her. Sometimes I'd stay, but most of the time I'd just take her a sandwich and leave her be. I didn't want to make her uncomfortable. She'd stopped coming as soon as the cold weather snapped into place, which was near Halloween of last year.

She hasn't been back since.

The school year flew by, winter came. Spring passed, and now summer had arrived.

Tonight, the music from down the road echoed through our open windows, along with the laughing and revving engines. My family found a way to ignore it, but to me it was an anthem, a call to go outside and see if my friend had come.

"I'm not a sore loser, I'm just tired," I said, pushing away from the table. I was lying, but I'd do anything to get him off my back.

"See if Jake wants a go."

Dustin stood and stretched his arms above his head. He was thirteen now, three years older than me, and two years younger than Jake.

"Nah, I want to go watch TV now that Mom and Dad went to bed."

Our parents were strict, and religious. Any chance of freedom we found, we grabbed hold of it. Watching television after hours was one of our favorite things about summer, but it still didn't hold a candle to my possible guest arriving tonight.

The house was quiet as I gathered two sleeping bags, two pillows, and my backpack. Thankfully, no one was watching. If they had been, there would be a lot of questions.

I made sure the screen door didn't slam as I exited and walked down the porch. Tonight, the moon was bright, and the crickets weren't as loud, but my insides seemed jumpier than normal.

Once I cleared the top of the treehouse, I began to roll out the sleep sacks, trying not to let my hopes get too high. As I waited, thoughts began to expand in my head.

*What if she didn't come? What if she never came back and I never saw her again?*

I must have drifted off to sleep at some point because I woke with a jolt as I heard the sound of the hatch opening.

"Wes?" Callie whispered, and hearing her voice again made sparks prance under my skin.

I sat up quickly and tried to adjust my vision to the dark.

"Callie?"

She crawled all the way inside and lowered the wooden door.

"Yeah, it's me."

I sat cross-legged, still wearing the shorts and T-shirt I had on earlier.

"I didn't know if you would come again," I finally said after the silence stretched too long.

She carefully situated the pillow on the sleeping bag.

"You brought this for me?"

I nodded, but then wasn't sure if she could see me.

"Figured we could leave it up here for you…in case you need it and I'm not out here."

"Are you going somewhere this summer?" she asked, tugging the backpack I had brought open.

I didn't want to go anywhere for the summer, but it was too late to change any of it. "Camp, in a week or so, then my grandparents' house for a bit. How about you?"

She pulled out the sandwiches.

"No. I never go anywhere."

I thought about that for a second… letting it sink in. We'd had a dozen or so conversations about her life, but I still felt like I didn't know her. I hated that pity knitting together in the bottom of my stomach.

I always felt it for her before, but now it felt a little different. It felt more like anger.

"How come I didn't see you at school ever?" Callie bit into one of the peanut butter and jelly sandwiches. Her eyes stayed on me as she chewed.

It was stupid to feel embarrassed by this, but people always treated us weird when we said it.

"I'm homeschooled."

Callie's eyes rounded.

"Oh. I looked for you a few times…"

My chest felt like a firecracker had been shoved inside it. I had looked for her, too, but only when I rode my bike, or when I was brave enough to stop by her mailbox. I was always too scared to go any further.

"Do you like being homeschooled?"

I shrugged, toying with the sleeping bag string. The moon was bright enough that with the sheet pulled to the side, I could see Callie, and she could see me.

"It's okay…gets boring from time to time, and my siblings are annoying, but my mom finds us a lot of stuff to do in town, with other homeschool groups."

Callie pulled the water bottle free and twisted the cap.

"You have brothers, right?"

I nodded. "Two…and two little sisters."

She tipped her head back, drinking, and then let out a sigh.

"That must be nice not to feel alone."

"You don't have any siblings?" I wanted to be closer to her for some reason, but I wasn't sure why. Still, I straightened my legs so my toes were near the edge of the sleeping bag.

She shook her head.

"Nope. Just me. My mom died a while back, so it's just me and Dad…plus all his girlfriends and the guys in his club."

She'd mentioned the club before, and it intrigued me now, just like it did the first time I'd heard it.

"So the club…they all ride motorcycles, right?"

Snatching up the bag of potato chips, she pulled it open and tossed a crisp into her mouth.

"Dad says it's like a family. The members are usually all hairy and old…but they're nice. They just scare me sometimes when they get really loud, and they do grown-up stuff with the girls around the clubhouse."

"There are *girls* around the clubhouse?" I couldn't help but ask, because all I could picture were girls her age.

"Yeah, there are always girls around. I only like the old ladies, though; they're the permanent ones that aren't going anywhere."

A yawn interrupted the tail end of her sentence, and I realized she was tired.

But a part of me didn't care. A part of me wanted to be selfish, because like every other time, she would slip away as soon as the sun rose, and as badly as I wanted to be awake and one of these days walk her back, she always beat me.

"Have you told your dad that you don't like it when he throws the loud parties?"

Her lips twisted to the side and some of her dark hair fell in front of her face.

"I try, but my dad doesn't really hear me. He likes to smile and pat my head, but he always tells me to just go see Red when I'm upset."

My brows furrowed. "Who's Red?"

Another yawn emitted from her.

"She's the main old lady. She runs the kitchen, and club money. She buys groceries and has a soft spot for me. I like her, but on club nights like this, she gets just as involved with all the chaos as the rest of them."

Her dainty hand flipped the top of the sleeping bag over, and she crawled in. She wore another one of her big T-shirts that swallowed her.

"Can you tell me a story?" Her voice came out as a whisper, and I decided to lay down too and just let her sleep.

I slid into my sleeping bag and rested my head on the pillow, propping my hands underneath me.

"What kind do you want tonight?"

Another yawn. "Adventure this time."

I started in on the story of *Peter Pan*, still confused as to how she never seemed to know any of these movies or story lines. Last summer I had spent the few times I did sleep up here with her retelling the story of Cinderella. Not that I wanted to, but she'd asked me for something with love and a happy ending, and my sisters had watched the movie that afternoon. So, I started, and she didn't let me stop until she'd heard the very end.

"Does Peter love Wendy?" Callie suddenly asked, the sound of sleep heavy on her voice.

I stared at the ceiling of the tree house and considered her question.

The story of Peter Pan was always something I associated with pirates, cannon fire, and sword fights...but love? I had no clue...but I suppose—

"I think he did love her."

Callie waited a second. "Why?"

I thought it over and just went with the first thing that popped into my head.

"I think he loved her because she wasn't lost, she just wanted an adventure. She was always sure of who she was. She knew what her role was in Neverland...and with Peter."

"But he rescued her so many times..." Callie argued softly.

I shook my head, knowing she couldn't see me.

"Sometimes rescuing someone can lead to a pretty fun adventure. I bet Peter enjoyed it."

She didn't ask anything else, and I started to drift off.

Right before I fell asleep, I heard her whisper.

"I think Wendy loved Peter more."

# FIVE
## CALLIE

MAXWELL RESTED HIS JAW ON MY RAISED KNEES.

My Great Dane was a cuddler, like an oversized emotional support dog. He could always sense when I was upset or hurt…or just needed extra love. He was a gorgeous blue breed with floppy ears and practically no manners whatsoever. I found him at a shelter as a puppy, and at the time they had him labeled as a mutt, likely a heeler breed, but I didn't even care. His eyes met mine, and it was like we both just knew.

I'd driven home from the lawyer's office under a cloudy sky, with rain pelting my windshield. It was good. It made me focus on the road and not my raging emotions. The reality that I had spoken to Wes sank into my mind like mud. Not really spoke—we argued. His words were tiny pebbles in my mind that I kept turning over and over.

Did I want a war with him? With the club?

Obviously not, but at the same time, I wanted what was left to me.

The funeral was still heavy on my heart as well, regardless that I tried to act unfazed. It really hurt that my dad was gone. I assumed I'd made peace with the fact that he and I would never have a relationship, that my dad was set in his ways and would never care what I did one way or the other, but as I sat reading his letter from the will, tears stuck to my lashes and a sob gathered in my throat.

*My Dearest Callie,*

*Don't know how I even got to this point…the one where I can't pick up the phone and just call you. It's my own fault, I know that. So, before I lay anything out, you should know that I'm sorry.*

*I am so sorry, sweetheart.*

*I was a failure as a father and have so many regrets…more than you'll ever know.*

*I found out I was sick about six months ago; I didn't tell a soul, and I know that I could have tracked you down. I could have had Hamish look you up. He's old as hell but he knows how to track. Never left those bounty hunting days behind. But I was scared, sweetie. I was scared you'd reject me, even knowing I was sick, knowing my time was limited. Then I thought about what I'd even say to you, and I panicked.*

*You need to know that you were my sun, Callie. Everything since has just been cloud cover and rain. I've learned how to live with it, but I've been miserable every day since. I hate what happened to you. There's a part of me that can never forgive myself for them taking you. After the incident, I sort of just shut down, and I knew back then you'd take it personal. I knew it, and I still did it.*

*It may be hard to understand, but me shutting you out forced you away, and by you leaving, it meant you'd live.*

*That had to be enough for me.*

*I never wanted any of this, never wanted you in this life, but I didn't know any other way of living.*

*I can't make up for a lifetime of wrongdoings in one letter, but I can try and fix what's left of my legacy.*

*I'm leaving you the club.*

*It was the thing that drove us apart, Callie.*

*I know that now. I wish I could go back in time and choose you. I would have chosen you a thousand times over. This club was a placeholder in my life, and while it did mean something, because it gave me a family, it also cost me the only family that mattered.*

*I'm leaving it to you because you, of all people, deserve to choose its fate.*

*The Riders can move somewhere else. With me gone, maybe they'll disband and gather under a new name. Maybe all my sins can be washed away with what-ever you decide to do with it. Sell it. Burn it. Do whatever you want with it, honey. Just don't live there. Don't tie yourself to that place, or that property. You can get a*

*decent price for it since it's paid off. Keep the cash and enjoy what's left of this life.*
*I love you my beautiful girl, and I wish I would have done better by you.*
    *Allow me, in death, to correct some wrongs.*
    *-Dad.*

I was slightly shocked that he didn't reference his other letters that he'd sent for the past three years, nor did he mention Wes a single time. I was jealous of the boy I once loved, who used to rescue me from the chaos of the club. I still could not figure out why he had continued to stay with the Stone Riders.

It didn't make any sense.

Wes came from one of those families that went to church, did family photos, and took summer vacations. He was smart. Graduated at sixteen, then started his college courses as I was still struggling with my basic level classes in high school.

He used to help me.

I'd recline against his chest while he held my textbook and began to instruct me on the topic in a way that made sense. He was the reason I graduated from high school.

I assumed he'd go to some specialty school…maybe something for mechanics. He was always so good with his hands. When we broke up, he was still deciding where he wanted to go and what he wanted to do.

My throat grew tight, like a golf-ball sized regret was suddenly stuck inside. Every now and then I'd mentally trace over the way we'd ended and rehash all the ways we broke apart, inspecting it for places I could have had a different outcome. But most of the time, I'd just shake my head and the pain would storm my emotions like a thunderhead.

I focused back on the letter, thinking over the other letters in my top drawer.

Wes was wrong. My father was literally telling me to get rid of the clubhouse.

To be honest, there was a tiny flicker in the back of my mind that made me inspect his choice of words carefully. He seemed insistent on it, and from everything I knew about the man, it did seem like the last thing he would have wanted. Maybe getting sick had changed him.

Maybe he really did have time to reflect on his failures.

Still…something was bothering me, and I couldn't put my finger on what.

I tucked the letter away, preparing my heart for tearing into the rest. What did he have to say to me once a month for three years? Possibly that he was sick? Perhaps that he wanted to see me again or that he missed me.

Max whined at the door right before a soft knock sounded on the other side. He tilted his head back like he knew who was on the other side then gazed at me, as if he wanted me to hurry up. Which meant my visitor was Laura. I didn't have any other friends in the city that I knew well enough for Max not to bark when they came over. Just to be safe, I peeked through the eyehole and smiled.

Laura was five foot two and practically my twin in every way, save for her cascade of blonde curls and sharp blue eyes. I had a milder temper, and I was quiet. If someone cut me off in traffic, I'd curse them out in my car, but if our windows were down, I wouldn't say a thing. Whereas Laura would crawl through her window to get to their car just to wring their neck. She was dynamite walking on two legs. There was something about her that reminded me of Rose Ridge, and while I had no illusions about my life growing up, I still missed home.

Unlocking the deadbolt, I swung the door open with a sigh.

"You brought me wine?"

Shouldering past me, she headed straight for the kitchen, scoffing as she went.

"This is my security blanket and not for drinking."

Max fell into a trot, moving past me toward Laura.

"What exactly about a bottle of wine acts as a security blanket?"

With her back to me, she set the bottle down and moved to the fridge.

Ducking inside and pulling out a Gogurt, she straightened while tearing off the top.

"Are we ever going to talk about why you get kids' yogurt pouches? And I just got off the train. Cops were called to the platform again because two people were reenacting some scene from *The Avengers*. One of them kept saying he was Thanos and making everyone uncomfortable. Also, your apartment is shady as fuck. There were two drug deals happening when I walked in, and one of the guys watched me like I was hiding a dime bag in my bra."

The Gogurt she was sucking on actually looked kind of good, and if I couldn't have wine, it would be the next best thing.

"Give me a strawberry one, please."

Laura dipped back into my fridge to retrieve it while I sunk onto one of the stools at my breakfast nook.

"So you carry the bottle as a means of protection?"

Her lips wrapped around the yogurt pouch as she tried to get the last remnants out. "I just have this theory that women holding bottles of wine don't get kidnapped or approached."

I shook my head, sucking on the tip of the pouch until the strawberry yogurt hit my tongue.

"Can't argue with that logic."

My best friend smiled wickedly as she grabbed a glass. "Right? It sort of makes sense, the more you think about it."

"So" —she focused on me, sliding her elbows onto the counter— "you look like you've been crying. Wanna talk about it?"

*No.*

I shrugged. "My dad left me ten acres of property, his clubhouse, and a letter where he basically apologized for the past twenty-eight years of my life."

Her hazel eyes rounded.

"Damn."

Maxwell whined, laying his chin onto his paws as he watched the both of us from his spot on the floor. It was something he did whenever Laura or I were together. It made me think of when I first met her. She was on a delivery route, looking for someone on my floor. She couldn't find them, and when she knocked on my door, she was so frustrated she just gave me the food for free and asked if I had any beer. I invited her in, we ate the guy's food, and she ended up staying for four hours, effectively quitting her job. Max laid on the floor watching us that night, just like he was now. We've been best friends ever since.

"You're a homeowner now. In some countries owning land makes you titled, like a duchess or countess. Either way, you're out of this shit hole." She did a little dance, clicking her shoes on the ancient linoleum of my kitchen.

Max raised his head at the echoing sound.

I waved my hands at her, half reaching for her. "Stop, you're going to wake up my neighbor." With a small laugh and roll of her eyes, she settled.

"So, when do we go collect on the inheritance?" she asked, taking a sip of her water. She bent down to pat Max's head.

He loved it, leaning into her touch and letting his tongue fall out of his mouth.

"We?" There was no way I would be taking her down to Rose Ridge. It could be dangerous; besides, she'd go to jail. Her temper could *never*.

Standing to her full height, she planted her hands on her hips.

"Yes, *we*. I'm coming. You know I work like two shitty jobs at once, but I'm always two strikes away from losing them both."

She wasn't wrong, and I knew her lust for adventure would always compete with her willingness to keep a roof over her head. As it was, she shared an apartment with two other roommates and didn't get along with either of them. The only reason I had this tiny place to myself was because I didn't mind living on this side of the city. The rent was nearly a third of what she chose to pay near Capitol Hill.

"Laura, this isn't like a normal family inheritance. My dad was the president of a biker club, and not the nice kind that does teddy bear runs. Their club did illegal stuff—and somehow my ex-boyfriend is the new president."

My friends' eyes didn't shift or move. In fact, she began inspecting her nails while I spoke.

"Sounds juicy, I can't wait."

"Laura, I'm serious. It's dangerous."

She clicked her tongue and slumped onto my two-seater couch, while Maxwell tracked the movement with his eyes.

"Look, if you really don't want me to go, I won't. I can watch Max and let you go take care of business, but I would love to go and see all the craziness that made you who you are."

I tipped my head and stared up at the ceiling. A water spot was in the corner above the window. I liked to keep tabs on it to ensure it didn't grow. I honestly didn't mind her tagging along, but the idea of putting anyone in harm's way made my stomach sour.

Growing up, I was shielded from a lot of the realities of club life because of who my dad was. No one touched me, no one hurt me, no one did anything harmful at all except forget that I even existed. Still, the parties got to me. The noise, all the chaos of having people in my house all the time. It was manageable until other clubs mingled and Dad would drink too much. Those nights were the scariest, because the new people didn't realize I was Simon Stone's daughter. I had way too many close calls, one of which had initially run me out of the house that night and down the road to Wesley's.

"What are you going to tell Jacks? Didn't he just threaten to give your chair away like last week?" Laura turned her head until her blue eyes were on me.

I hated the way worry feathered her brows. She didn't like my boss, and not just because he'd hit on her with a little too much enthusiasm. He was an asshole, through and through.

I shrugged. "I have the office job, too. The tattoo shop is only part-time anyway, and it's not like I have a ton of clients. Jacks refusing to put my card out there until I paid the advance for the space sort of ensured that. I get it, but I don't have that kind of cash."

Laura sat up and pointed at me. "Yet! Here's the plan: you go down to Rose Town by the end of the week."

"Rose Ridge," I corrected her.

She waved me off and powered on. "Rose whatever. You talk to a realtor about selling the place, get an estimate, and who knows? Maybe it will be enough to open your own shop and you'll become Jacks's competition."

While that did sound amazing, there was still that tiny flicker in the back of my mind that wanted the shop I settled in to be facing Main Street in Rose Ridge. In this fantasy, I lived right above it, and

Maxwell had his own space to lounge while I worked. Afterward, we'd walk downtown for dinner, and he'd play at the park. Every time I conjured up that image, it felt safe and peaceful. Which always made my stomach flutter with excitement. Maybe while I was there, I could see if there were even any potential storefronts that would work. But that would mean I'd be returning home, and was I really ready to go back?

Wes would be everywhere, and my clientele would frequently mix with club members.

Doubt sank my dream like a paper boat, making me reconsider the whole thing.

"What about the law office where I work four days a week? That's a good gig, and they pretty much let me do whatever I want." I bit my lip as I fussed over the idea of losing my place there. It was good money, and reliable.

Max took this opportunity to crawl on top of us, which made us both groan.

"Max!"

Laura held his face, so it was pointed away from hers.

"No offense, Cal, but all you do is make copies, get their coffee, and sit there looking pretty for the disgusting windbags to stare at. You get paid barely above minimum wage."

Ouch. I had worked hard to secure my spot at that law office, and yes, it was practically meaningless, but it came with some tiny scrap of pride when I was able to tell people I worked at the Law Offices of Welsh & Meyer. I felt respected when I was there. If the windbags she mentioned did stare at me, I never noticed it.

"Look." She reached around Max's chest and grabbed my hand. "Just ask if you can take a week off. Start with a week, and we'll figure it out from there. Okay?"

One week. I could do that.

"Okay, fine. You can come with me, but that means we're going to have to take this beast with us." I patted my dog's stomach and tried to push him off the couch. He wouldn't budge.

"Max is good people. He'll love it down in Rose Town."

"Ridge!"

"Rose Ridge! Right, sorry." She winced, but her mouth tipped with laughter.

I shoved her with my foot, but it made Max shift as well, forcing his tail to whip around and nail me in the face.

"Ow! Maxwell!"

Laura laughed, and I pushed her off the couch.

"This is going to be fun."

# SIX
## WES
### AGE 13

My school year was officially over. Being homeschooled had a few perks, and ending a whole week before the public school was always one of them. Usually, I was already busy with fishing and swimming, but this year, I found myself riding my bike down to Rose Ridge Middle School.

Red brick surrounded the one-story school, guarded by a chain-link fence. A few trees were spaced out along the property, edging around the parking lot. I rode, watching the double doors for students. The bell rang, and kids streamed out the doors. There were so many faces I didn't recognize.

How could I live here my entire life and not know any kids my own age? I knew the kids from the homeschool group, but most of them were from a different county. That left the girl who still snuck into my treehouse on hot summer nights when her dad's clubhouse got too wild. Her visits were becoming less frequent—at least they were last summer. The first time she popped in wasn't until July, and we only had a few times to hang out before school started up again.

I didn't particularly like it.

Which was why I was here, inserting myself into Callie's summer so she had no other choice but to talk to me on my terms and not hers.

I waited on the curb outside as guys my age came out, pushing, laughing, and joking. Girls came, too. They all wore shorts so small I could see all the way up their legs to the crease of their butt cheeks. It made my face heat, for some reason. Maybe because girls didn't dress like that in the homeschool groups, or at church…

Still, none of these girls were Callie, so I didn't really care.

I waited until I saw that glossy dark hair, and that familiar expression. Her pink lips always tugged down, like she was thinking about something sad. Her hazel eyes focused on the ground as she walked, until she reached the bike rack.

She didn't even put a lock around hers, which, with how much rust was on it, didn't surprise me. I watched her every move, especially how she looked in real clothes. Every time I had ever seen her, she was wearing an oversized T-shirt. Now, she wore shorts that went just as high as the other girls, but on her they looked different. *Better.*

That firecracker-in-my-chest feeling came back as I took in the shirt hanging off her shoulder, revealing more skin on her than I had ever seen. Her long hair hung down her back in a slick sheet of silk, and a horrifying realization settled in my chest: she was breathtakingly beautiful.

Callie walked her bike along the sidewalk, away from the school and toward me. My throat suddenly felt dry, and my face felt too warm. It was hot out, but not that hot…it was still only May.

How had I not noticed it before, how stunning she was? It was like I couldn't take my eyes off her. Perhaps that was why I didn't care if the other girls wore shorts, because Callie was all I could see.

My hands sweated on the handlebars of my bike as I held it up. Callie didn't see me yet, but she would as soon as she cleared the gate. Panicked anxiety made my mind spin with ideas of what I would say to her.

*Hey, how was school?*

No, that would be stupid.

*Nice to see you outside of the treehouse. You look really pretty in the daylight.*

I blushed, hating myself for feeling so anxious. She was just Callie the tree house girl, nothing special about her.

But then some guy my age ran up next to her and covered her hands with his on the handlebars, and suddenly she *wasn't* just Callie. She was the girl I was supposed to keep safe. The one who trusted me to give her a place to sleep. The one who smiled when I told her Disney stories and acted like they'd really happened.

She jolted to a stop, a look of alarm forced her eyebrows up and her lips down.

They were saying something, but I couldn't hear. She tried to move her hands, but he wouldn't let her go. The guy lowered his face until he was whispering in her ear, then laughing at her as she pulled her face away and blushed.

There was a fire in my chest, burning my lungs to ash, as I shoved my bike down and began walking forward.

My eyes focused on the distance between me and Callie, and how tears began to trail down her cheeks.

I was in front of them within seconds. I guess I had started running at some point.

Then my fist flew.

The fire came out, and all I could see was red. *He had made her cry.* He made her blush. *He touched her.*

I swung again and again. My fist hurt, but I couldn't process it.

"Wes!" I heard Callie yelling, but I couldn't stop.

I'd never been in a fight before, didn't even know how to throw a punch, but all I knew was that he needed to remember this moment. He needed to remember *me*, and never go near her again. I felt my knuckles slam into his jaw, heard him cry and beg me to stop.

I couldn't. I knew there was a crowd of kids around us, and one of them tried to push me. Callie was screaming my name now, her voice sounding hoarse.

I still couldn't stop. Not until someone much bigger than me was pulling me away.

"Come here, little man...you're going to break your hand. This little asswipe isn't worth it."

I blinked and saw chrome, leather, and Callie.

She was following us, pushing her bike as I was being guided back to mine.

"Callie, this a friend of yours?" the man asked, and that's when I looked behind me at the kid I'd hit. He was sitting up on his elbow, staring at me, his nose busted and his eye swollen shut. Teachers were starting to huddle around him, their eyes landing on us as the kid pointed.

Crap.

"He's my friend," Callie said softly, and it put my focus back on the person leading me to my bike.

The guy grunted and then laughed. "He's got heart. I'm going to mention him to your pops, see if he can be the new detail."

"Don't say anything about this to my dad!" Callie snapped angrily.

The guy laughing at us was just a few years older than us…he looked like a high schooler. He had a leather vest with a skull and roses blooming out of the eye sockets on the back, and a motorcycle just like the other guys from the club.

He mussed Callie's hair then let out a sigh.

"Calm down, Little Fox. You're gettin' all red in the face. Take your friend to get some ice. His knuckles are going to swell up tomorrow. Clean him up so his parents don't get pissed."

Callie's hazel eyes finally shifted to me, and the air seemed to get caught inside my lungs.

"I'll take him." She paused as the guy nodded and then straddled his bike. "Thank you, Killian."

He smirked at her then winked at me and started his bike. I watched as Killian twisted the handle, forcing the engine to rev louder and louder, then he pushed the kickstand up and darted off down the road, kicking up dirt as he went.

Once he was gone, I picked up my bike and waited for Callie to lead the way. I had no idea where she was going to take me, but I liked the idea of icing my hand. It throbbed, and I really didn't want to show that it hurt in front of Callie.

She walked next to me, calm and quiet.

My thoughts were all mixed up, swirling and spinning in places they had no business going.

"Why'd you come?" Callie asked, breaking into my thoughts.

I stared ahead, suddenly feeling shy.

"Who was that guy?"

She kicked a pebble in her way, then veered off the road through a few bushes.

"Come this way. We're going to clean you up."

I guided my bike without a second thought. The trail was dense and hard to see as the canopy mostly blocked the sun, but it was only a short trek before there was a babbling stream cutting through the woods.

She tossed her bike on the bank and then slowly climbed down to the river.

"Here, come on. You want to stick your hands in. It's cold, so it'll be like sticking it into an ice bath."

I did as she said, taking my shoes and socks off, then wading into the water.

"It's freezing!" I hissed.

Callie laughed, and it sounded like something I wanted to hold onto, like a lucky rock or a charm. I found myself smiling up at her.

She joined me moments later, removing her ripped tennis shoes and mismatched socks.

"I like this spot. I mean, it doesn't go super deep for swimming, but it's private. I almost ran here that first night, instead of your house."

Callie walked in far enough for the water to reach the hem of her shorts, and I tried to ignore how pretty she looked with the fingers trailing the top surface and how her eyes lit up.

"Why did you come to my treehouse?"

She shrugged. "Remembered seeing it on one of my bike rides and wondered what it would be like to sleep inside it. Sleeping in a tree seemed like a safe idea—away from predators, away from people, drunks, and bikes."

I didn't like her words. They made me feel like I did when I was hitting that idiot.

"Who was that guy back there?" I asked again.

She let out a sigh and began taking water and wetting the back of her neck.

"Logan Linton. He's an asshole. Football player, and thinks everyone in the school is there to please him. He's always grabbing me and hurting me."

I clenched my aching fist that was already starting to swell and dipped it under the water.

"So…he's not your boyfriend?" I only asked to make sure she wasn't letting him treat her like this.

Callie's lips slung to the side as her eyes found mine. "If he were, he wouldn't be after today."

"Why?" I couldn't quite work out what she was saying.

She let out a laugh.

"Because you beat him up! That would be sort of embarrassing, to keep dating him, wouldn't it?"

I thought that over and let my next question slide between us before I chickened out. "And who was the other guy, Killian?"

Her gaze stayed on the water gently pushing at our legs as she let out a happy sigh. "Killian is like my older brother. He's a prospect, even though he's only sixteen. His daddy is a bad guy, just got sent away for twenty years, so my dad took Killian under his wing, patched him in, and now he's family. He's supposed to follow me home every day, but he's always late."

I thought that over, oddly glad that her dad had someone looking out for her.

"Why did you come, Wes? Why did you hit Logan like you couldn't stop?"

My gaze raised, clashing with hers. Somehow, we'd wandered closer to each other in the river. Our fingers were just inches apart now.

I thought over what I should say and what I wanted to say. I should tell her I did it because I just felt like it…but I wanted her to know the real reason. I was curious how she'd respond. "I came because I didn't want to wait to see you. I hit him because he was touching you, and he made you cry."

She watched me as the trees swayed above us and the water burbled. It felt like we were the only two people on the planet.

When I assumed she wasn't going to say anything else, I felt her finger barely touch mine under the water.

I kept still as her entire hand suddenly found mine, her fingers lightly brushing over my bruised knuckles.

I closed my hand around hers, and we continued walking around the river, holding hands under the surface where no one could see.

With one hand, the girl I couldn't stop thinking about hung on, and with the other, I felt the ache of a battle I knew I'd rage again if anyone else ever tried to hurt her.

# SEVEN
# CALLIE

Laura was riding shotgun, with a red rope of licorice dangling from her mouth. She had on a pair of oversized sunglasses and her feet up on the dash. Maxwell was in the backseat with his head out the window. From the outside, it seemed as though we were on a fun road trip, one where the AC had died in my car and my best friend kept telling me to let my hair down. It was tied back into a low bun so no annoying pieces would hit my face while I was driving.

It took two days for me to notify my employers and clear the time off work.

Considering I had just taken three days for the funeral, none of them were very pleased with the idea of me taking even more time. Jacks told me he wasn't holding my chair or space. Mr. Meyers from the law office told me he wouldn't fire me, but I would need to get in touch with them by midweek to discuss my return.

The trip took four hours, but we'd left late, so by the time we rolled into Rose Ridge it was already evening, with purple and orange streaking across the sky. The stagnant air was still thick and sticky as I climbed out of the car and stretched. It felt so strange to be back so soon, considering this was the most I'd seen my hometown in the last seven years. Out of habit, I looked around for any motorcycle members or menacing glares. Wes had promised a war when I arrived, and I wasn't sure what form that would take.

"This is the motel?" Laura looked it up and down as she pushed her sunglasses into her hair. It was as wild as a thistle patch, with strands sticking up. I smiled, grabbing Max's leash. I had forgotten she grew up rich, and while her parents didn't fund her lifestyle now, she was accustomed to a very different way of living than what I had grown up with.

"Yep. Only one in town." I walked toward the office and prepared myself for the scent of homemade soap. Gerald, the owner, liked to sell it in the office, like a gift shop. Last time I had arrived, the elderly man with graying hair and a round belly had greeted me with a smile. This time, as the bell dinged and we pushed through the door, his smile was replaced with a frown.

My gut sank.

Without even hearing a word, I already knew what he was about to say.

"Sorry, ladies. No vacancy."

Laura scoffed, thinking it was a joke.

"Your sign says vacancy, and there's not a single car in the parking lot."

Gerald busied himself with brochures, fixing and straightening them.

"Private party booked all the rooms."

Translation: Wes had told him not to rent a room to me.

There was already someone watching the motel, or us. Fuck, he'd probably had us followed. Wes had likely investigated why Gerald had allowed members of the Death Raiders to party here, as well, which would give the motel owner extra incentive not to help me.

"Okay. Thanks anyway, Gerald." I turned away, taking Max with me.

Laura chased after me, right on my heels with her hands held wide. "Wait, you're just going to leave? He's lying, Callie. He doesn't have a private party, that's bullshit. He must have a room available."

Tugging on the car door, I loaded Max and then reclaimed my seat in the driver's side. Laura reluctantly followed, slumping into the passenger seat.

"You're not surprised. Why?"

The engine came to life as I turned the ignition over. There had to be a vacation rental or something else in town. Laura was already scrolling on her phone as I pulled out of the parking lot, veering toward the river. Tourists loved the river.

"Anything?" I looked over at my best friend, while also stealing a peek into my rearview mirror. No motorcycles yet.

"None that have a vacancy." She swiped some more, her brows furrowed in concentration. "Okay, this one might work, let me call."

Ten minutes later we were parked on the side of the road, letting Max relieve himself in a patch of weeds.

Laura was fuming, and I was trying to come to terms with my new reality.

"Five places, Callie. *Five.*"

She was referencing the number of places that had turned us down. Not because they were full, or even because of my dog. They had all given the same cryptic reason, which all led back to Wes.

*Private party booked through the rest of the summer.*

That was bullshit, and Laura knew it. I knew it. Max knew it.

We all fucking knew it.

"You wanted to know why I wasn't surprised...this is why. These guys run this town. You can't argue with it or fight against it."

Laura kept her head down, hands tethered to her hips. The silence was interrupted by a chorus of crickets in the tall grass off in the distance.

"The next town is like fifteen miles away. I mean, it's going to have to work, so let's go."

My temper was usually mild, and I didn't try to cling to things I couldn't change. When Wes and I broke up and I decided to leave, he let me, and so did Dad. No one tried to stop me, and that was response enough for me. What good would it have done to get upset, yell, or scream? None of it would have made a damn difference. But now, I was feeling this fire build in my chest. The war Wes had mentioned was here, quiet and calm on the surface but bubbling and vivid underneath.

I should have known this would be his play.

Pushing off the side of the car, I let out a sigh. The last pieces of daylight were waning, leaving stars in their wake. The moon was just a tiny thumbnail in the sky, and the heat was finally starting to succumb to the night.

With the receding light, the fucks I gave regarding this entire situation with Wes began to lessen, as well. He was keeping me from my home, the one thing my father had left to me. Fuck the club, and fuck Wes.

"We're going to the source."

Laura shoved her hair up off her neck and pulled the mass into a bun.

"Damn straight we are."

Cicadas sang a familiar tune as we drove toward Belvin Drive with our windows down.

Nostalgia tugged at my memories like phantom talons, clawing and piercing through me. We drove along the dirt path that led back to my childhood home, and my heart raced for what would come next.

I hadn't laid eyes on the clubhouse in seven years, I hadn't returned home one time after I left, and while I was still mourning my father's passing, I could also feel guilt flare the tiniest bit. I realized staying away was due to stubbornness and just being angry at the club, and when Wes joined it was the final straw for me. Back then, my anger and bitterness felt justified. I clung to those reasons until my fingers bled, but now, I just felt foolish. I was the one who had missed out on nearly a decade of memories, and now I was the one who was the stranger in my own home.

As we rounded the curve in the drive, I imagined a small, dark-haired me learning to ride a rusty bike while club members watched and laughed, most of them drunk, several of them high.

My dad wasn't even the one to physically help me; it was always Brooks or Rhodes who held on to the back of my seat and guided my old bike around.

The being-poor part was difficult too. We never had any money.

Stone Riders had been my grandpa's creation, from what I understood, based off an era of mistrust and bad deeds from a local factory. My dad was a big reason it had flourished and grew to the expansive size. Seven years ago, he'd reached nearly three hundred members, scattered throughout the area. Based on the funeral size, those numbers had held. Growing up, the club didn't pay the bills, at least not as far as I ever experienced. If they did illegal things, I was never the beneficiary of any cash flow from it.

My clothes came from donation bins, and whatever Red found for me at the big box stores she went to. My shoes never fit right, and my hair was a greasy mess until I was old enough to use Google and hustle my own products.

It wasn't until I was in high school that Dad's club was suddenly flush with money, and I was too in love with Wes to pay it any mind or realize they'd likely started moving bigger, or better, product.

Laura gasped next to me, which brought me back to the moment.

"This is where you grew up?"

I stared at the massive structure in front of me. It wasn't *at all* where I grew up.

"No. I was raised in an old two-story house that was in serious need of a renovation. This…this is something else."

I stared at the enormous windows at the top story, at least ten feet long, and arched into a beautiful design boasting of tall ceilings and opulence. A few feet below were oversized French doors that led out to an expansive patio, and there on the first floor was a deep inset porch that wrapped around the whole house. The home was divided, with a nice private, covered patio and gated entry. Off to the other side was a huge glass garage door that was currently open, showcasing a myriad of club members drinking, laughing, and even working on their motorcycles.

"This is wild," Laura muttered, still staring.

A large fire pit with several chairs surrounding it was off to the edge of the yard, and a row of motorcycles were parked off to the right. Gone were all the rusted cars, bikes, and junk. The weeds were controlled, the grass cut and there were even river rocks filling some of the pathways around the house. It looked like something you'd find on a magazine cover.

"Where do we park?"

I dug for the same confidence I felt earlier. "Wherever I fucking want. I own this place now."

Laura gripped her thighs and let out a low whistle.

"I've never seen this side of you before, Callie. I'm equal parts excited and terrified."

Feeling empowered, I pulled right up to the front, ignoring the club members gawking and staring at me.

Max started barking immediately as more eyes were drawn to us, but I didn't care. I grabbed his leash and helped him exit the car.

"Just stay close to me, okay?" I whispered to Laura.

The sound system from inside the house was blaring Hozier, and there was something weirdly soothing about the fact that it wasn't the same classic rock I grew up with. Maxwell had calmed as he walked next to me, his head reaching my waist. I kept my eyes forward, not bothering to give into the men whispering, laughing, and milling around me. I heard a few whistles and a few cat calls, but my eyes stayed ahead.

Laura was right next to me as we pushed forward into the club house. Her gait was looser than mine, almost like she was comfortable here. Or like she wasn't concerned in the least that danger surrounded her.

Through the wide-open doors was what looked like a high-end mechanic shop, with waxed floors and several motorcycles being worked on. On the opposite side was a long bar filled with a dozen or so different people scattered around it. Two women were dancing on top of the bar, pouring drinks into glasses like they were extras in *Coyote Ugly*.

There were couches, pool tables, a massive flat screen, but there were still a few original fixtures from when I had lived in this house. The fireplace under the mounted screen was one of those things. The brick was still exposed, but inside was screened off, as though the chimney had been removed.

"Is that a fucking horse?!" someone slurred, and Max barked as if he knew they were referring to him.

Another shout echoed through the loud space. "Yes, new sweet-butts! Who the fuck brought them, and how do I thank you?"

I heard a few members curse and then someone ran out the back door.

Wes was around here somewhere, and I didn't want to see him before I saw Red.

"Why did he call us Sweetbutt?" Laura asked in a rushed whisper, stepping closer to me, "They aren't going to do stuff to our butts, are they? I'm a kinky, girl, but only for the right guy and only if I'm lubed appropriately."

Biting back a laugh, I whispered back, "Sweetbutt is just a term for girls who come by to fuck the guys. They're just passing pussy, essentially." I hated summarizing the term so dully, especially after knowing so many kind women throughout my life that were just considered a Sweetbutt, never transitioning into a property patch or becoming an old lady to any of the members. Still, I couldn't change what the term meant.

"So they think we're here to fuck?" Laura gripped my arm.

I ignored her as I searched the faces, a few familiar…a few finally processing who I might be. I had my father's eyes and my mother's lips. It was something the club members had commented on regularly, and I had no idea what their fascination was. I also had a tattoo on the inside of my wrist of their patch. I had gotten it done when I was eighteen in an attempt to grow closer to my father.

"Holy fuck, that's Stone's daughter!" boomed someone from behind the counter, and right as they did, three things happened at once.

The back door slammed open, the music cut, and I heard a familiar voice that had my head swiveling and relief swimming through me.

"Cheese, rice, and all the holy saints, is that you, Callie Ray Stone?"

Red made her way around the bar right as Wes stormed down the hall, coming in from the back. He wore his leather cut over an oil-stained T-shirt and dark denim jeans that were tucked into untied motorcycle boots. His dark hair was greasy, with pieces falling over his dark, furrowed brows. His face was cut into angry strokes of determination and chiseled perfection, but I was determined, too, and he could go fuck himself.

I focused on the woman behind the bar who had sugar-white hair tied up into a high bun, and a face done up beautifully with exaggerated makeup. Huge lashes; filled, arched eyebrows; contoured cheekbones, and of course, apple red lipstick, which didn't hide her age at all but also didn't dull her shine.

"Honey, how the hell have you been?" She swept me into a tight hug, which made Maxwell bark and nudge my waist with his head.

"That fucking horse can't be in here," Wes roared, storming up next to us, aggressively pointing at my dog.

I put my hand on my hip, noticing that Laura had her arms folded over her chest, her resting bitch face firmly focused on my ex.

I looped Max's leash around my knuckles. "Well, we wouldn't even *be here* if you didn't blacklist us from every single hotel and establishment in the city."

Wes smirked. "Then better go find a different city."

"Wesley, you didn't!" Red scolded, throwing a hand to her hip, her voice going stern.

The other club members began flitting in and out, trying to catch onto what was going on. The music restarted, but it was softer now.

Wes didn't reply. His arms were linked over his chest, his legs spread apart, and his face unmoving. I tried not to notice his eyes or the way the whiskey brown seemed so stark against his features. He looked older. The tiny lines around his mouth, the few days' worth of growth along his jaw that he never allowed to grow before. The scar running through his lip, even the arch of his dark brows, felt like he'd lived an entire lifetime already. All without me.

"She's trying to sell the club," he finally explained as Red's glare intensified.

"He hasn't even given me a chance to figure out *what* I want to do. But this is my home, always has been," I argued.

Wes threw his hand out, stepping closer.

"Look around, Princess. Does this look like anything you grew up with? This hasn't been your home for a long fucking time."

Hot rage reached for my heart, making me feel like a bullied teenager again, fighting against horrible insults and rumors that were never true. I was always the outcast, the freak. The girl being raised by wolves. Boys used to ask me to spread my thighs and show them what biker princess pussy looked like. Others would ask if my knees hurt from sucking club cock. The kids I grew up with were vicious, and Wes knew this.

He understood my past, and it felt like he was just throwing it all in my face. Of course this modern, recently remodeled place didn't resemble where I had grown up. We had mold in the bathrooms, odd stains in the tub, broken mirrors, mice, and shag carpet. This place looked like it belonged on Wesley's television show.

Red's expression turned glacier as she snapped, "Wesley Ryan! You better watch how you speak to this girl. She is the bones of this place, no matter how much money you throw at it. She is Simon's blood, and you'd be dead where you're standing if he ever heard you speaking like this to her."

Wes looked like he'd been slapped across the face with the way his eyes lowered and the muscle in his jaw began to tick.

The members around us went quiet until suddenly there was a loud shout that went up from the back.

"If it isn't our Little Fox, finally back home, with a pixie and a horse in tow."

I watched as three men crossed the room. All in their late sixties, with graying beards, scruff, pot bellies, and faded leather cuts. These were the Stone Riders original members, who had ridden with my grandpa as young prospects. They used to tell me stories about how cruel and hard my grandpa was, especially on my dad.

"Brooks, you're still here?" I asked jokingly and opened my arms as one of my father's oldest friends swept me up into a hug.

"He's still making me miserable, too." Red joked, pulling Brooks in for a kiss.

They had been together long before I even knew what a property patch meant, or the term old lady. I just remembered the obsession Brooks had over Red, and the way she wore her vest that boasted of being his property. She was his, and it was nice to see that he had only ever been hers.

"Don't forget me," a shaky voice requested.

I turned and found a pair of soft brown eyes on a weathered face attached to a beard so long it nearly reached his navel.

"Hamish, I would never forget you," I rasped, emotion clogging my throat.

Memories of him helping me read came back swift and harsh. Me on the back porch, him tipping a glass bottle, the dim light of the porch light catching on the amber. He was the only one sober enough to help me with my homework. Each night, he'd hold off on hitting the next beer until I'd gotten through all my work. My father made fun of him for it.

"How are you, my girl?" His tight embrace had Maxwell growling.

I stepped back and patted my dog's head to put him at ease.

"Nice hound you have there." Hamish dipped his face and lowered to get a better look, then he laughed. "The fox and the hound. Where's Killian? He's going to shit his pants when he sees you."

I looked up in time to see Wes whisper something to a guy standing next to him.

The man wasn't listening to Wes. His eyes were on me, and as I caught his expression, a small smile crept along his face, and I felt mine do the same.

This time I moved first.

People parted, and Wes stood staring, as if I'd grown horns, but the man next to him took a long step forward and then scooped me up.

"How the fuck have you been, Little Fox?"

Tears finally broke through and were trailing happily down my face. I heard Wes mutter a curse next to us, but I didn't care. He could fuck all the way off.

"I've been good."

He set me down and continued to smile at me.

"You look good. You miss me?"

His eyes quickly flitted behind me to Laura, who was still standing with her arms crossed and her lips thin. She was watching our interaction with both wariness and fascination.

"I'm always missing you, Killian."

"You look every inch the club princess you were born to be. You still designing tattoos?"

I put my hand on his shoulder to steady myself. The high-heeled boots I was wearing weren't the most stable. I didn't miss the way Wesley's face swept briskly to the left to catch Kilian's expression. He seemed surprised to hear that Killian and I had somewhat kept in touch. He was one of the only assholes here who had social media.

"She inks them now, too," Laura said, lifting her shirt, brazenly showing off the massive mermaid tail I had inked into her rib cage. She looked like she had scales.

"Oh shit!" Killian said, moving past me to Laura. He skimmed a finger down her side as he inspected the ink.

"This is fucking good, Little Fox. Look at you." He turned his head, a big smile in place. Pride engulfed my entire heart, soothing out old hurts and the tiny piece inside that craved approval from my dad. He wasn't here, but Killian was like my brother, and the next best thing.

"Jesus Christ. This isn't a fucking reunion," Wes barked as he watched Killian smirk.

I didn't miss how his eyes moved right where Killian's arm slid around my waist.

He was staring at him like he'd just touched something of his.

"Look, we'll get out of everyone's hair just as soon as Wes lifts the lodging ban on us. We were blacklisted from every establishment in town."

Wes glared, showing his teeth.

"Like I said, find a different town."

I tilted my head, feeling a fight coming on. "I don't want to. I want to stay in *this* town."

Red suddenly stepped between us.

"This is nonsense. Callie, honey, you can have your dad's old cabin. It's on the back end of the property. It's been recently—"

"She can't stay on the property," Wes declared flatly, interrupting Red. He acted as though I was an unwanted stray and not the rightful heir to this clubhouse. That rage in my chest roared with a silent scream, forcing me to step closer to my ex.

"Need I remind you that this property is legally mine, and I can technically have any room or space that I want?"

Wes glowered. A muscle jumped along his firm, square jawline, and I hated that I realized I'd never seen him look so angry so many instances in a row. He used to be pure sunshine; now he was all storm clouds.

"They can stay with me," Killian offered with a wide smile.

Wes darted his eyes to the man right at the same time as I did. I had no clue where he lived, but it had to be better than some rundown cabin on the edge of the property. I was exhausted, and all I wanted was a bed to collapse into.

"Do you have space for us?"

Killian eyed me, lingering on Laura then took in Max.

"I do."

"Killian," Wes warned.

It made me curious at their relationship. When I left, Killian was my dad's second in command, and Wes looked up to him for some unknown reason. While Wes wasn't a part of the club, he was considered a hang-around by the other club members. Someone who wanted to join, or was interested, but hadn't pledged or become a prospect. I hated it, because I did everything within my power to ensure they never saw him as a potential member. Still, he and Killian were good friends, but Kill was always in charge, so it was strange to hear Wes bossing him around.

I watched Wesley as I responded to Killian.

"We'd love to stay with you."

"Not fucking happening." Wes stepped in between us, and his hand was suddenly on my hip, guiding me backward.

Because I'd let go of Max's leash to hug Killian, I had nothing to keep me from moving with Wes. Killian laughed as he stepped in front of Laura to stop her from coming after me. Max began barking, but it was muffled a second later when Wes shut us into a storage closet.

He clicked the string above my face, illuminating the small space.

Our bodies were nearly flush as his chest heaved, and mine did the same. His hand was still on my hip, and I had no idea if he was aware of it or not, but there wasn't even enough room to shake it off.

"You're not staying with him," Wes stated, towering over me.

I tilted my head back, watching his jaw work back and forth. I could feel the strain in the air between us, and while I knew Wes didn't want me anymore, it didn't stop my nipples from hardening under my shirt, or that my body felt like liquid moonlight was suddenly thrumming under my skin. This was the effect Wes had always had over me. He was sunshine, and I was always the sleepy flower, waking up to bask in his warmth.

"Where am I supposed to stay, Wes?"

I was practically whispering at this point, and while it was quieter in here, I didn't need to soften my tone. Words just felt heavy and burdensome.

Wes searched my face, that conflict twisting and forcing his hand at my hip to cinch the fabric in his fist.

"I told you—"

Shaking my head, I cut him off. "I'm not driving fifteen miles to the next town."

His voice dropped to a whisper. "I warned you if you came for the club you'd be met with war."

His mouth spoke of war, but his hands at my waist, and the way he kept closing the space between us, spoke of something else. Something we'd both left behind and closed the book on seven years ago.

I wanted to smile again, act cocky like I did last time, but I was so tired. And more than anything, I wanted to get away from him, because these feelings he was stirring weren't welcome or convenient.

Right as I was about to open my mouth and wave the white flag, the door opened, and Laura snatched my wrist and yanked.

"Found us a spot."

I reeled, falling after her as she pulled me behind her. Wesley's hands fell away, but he was on my heels a second later. Killian was nowhere to be found, and the rest of the club looked like they'd fallen back into their previous chaos.

"Where?" I asked, searching the room, but Laura kept pulling until we were near the front door. A woman with thick black hair, wearing jeans so tight they could have been painted on, waited. Her face was down, staring at her cell, and my dog's leash was wrapped around her fist.

Wes groaned from behind me. "You've got to be fucking kidding me."

The woman looked up from her phone and gave us a blinding smile. Her big blue eyes were framed by dark lashes and flawless wing-tipped eyeliner. Her heart shaped face was beautiful, but my gaze was drawn to the bar through her eyebrow and the ring in her nose. Outside, she looked hard and edgy, but there was a sorrow about her that made my heart ping around in my chest with familiarity.

"Hello, Wesley. Heard your girl needs a place to stay." The woman winked at me.

Wes shook his head, slowing his steps until he was far enough away to resume his power stance—legs wide, arms crossed, face obstinate.

"Sasha."

She tucked her cell into her bra, then blew him a kiss. Her tall boots shifted on the hardwood as she turned to open the door.

I didn't know what their relationship was, but for some reason I felt the need to blurt, "I'm *not* his girl."

Sasha paused and threw me a look over her shoulder.

"Yes, you are, honey. The sooner you accept that, the easier all of this will be."

"Stone Riders don't condone this. You'll be going against the club," Wes muttered in a deathly quiet tone.

With one last crinkle to her eyes and pop to her pink gum, Sasha smiled and said, "All my allegiance to this club was buried with Simon. The only other person on this planet that could summon any more from me is this girl right here."

She slipped out, and Laura was on her heels. For some reason, I gave Wes one last look before following them.

As exhausted as I was, my mind still tumbled over the painful interaction with him. Why didn't he want me here? Why on earth was I so delusional where he was concerned? It wasn't as though he were harboring a secret crush on me all these years later, or wanted me back.

It's been seven years, and it was fucking high time to get over my first love.

# EIGHT
## WES
### AGE 15

My dad often took my brothers and me out to the river to fish. We'd sit on the boardwalk with our lines dangling in the water while we relaxed in our camping chairs. This time of year, half the town was out there trying to catch something. I used to love it. I'd look forward to it all week, since my dad worked and the only free time he had was on the weekends. Now, all I could do was stare at my watch as the day waned and time ticked by.

"You're not even trying, Wesley," my dad chided as my shoulders slumped and my line followed suit.

"He's distracted," my brother joked, pulling on his rod to tighten his line.

My dad watched me carefully, chewing his spearmint gum, making his jawline look intense. He reminded me of Pete Carol when he did that. Dad watched us with the same intensity as when the head coach watched his team execute a play. A lot of unnerving silence. He even had slightly graying hair like the coach, plus a narrow face and slender nose.

"What has you distracted?"

I hoped with all my might my brother didn't know. I had worked so hard to keep Callie a secret for this reason right here. I didn't want anyone to ruin what we had, or to do anything to mess it up. As it was, she wasn't something I had to explain or share with my brothers, and I'd do just about anything to keep it that way.

I said nothing right as Dustin said, "He's distracted by that Stone girl, from down the road."

My neck grew warm as I stared out over the water. My dad's gaze was laser focused on me, and I knew I had to be careful with what I said next.

"The biker's daughter?"

His tone was curt but curious, like he wasn't sure that could be true and maybe he had it wrong.

I swallowed the thick lump lodging itself in my throat.

"We're just friends."

Dustin scoffed with his entire chest, making him look like an idiot. I glared a hole into the side of his stupid face.

"I can't imagine being friends with that girl is prudent. She's from a pretty rough family. I'd like you to steer clear of her."

He said rough family, but all I heard was *real* family.

My parents shoved faith and family values down my throat so often I wanted to tear through them with my teeth just to get some air. Dad was strict, but he was also a hypocrite. He didn't think we knew about the lipstick on his collar when he came home, or the fact that he smelled like a perfume brand that Mom didn't own. He didn't think we saw Mom's jaw grow tight when she greeted him or how she swiped at her eyes when she wandered back toward the back of the house.

They had five children together, but he wasn't faithful.

Regardless, if I spoke any of these thoughts out loud, it would be a big production of yelling, grabbing my collar, and shoving me into the basement to think about my mouth. I'd miss seeing Callie, and it wasn't worth it.

I smashed my back molars together hard, feeling my jaw tighten, and tried to focus on the future, on the good things. I'd be turning sixteen in three months. Callie was sixteen in two.

For the past few summers, we had continued sharing the tree-house, but our legs were getting long for the space, and our innocent kisses started turning much less innocent. Two weeks ago, when the weather had shifted and school let out, Callie had snuck over like usual. But that shirt she wore that was too big for her wasn't as big, and curiosity finally got the better of me.

I pulled it up over her head and saw her in a sports bra for the first time, and I realized I really liked getting to see her skin. I had pulled the pillow from behind my head and pushed it over my lap so she wouldn't see how badly I wanted to touch her. Since then, we'd done a lot of kissing and exploring with our hands, but there was a part of me that wanted to do more. Feel more. See more.

We continued fishing and drinking sodas, and I ended up betting Dustin five dollars that I'd catch something before he did.

I won, just like I usually did. On our way home, we stopped for gas, at which point an idea formed in my head.

"I have to go to the bathroom," I declared to my dad and brother and then darted inside.

I knew I didn't have much time, so I searched carefully for what I wanted. The options were limited, but I found what I needed and took it up to the front, silently praying I was able to pay before my dad came inside.

"Just this?" Old man Barker eyed me suspiciously.

I blushed under his scrutiny. "Yeah, just that."

He rang me up and slid the item into a bag as I handed over the five I had won. I gave him a brief nod of thanks and then hurried outside. Instead of keeping it in the bag, I removed it and shoved it into my back pocket so there'd be no questions whatsoever about what I had purchased.

Once we were back home and I'd helped put everything away, I began pacing the backyard. It was late June, and while I knew Callie would come by later, a part of me didn't want to wait to give her what I'd bought. I wanted to see her face when she held it in her hand and realized I was thinking of her while I was out today.

"Mom, I'm going to ride my bike down to the park," I called out, knowing she was in the kitchen.

She made eye contact with me, her sharp brown eyes assessing me for lies.

"Be back by dinner."

I nodded and took off down the road.

If she talked to my dad, he might put two and two together and realize I was trying to see Callie, but I didn't have a phone yet, and it wasn't like they could track me or call and ask me to come back. I rode hard, standing up on my pedals to gain speed and distance from my house. The sun was setting, leaving pastel streaks across the horizon, but it was still sandwiched against a pale blue sky.

Within minutes, I was at the top of Callie's driveway, staring at the rusted mailbox and the painted image of a skull with roses blooming from the eye sockets. Not once had I ever ventured down the gravel path or dared to get any closer to her house, but I was almost sixteen. Soon, I'd be driving, and my hope was that I could pick her up on dates, which would require me to get closer than her mailbox.

With a nervous swallow, I pedaled down the path.

Every few feet, rusty metal littered the patch of grass on either side of the dirt drive. Bike parts, truck frames, old wheels. Wildflowers grew among some of the rust, which was oddly beautiful.

Soon enough I was right in front of Callie's house. It was two stories, but it looked even older than my house.

Dull windows, some patched up with plywood, lined the top story of the house, and the lower story was much of the same. Bed sheets hung as curtains, and car parts littered the ground and porch.

There didn't seem to be anyone around until I heard the screen door screech open and a man with long, dark hair walked out. He wore a leather vest with a few white and red patches covering the right side, and in white lettering, the word "President," was sewn into the left side of his vest. Dark ink covered his arms, down to his knuckles, and under the loose shirt he wore there was even more ink along his torso.

I knew this was Callie's dad.

He was staring at me from a pair of eyes that seemed to match hers, and even his expression was similar to hers when she got upset.

"Who are you?" he asked harshly.

Words died on my tongue as I stared at him. All the warnings about him being dangerous came rushing back, freezing my limbs. I probably looked like an idiot just straddling my bicycle not saying anything.

"Well… you here sellin' something or what?"

Sweat trickled down my neck as I stared up at him, until finally words came.

"I'm here to see Callie."

By the way the man's eyebrows lifted, this answer amused him.

"You the boy that got into a fight for her?"

I nodded, trying to think back to that day when everything changed between Callie and me. There'd been more fights since then. Turns out the boys at her school were pricks and liked to make jokes about her. It only took one time for me to overhear them joke about her being club pussy for me to lose it.

The man laughed, walking closer. "I was wondering when you'd finally show your face."

Was I in trouble? Was he going to hit me?

"Killian says you fight like you have nothing to lose, like you can't stop." He lifted his chin in my direction. "That true?"

There was a big fire pit between us, dead grass, a rusted barrel of ash and debris.

"Yes, sir."

He laughed, tipping his head back.

"Call me Stone, or Prez, but not sir."

I nodded, not wanting to speak another blunder.

"What's your name?"

A slight breeze blew between us, making his hair shift the slightest bit.

"Wesley Ryan. I go by Wes."

His long legs ate up the space between us, and his hand came down on my shoulder.

"You Terrance Ryan's kid?"

I nodded, having no idea what he'd heard of my father. Probably that he was a good guy who attended church, paid his taxes, and had a handful of kids at home. Maybe he'd heard something else, because the look that passed over his face was almost pitiful.

"Okay, Wes. Let's see if you can hit a heavy bag, then you can help me clean up some of these beer bottles."

I didn't want to clean up beer bottles or really learn to hit, but he was being nice to me. Besides, maybe it would allow me the chance to see more of where Callie grew up.

An hour went by. I learned to hit a heavy bag with my bare fists and push through the pain. My knuckles were puffy and red, but I still felt a small thrill inside that Stone had taught me something. He'd stayed the entire hour, explaining where to move, how to shift, where to land the blow to get a better outcome.

A few of his guys came and watched, talking, drinking, and laughing while I continued to hit. It felt good. To fuel my hits, I thought about my dad and my brothers. I thought about how they wanted me to go see my grandparents again, which would take me from Callie. I thought about the boys I saw talking to Callie when we were outside the local swimming pool. I thought about the way their eyes traced her body when she wore her two-piece swimsuit.

I had a lot of rage inside, and hitting the bag felt better than anything I'd done besides spend time with Callie.

Finally, there was a soft laugh that pulled me away from the heavy bag. I turned around and saw Callie making her way into the large garage. She wore a pink skirt and a flowy white top. Her hair was braided, and her lips were glossy. I felt my stomach dip, and suddenly I swiped at my forehead to get rid of any sweat lingering there. Her dad watched me with a smirk.

"Well, look who finally showed up. Callie, your boyfriend here is a good egg. I assumed he'd crack a long time ago. Bring him around more often. He's got a killer right hook."

I beamed, feeling seen for the first time in years. His approval of me being her boyfriend also felt oddly fulfilling, like a soothing balm over a cut. I knew they said her dad was bad news, but I liked him. He was calm while instructing me how to hit, and he made me laugh.

The guy I recognized as Killian handed me a water bottle with a grin. He was a few years older than me, and ever since I'd met the guy, there was something about him that made me want to be just like him when I was older. He had confidence and a sense of belonging that I couldn't begin to fathom.

Callie's expression was hard to decipher. Her brows were drawn tight, her jaw was clenched, and her eyes had a strange sheen to them. She gave a piercing glare to her dad as soon as he turned his back then pulled on my hand, leading me outside. I heard a chorus of laughter as we went. Once outside, I noticed her face was turning a reddish color and that sheen in her eyes had turned to tears.

"What are you doing here?" Her voice came out crisp and harsh, so unlike anything I'd ever heard muttered from her lips before.

The sun was setting, and I was positive I'd missed dinner. Mom would be pissed.

"I wanted to bring you something, but you weren't here. Your dad came out and talked to me, and I ended up hitting the heavy bag for a while."

Her arms crossed over her chest, like she was upset. I wasn't sure why; I hadn't done anything.

"Are you mad that I came?"

Her eyes flashed, her nose flared, and then she stomped off toward the woods that separated our properties.

"Callie! Wait!"

I nearly tripped over a branch trying to keep up with her.

"What's wrong?"

Finally, once we were far enough away from her house, she spun on me.

"You weren't supposed to come. I didn't want you to see my house, or my broken dad, or my pathetic life!" she screamed at me, her face flushing with anger.

"Why?"

Her hands went up as she paced the clearing around us. There was an old cabin off to our left that looked like someone had recently visited. She glared over my shoulder at it as more tears clouded her vision. I couldn't stop watching her legs, or thinking about how tan they looked in her skirt.

With a choked sob, she explained, "Because you come from this perfect life, Wes. A big family that takes vacations and goes to church. You've been on a plane; you get new clothes at the start of every school year, and you don't even go to school! I don't have that. I have a dad who barely looks at me, never asks where I've been, and thinks it's perfectly appropriate to let me be around this life *he* chose. I grew up without a schedule; there's no normalcy in my life. I drank my first beer at *nine*, Wes. Found my first blunt at ten. Saw people having sex when I was too young to even understand what they were doing. I've been offered a tattoo more times than I can count. I made my own lock system on my door because of how many times guys have tried to sneak into my room. Sometimes there's not food here if Dad drinks and forgets to cash his checks or go shopping. The only way I get new clothes is if Red takes me."

Her voice began to shake as she neared the end of her tirade. Chest heaving, she stared at me, waiting for me to reply. All I could focus on were the images she'd shared and having to go through all that at such a young age. I clenched my fists tightly, embracing the pain and tenderness from using them against the heavy bag for the past hour.

The sun had officially dipped below the hills, leaving a dusky sky overhead and a few stars beginning to peek through. There was a lot I wanted to say, but I wasn't sure how to say it all, so instead, I stepped closer and pulled her hand into mine.

"What are you afraid of?"

Her dark brows pulled together as she searched my face, "What do you mean?"

"You don't want me to see it…what are you afraid of? Do you think I'll judge you?"

She wrapped her arms around her middle, as if she was trying to become smaller. I hated it.

"I'm afraid of losing you because of it. Like it will be too much for you, and you'll cut me loose like one of those fish you're always catching."

A laugh loosened the tightness in my chest. "I legally have to throw those back."

She tried to smack my chest, but I caught her hand.

"You fish for the thrill, to hold it in your hand for a pretty photo. A memory. Then you toss it back, never to think of it again. I think I'm something you'll remember one day when thinking back over your youth, while you sip expensive wine with your fancy wife. I'm the memory you'll have, not the moment you want to keep."

I kissed her forehead, then wrapped my arms around her. Fuck, she had no clue, did she? No idea how embedded in my life she'd become.

"I got you something today. I know it's small and cheap…but it made me think of you."

She leaned back, tilting her head. "You did?"

"Mmmhmm." I pressed the key into her palm, hoping it wouldn't be a big deal, but she disconnected from our hug and took a step back.

Her pink nails curled around it, and the tightening in my chest made it seem like she'd curled them around my heart.

"A key?" Her blue eyes lifted. "What's it go to?"

The small key was painted a light purple with stars, made to replicate the night sky. The key didn't even go to anything, it was a blank, but I didn't have time to think all that through when I was in the store earlier.

I stumbled through explaining myself. "Right now, it doesn't go to anything, but I was thinking maybe one day we can get it made for our house—"

Her pink lips parted on a gasp.

I shut my eyes and powered on. "You think I want to get rid of you, or throw you back." I shook my head. "Callie, if you want to use a fishing metaphor, then you'd be the river, not the fish inside it. You cut a path through me, filled it, and now it's always shifting and moving. I can't wait to see what our life will look like someday, but for now, I'm happy taking it one day at a time."

She stepped forward and threw her arms around my neck.

"I love you, Wes."

I gripped her waist, pulling her closer, feeling my chest ache with how long I've waited to hear her say those words. "I love you too, and one day, when I have a house for us, that key will be the one to open it."

She giggled into my neck, a slightly watery sound that had me realizing she was crying happy tears.

"Okay."

I shifted back to catch her gaze. "You realize that will mean you have to get used to me hanging around your dad, right?"

She pushed her bottom lip out then rolled her eyes. "That's exactly what they'll call you if you're not careful."

My brows caved in confusion. "They'll call me what?"

"A hang-around. They're going to think you want to become a prospect, Wes. You have to make it clear you're only there for me, otherwise they'll take you from me."

I laughed at the mere idea of not only them accepting me but me ever wanting anything more than her.

"I'd never choose anything over you."

I grabbed her hand and pulled her along with me as I headed back to her house. No way was I letting her walk home in the dark, and I'd be in trouble once I got home, so I couldn't go out to the treehouse.

I pulled her to a stop and kissed her.

She moved with the kiss, returning it breathlessly, then adding, "You do realize you sort of make it seem like you might want to marry me someday, Wes, with this sort of thing?"

I laughed into her neck.

"One day at a time, River."

# NINE
## CALLIE

SASHA LIVED IN A BARN.

On the outside, it was plain, with weathered gray, chipped boards, and a dark, pitched roof, the inside had been renovated to near perfection. Natural light spilled through the overarching windows, illuminating the hardwood under our feet. Thick rugs softened the space, along with cushioned chairs and a long, L-shaped couch. The walls were redone with shiplap so they were smooth to the touch.

I sipped my coffee, taking in the decor and enjoying the sound of a nearby rooster crowing. A tin can holding faux wheat stalks was in the corner, and so was Max, curled into a ball on his dog bed. The guest bed she put me in was one of the softest I'd ever slept in, and from the fact that Laura was still sleeping, I had to assume hers was just as soft.

Overall, this place was incredible, but my eyes kept catching on little things that had my breath hitching the slightest bit. Sasha had photos of my dad all over the place, and pictures of me as a little girl…and pictures of me and my dad together. My heart squeezed painfully tight as I left the safety of my chair and walked over the scattered rugs to trace one of the images sitting on the mantel. In the image, I'm wearing overalls, and in my hand is a big beach ball. I remembered that day.

How did she have all these photos?

"Oh good, you're up." Sasha yawned from behind me. "Did you find the coffee?"

I turned, lifting my cup. "Yeah, thanks for leaving it ready to go and having creamer."

Fluffing one of the couch cushions, her thin robe swayed until she tied it more securely at her waist. This morning, without her makeup, she looked a few years older. I had placed her at mid-thirties, but now I was wondering if I was a few years off.

"What should we have for breakfast? I was thinking of grabbing some—"

"Why do you have pictures of my dad all over your house?" I cut in, then gestured to the photo on the mantel. "And of me? What is all this and who were you to my dad?"

Her arms fell to her sides, the pillow she was fluffing dropping with the movement. I watched her countenance transition from caring host to guarded and emotionally distant.

She blew out a breath, making some of her falling hair lift from her face.

"Could we at least have breakfast before we dive into all of it?"

She moved around the living room, briskly darting toward the kitchen.

I trailed her, hugging my coffee mug like it was a raft in the middle of the ocean. I knew her question was rhetorical, but a part of me wanted to sass back that breakfast could wait. It was really freaking strange that she had images of my entire life in here.

A cupboard creaked open as Sasha grabbed a mug and began pouring herself a cup of coffee. When she didn't respond, I slid onto the bench, tucking my legs below her breakfast nook.

"Okay, can you at least tell me what you were to my dad? You two seemed close."

She half turned, giving me a tiny laugh that came out strained. Her eyes watered as she leaned against the counter and sipped from her mug.

"Simon and I—" Her voice cracked, and suddenly my own seemed to be caught in my lungs. "We were together, romantically, for the past five years."

My breath stalled for a moment as I processed what she'd said. My dad had been single for most of my life, save for the one-night stands. A part of me hated that I had missed seeing him in a committed relationship. To see him smile and laugh, to see him in love. By the way he looked in the pictures, I knew he loved Sasha. Sorrow sharp and deep cut through me as the reality of how much I had missed of his life sank in.

"I didn't realize…" I softly said, staring down into my cup.

Sasha moved forward and gripped my hand tightly.

"There's so much behind my relationship with your dad, and more history than I have time to get into, but here are the facts. I loved him. He lived here with me. That's why there are a million photos of you around here. He loved you so much. All the stories he'd tell…"

She looked off to the side, her lip trembling as tears trailed down her cheeks. "I can't bring myself to take them down. You were a part of him, Callie. Even if you didn't realize it, you lived in that man's heart more than anyone else on this earth ever did or ever would. Even more than me. I loved him, and because of him, I grew to love you, too."

A tear slipped from between my lashes, trailing my cold face. I hadn't even realized my face had gotten so frigid; my hands were practically blocks of ice as well.

Sasha sniffed, then took my face in between her palms.

"You got the letter from your daddy, right? The one from the reading of the will?"

I nodded, even as new questions formed in my head. Like why he didn't leave anything to Sasha, or the bigger question—why wasn't she at his funeral? She would have known about his sickness, and even cared for him as he transitioned into hospice.

Sasha searched my face and dropped her voice into a whisper.

"You have to sell that place, Callie. There are too many skeletons in the closet. Get rid of it, honey. No matter what Wes has to say, you have to sell. Okay?"

My stomach twisted with those same familiar knots I'd felt the first time I had read my father's words requesting that I sell. It just seemed strange. Why would he want to give up something that had been in the family for so long? That had been with his club?

"What if I keep it?" I asked, tilting my head just the smallest bit.

Sasha's lips thinned and her grip on my face hardened, though not painfully—more like she was terrified of letting me go.

"You just can't, honey. Your daddy barely made it through the last time you were hurt by that rival club. You keep that property, and it's like having a target on your back. You've got to sell it, take the money, and move far, far away from here. Go out west, settle down with some handsome banker, and pop out a few babies. Smile, be free, live a safe life. That's what your daddy wanted."

"But what if—"

A loud yawn interrupted our conversation as Laura made her way downstairs, and then immediately following her traipse down each step, a loud motorcycle engine reverberated through the walls.

Sasha popped up, her face swinging toward the window like she was nervous about who had just pulled up. I watched carefully as she drew the sash of her robe tighter. My old instincts were kicking in too; my dad would always give cues as to when we should be afraid of who had rolled onto our property. The space near his eyes would always tighten, his mouth would turn down, and his finger would tap. It was barely noticeable to anyone else, unless you were around him all the time. I didn't know Sasha to know if she gave anything away, but the way she dropped to her knees and tugged out a nickel-plated revolver, then slid it under the bag of bread in front of us, told me whoever was coming was dangerous.

"He's going to knock, and then he's going to open the door. Tell him nothing about yourselves. Don't even tell him your names." Sasha's voice shook the smallest bit, making my stomach churn.

Laura was next to me in a heartbeat, hugging my wrist with a death grip.

"Callie, hide your tattoo. Throw on a sweater or something, but don't engage with him at all. He already knows you're here because of your car, otherwise I'd have you just hide upstairs. This will prevent him from getting suspicious. Ignore everything that comes out of my mouth in the next few minutes."

Sasha walked forward as someone pounded on her front door, rattling a few of the picture frames near the trim. Max began barking, but I snapped my fingers, indicating he needed to sit next to me. He obeyed, morosely as he stared at the door.

"Go grab coffee. You have to act like we aren't scared as shit right now," I whispered to Laura, so she'd let go of my wrist. She snapped out of it a second later and did as I said, keeping her eyes lowered to the counter and the task at hand.

Sasha smiled widely as she opened the door, and a man walked in. Max made a sound, but I put my hand on his head, indicating he needed to calm.

The man wore a faded leather cut with a red, gaping shirt underneath, leaving all the ink on his arms available for me to see. The Grim Reaper was inked into his skin over and over in varying ways. That, and a few snakes, some military sigil that I wasn't familiar with, and a few other faded lines I couldn't make out, but it was enough to identify him as a Death Raider.

My skin pebbled with goosebumps as fear gripped me and my fingers itched to reach for the revolver hiding just inches in front of me.

"Thought you were coming over last night?" the man asked, walking further into Sasha's home like he owned it. His boots tracked in dirt, and his greasy hair was held back by a black bandanna. His skin was tan, likely from riding, but it also looked weathered and hairy. He looked to be roughly around the same age my dad was before he passed. Well shit, I hadn't seen him in seven years, he likely looked older. I pushed the thought away, so I could focus on the interaction in front of me, regardless of the painful lump in my throat.

Sasha ducked her head to the side as he stepped closer and gripped her chin.

I had no idea what was happening, but I knew she didn't like this man, nor did she want him touching her.

As if he could feel my gaze on him, his eyes suddenly jumped up, landing on mine.

"Who are your friends?"

I doubted very much this man was smart enough to make the connection of who I was based off the pictures around the room. I wasn't any older than fifteen in any of them.

Sasha led the way, smiling as she gestured toward us.

"This is Sheila, the daughter of one of my best friends. Her and her friend were just passing through for the night, but I made them promise to stop in and see me."

The man drew closer, and my breathing hitched. I didn't like him this close, and my head and gut were screaming at me to grab the gun.

His eyes were dark as they lingered on Laura's exposed legs, and then ever so slowly, he slid his gaze to me.

With an oil-stained finger, he pointed at me. "You're familiar. Why are you so familiar?"

Max barked, loudly, and it reverberated around the walls so much the man cursed.

"Fuck, that a horse or some shit?"

I was thankful for the distraction Max provided, but the man's gaze returned to me a second later. I shrugged; a knot stuck in my throat. Sasha laughed him off, tugging on his vest to get his attention off me, but his gaze was laser focused.

I finally made my voice work, just so he'd stop looking at me. "I've never been here before, no idea."

Sasha glanced at the bag of bread then flicked her gaze to me. The message was clear.

If he made a move, shoot him.

"No. I know you from somewhere...I've seen you. That nose, and those lips...I recognize you."

My heart hammered in my chest as he spoke. Was he there that night? Was he one of the men in the van?

"Spider, stop scaring the girl. She said she doesn't know you, so let it go," Sasha teased, tugging on him again.

He finally relented, shifting away with Sasha's pull. His lips landed on hers a second later, his hands shoved deep into her hair as he deepened the kiss. Sasha moved backward, so they were shifting further from us.

I eyed Laura, silently telling her to stay where she was. I noticed her eyes were huge, and her fingers were shaking as she held her mug in front of her.

While Spider and Sasha kissed, his eyes flicked my way once more before another loud engine echoed in the air.

Spider broke away first. "You expecting one of them?"

Sasha's mouth was swollen as she shook her head. "No, Simon died. I haven't stepped foot in their club since."

Hearing her say my dad's name to this man so flippantly felt like a punch to my stomach. Was Sasha playing both sides?

Spider watched her carefully before turning toward the door. His jaw flexed as the sound drew closer, until a second and third engine could be heard. My heart was a terrified thing, searching for some form of safety. I found myself praying that Killian or Wesley were on their way, because even if we were at war, they'd never hurt me.

"Fuck, there's more than one of them. I have to get out of here. You better have your ass in my bed by tonight. Understand?" Spider slapped Sasha's butt as if she needed the physical example. She stared at him, dopey eyed, but I didn't miss the way her fingers shook as she tucked away a piece of hair, or the way her lower lip trembled as she watched him stalk away.

Spider started his bike and took off through the back side of Sasha's property, avoiding the main road, and within a few seconds, three new bikes were parked in front of her house in a plume of dust. Sasha swiped at her eyes, then seemed to mess with her hair, as if she could erase the imprint of his fingers in it.

The door was still open, and within the span of a few breaths, Wesley was walking through it, followed by Killian. The third person was someone I didn't recognize. Max barked again, and this time, I removed my hand, allowing him the chance to go sniff and inspect the newcomers.

I hated how my eyes searched for Wesley's, and I hated even more that his gaze skipped Sasha completely and landed on me first. He stood frozen on the threshold, as if he needed to work out what had just happened.

"Who the fuck was just here, Sasha?" he asked, his voice as turbulent and violent as any tempest in the ocean.

I let out a shuddered breath, needing a second to regroup. My fingers were numb from how hard I was gripping my mug.

Sasha seemed just as shaken as she rasped, "Spider. He heard you and took off."

Killian's gaze snapped over to me, then landed like a soft blanket over Laura. He took three steps closer to us, crowding the opposite side of the counter that Laura was huddled against. His worry wasn't for me. Killian knew I would know how to handle a random rival member showing up, regardless that it was the one rival group that had kidnapped me when I was just eighteen years old. Still, deep down, I knew he was standing there for my best friend, and a piece of me wanted to reach out and thank him for it. As it was, I was far too selfish to care for Laura myself, right now.

Wes was across the room within seconds, their third member hanging back near the door, watching the road through one of Sasha's windows.

"You had a fucking Death Raider in your house while Callie was here?"

I flinched at how loud and angry Wesley's voice carried through the room.

Sasha lowered her head, as if she were ashamed. "I forgot that he was expecting me last night. I heard she'd arrived in town, and you refused to let the poor girl stay anywhere, so I brought them here and forgot about my meetup."

Wes ran his large hand through his dark hair. Worry lined his face, and fear marked his movements. I wanted some answers, but I knew if I asked, no one would give them to me. It was club business, and I wasn't in the club.

"Did he recognize her?" Wesley's voice pitched the slightest bit, which was the only indication that somewhere down deep inside was the boy I once loved.

Sasha shook her head, but I was nodding. Wesley's eyes narrowed on us both.

"Which is it? Did he fucking recognize her or not?"

I lifted my hands like I was weighing something and shrugged. "Well, he said I was familiar…but he couldn't place me."

Laura scoffed, stepping closer, and I noticed Killian's jaw clench as she stepped closer to him.

"No, he knew her. He might not have acknowledged her name, but he knew her face. Sasha had to practically offer a lap dance to get him to stop looking at Callie."

That was exactly the wrong thing to say to Wes. I knew it the second his dark brows formed a shelf and his eyes narrowed, all while that deliciously firm jaw of his ticked.

"Get your things." He said it to me, but he was staring at Sasha as if she had somehow let him down.

"Wes, I had no idea," Sasha started, but Wes cut her off.

"No idea?" he snarled.

I flinched, and so did Laura, and while I would normally never do anything my stupid ex-boyfriend ordered me to do, I was scrambling off the stool and rushing up to the loft with my best friend and dog on my heels.

I hurriedly tore off my pajamas and pulled on a pair of shorts and tank top, tossing my remaining things into my bag. Then I tiptoed closer to the banister to eavesdrop.

I heard Sasha apologizing again and saw Wesley gesturing wildly with his arms.

"What if he had realized who she was, Sasha? You wanted to protect her, and you threw her right into the mouth of the fucking lion."

Sasha stepped up, pushing against his chest. "What about you? You refused to keep her safe by denying her entry anywhere."

Wes scoffed and ran his hands through his hair. "So she would leave!"

Sasha spun in a circle, gesturing for Killian's help.

"What would have stopped her from stopping in Rauland, or Coulder…both towns are newer Raider territory, she wouldn't even know she was walking into danger. You weren't thinking, Wes, and you're pissed because one slipped past your defenses. You can't keep that girl from what's owed to her."

Wes stared off to the side for long enough that the conversation died down. Killian took a call, glancing up every few minutes. Laura had her things packed and was just patting Max's side while we waited. Finally, Wes looked up and made eye contact with me, then slid his gaze to my friend.

"You're following us back."

Laura squeezed my hand, and I nearly choked on my spit.

He better not mean what I think he means. I slowly got to my feet and strangled the handrail as I glared back at him. He must have known what I was about to say, because he cut me off.

"I can't trust that you won't drive off. So you're riding with me."

Shaking my head, I started to protest, but Wes glared, clenching his jaw.

"It's not up for debate, River. Get your ass down here, now."

*That name.*

I could hardly breathe as I reeled from the way that name rolled over me and struck at my heart. Laura rubbed my shoulder encouragingly, which helped me focus on moving. I gripped the handle on my suitcase and began descending the stairs. I didn't want to ride on the back of Wesley's bike. I couldn't fathom being that close to him again, and a part of me wondered why he asked me and not Laura. It didn't matter, I didn't want to be mixed up with Death Raiders, and considering they'd been at the motel we wanted to stay at, and now were at Sasha's, I was willing to go with my ex wherever he decided because I knew at least it would be Death Raider free.

I had traded cell phone numbers with Sasha, much to Wesley's frustration and multiple protests, but she had been kind to me, and regardless of whatever sort of weird Raider situation she had going on, I liked her. She hugged me tight, as I always imagined my own mother would, and sent us on our way.

Once we were outside, I tossed my things in the back hatch of my car and clutched my best friend in a tight hug.

"I'll make sure you don't get lost, just follow close."

She nodded and took the keys from me, while I helped Max into the backseat.

Wesley waited near his bike, standing like a god clad in leather and denim. He watched me walk over, hesitant and unsure. I had on my heeled boots, but I was wearing shorts, and after burning my calf on my dad's exhaust pipe as a kid, I swore I'd never do it again.

Wes caught my eye, holding my gaze as I trailed my fingers over the leather seat positioned behind where he'd be sitting.

"You remember how to ride bitch, right?" His tone came out mocking as he handed me a bucket helmet.

I was practically born on the back of a bike, and he knew it. I rolled my eyes and snatched the helmet from him, buckling it under my chin without his help. What I hadn't ever done was ride with *him*. He'd never owned a bike while we dated, and even up till the end, after he'd become a member, he wasn't riding. Or if he was, I wasn't aware of it. Seeing him straddling the bike now was an odd sensation. My stomach tilted in excitement, but nerves threatened to burrow deep enough to make me sick.

Inhaling a sharp breath, I placed my boot on the buddy peg and then my hand tentatively on his shoulder while swinging my leg over the bike, until I was resting my ass on the leather. It was warm under my legs as I adjusted. His large, calloused hand skimmed down each of my calves as if to ensure they were set properly on the pegs. I resisted the urge to lean into his back. In fact, I was sitting as far away from him as I possibly could. I could hold onto the sissy bars attached to the small chair at my back and be perfectly fine to stay on the bike. I didn't need to touch him to be safe.

The engine roared to life as Wes tugged under my knees, moving me until my thighs were cradling his hips. His silent way of telling me I would be holding on to him, and not the bars at my back.

I yelled in his ear a reminder and a way to distract from what he'd just done. "Don't lose Laura. She's not from here, and she'll have no idea where to go."

He gave me a slight nod as his wrists rotated on the throttle and clutch, and right as we were about to pull forward, I slipped my arms around him, linking my fingers together over his stomach. It felt so strange to be touching him again, much less riding with him. I couldn't deny it felt good, like it fit him in a way that nothing else ever had.

We sped down the road, as the wind whipped my hair behind me.

I decided to ignore the tiny thrill in my chest as we made our way, and I aptly ignored the butterflies that had taken flight as excitement unfurled like a waking flower in my chest. I'd never admit how badly I missed riding, nor would I admit that being this close to Wes while the wind whipped against us felt akin to flying.

Wes led us down the highway, until he turned off on a familiar road. It was the back way to his old place, which confused me. I assumed he didn't live at his old house, merely because of how much he detested the house after he'd moved out, but maybe I was wrong.

We passed the switchback that would lead to my old house, and he continued down the dirt path until we were skirting an overgrown field that was once his front yard. Weeds as tall as a kindergartner bordered his old house. The three-story home was empty and weathered. It was as if not a soul on earth remembered it was here. Wes slowed his bike, skirting the house, going around back where his tree house sat, and the property line that once divided our lands.

My eyes flicked upward to the fort, just to be sure it hadn't been torn down. The pine boards still held, as if time had forgotten them altogether. I refocused in front of me, curious where we were headed if Wes wasn't taking us to his house to stay.

Grass and sand shifted under our tires as we continued toward the thin road that separated our properties. There was never anything here that blocked either of us from moving from place to place. It was how I ran so easily to his treehouse when I was only nine years old. Now, however, there was a shiny metal fence that divided our two lands. Wes slowed as he approached a small patch of fence that began to slide open as he pressed a button on the small key fob on his key ring.

This entire setup was so advanced compared to anything my dad ever had while growing up. We had enemies, but Dad chose to protect the property closer to the house. Ten acres was too much to monitor…at least that was what I had overheard him say when the subject had come up. I was loosely hanging onto Wes now that our speed had decreased enough. I sat up tall, watching as we finally cleared the fence, and small hill, until my dad's old cabin came into view.

So many emotions rushed me as we ventured toward it. I had initially assumed Wes wanted us to stay with him, and now I realized we would be alone in the cabin. I wasn't sure which one I was more reluctant to accept. I missed the cabin, and would have loved a chance to see it, but staying in it? *Never again.*

Wesley parked and straddled the bike while taking out his cell, acting as though I wasn't on the back of his bike at all. It needled my nerves, but I pushed it away and dismounted, using his shoulders and the foot peg to keep my balance. Laura pulled in next to us and put the car in park. I stared at the front door, feeling my stomach twist into a knot.

"What is this place?" Laura asked, sounding gentle as she exited with Max and came to stand next to me.

Looking over the humble one-story cabin, a smile tilted my lips in an effort to find the joy in this scenario.

"This was my dad's cabin. We used to come out here when I was a kid and camp."

I wouldn't mention the significance the cabin had to Wes and me. No one needed to know about that, and I certainly wasn't going to dredge up old memories.

Max began to bark at a rodent hanging out near a tree and suddenly took off in a gallop toward it. Laura went after him, leaving me all alone with Wes. He had cleared his bike and strode toward the front door.

Dad's old cabin was made from logs my grandfather had cut down with his bare hands. It had an old red tin roof and a chipped green front door. All of it was in disrepair, including the half porch that used to be fully enclosed and was now mostly only framed, the screens ripped and tattered. The rocking chairs that once sat side by side under the covered porch were rotted and covered in mildew.

"It's not in the best shape, but at least you'll be safe," Wes muttered while unlocking the door and pushing inside.

I followed him, coughing into my shirt as I cleared the threshold. There was a thick blanket of dust on everything, along with a generous scattering of cobwebs. The place had been overlooked and forgotten, and while there was a small piece of me that wanted to cater to it and bring it back to life, the memories were too much.

"Wes, I can't stay here…just let me stay in town at the motel." I'd risk it at this point, if he didn't want to be responsible for us, which it seemed as though he didn't.

His eyes scanned the space, as if he was trying to see what he could fix. He dipped low and grabbed the back of a chair, righting it until it sat on all four legs, then he dusted it off with a rag from his back pocket.

"It's fine. Just a little dusting and you'll be good."

He was ignoring the real issue, which I knew I hadn't stated, but like hell would he force it out of me.

I turned toward him and gripped his elbow, so he'd look at me.

"Why do you care if I'm safe? You want me out of your life, remember? Wouldn't it move faster if the Death Raiders found me? You'd get your clubhouse then."

His gaze dropped to where our skin made contact. I'd assume he wasn't affected at all if it wasn't for the way his eyes widened or the way his lips parted when he focused on my hand.

"How could you even ask that?" His voice came like a whisper, caressing my heart in a way it had no business touching.

Shaking his head, he shifted out of my hold and took a step away.

"You hurt me, Callie. Broke my fucking heart seven years ago, and sure, it took a while to get over you, but rest assured, I did get over you. But I also promised your dad if you were to ever come back, I'd ensure you were safe. I don't owe you a place in town, or anything else, but I will always be sure you're protected."

It was on the tip of my tongue to argue that he'd broken my heart by joining the club. He knew we'd never recover if he did. It was the one request I had made of him when he started getting close to Killian and my dad. He promised me, even after I tried to make it work. I knew deep down we never would. Not when the road would always lead back to where I came from and how I grew up. *This fucking place.*

"Please, Wes. Just lift the ban and let me stay in town. Anything but here."

Suddenly he turned around, pinning me with a hard gaze.

Then, within a single breath, Wes was pushing me back toward the wall until he was towering over me, pinning my hands above my head. My shirt rose with the movement, and the brash way he handled my body was somehow so familiar it made me dizzy.

"Are you that much of a pretentious princess that you can't stay in a dusty cabin?" His nose skimmed my cheek, his knee moving in between my legs until his entire body was flush with mine. "Or is it that you're remembering our time here together…maybe that night I first fucked you?"

My arms being suspended didn't hurt, neither did the way my body was being pinned to the wall. But going back to that night, and all the nights after, was akin to dragging a knife down my chest and tugging my heart out. Of course I didn't want to think of any of our nights together. But he was wrong—I wasn't thinking of our first time here; I was still thinking of our last.

I pulled at his hold to try to end his line of questioning, but he held firm, his other hand moving to my hip.

"Do you remember what you would say to me when my head would disappear between your legs?"

Why was he doing this? I didn't want to think about it. It burned me to remember, to go back, when all I had been doing was trying to move forward. He was also acting as though all we did was hook up here. He was completely ignoring that we'd made this place a home. *Our home.*

I shook my head defiantly.

"You don't want to remember how you begged me to fuck you?" His knee pressed harder in between my thighs, taunting me to tilt my hips and engage with the friction he was providing.

His hot breath fanned my face as he whispered, "I remember how you'd tug my hair and scream for me to go deeper with my tongue, to suck your clit. Remember that time I flipped you on your stomach and spread your cheeks, until I was circling your—"

"Callie! There's an archery range out back and a target for ax throwing. This place is wild, but I'm here for it!" Laura yelled from outside, making her way in.

Wes released me and stepped back, all while keeping his gaze on me.

Once Laura was on the porch, he scoffed, derision creeping into his focus.

"I hope you think of it all night, Callie. *All of it.* I hope you remember why you should have just stayed away, and then I hope you wake up in this shithole and realize how irrelevant you've become. You left, and you should have stayed gone. Now you're just creating work for me, so do me a favor and stay here like a good little princess, unless you're ready to give up and go back home."

With that, he walked away, the scuff of his boots rumbling against the hardwood and a million dust motes gleaming in the slice of sunlight from the open door.

Laura stood in the doorway watching, her face blanching. Obviously she'd heard the tail end of what he said. Then Max ran inside with a loud bark, and I couldn't hold myself up any longer.

I slid to the floor and watched as my dog moved in to support mode, placing his head into my lap. My best friend curled in on the other side of me, and we stared at the tattered cabin in front of us, unsure what to do.

Laura spoke first.

"So to be clear, we'll get in trouble if we go back to Sasha's?"

I sighed, "yep."

She made a sound of understanding.

"And we're still blacklisted from town?"

"Correct." I slid my fingers through Max's silky coat, trying to calm my nerves.

"Okay, well, that's bullshit. We are so getting that asshole back. We still have a good chunk of the day left, let's go talk to a few realtors."

As if any would work with us.

Laura could likely feel my mood, because she slipped her arm under mine and helped me up.

"There is no way Wes has every single one under his thumb. He's not that crafty. Let's talk to one out of DC, or at least a few cities over."

I hated this, because I knew how delicate this situation was, and it wasn't as simple as just going a few cities over to find a realtor. If that one person had any ties to a rival club, then there would be a war. They couldn't know that the club was for sale, but what option was Wes leaving me?

I had to figure out some way to get the upper hand.

Sasha wanted me to sell so badly…surely she would know of someone I could talk to.

Decision made. I'd reach out, but be discreet about it. Wes didn't control everything; it was high time someone stepped up and showed him that.

# TEN
## WES
### AGE 17

I tugged on the back door one last time to ensure it was locked before flipping the lights.

It was part of closing procedures, but even if it wasn't, I'd still do two rounds, double checking all the locks. It was one of the reasons my boss loved me, and why he gave me whatever shift I wanted.

I got myself a job at the local mechanic shop, called Henry's Auto Body. It wasn't anything fancy, but the town trusted Mr. Henry with their vehicles, which in turn kept his doors open and customers coming back. I had requested the closing shift two months ago as summer approached, because I wanted the chance to be with Callie without raising suspicion from my parents. They knew I usually closed things around nine, but that I stayed after to help with custom work. They just had no idea how long that usually took. That was before when I actually had a family who gave a fuck about my life.

Now, it was just convenient to have a similar schedule as Callie.

Finally moving to the side door, I grabbed my stuff and exited the shop. My head was down, peering at my cell phone as I walked toward my truck. The summer heat was heavy against my skin as I tugged open my door and tossed my lunch box and extra shirt inside.

I smiled, peering at the screen as an image popped up on my

phone of Callie serving ice cream at work. She'd grabbed a part-time shift down at the Shake Shack, which was the only thing in town open past nine p.m. Her shift would be over in roughly an hour, which left me a little time to clean up before I saw her. I punched out a quick reply to her text.

> Me: cute, but is it just me or Travis staring awfully hard at your ass?

In the picture, she wore her long hair in two braids down her back that somehow framed her face like a goddamn dream, with little wisps and curls from the heat. Her thick lashes were dark, her hazel eyes lined in black, and her lips glossy with that pink shit she used that tasted like marshmallows. Her denim cutoffs were marginally longer than others she liked to wear in the summer and her tank top was loose, showing just the straps of her sports bra. I understood why guys looked. I just didn't fucking like it. She wasn't just beautiful; she grew up to be stunning in a way that made men stop walking to stare, even if they were on dates. In a way that drew unwanted attention and eyes on her, all the goddamned time.

> Callie: yeah, that talk you had with him did nothing. Think you might need to drive down here and give it another go, maybe this time with your fist.

She had no idea how difficult it was for me not to do exactly that.

She was bullied a lot growing up, guys making her feel unworthy because of her home life and circumstances, but it made her hard as nails. She took zero shit from anyone, including me. When we argued, it always ended with my mouth on her, or my dick sliding inside her, but never with her cowering or backing down.

My seventeenth birthday was celebrated by getting to discover Callie's body. Every inch, curve, and dip…and I made this discovery mostly with my tongue. We were in her dad's cabin when those kisses turned frantic, and before either of us knew what was happening, she was begging me for something I had been dying to give her. We took from each other, marking a first for us both. She gave me her virginity, and I gave her mine.

So as desperate as I was to drive down there and handle that motherfucker for staring at my girlfriend's ass, she was perfectly capable of handling it on her own. Besides, I wanted to shower before I saw her and hopefully talk to my mom about what she was planning to do. My brothers had moved out but kept asking me to talk to her. My parents were clearly not together, and for whatever reason, not divorcing. It made us all worry about what the future looked like for them both.

> Me: I love you, baby. I'll see you the second you get off work, but I gotta run home real quick.

Her text came in within seconds again.

> Callie: Fine, I'll handle him. Love you too, see you soon. And I'm picking the show tonight, no more of that sci-fi stuff.

Pocketing my phone, I made quick work of driving home. The small kitchen light was on and visible through the green and white curtains Mom kept over the sink, which meant my mom was home. Things between her and my dad had gotten to an all-time low, with him coming home less and less and her starting to hang out with my Aunt Stacy more often.

My siblings were all old enough that we didn't rely on her as much anymore. I was the last boy in the house, and my sisters were doing their own things, spending time at their friends' houses more than home. Honestly, it was shitty. I missed my family. It felt as though we'd slowly broken apart like an old building. Over time, piece by piece.

Sometimes I wondered if it would have been better if it had all just ended at once, like a bomb going off. Blowing everything we knew up, but then allowed us the chance to start over.

I walked through the front door, setting my stuff down, and tugged off my oil-stained shirt, leaving me in my tank top. "Mom?"

Rounding the corner to the kitchen revealed a shadowed figure sitting at my kitchen table, but it wasn't my mother.

"Simon?" My brows furrowed, my hand paused in the air, gripping my stained shirt.

The leader of the Stone Riders Motorcycle Club was sitting in my house, reclining at my kitchen table, drinking sweet tea, of all things. His hair was pulled back into a messy knot at the base of his skull, revealing his strong jaw and those eyes that looked so similar to Callie's.

The chair across from him slid backward as his boot nudged it. "Take a seat, Balboa."

Balboa was the shitty nickname I'd been given when I was fifteen and he'd helped me learn how to hit a heavy bag. It was supposed to be after Rocky Balboa. Those lessons didn't stop that day. I had gone back several days a week to meet with Killian and Simon, and eventually Hamish, and Brooks all joined in on teaching me. Callie didn't know, and I didn't like keeping it from her, but my dad had started showing up less and less in my life, and I discovered that I liked her old man, I liked his friends, and I enjoyed the lessons they taught me. Over the years, he'd become a mentor to me.

"What's goin' on?" I asked, warily taking a seat.

I would ask about my mom or sisters, but if Simon was sitting here like this that meant no one was home. *Typical.*

Simon let out a heavy sigh and toyed with the condensation on his cup before leaning in.

"I have never wanted you wrapped up in any of our club business. You know we've never talked about it in front of you. We've never done anything to mess with your relationship with Callie. I know she hates this life. Every now and then she hates me simply because of it."

I began shaking my head, because I knew Callie hated the club, but she didn't hate her dad.

Simon stopped me with a wave of his hand. "It's okay. I know where I stand with her. As long as she's safe, I don't really care, and honestly, I can't wait for her to leave this shitty town behind and start a life free of the club entirely."

That thought soured as I considered living a life without Killian's friendship, or hearing the stories Brooks made up, or seeing Simon every day. If I had my choice, my life would start and finish here with this family I was gifted.

I had to push those thoughts aside and focus on what Simon was saying. Something had changed. Simon was right—he'd never once risked bringing me into their business. Even as other guys asked if I was a new prospect, or if I was going to learn how to ride a motorcycle, Simon always shut it down. If he wasn't there, then Killian would. They both worked to ensure I was never brought into church or allowed around anyone who would spill secrets from their time in the meetings. My stomach twisted as I waited for him to explain what had changed.

"There's a war brewing, and Callie is old enough now that she could become collateral damage."

I blinked, my mind processing what he was saying. I wasn't stupid enough to assume the daughter of the president would be untouchable. I just assumed there would never be a war that would actually involve anyone getting hurt. I had seen this shit on television shows, but it didn't feel like there was a possibility that it could ever be real.

My mind was so tangled that the only words I could manage to put together were, "Who?"

Simon didn't miss a beat. "Death Raiders."

His silence stretched, and his contemplative eyes focused on the wood table in front of us.

I cleared my throat and tried to create more of a coherent sentence. "What changed?"

A heavy sigh left Simon's chest as he took a long draw of his tea. Once he set it down he answered. "Can't get into all that with you… just know, it's a dangerous development."

Simon slid backward, standing from the chair. I mimicked his movement, so I didn't have to stare up at him.

"What I came here for is to tell you that I need you to keep an eye on Callie. I want her with you as often as possible. I know you both have been sneaking down to the cabin."

My face flushed. If he knew why we were sneaking down there, he might just kill me.

"It's fine. I trust you, Wes. You're a good kid, and I know you love her. Here's a key to the cabin. You take her there and you stay there. I have no idea what the fuck is happening here with your folks, but I'm asking you to move in. Tell her whatever you want to tell her, but keep her away from the main house. I have scouts on her while she's working, but you need to be more aware of the danger. Also—"

He stood in front of me, staring me right in the eye as he handed me a nickel-plated gun.

I had hunted with my dad and grandpa from time to time, but we used rifles. I knew shit about handguns. Regardless, I wrapped my hand around it, accepting it from him.

"You're gonna learn how to use this. I wanted to keep you clear of this shit, but you're the best chance I have at keeping my daughter safe. Do you accept?"

Tucking the gun into the back of my jeans, I nodded. Sweat threatened to fall from my hairline, I only hoped it would stay in place. I wanted him to be able to count on me. Right as I went to shake his hand, my phone rang.

Callie's name lit up the screen from where it sat on the table.

Simon's eyes cut to the phone and smiled.

"She's in your hands now, son. Keep her safe."

"So my dad just gave you a key and you're moving in?" Callie didn't sound convinced.

I shrugged, unlocking the cabin door.

"I'm paying rent. Guess he was looking to rent it out since he doesn't come back here much."

She followed me inside. It was dark, but the light switch was immediately to my left. I flicked the lights, and the soft glow lit up the sparse space. Simon's cabin was small, with a tiny love seat in front of the fireplace, a rocking chair adjacent to it, and just a small bookshelf with a spot for wood. The kitchen was practically connected to the living room, it was merely a square, big enough to turn around in. A

fridge about as tall as Callie sat next to a tiny slice of counter, brack-
eted by the gas range stove. If you were to spin, you'd be at the
shallow sink, deep enough to stash roughly three or four dishes and
that's it.

Directly on the other side of the sink was enough room for a small
circular table and two chairs, then there was the bedroom door, which
led to a room big enough for a queen-sized bed, and a bathroom
where the toilet touched the shower and the simple porcelain sink.
Everything about this cabin was small, but it would be a fucking
dream compared to living at home in that huge, empty house.

Callie set her things down on the table with a sigh.

"So, my dad knows I'm staying here with you?"

I dipped to put a few logs into the wood stove before looking over
my shoulder. "You could always ask him yourself." Her relationship
with him was rocky at best. She strove for his attention, even tried to
fit in with the club from time to time, only to reject it with prejudice
the next second. It was somewhat confusing to keep up with, but in
her heart, I knew it all revolved around their relationship.

She laughed, moving to the kitchen. I had no idea what was in the
fridge or cupboards. The last time I was here with her, we fucked for
hours then passed out.

"I guess it could work. We're almost eighteen, and you already
graduated…"

She sounded like she was still trying to piece this whole thing
together, which was crazy to me. She'd had zero structure growing up.
Her dad was protective, but he rarely knew where his daughter was or
what she was doing. My parents were *constantly* asking where I was,
how long I'd be gone and who I was with, and while at the time it was
annoying, as I grew older, I could appreciate the boundaries it
provided.

"And you have a job," I added to her list of reasons why we could
live here.

I moved from the fire that was now glowing in the wood stove and
lifted her onto the counter, stepping in between her thighs.

"This isn't the place I want you to use that key on…but I also
wouldn't mind waking up to you every day. Or nearly every day…

whatever you're comfortable with. You can always go back home, but this would be nice too."

Her hands tangled together at my neck, her pink lips spread over white teeth, smiling brightly. She didn't know because I was too chickenshit to tell her, but seeing her smile nearly robbed me of breath. Holding her was the only dream I had at present, and I knew that was pathetic as fuck, but she'd been it for me for so long, I had no idea what would ever compare. I wasn't eager to find out, either. If I could have her and just support whatever dreams or aspirations she had, I'd be the happiest man alive.

"What would we do when we wake up? Would we be that couple that just get out of bed, or would we—"

I cut her off by tilting her backward and shoving her shirt up.

My tongue trailed over her belly button and lower to where her shorts buttoned. I tugged the copper tab and then slid the zipper down before responding.

"We would never be that couple, Callie." My fingers gathered at her hips and tugged her jean shorts down until she was just in her blue thong.

She watched as my nose trailed over her slit, inhaling her scent. When I'd first gone down on her and spread her puffy pussy lips with my tongue, she freaked over me smelling her, but fuck, she didn't realize what it did to me. My cock was currently granite in my jeans as I pressed a kiss to the inside of her thigh.

"What sort of couple would we be then?" Her question was breathy and held the smallest hint of excitement.

With my finger, I pulled her underwear to the side and groaned a curse.

She was glistening, her slit wet and ready for me.

"Well, I can't speak for you, but I know for me, I plan to start every morning like this, my nose in your cunt." I bent down and inhaled again. *Fuckkkkkkkkk.*

With my tongue, I slowly trailed up the length of her center without parting her.

"Each morning, I'd be buried inside you, until you screamed."

Pressing a kiss to her mound, I used my tongue to part her slit and lick slowly along her heat, drawing a moan from her. She loved when I went down on her now.

It took some time to get her used to it, just like it took me some time getting used to her taking me in her mouth, but we were adjusting. I was working on not blowing my load five fucking seconds after she started. Mostly, I savored her sounds and took her sultry moans, hoarding them like a fucking dragon would treasure. I loved her reaction to me, to everything and anything I did.

"Then what?" she asked, her voice cracking as her fingers dug into my hair.

I circled her clit and sucked, making her cry out.

"Then this," I muttered, adding two fingers to her slickness, sinking them into her pussy. My thumb found her clit, and I began to finger fuck her, watching her face as she fell apart under my touch. I knew if I moved my wrist fast enough, I could make her soak the counter, but I also knew she became too sensitive for my cock when I did that. So, I slowed my movements and kept applying pressure to her clit.

"But what if I want more than this every morning?" she asked, spreading her thighs wider. "What if I want dick every single morning, Wes? What if I become this unhinged fan, desperate for you to fill me up and fuck me every morning?"

The things she did to me with that mouth.

"Then that's exactly what you'll get," I promised before diving in with my tongue once more to make her come. Her heels dug into my back as I sucked and licked, and her fingers pulled at my hair, but within minutes, she was fucking my face without holding anything back, rocking her hips and then falling to pieces under me as she shouted out my name with a string of curses.

I gently kissed her stomach and smiled up at her.

"You ready to go to bed?"

The way she smiled back at me would stick with me forever. Pink, plump lips, white teeth, glowing olive skin, and that dark hair swaying as she let me touch her.

"Never been more ready for anything in my life."

We both laughed as I picked her up and carried her to the room. Our room.

"First, let's do something!" she said excitedly. I let her down from my arms as she ran over to her purse, her ass swaying in that thong as she pulled something out.

"Let's hang this up, as a good luck token." She held the key I'd given her when we were fifteen, making my heart stutter.

"You just carry that with you?"

She laughed, pressing the metal to her lips. "If I could ink it into my skin and carry it as a constant reminder that one day we'd be married and a happy family, I'd do it, Wes. For now, it hangs out on my keychain."

I stalked closer, feeling my chest grow significantly tighter. My nose burned, which was the oddest fucking feeling. How was it possible to love someone this much?

"Where do you want me to hang it?" I gently pulled the key from her fingers.

Her dopey smile made my knees weak.

"Above the mantel, see where that picture is? Slide the key over the nail then replace the picture. That way only the two of us will know about it."

Grinning, I did as she asked. Once the picture swung back into place, Callie was on me. Her arms went around my neck, her lips crashed against mine, and then her legs were around my waist.

We never made it to the bed that night. We ended up on the couch, and after a few rounds, I just tucked her into my chest and held her tight against me.

I thought over the conversation with her dad, then decided to push it out of my mind.

That was my first mistake.

# ELEVEN
## CALLIE

IT WAS EARLY.

The sun had just barely cleared the ridge surrounding the valley as I sat on the front porch, sipping my coffee. I had an oversized sweater over my pajama shorts. The sweater stopped mid thigh, but no one was out here to see me flash my ass if I bent over. The night spent in the cabin was as frustrating and exhausting as I assumed it would be.

After Laura and I cleaned, we went into town for food to stock the kitchen. As soon as we reached the fence to exit, there was a member from the club there to meet us and trail us into town. It annoyed Laura, but I was beyond caring anymore. I had grown up with members tailing me and following me around, so I just shoved it into the back of my mind. Once we'd returned, we began drinking. We were trying to find the silver lining of this trip, but Laura ended up passing out on the couch early, leaving me to an empty cabin full of memories.

The itch under my skin to check behind that picture for a certain key had gotten the best of me. I didn't know why I thought it would still be there, or why I assumed Wes didn't throw it away when he moved out. I should have just taken it with me when I left, but I was too proud and too damn angry. Sure enough, as I slid that old picture to the left, there was an outline of where the key had once been. I searched the mantel to ensure it hadn't fallen or slipped into a crevice somewhere, but it was gone.

Now, under an early dawn, I felt foolish and annoyed. Why was I allowing my memories of Wes to define my connection to this place? It was always mine and my father's before it was anything to Wes and me. I took another sip, allowing the foundation of this place to wash over me. When I was a little girl, my dad used to bring me out here to camp. It only lasted until I turned fourteen or so, but when I was little, it felt magical. He'd take off his leather vest and simply become my dad. Not the president, or any other person to anyone. He was just mine. We'd spend the whole weekend eating hotdogs, telling stories, and burying treasure. I wondered if any of that treasure was still buried around the property.

Leaving my mug behind, I walked behind the house and began toeing different patches of dirt with the tip of my boot. It had been years since I even looked at this part of the property, so I was a little unsure of where to even begin. Even when I briefly lived here with Wes, I didn't come outside and look around for treasure, except for that one night, but I couldn't even remember where we'd buried that jar, or why it hurt so much to remember that moment with my father. Sorrow crowded my chest and made it ache.

Remembering how he'd helped me get past one of the hardest chapters of my life, using our buried treasure, was something that I had always clung to. Now, my dad was gone forever. There was no reconciliation talk. No rumble of his engine, which I used to wish for when I was in my apartment in DC. No bear hug where he wrapped me in his arms, and I finally felt safe again. None of that was ever going to happen again, and for all my bravado at the funeral, grief was a knife point in my sternum, threatening to tear me open.

A tight, painful sob caught in my throat as I searched the ground.

The glass jars we used weren't buried that deep, and the landscape didn't seem to have changed that much. So, it should be around here, easily available.

When the ground blurred and a tear fell down my cheek, I realized this might be more of a daunting task than I originally thought. The sun made it over the hills, pouring into the valley and bathing me in gold. I sniffed, allowing more tears to fall free as I shut my eyes. Maybe I needed this.

To cry, let out all the anguish and hurt.

Fuck, I needed therapy. It was a luxury I couldn't afford, but if I saved, or skimped on eating out, I could make it happen. I really needed to, because this shit hurt. Eventually I sunk to the ground, wrapping my arms around my knees as the new day expanded around me. The heat from the sun was already soaking into my sweater and drying my tears, when I heard someone walking.

My head snapped up, my eyes landing on the tall form roughly fifty feet from me. Here in the early morning light, Wes looked like a fallen angel. Devastatingly handsome, a look of determination and wrath painting his features in harsh lines and shadow.

My gaze narrowed, with streaks of tears still clinging to my cheeks. He was the absolute last person I wanted to see.

"What?" I yelled.

I must look ridiculous. Sitting among weeds and dead grass, dirt smudging my ass from where my pajamas had ridden up.

He stalked closer, his face an unreadable mask, like stone. There was no warmth left in him, and whatever used to be there once upon a time was long gone.

The sun created a halo effect around his head as he neared, until finally his motorcycle boots kicked up dirt near my toe and he lowered into a crouch, peering at me from wary eyes.

"I need the letter your dad left you."

His voice came out clear and deep, like a cold river running in the depths of a cave. Those familiar eyes squinted at me as I sat in the dirt, tears staining my cheeks. Just to ground myself, I dug my nails into the earth at my sides and inhaled a shallow breath.

"What, no 'Good morning, *River?*'" I tilted my head, taunting him with the nickname he had used yesterday. Wes used to love waking me up and pulling me outside to catch the sunrise. He'd set me on his lap, wrap his arms around me, and we'd sit there, watching as a new day started.

Staring at me, Wes didn't so much as flinch or shift at my retort.

"The letter, Callie. I'm serious."

Heaving a tiny sigh, I drug my nails through the dirt like I was a kid again. "Which letter?"

I knew it was the one from the attorney's office, but I needed time to figure out exactly how I was going to get out of this. Wes was cold yesterday, almost cruel. I had to assume the doting, obsessive love of my life from seven years prior was completely gone and in its place was a vicious motorcycle club leader.

His expression stayed calculated, his gaze pinning me in place. The way his focus dropped to my lips was the only indication I had at all that there was a heart beating behind that chest of his.

"The one from the will. This is important. I need to know what he told you."

Tilting my head back, I smiled with fake bravado. "He told me to sell the property, Wes. All of it. Every single speck of dirt." I pulled my hand up and let a small pile of earth fall from my palm.

Wes's gaze tracked the movement, his lips thinned into a firm line. This wasn't funny to him. I dusted my hands together to rid myself of the filth and then moved to get up, but Wes moved at the same time.

With one palm behind me, he hovered over me, nearly pinning me to the ground. A rush of air left my lungs with how close he was. His chest brushed against mine, his knee came down between my thighs, and his face…

Fuck, his face was equal parts menace and mirth.

"This isn't a fucking joke, Callie. Lives are at stake. Now, tell me where the letter is." His breath fanned my face, and how unfair was it that he smelled like peppermint?

With all the strength I had, I glared at him. Our faces were inches apart, one of his hands was behind me, the other had drifted to my waist, and I could feel the heat of his palm teasing the exposed skin where my sweater had risen up.

There under my chest, deep in the rivets of my heart, was a tiny spark, bursting to life with vengeance. The meek mask I pulled on to hide and stay out of everyone's way was slipping off, and a tempest was raging inside my breast.

"Why is it you think you can treat me this way?" I asked, my voice shaking.

I wanted him out of my space, off me and away from me. This close, I could feel the embers of what used to be between us, and all it did was uncover how badly he'd burned me.

Wesley's expression shifted to curiosity for a single moment, his eyes drifting across my face like he couldn't figure out what I was referring to.

His voice was even and low as he replied, "I'm not treating you any differently than how you treat me."

"You are!" I tried to push at his shoulder to get him to move, but he only leaned closer.

"This isn't about being nice, Callie. It's about life and death. I'm not playing a fucking game here. I need to see that letter, and I don't frankly give a shit if you think I'm mean by asking for it."

A burning sensation was starting up in my nose, which meant tears weren't far away. Why the fuck was he on top of me right now? I pushed again, and this time a small growl reverberated in his chest.

"I'll move as soon as you tell me where the letter is."

I sagged back, frustrated and annoyingly turned on.

"Fuck you, Wes. I'm not giving you anything, especially when you treat me this way."

His lips skimmed my jaw as they traveled near the lobe of my ear. Hot breath slid across my skin, and even with the sun caressing the field, his trail left goosebumps behind.

"How is it you want to be treated, Callie? Do you want to be treated like the victim you're begging to be seen as?" His hand at my waist slid under the fabric of my tank, and his heated touch moved along my back, up my spine. His mouth stayed level with my ear as he continued to whisper. "Or did you want to be treated like the princess you've always been? Worshiped and adored by everyone in your daddy's club but too blind to see it?"

What was he talking abou—

"Or,"—his teeth snagged my ear lobe, right as his hand moved down to my ass, sliding underneath my shorts to grip my cheek—"did you want to be treated like a dirty slut and have me fuck the answers out of you?"

A gasp left my chest right as he licked the space he'd just snagged with his harsh bite. That tongue traveled down the length of my jawline, until he was sucking on my neck.

Oh shit. That felt good, too good.

I slammed my eyes closed as I tried to focus. Wes was playing me, toying with me like I was an idiot who didn't have a brain. He wanted my letter, and I wanted my property. There was no way forward for us, but it didn't change how hurt I was over his words.

*Victim. Princess.*

Anger surged in my chest as I bucked my hips and screamed.

"Get off me!"

He sat up immediately, removing his body from mine. Confusion then worry flashed across his face as he searched my body for the reason I yelled. As if he'd hurt me physically.

Like he'd fucking care.

I scrambled up to stand and began dusting myself off as I turned away from him.

"Do not come near me, Wes. I mean it. I'm not a fucking toy. I'm not a…a—"

I couldn't even process what I wanted to say with how hard my heart pounded in my chest, and how hurt I was over what he'd just done. Why was it so easy for him to pretend like nothing had ever happened between us?

Suddenly I turned, needing to shout that at him, because there was so much venom built up inside me that I needed to let it out.

"What did I ever do to you to make you hate me like this?"

My voice cracked as a few angry tears slid down my face.

He was standing now, dirt streaking the knee of his jeans and down the length of his legs. That strong jaw tensed again as he stared down at the ground.

I continued yelling. "I loved you, Wes! I was so in love with you, and then you changed. Overnight, you became a different person. Losing you, it made me feel..."

"Made you feel what?" He took a step forward, abruptly cutting me off. "Helpless, out of options, left with no other choice...did it make you feel like you were forced to cut out your own fucking heart?" The way his voice shook, the determined but lost look in his eyes, robbed me of breath.

What was he talking about?

Gold-brown eyes searched my face as though he was trying to silently communicate something, but my heart was pounding too hard to see clearly. I couldn't look past this immediate situation long enough to go back and inspect what happened. Nevermind that I was basically asking him to do the same exact thing.

Shaking my head, I retreated another step, but he stepped forward and tugged my hand.

"I made a decision, Callie, and you left me because of it. What did you want me to do?"

My eyes widened as more tears flowed freely and unchecked down my face.

"I wanted you to choose me, Wes. I needed you to be different from my dad."

He clenched his jaw tightly letting my hand go. "Yeah, well, at some point, it stopped being just about what you wanted. I wanted you, and you wanted out. Your dad was my family. Brooks, Killian, Hamish...they became my family, too."

I pushed his shoulder again, hating the vile anger burning through me like a virus.

"What? Your perfect fucking family wasn't enough, you needed mine too?"

Gripping my wrist, he glared down at me.

"Yes. I wanted yours too, *River*. I wanted all of you, everything you touched, all the air you breathed, the fucking dirt under your nails. I wanted it all. You knew I didn't have a choice after that night, yet you punished me regardless."

I didn't punish him. He—my memories came in and out from around the time we'd broken up. He joined right around the same time I was taken. I came back, and everything was a whirlwind, but I accepted that he'd joined. For an entire year I stood by him while they put him through all the club shit, while he joined their church meetings and slowly slipped through my fingers. I hung on as long as I could, until I noticed my life looping, and I couldn't bear the image of my own kids growing up like I did.

"All I remember, Wes, is you choosing a life you were too privileged to ever know anything about, and you chose it over me, effectively breaking my heart," I whispered. "But it doesn't matter anymore." Seven years had swept us both away in different directions. So, no. It really did not matter because it wasn't like we could go back in time and fix any of it.

"It wasn't like I could leave, Cal. I made an oath."

His arrogant tone wrapped around me like a rope, burning and chafing at my memories.

"That oath was mine, Wes. You owed it to *me*; you *promised it* to me."

I shook my head, turning on my heel. I watched the cabin as I took each step, making an imprint in the dirt. The sun hit my back, soaking through my sweater, heating my exposed legs. This was all such a big mistake. Staying here, seeing him…being on my dad's land again.

There wasn't even any echo of Wes walking when he pulled my elbow and spun me around. His face was emotionally closed off. Whatever had just happened to open him up, he'd already shut down.

"You can either give me the letter, or I will have two men drive to DC and toss your apartment. If it's not there, then I'll physically go through every single piece of personal property you brought with you."

I opened my mouth to argue but he spoke before I could. "You have two days."

Without a second glance, he let me go and began walking away.

My first plan was to talk to Sasha, knowing she would have helped me to fight off Wesley's curiosity. However, the incessant frustration over not knowing what was going on with the club and the idea that Wesley was hiding something seemed to crowd all my other thoughts. I had a few options ahead of me. I could go behind his back and continue to try to sell the property, knowing Wes would put up a fight, in which case I may end up having to sell to him, assuming he had the flexibility to buy it.

I could go to Sasha and get her to help me, knowing she could find a buyer outside of Rose Ridge who wouldn't ask any questions and would probably pay cash. I could sell it, and go back to my life, and leave all the cryptic bullshit to the club.

But...

My heart was tangled in the same barbed wire that Wes had tossed around it back when we were kids. It had never gotten free, no matter how much time had passed, or how good I had gotten at functioning without the use of my heart. That bloodied organ belonged to him. I'd never tell him in a thousand years, but because of it, I cared what happened to the idiot.

That left me with another option.

Uncover what secrets were being hidden in the club and figure out a way to help.

"Okay, so we are walking to the clubhouse...am I understanding you correctly?" Laura asked, swiping under her arms with a stick of deodorant.

I stood in the doorway with my arms crossed, still thinking through my plan.

"Yeah...we need to start showing up and digging for information."

That could work. The older members would all talk to me, and I had a feeling the newer members could be swayed by Laura.

"No, wear the one that shows more cleavage." I shook my head, seeing her toss on an old, tattered crop top that showed off her midriff.

She looked down and frowned. "My stomach is way more attractive than my boobs. Let me keep this one on."

"Your boobs are fantastic."

She gently caressed the mermaid scales on her ribcage. "But this shirt shows my tattoo."

Letting out a sigh, I gave in, realizing it was foolish to try and tempt answers out of Wesley's club to begin with. These guys would respect her if she said to stop, as far as I knew. I mean, if Wes was in charge, there was no way any of his men would lay a finger on her without her consent, but I still worried about it.

"What about you, aren't you going to dress up even a little bit?" Laura pulled on a pair of high-heeled boots.

I shook my head. "Wear the flat boots on the way over, then change once we get there. It's a good half-mile up to the clubhouse."

"Right, shoot." Laura tore off the kicks as I peered down at my outfit. I was in a cropped black tank top and a pair of ripped jeans.

"This outfit works, doesn't it?" I was nervous now that she'd said something.

Laura stood and tossed a pair of shorts at me, teasing.

"Show off your best *ass*et, Callie."

The way she emphasized the word ass in asset had me laughing, but I knew what she meant. The shorts she gave me would leave the lower part of my ass hanging out, but it would make me fit right in with the other women in the club. I changed into the shorts, pulled my heeled boots back on, and then did my makeup.

"Will Max be okay while we're gone?" Laura's hands were on her hips as she stared down at my pup. With his chin on his paws, his eyes moved back and forth between us with a little huff.

"He's fine for a few hours, as long as he's fed and has water. He actually knows how to twist door knobs to let himself out, did you know that?" I applied some lip gloss, forgetting we'd encounter gnats and other flying insects on our way over to the clubhouse.

Laura scoffed, "Oh I remember. He did that when I took him with me to a friend's house. Scared the shit out of me."

I checked Max's water bowl and then pressed a kiss to the top of his head before walking out the front door. By the time we were headed down the road toward the clubhouse, Laura and I both looked like we'd just stepped from a magazine, so long as it was one that featured tattoos, ripped clothes, and smoky eyes. My hair was curled down my back, Laura's was tossed into an updo, and our shaved and moisturized legs were on display.

We were on a mission, and with the way my heart kicked inside my chest, I was nervous that someone might catch on.

The sound of revving engines echoed as we came upon the back entrance to the club. A large patch of grass with cornhole and yard darts stretched in front of us. Off to the side, there was a nice, paved patio with cushioned furniture, and a fire pit that was contained to a circular stove, all neat and tidy.

My gaze kept bouncing from feature to feature, practically laughing as thoughts of some HGTV episode kept popping into my head. How was this the same club that my grandfather had started? Growing up, everything we had was broken, chipped, rusted, or busted. Nothing was new, and the members of Stone Riders preferred it that way. I couldn't imagine they were happy with this manicured getup.

Up the stairs led to the club, and I noticed again, there was a partitioned privacy fence along half the back of the house, dividing it from the club and someone's living space.

With hardly anyone out back, we went unnoticed as we slipped inside through the rear door. Creeping down the hallway, we rounded the back of the kitchen where Red was wiping out glasses, joking with one of the girls.

Several of the older members were scattered around a jumbled mess of tables all pushed together, playing cards, while the younger ones seemed busy around the garage area.

"This round there's no cheating," Hamish hollered around the cigarette dangling from his mouth. Brooks and Raif laughed, staring at the cards in their hands while the overhead speakers played something older, drowning out the sounds from the garage across the building. Laura came up to my side, giving me a curious look.

My eyebrows were arched too, confused as to how exactly we'd timed this so poorly. The place was practically empty. No sweetbutts were hanging around, no prospects were doing any projects or big overhauls. From what I could tell, it was just the old timers.

"Looks like you're up." Laura pushed at my waist, forcing me to move.

I skirted the bar top, sliding onto a stool as Laura busied herself around the club, likely snooping as much as she could before getting caught.

The men playing cards weren't looking up, so they didn't see me, but Red caught my eye from the kitchen. With a small gesture from her, I was off the stool and making my way toward the kitchen.

Once I was far enough back, I sidled up near Red and waited.

"You came back." She looked up, palming an onion. The girl with her was about my age but seemed a bit skittish. With a quick glance up at me, she blushed and went back to sorting through a box of vegetables.

"I did…" I answered, letting my response drag out. I flicked my gaze back over the room to ensure Wes wasn't around. "Red, you wouldn't have a way to get into Wesley's room, would you?"

Growing up here, the clubhouse was always my home, but it was the club first and foremost. The top floor had eight bedrooms and the bottom level had seven makeshift rooms, all for members. Then there was the garage and attached spaces that housed even more, so I knew without a doubt that Wes had to have a room in the club somewhere, especially as the new president.

Red gave me a sly smile as she focused on the onions, sorting through a large box, tossing out the bad and bringing a few to her nose. After a few seconds, she let out a sigh.

"I was just telling Natty here how much things have changed over the years in this club." Red glanced over her shoulder at the girl, presumably Natty. The girl with long hair the color of honey, smiled up at me and then ducked her head again.

Red continued talking. "Before, when your daddy ran things, the president would stay here in the clubhouse with everyone else. It was a family, a chaotic mess of limbs and smells I didn't care for but had gotten used to after so many years. You get used to seeing a pair of tits and a swinging dick or two.

Now, it's not like that. The president lives privately from the club, in his own quarters. There's not even an entrance to his house from this side of the club…you'd have to go outside and use the door or find a window. He doesn't have a room like our old prez, our new one needed half the goddamn club to call his home. But he keeps us safe, and his fancy show paid for all these nice upgrades, so I can't complain."

I was picking up on what she was saying. She was telling me how to get into Wesley's house, without coming right out and saying it. I nodded along with her story, digging my hands into the box of onions and moving on to a smaller box of tomatoes.

"Do you think my dad would have approved of this new president?"

I wasn't really sure why I was asking. Red had given me my answer, and I was free to go. It would be smart to try to snoop while Wesley was gone. Assuming he even *was* gone.

Red clicked her tongue, tilting her head to the side. "Your daddy loved that boy. He had wanted him to join after the first time he met him. But he knew Wes never would; he'd never risk losing you."

My stomach flipped unexpectedly. I wasn't prepared for that story to come up, and even worse, I didn't want her to stop, so I stayed quiet.

"Your daddy often talked about how there was no love on this planet like the kind Wes had for Callie. The whole club joked and razed them for it, but behind closed doors, it was an awe-inspiring thing. Their love was the most solid thing we'd ever witnessed, and the way it kept flourishing year after year…then everything changed when that Raider took you." Red's gentle gaze landed on mine, and suddenly I was eighteen again, trying to breathe through another panic attack as memories of the kidnapping would slam back into me.

Red used to help me through them…after the event.

I decided that was enough story time for me. I reached out and gently squeezed Red's wrist while giving her a smile before slipping out of the kitchen. I still had no idea where Laura was, but it was probably for the best. She wouldn't know what to look for in Wesley's house, but I did. I knew exactly where to search.

I just had to get in and out without being noticed.

It wasn't until after I had snuck outside and crept around the privacy partition that I realized I never asked Red where Wesley was, or if he was home.

My shoes were stashed near the back of the house, on top of the gas meter. My tiny black ankle socks moved silently up the small set of stairs leading to the private patio. Once I was behind the lattice, I peered around and then tested the door. The handle held firm as I jiggled it.

"Shit."

There had to be a key somewhere. When Wes and I lived together in the cabin, we'd always leave the key above eye level, simply because people always looked down when they were trying to find the spare key.

My hands moved along the surface of one of the beams, holding the awning in place, and sure enough there was a tiny scrap of electrical tape covering something shaped awfully similar to a key. Tugging it up, I smiled at the silver key in my hand then jumped down from the patio chair and slid the lock open.

This part of the club was renovated into his personal apartment, from the looks of it. I had assumed as much from the outside, but inside, there wasn't even a hint that there was a chaotic motorcycle club on the other side of his wall. Hardwood floors ran beneath my feet, but it was the laminate kind. Still looked fresh with the light gray walls and dark, walnut-colored baseboards and trim.

"Why did he go this dark?" I mused out loud, taking in all the black-and-white photos on his walls, and the stainless-steel appliances in his kitchen. There wasn't a single dish in the sink or the drying rack. The counters were clear, free of any clutter or personal items. It almost looked like he didn't even live here. Just to be sure, I tugged on the fridge door that had a touch screen on the front. Fresh vegetables, beer, milk, eggs, condiments…nothing spoiled or out of date. He definitely lived here.

I moved past the dining room area, where the small table and four chairs sat, and past the living room with a leather sofa facing a massive flat-screen TV mounted on the wall. There was another door, leading out to the backyard, but I moved to the staircase.

Pictures of restored bikes covered his walls, but there were a few of him and my dad, him and Killian, along with him and a few other guys. None of any women so far, and for some reason I felt like I was holding my breath for the moment I came across something that would confirm that he'd moved on and had someone else in his life. With seven years passing between us, I already knew he likely had other girlfriends, lovers, whatever they were to him…but seeing evidence of it might be too much. I certainly never framed photos of any other boyfriends. I'd never even had another serious relationship after Wes. I had a few one-night stands, and one time a guy stuck around long enough to fuck me three different times, but that was it.

They all left, and I wanted them to. My heart had never recovered after Wes, and I didn't see the sense in trying to fix it just so I could risk it with someone else. Once you love someone so thoroughly, there's pieces of you they claim, and whether you work out or not, the tear in your soul can't be mended. If Wes had been bad to me, or mean and abusive, then I'd get over him and release those feelings, but he'd only ever loved me. It was me who did the hurting when I told him to choose between me and the club.

Back then, it had gutted me, and I didn't stick around long enough to challenge his words. But his lack of actions after I left told me enough of how much he'd meant them.

The stairs led to a small landing that held a bathroom to the left and a small open space to the right.

"Bingo."

I walked toward the desk and began thumbing through envelopes and mail.

There was a laptop sitting there, and while I knew eventually, I might have to peek at it, I wasn't ready to yet. There was no telling how much time I had before he came home, and I wanted to snoop first.

The drawers revealed files, but nothing outside of his legal garage business. He'd filed an LLC, and there were contracts and other legal documentation from the show he'd worked with. I was slightly curious if he was doing another season with them, and if so, when they'd start shooting. I recalled all the times I'd been brave enough to watch the show. There was never a single time I'd noticed anything familiar in the background or landscape when they'd roll the restored bikes out.

He was always in some high-end garage, surrounded by asphalt. Which likely meant he didn't do any of the filming here. That made sense. Why would he invite the world into his super-secret hideout?

"Where would I keep secret stuff about my club?" I asked aloud, setting my hands on my hips as I looked around his makeshift office. I'd found nothing, and my eyes kept trailing down the hall to the open doorway where I knew his bedroom had to be.

Snooping in the open spaces of his home was one thing, but his bedroom…my stomach tilted at the notion of crossing that line. I knew Wes longer and more intimately than probably any other human on this planet, but a lot could change in seven years. What if he did have a girlfriend, and there was evidence of her living here, in there? What if seeing it destroyed me all over again?

What if Wes had changed and was now into illegal stuff?

My heart rammed against my chest as I slowly made my way down the hall. I was just about to push open the door when I heard one slam from downstairs.

My eyes went huge as I searched for a place to hide. There were no linen closets, just the bathroom, but it was too close to the edge of the staircase to run into. Which left his bedroom.

Hearing his boots hit the stairs, I quickly darted inside his room and pushed down the way my nose flared at his familiar scent. I tucked myself into the back part of his walk-in closet where a few garment bags hung. The carpet under my feet felt stiff and new, and the smell of leather invaded my nose as I carefully slid further behind his clothing.

He pushed through his bedroom door a few seconds later, and

from the sounds of it, he had started the shower in his attached bathroom. I held my breath as I heard his movements bring him closer to my hiding spot. The closet light came on, illuminating the rows of shelves on the opposite side where he had his jeans and boxers folded, along with a few T-shirts. Below that were three different levels of shoes. He had nice shiny ones that he'd have to wear with a suit or tux, he had running shoes, and of course several pair of motorcycle boots. He had ties, watches, hats all arranged in hereas if someone had set all this up for him.

Knowing Wes, and how he used to keep his things, this wasn't him. Someone had done this, and the sinking feeling in my chest only intensified as I let that realization roll through me. Wes was seeing someone.

He'd shed his shirt, and with his back turned to me I could see the ink he'd gotten since our breakup. Before, he had tattoos along his arms, a few on his wrists and across his chest, but his back was always bare. Now, under the strong muscles and broad shoulders were black lines that made up a skull with roses blooming from its eye sockets, marking the insignia for the MC he was now leading.

There was a deep part of me that wanted to trace the dark lines with my fingers and feel his soft skin again. My mind went back to what he'd said during our exchange outside of the cabin, and I tried to erect a wall of indifference.

Wes was staring at his phone, his back still to me, and my eyes drifted lower, to where the band of his boxers peeked out from the waistline of his jeans. I'd always loved the way his muscled back looked, but it was even more mouthwatering now. Strong, defined muscles all tapered into a narrow waist, and his ass was just as delicious as it always was.

"Enjoying the view?"

His deep voice startled me so much, my head snapped up, right as I stepped to the side. Unfortunately for my ankle, there was a kettlebell to the left, and I ended up falling. Through several muttered curses, I was finally up and crawling out from behind the hanging items in his closet.

"How did you know I was here?"

Wes stood over me with his arms crossed, a soft smirk in place as he watched me.

"I have cameras, River. So I watched as you made your way through my house, snooped through all my shit, and then contemplated whether you should go inside my room."

*Oh shit.*

There was no way to talk my way out of this now, so I stood up and tugged my shirt down, so it was straightened out.

"So…you knew I was here, what are you going to do about it?"

I knew he'd never hurt me, but he might get pissed enough to kick me out of town or something.

Wes stepped closer, erasing the space between us.

"I think you're going to tell me what you're looking for, and for your sake, I hope you brought your letter."

Under these lights, his eyes almost glowed against his sun-kissed face and dark hair—it wasn't fair how shamelessly attractive he was. I closed my eyes and looked to the side, just to help with the heat growing between my legs.

"I don't have the letter," I started, but cleared my throat to gain steam. He was standing too damn close for my brain to function properly. "However, as far as why I was here, I wanted to—"

My eyes found his again, and my explanation faltered. If I told him why I was here, he'd shut me out…ensure I was as far away from his house and club as possible. He couldn't know that I was after secrets, or what might be on this property.

My face flushed as I mentally reached for another thought that had been bugging me, hanging out in the peripheral of my mind.

"Wanted to what?" Wes breathed softly while his hand rested on the copper button of his jeans. With one tiny flick they opened, and I watched as he slid the denim down his legs, leaving him standing in just a pair of snug boxer briefs. He'd always worn this type of underwear when we were dating, but his thighs were never this muscular, and his abs were never this pronounced. The dusting of dark hair leading from his navel down below the line of his briefs had my mouth parting.

This was new, as well.

Wes dipped his head, grabbing a fresh pair of boxers before repeating himself. "Wanted to what?"

Recovering, I slammed my eyes shut and trailed after him as he headed toward the bathroom. "I wanted to know if you were dating someone."

I did want to know, but I also would rather die than hear him talk about dating someone.

He suddenly turned in place, his gaze searching mine as if he knew I was lying, but there was something else there too. Something primal and full of hurt and need.

"I mean, I know I don't have a right to ask but I—"

"You don't have a right." He cut me off, his voice stern and laced with venom.

I glared, tilting my head so he'd have an unobstructed view of my entire face.

"I mean, I do have some right, considering."

That firm jaw clenched as he stared down at me with what felt like a twinge of madness.

"You think because I used to know you almost a decade ago, you have a right to break into my home and snoop around my shit, just to see if I'm dating someone?"

Heat engulfed my face as he continued to stare, and his statement washed over us. It wasn't a question, we both knew the answer. I didn't have any right to be here or to care about him anymore. I had to remember that I wasn't really here just to see if he was dating; I was here to gather intel. The reassurance had me straightening my spine under his scrutiny.

"I'll always have that right, Wes."

His incredulous laugh snuck under my skin, swelling painfully inside my chest.

"You are un-fucking-believable, Callie." With a shake of his head, he turned once more and continued to the bathroom where his hot water had likely turned cold by now.

I moved forward, wild and hurt…unsure why I was pushing this so hard. I should let him get in the shower and live to snoop another day.

Instead, I followed him into the bathroom, where his bare ass greeted me.

I sucked in a sharp breath.

From over his shoulder, he glared at me. "You come any closer, and I'm pulling you in here. Clothed, naked, I don't care, I can fuck that mouth just as easily either way. But rest assured, if you step foot into my bathroom right now, I will fuck you."

With that he stepped behind the glass door. His eyes closed as he stood under the spray, his hands went to his hair as he washed, all while I stood from the threshold of the bathroom and watched.

I wasn't sure why I was still there, when I had a clear opportunity to leave. He'd even warned me off, and yet I was caught between exiting and stripping. His threat was an answer— veiled behind a curt tone and derogatory language—but an answer just the same.

Wes was single.

He'd never promise to fuck me otherwise. He wasn't a cheater. He may have girls he fucks from time to time, but he didn't have a long-term or serious person in his life at the moment, and there was something about that revelation that pulled a sigh of contentment from my lungs.

Tucking my arms under my elbows, I leaned into the door frame to continue watching his defined torso twist and bend as he washed his body. I was enjoying the show a little too much as that familiar ache began to grow between my legs. Then Wes turned in the shower and locked eyes with me while gripping himself.

My mouth parted, my eyes widened, and my breath stalled as I took in the perfection of him. He was the same but different—more defined, and his muscles had increased, which somehow made him broader, which only amplified his girthy, longer-than-I-remembered cock.

Placing a palm on the glass wall beside the door, Wes watched me as he began stroking himself. His abs contracted as his hips dipped forward, pushing his length into his closed palm. His breath clouded the glass in front of him as he groaned, his eyes still locked on me.

I watched in shock and stupor as my own wetness increased and the urge to relieve the ache with my fingers increased. This was so dangerous. So fucking dangerous.

"Come here, River. Bring that smart mouth over here and let me answer your earlier question."

His voice echoed around the room, but even with the water, I caught every word.

I was two seconds from taking a step forward.

With a heaving chest, I stayed still while his fist moved at a leisure pace, pumping his orgasm out. He emanated another groan as he watched me.

"You come in here, looking hot as fuck with those shorts and those fucking tits and think I actually care why you're here? You have no fucking clue how long I've waited for this. Now, this is your last warning. If you're still standing there by the time I finish, I'm going to help you remember why it's not a good idea to sneak into the club president's house without permission."

That was like a bucket of cold water hitting me in the face. Why was I so eternally stupid when it came to this man? He wasn't Wes. He was the club president, and this wasn't personal. He'd fuck any piece of willing ass that snuck into his house, because that's what club presidents did. They had eternal pussy at their disposal, and a reputation to uphold. He wasn't seeing anyone, but it was obvious that he wasn't hurting for a warm hole to fill.

"River," he called, but my eyes were already on the floor.

Why was I watching? Why was I still here?

Shoving off the door frame, I turned on my heel to leave. My feet pushed into the carpet as I heard him curse from the bathroom behind me. The water turned off, and I didn't hear the rest because I was already taking the stairs.

He was soaking wet and naked as he reached the banister, and peered over it to stare down at me.

"Callie."

I kept moving until I was at his door, and without giving another glance over my shoulder, I slipped outside. As soon as I tugged on the door, I heard his feet slapping against the hardwood. His muttered curse reverberated in my ears as I slammed his door shut and darted around the side of the house, grabbing my shoes from the gas meter.

I hated that I cared.

I hated myself for thinking he'd be different when he was exactly like them.

Which was why I knew I could never stay with him while he had the club. I was glad I left. I knew he'd never be any different once this life lured him in.

Wes had made his choice, and I needed to get a fucking grip.

# TWELVE
## WES
### AGE 18

Waking up with Callie in my arms was the best part of my day.

Hands down.

There was no comparison to anything I'd found. Her pink lips were barely parted, and her dark lashes fanned the tops of her cheeks. She was naked every night she slept with me, and every single morning, I'd wake up with a cock hard as stone, ready to fuck her.

It was routine at this point, and while I watched her sleep, I did so with rapt attention to her breathing. I had once mentioned that sometimes she slept so soundly I wondered if she would even notice if I started fucking her. She joked that I should try it sometime. She had no idea, but the time had come, as she wasn't waking to my tiny touches or kisses. It was nearly seven in the morning, and I was going to be late for work if I didn't get up and leave soon.

But I needed her.

Callie was more than an obsession. She was my reason for waking, my reason for trying. She was all of it, and without the opportunity to touch her and claim her before I started my day, there wasn't a point in starting it.

Gently rolling until I was on my forearms, I watched as her rhythmic breathing continued and her eyes remained shut. Fuck, even with her permission, this felt weird. But it was Callie. My Callie. And she'd never be upset at the prospect of me touching her. Besides, there was some tiny thrill at the prospect of getting to fuck her so thoroughly that she'd wake up while completely full of my cock.

Still, something gave me pause. I'd start slow, and maybe work my way up to fucking her. I'd touch her first.

So, I gently pushed her thighs open and slid my hand over her bare mound and through her silken pussy lips, groaning at how perfect she felt. Her eyes fluttered as I went up her slit and then drug my fingers back down her center. She shifted, letting out a tiny moan as I decided to lower my head between her thighs.

This right here was perfection.

Using my thumb, I pushed her lips apart and licked through her seam, slowly circling her clit. The fact that she was sleeping turned me on, making the tip of my cock weep against the sheets and my hips thrust on their own into the mattress. I tossed her leg over my shoulder, and my delicate touch roughened as I devoured her, sucking and licking as she let out little moans of pleasure, showing she was starting to wake.

Sure enough, a tight grip on my hair and her hips tipping forward was the final straw before she woke and sleepily watched through parted lashes. I had my tongue buried inside her cunt, fucking the mattress as I lapped up her arousal, unwilling to relent until she let out a breathy cry.

"Wes," Callie moaned, slowing her hips while pressing on my forehead to stave the sensation of my tongue dragging across her sensitive center.

I sucked her clit into my mouth with a devious growl, and she snapped.

"Fuck me. Please, baby, fuck me. I need it."

I loved when she lost her resolve like that and began to unravel.

Moving over her, I gripped the headboard, staring down at her as I guided my erection along her completely soaked pussy.

"You want this?" I asked, breathless.

Her eyes were wide and glassy as she licked her lips. "Yes."

I slid the head of my cock through her folds, groaning as her hips bucked.

"Hmmm, but you interrupted my fun."

Callie touched my chest, wrapping her hands around my neck.

"What did I do?"

I was sliding into her ever so gently. "You woke up."

Moaning, she tethered her fingers at the back of my neck.

"You wanted to play while I was unconscious?"

I scoffed. "You're always cognizant when you're with me. You clawed me open, Callie Stone, and demanded a position inside as queen of my heart. We can't be apart. Even in death I'm pretty sure I'd follow you."

"How do you make that sound so hot?" she breathed, tilting her pelvis, trying to guide more of my cock inside her.

I held her hip in place so she couldn't.

"How are we going to rectify this?"

She seemed to think it over, then went limp in my arms, smiling up at me. "Tie me up."

The idea shot off like a rocket, the image of her at my mercy, unable to stop me from playing, from touching. It was like she'd unlocked a kink I didn't even realize I had.

"You're sure?" My eyes were huge as I began to sink inside her, no longer able to hold back.

She nodded, wetting her lips again. I bit down on her plump bottom lip as I pulled out of her and sunk back in, thrusting as hard as I could go. She let out a tiny yelp, but her hands came up, clinging to me.

"More of that. I love when you do that, Wes."

I didn't have a rope, or the resolve to pull out of her at the moment, but it would have to be something we tried another time. I did, however, pull her hands above her head and hold them there as I ruthlessly fucked her. I slammed into her heat repeatedly, watching as her tits bobbed and swayed with the movement. Her ankles connected over my ass as my free hand went to her right ass cheek, where I roughly grabbed her and thrust my hips without restraint.

The sound of our bodies slapping together filled the room, our moans and heavy breaths mingling with the mewling sound she was making now as her climax began to build.

I gripped her wrists harder as I plunged my swollen cock so deep inside her that she let out a string of curses.

"You're so perfect, River. So fucking perfect and so fucking mine. I can't believe I get to wake up to this every morning," I breathed, moments away from blowing my load inside her.

We'd been sloppy and impulsive for the last few months, which resulted in a pregnancy scare. After the test came back negative, we stopped relying on condoms and Callie went in, getting on something more effective. I was thankful, because it allowed me to fuck her bareback, and shit, that felt good, to not have to worry.

Callie screamed as her back arched, her tits pushed up against my chest, and her mouth gaped open. "Oh my—Wes. Fuck!"

She came hard, right as I did. Groaning into her neck, I finally released her hands.

Lifting off her, I carefully pushed back a few strands of hair from her forehead and relished the soft smile she gave me. I cherished her after-sex smiles, because they were unlike any other smiles she gave to me or anyone else. Dreamy, sated, as if she was high purely from my touch. It always made my chest feel warm. It was familiar and safe… like coming home.

"I have to go to work," Callie whispered sleepily, dragging a finger down my nose and over my lips.

I did, too, but with the way the sun washed over her face, highlighting her dark lashes and skin, it was too tempting to stay here with her. All I had to do was lean in and kiss her, slide into her slick heat that'd still be dripping with my release, and we could just keep fucking.

Kissing her neck, I released a heavy breath and began to move. We had bills, and I was saving up for a ring. I had nearly all of it saved so I could buy her a ring that wouldn't embarrass her. I knew it wasn't going to be massive or boast that we were rich, but it would be hers, and it would remind her of us. I had the ring picked out. I just needed the last three hundred dollars to secure it, which would come by my next paycheck.

"What do you want for breakfast?" I tugged her hand, helping her out of bed. She smiled sweetly up at me, then pressed a kiss to my sternum.

"I made overnight oats, knowing you'd keep me in bed longer than I had time for."

I smacked her ass lightly as she jogged past me and out of the bedroom. We were still in her dad's cabin, but we'd made it ours with tiny touches and framed photos of us covering nearly every surface. We'd taken a road trip last summer and saw the Grand Canyon, and we'd come too fucking close to getting hitched in Vegas before sense returned and we started our journey back.

Callie wanted everyone there when she got married. Her dad, Red, Brooks, Hamish…even Killian. A part of me wanted that too, because as I'd grown close to Callie, I'd grown close to her family, and even Killian was like a brother to me now.

As for my own family…Mom finally left Dad. She lived in Maryland now with her sister, as did my sisters. My dad moved in with his secretary, last I heard, and the house was being lived in by my older brothers. I wouldn't mind them attending my wedding, but they'd give me shit for not inviting my dad or not wanting to put up with my mom's opinions regarding Callie. She'd made herself clear when she found out we were dating at fifteen. The second she made the connection to who Callie's dad was, she began her quest to break us up.

I never once told Callie about it. It worked because my mother was always sickly sweet to Callie's face. I'd hear all her real feelings behind closed doors.

I showered, then brushed my teeth, and by the time I had ventured back into the kitchen, Callie was tossing her hair up and sliding a mug of coffee into my hand.

"Can we go to that cute little food truck place tonight?" Callie asked, digging through her purse, probably for her keys.

I was hesitant to make any plans that included leaving Rose Ridge without consulting her dad. I realized that made me seem weak, but her dad was acting more worried than usual, and Killian had made a cryptic comment the other day about including them if we made plans to go anywhere.

They treated me like I was just her boyfriend, not a prospect or a hang-around. I was in a category reserved for family, but with that came the cold shoulder more often than I liked. I caught sight of the group attending their weekly church meetings—which was an odd term, at least in my world—but in theirs it was basically where they gathered to talk about club business. No women, no prospects, no outsiders were ever invited in. I never missed how Killian would throw a look over his shoulder when he'd head inside, and I'd be at the bar eating breakfast with Callie while she talked to Red.

He'd stare at me like I was supposed to be in there with them, like he was just waiting for me to make the decision to join. It was on my mind more than it should have been, honestly. I knew Callie wanted to leave Rose Ridge. She'd started making lists of the places we could live once we'd saved up enough. Texas was on her list, so was Kentucky, and then randomly Wyoming. No idea why. I just let her dream, holding tight to the fact that she was the dream I was following.

I took a generous sip of my coffee before responding, already feeling my gut twist with anxiety. "Maybe, let me check with work."

She waved me off. "Okay, but fair warning, I am probably going to head to that farm store that's on the way, regardless if we go or not."

Shit, I didn't like that.

"Just wait for me, okay?"

She stood, one hand on the wall as she slid her foot into her shoe. Her eyes focused on my face, and I prayed she'd understand how serious I was. Giving me a sweet smile, she nodded.

"Okay, I'll wait."

Once her shoes were on, she stepped forward and kissed me. Something in my chest churned, but I pushed it down. Dating the daughter of Simon Stone was never going to feel normal, and I likely would never stop worrying about her. When I married her, and we had kids, that worry would double or triple. But as I watched her walk out the door, I knew deep in my bones, to my very marrow, that I wouldn't want it any other way. I'd wage war for that girl. I'd go to hell and pick a fight with the devil if I had to. In every scenario, she was on my mind. How to keep her, how to love her, how to make her mine.

Nothing would ever change that.

The day passed with nothing but fuckup and after fuckup.

My boss had called in sick, so I was in charge. We had a few oil changes on the schedule, but then there was an accident down on Fir Street, and all three vehicles were towed to our shop. Because we were down a member, and the other two employees were still new, it fell to me to assess the cars so the insurance companies would have their quotes. It was frustrating, and the heat didn't help. I was sweaty and annoyed by the end of the day, and all I wanted was to see my girl-friend and take her to that favorite food truck of hers that sold the mango-flavored street tacos.

I was supposed to head right over to Callie's work to meet up with her, but I texted her to meet me at home instead.

By the time I was finally off work, I noticed she'd replied to my text

over an hour ago.

> Callie: don't be mad, but I got off early and wanted to surprise you with something. I'm already here, browsing the farm store. Love you, hurry up so we can eat.

Fuck.

I had yet to even get a free moment to talk to her dad. I was hoping by the time I got home, she'd shower, and I'd slip outside to call him and run this by him or Killian, just to be sure. But perhaps, if things were bad, they had a tail on her.

I pressed her contact, hearing the phone ring while I started the truck. It went to voicemail after a few rings. I tried her again, this time it went to voicemail on the third ring, which was suspicious or maybe it was an accident.

Still, I called again.

This time she picked up.

"Hello?" a female voice answered, but it wasn't Callie.

"Hi…ugh, sorry, I'm trying to call Callie Stone?"

My foot was on the gas, pushing my truck faster toward home.

The female made some sort of sound, there was noise in the background then she came back on. "Sorry, I found this phone in the parking lot. I was trying to see who it might belong to here at the food trucks, but no one recognizes it. I can keep it here for you, if you know her."

The rock that had been churning in my gut all day sank as fear gripped my chest.

I hung up and dialed Simon, almost on autopilot. My truck was flying down the road at a breakneck speed. I saw a few club members passing me, heading the wrong direction. I didn't care. I had to keep going.

Simon didn't answer.

"Fuck!" I threw my phone right as I rounded the dirt road leading to the club. I'd never sped down the road before because of the dirt it'd kick up. It was disrespectful, but right then, I didn't care. I needed to find Callie.

I slid to a stop, hearing gravel spray as I pushed the gear up and parked.

"Simon!" I ran for the clubhouse right as Hamish was walking out. His eyes grew large and shocked as I ran past him.

"Where is Simon?" I shoved inside the door, seeing dazed club members and Red behind the counter, her eyes narrowed in concern.

"Where's Killian? Fuck, I need someone. Callie is missing."

That got everyone moving.

Red came from around the counter, right as the church doors flung open and Simon, Killian, Brooks, and Raif all walked out. Their vests were on, their boots thudding against the floor as their eyes hardened on me.

"What the fuck happened?" Simon's voice carried a sliver of worry, but he masked it well.

Shaking my head, I tried to breathe and force my voice not to waver.

"I don't know. She texted me over an hour ago that she was going to the food trucks early. I asked her to wait for me, but she said she'd meet me there."

Killian came up next to me and gently took my cell so he could read the text.

"I called and some girl answered it, said the phone was on the ground. Said she was asking around for who it belonged to, but no one was claiming it."

My body was tense, my knees and legs shaky, but my adrenaline was pumping. I wanted to go get in the truck and just start driving, but I knew Simon would have a better plan.

Simon stared at Killian for a moment before Killian said, "You think this is the demonstration they were talking about?"

Simon's jaw clenched before he glanced at me and shook his head. "Not here."

"Something happened. I know something is going on, tell me so I can help!" I shouted, trying to get Simon's attention but he was already delving out orders.

"Brooks and Raif, you two go to Pyle, scout and see if you can find tracks. Get eyes out there."

There were people moving around, guns were grabbed, and Killian walked toward the back wall, grabbing a bulletproof vest and pulling it over his head. My heart was thundering in my chest.

Simon walked past me, and I felt fucking invisible. I always hated this feeling, but now that Callie was at the center, I couldn't take it.

"Please, Simon," I begged, gritting my teeth as I walked up to his side.

He turned, setting those hazel eyes on me, and his head dipped. It was enough of an answer.

He wasn't going to tell me shit.

"You know I would bring you in, Wes. I can't, son. She'd kill me."

I needed to hit something. "She might not even fucking be alive, and you're worried about her being mad at you?"

This was fucking bullshit.

Killian walked over, keeping his gaze anywhere but on us.

Fucker.

I loved the dude, but in that moment, I was so jealous of his place in this life. Why should he get to be privy to what's happening with *my* girlfriend?

Why should *any* of these fuckers?

"She's mine, Simon. Make an exception." My voice was harsh, with a biting tone.

Harsh enough that it warranted attention from people around us. No one spoke to the president like that.

My girlfriend's dad just stared at me with pity.

"I would, Wes. You know I would."

Panic surged as they started moving past me.

"I will not be put on the fringes of this," I warned, but the threat held no heat. What the hell would I do to a club of bikers, following orders? All I knew was someone had to start talking to me and soon. Tears were burning my eyes and I just wanted to scream until somebody could actually hear what I was trying to say.

Nothing mattered. Nothing but her.

"Just give us a few hours, let us figure out what happened. Killian will keep you updated as much as possible." Simon gripped my shoulder as I hurried with them to the porch. Killian gave me a sympathetic look then followed suit. Hamish, Brooks, Raif, they all followed their leader, leaving me back with the women.

Red stood with her arms crossed, her face stern, and then she ducked back into the storage room. I stood there clenching my fists so tight I was worried I'd break a knuckle or pop a vessel. I needed to go with them, but I knew if I tried to follow, Simon would have someone knock me out or some shit. Their engines blared as the group of them took off from the property.

Moments later, Red returned, holding a black leather vest over her arm.

"Simon had this made a year ago. He'd kill me if he knew I showed it to you, but I know what you're feeling. I felt it ten years ago when Brooks went missing for three days. I wanted to scream, to tear the very skin from my bones, when no one could tell me anything. It was a really dark time for me, and I wouldn't wish that on anyone. I know what you need, honey"—she placed the vest in my hands—"question is, do you?"

Peering down at the leather, I skimmed my thumb over the patches sewn into the cut. My name was on the right side of the vest, the Stone Riders patch was under it, along with the acronym, SRMC, then Virginia. My throat was tight as I realized what this was.

My head snapped up. "It doesn't say prospect."

Red smiled with tears in her eyes. "Honey, you must have wildly misunderstood where you stand with that man. He loves you like his own flesh and blood. You'd never be anything but royalty in this club. Besides, you forget how many chores you did with Killian around here when we didn't have any prospects. Remember when Lucky started and you felt bad for him, so you joined in and helped him out?"

Back then I just wanted to be a part of what they were doing. Anything that allowed me to stay, I'd do.

Holding the vest up, I noticed on the back of the vest there was a tiny fox patch, which was the nickname the club had given to Callie. Suddenly all I could think of was getting her a vest that said *Property of Wes*. The idea sent a rush of heat to my cock, which was the wrong fucking timing, but still the image played out. Then several more of Callie wearing that cut and nothing else, while she straddled me.

Another with her wearing it while at a picnic with the club, holding a baby on her hip while tossing me a smile over her shoulder. That was the future I wanted. Suddenly I wanted it so bad that I could taste it. I wanted this club, and I wanted her by my side.

I wanted a future.

One where I could show her that the roots she hated so much were strong and beautiful. Where I could help her heal enough to love this life, to live it with me.

"You put that on, honey, and it'll mean something. It's not something you can easily take off. You become a Stone Rider, you stay one for life."

Anticipation fluttered under my veins, paired with fear over where Callie was. I knew I was choosing something right then, but in my heart, it was Callie. I'd choose her over and over again, and in that moment, it was with her in my heart that I slid the vest on. Red made some sound, then squeezed my hand before walking back to the kitchen.

Storming outside, I walked over to the garage, where we'd been restoring an old bike for me, one I had practiced riding with Killian when Callie wasn't around. I pulled the tarp off the top and dug out the storage box I kept on the shelf. It held the key to my bike, some cash, and the gun Simon had given me last year.

Tucking the gun into my jeans, I straddled the bike and slid the key into the ignition. Once it rumbled to life, I grabbed a bucket helmet and snapped it into place. The club had already started riding, but I was just a few miles behind. I sent up a silent prayer that Callie would be found safe, then I twisted my fist and shifted into first, taking off to join my club.

# THIRTEEN
## CALLIE

"If you need anything else, just come grab me."

I smiled up at the boy who used to flirt with me in English class. Garrick Rutherford had grown into a handsome man who now ran the local library. He happened to currently be single, the owner of a local vacation rental, and enthusiastic about doing everything within his power to help me.

"Thank you so much Garrick, I will." I placed my hand on his arm, hoping my flirting was paying off. It seemed I had finally found a source in Rose Ridge that wasn't loyal to the Stone Riders. The power clearly went straight to my head as Garrick grinned, knocking on the table before walking off. Once he was gone, I pulled my cell phone out and shot a text off to Laura.

> Me: Library is a success, how's the bar?

It was midafternoon, so I wasn't expecting much, but the local early birds might prove useful.

We'd devised this plan after our rather pathetic attempt the day prior to glean club secrets. After I left Wesley's house, I found Laura arguing with Killian over something and pulled her away, explaining we needed to regroup. I hid my emotions over Wes treating me like club pussy behind a careful mask of indifference. I knew my ex was used to getting any woman he wanted, and since I was in his space, it only made sense that he'd try to get me on my knees, or my back, but what made me angry was how close I had been to caving to his requests.

I loathed how attracted I still was to the man, so today I was determined to stay away from the club and begin my search outside of the fortified walls the Stone Riders had to keep the town out. I devised a new plan to poke around the town in hopes someone might spill random information about what's happened recently.

My search started with the library. While I knew the local reporters were likely still on the payroll of the local club, there was a chance some smaller papers or even local bloggers had put out their own reports that would have been buried. Since the cabin didn't have Wi-Fi, I had my laptop with me while sitting at an old wooden table. Old carpet ran under stacks of books all lined up in rows in front of me, keeping me hidden away in the back.

My phone buzzed on the table with a text.

> Laura: It's pretty slow here, all I've gotten so far is an invite to the Stone Riders infamous community barbeque where they allow the town to participate in judging their chili. I have one guy who keeps drinking and seems to have a loose tongue, I'll be in touch soon.

I smiled at my phone, excited that she seemed to be getting somewhere. I clicked on an article that seemed promising, all while I texted Killian, asking how Max was. When I concocted this plan, I knew I'd need something more stable for him today, considering we'd be gone for a while.

> Me: how's my boy doing?

Setting the phone back on the table, I opened the article I found. Titled "Dangerous and Ignored," the article was written by someone with an ambiguous screen name but seemed to know quite a lot about the different politics going on around the area.

Leaning forward, I squinted as I began scanning the text.

*The problem is no one will speak of what they see or know. There seems to be a rapid danger growing in this part of Virginia, where local authorities turn their heads every time one of these local motorcycle clubs get into yet another gun fight. Take the recent battle between the notorious Stone Riders and Death Raiders. It's been said the Stone Riders originated here in town from Cecil Stone, who started the club with fellow factory workers. His battle with the Death Raiders, said to hail from Pyle or close to it, has been ongoing for close to thirty years. Just when the rival clubs seem to make peace, there seems to be something new they're battling over. My source says Simon Stone, the current leader of the Stone Riders club, has engaged in close to fifteen deadly encounters with the Death Raiders. This wouldn't really be news for anyone who has ever read about various turbulence due to a small rough and tough group such as this, but the fact that this small slice of Virginia has not one but four different rival clubs that wear the one percenter patch makes for a terrifying situation. I have personally written the governor to make sense of why so much violence has been overlooked in our part of the state and have yet to hear a reply. There is even a group that has started pledging to eradicate the clubs from this part of Virginia for the safety of our children and local community.*

A vibration on the table made me jump.

> Killian: your boy is misbehaving and won't listen to a word I say—heads up, he's going to be a mess to deal with. But that's not new. He's been like this for a while...

My brows caved in confusion as I stared at his text. Max was usually a great listener, and a breeze to babysit, even for strangers, at least from what I've been told. Why would Killian have—

I peeked up in time to see Garrick making his way back to me. His pallid face and strong chin were ruddy, and he stormed toward me with an exasperated expression. It took me a second to piece together why he would look so upset, but the person trailing behind him finally had it clicking into place.

Wearing those brown motorcycle boots, and denim jeans loose in the legs yet tight enough to fit him perfectly in all the right places, Wes strolled through like he owned the whole entire world. His black cut was layered over a white tee and his face was clean shaven, revealing his wide, strong jawline that had become even more devastating over the past seven years, and gripped in his fist was a dark purple leash, nearly forcing a bubble of laughter out of me. Max trotted next to him, his mouth gaping, tongue out, and drool leaking from his mouth as they walked.

Killian was going to pay for this.

"Callie, this man keeps insisting on seeing you," Garrick explained in a terse tone, keeping his gaze low. The color of his face made me wonder what Wes said to get under his skin.

I smiled at my old friend and placed my hand on his arm. "Thank you, Garrick, sorry about the trouble."

Garrick gave me a small smile, ignoring the dog and motorcycle leader standing next to him. Wes put his arm out, against Garrick's chest, effectively pushing him away from me.

"Thanks for doing your job, Jerod."

With a severe glare, my friend corrected him. "It's Garrick."

Wes gave him a smirk. "I don't give a flying fuck. Get out of here."

Max ignored them both and found his way to my stomach, where he nuzzled me. My hand went to the soft fur on top of his head.

"Why do you have my dog?" I asked Wes as Garrick clenched his jaw and turned around, heading back to his desk. Wes took the opportunity to round the table I had been sitting at and steal my chair.

"Hey!"

His arm went up, pushing at my waist as I tried to protect what I'd been reading.

Wes scoffed, as he began reading out loud. "These rival clubs are more akin to gangs and need to be stopped. Click here to read more about what you can do this next election season to ensure we put a stop to these clubs. Every one of their members deserves to be behind bars, and it's my mission to see that accomplished."

My arms became a band of steel across my chest as he continued to scan the text.

"Wow, this is some riveting shit, River."

I hated that he was still calling me that, even more so because it still created a trail of goosebumps down my arms when he did.

"I was just reading up on the news from around here," I said offhandedly, as if I could keep him from discovering exactly what I was trying to do.

To make matters worse, a text came in, making my phone vibrate next to Wes's hand.

He picked it up and read it out loud.

> Laura: Killian just walked into the bar and pulled me away from the guy I was talking to. He said he's taking me somewhere to eat. If you don't hear from me by tonight, either I'm dead or he is. If you care for him at all, keep him in your prayers, because that mother fucker gets under my skin. *prayer hands*

Wes lifted his face, catching my gaze, with a small smile skirting his lips.

"You've been busy since you broke into my house, River. I'm curious what exactly it is that you're planning here. If I didn't know any better, I'd say you were digging for information."

I shoved past him and shut my laptop, then scooped up my phone.

"What I'm doing is none of your business, Wes."

He spun, gripping my wrist as I began shoving things into my bag.

"Wrong. You are my business, River, and I think it's time we had a little conversation."

Exhilaration tempted to pry my chest open with greedy fingers. A real conversation with him, where we sat down like two mature adults and explained what the other was thinking or planning? That's exactly what I wanted.

"Okay, what did you have in mind?" I held my laptop bag to my chest, while Max's leash strangled my fist. Thankfully he was being decent, sitting and just watching our exchange with those bright blue eyes.

Wes tugged the leash out of my hand, while he leaned close to whisper. "Your mouth wrapped around my cock, but we can figure out the semantics later if you want."

Annnnnd we were right where we ended yesterday, with him thinking I was just some sweetbutt he could boss around, assuming I'd fall in his lap, worshiping his dick.

I reached for the leash and pulled it away from him.

"You know what? Never mind."

Wes smiled and a peal of laughter tumbled out of his chest. I moved past him, even as the sound of him laughing sunk into me as sharp as any hook. These familiar things he did were painful, tearing at me in ways I wasn't ready to confront.

Wes gripped my retreating hip and pulled me back by my belt loop.

"Wait. Sorry, let me start over. You acted like this yesterday, too. Is my flirting game really that bad?"

I stared at my ex, unsure what this trap was but unable to avoid falling into it.

"You were flirting?"

His face flushed right below his lashes, but the way he dipped his face erased any trace of it.

"I was trying, yeah."

I shifted on my feet, unsure what to do with this version of Wes. He was the most like *my* Wes that I had encountered since being back.

"Why do you keep treating me like I'm just club pussy, then? I mean, unless you flirt with them too?"

His dark brows caved into the center of his forehead.

"What?"

Fuck, this was awkward. My bag shifted to my shoulder as I adjusted my stance and Max whined, pushing his nose into my stomach.

"Yesterday, the way you talked to me, and today—it was like you were trying to fuck me. But seeing as how you've made it clear how much you hate me, I feel as though I need to remind you that I'm not one of your sweetbutts. I'm not going to see the president patch and drool all over your dick. It does the opposite of impress me, in case you forgot."

His eyes glittered with amusement. I waited for him to say something, but his gaze drifted slowly down my body, then back up, freezing on my lips. I shifted under his scrutiny and tried to take a step back, but he advanced with an exhale and another smirk tilting his lips.

"I haven't forgotten a single thing about you, River."

I stared openly at him, my mouth parting the smallest bit.

Garrick suddenly interrupted us, popping out from behind one of the shelves.

"Callie, you have to get that dog out of here. I have people complaining."

Wes bit back a laugh as I furiously nodded. Right. Dog, library, *Wes.*

I tucked the chair under the table then yanked the leash away from my ex. Right as I was about to exit the library, Garrick walked up from behind me and gently tugged on my wrist.

"Wait, before you leave…" He paused, eyeing Wes at my back.

Hauling me to the side so we had a tiny bit of privacy, he asked, "Can I get your number?"

Oh crap.

I had flirted with Garrick and now he wanted to call me? Date me? Garrick was hot in a way that would at least distract me for a while, but just like every other date I'd been on since Wes, it would burn out quicker than it started.

Beaming at him, I was about to deliver a polite rejection that would leave his feelings intact when Wes took up the space behind me, pulling me flush against his chest.

"You can have my number, Jerod. You can call it and see if Callie wants to chat, seeing as she'll be staying with me."

Wait…what?

I tried to turn around, but Garrick was already walking away, and I felt like shit. We were finally outside when I slapped his chest. "Why did you do that?"

Wes caught my belt loop once more and steered me toward the car.

"Like fuck is another man going to date you while you're here. If you leave, then that's one thing. I can't control who you're with. But in this town, you're mine. It's me you'll date. Me you'll call. Me you'll fuck. You need romance, then read one of those books you love so much. When you go back to DC, you'll have your fuck buddies again, but here, there's not a chance I'll stand by and let you be with anyone else."

He didn't even wait for me to respond. He moved past me, opening the back door of the car for Max to jump in. "Come on, let's eat," he said casually while I was still trying to wrap my brain around what he'd just said.

Wes had done a one-eighty spin on me, and I had whiplash. Or heart flash. God, that was a stupid thing to call it, but why else did it feel like my heart had just been tossed inside a furnace, only to be snatched and thrown into a freezer?

"It's getting late. I know of a few spots along Main Street that have outdoor seating, so we can bring the horse." Wes held my door open for me.

Max tilted his head from inside, as if he were piecing together what we were doing.

Why was he asking me to dinner? He was so mean to me in the cabin, and then every encounter after… This had to be a trick.

"Well—" I started but Wes cut me off once more by grabbing my laptop bag and gently packing it away in the passenger side of the car.

Once it was put away, he straightened and moved so he was holding the frame of my door. It was a silent prompt for me to get in, but my feet were frozen. The heat-soaked asphalt at our feet made sweat trickle down my neck. Wesley's brows constricted to a point on his forehead, and I knew he was confused as to why I wasn't moving. Max barked from his spot in the back, as if he was wondering too.

"I'm hungry, River, and if you don't move soon, I doubt you'll appreciate the meal I select." His gaze flicked down my body in a slow, measured way, slowing at my waist until he was boldly staring at the space between my thighs.

This entire thing was scrambling my brain, but I finally slid inside, still feeling dazed and at a loss. Wes rounded the car, folding into the driver's seat, looking at odds with my vehicular aesthetic with his brooding stare and set jaw. Not to mention his leather cut, denim jeans, and boots.

As I buckled, I asked, "How did you get here with Max? Where's your bike?"

Wesley gripped the steering wheel as he guided us down Main Street, pausing at a red light.

"Got dropped off. Figured we'd take your car back home."

Hearing the word home come from his lips took me back to when we were fifteen and he'd placed that star-embellished key in my palm, promising a future he had no business swearing.

The reminder had my lips smashing shut instead of asking him what he meant by the term. Was he referring to the cabin, or was he saying that I was going to be staying with him?

Before I knew it, we were parking across the street from a cute restaurant with red awnings and stringed lights crossing over the patio seating. Music played from the interior of the restaurant, giving off a slow, summer evening vibe. Instantly I wanted to cocoon myself in the feeling.

Wes was already out, helping Max while I exited the car. We crossed the street side by side, and I took a moment to admire the area. The strip had changed since I'd lived here. There were a few more restaurants, a beauty salon, a home decor shop, bookstore, and a —*ohmygosh!*

My feet moved on their own, even as Wes was almost to the front door of the restaurant. I briskly moved down the sidewalk, passing glass window after glass window, keeping my sights on the one at the very end. I had no idea if Wes was following or if he'd grabbed a seat in the restaurant, and I didn't care.

The shop was highlighted with teal trim and a trendy sign swaying overhead with the outline of a skull with flowers growing from the top of the empty skull.

*Dead Roses.*

Smirking at the clever use of the town name, I pushed inside the shop and let out a small, happy exhale. A waiting room with laminate hardwood welcomed me as classic rock played from a speaker at the receptionist's desk. It was louder in the back, where the chairs likely were. Low-hanging lights were artfully placed over the leather couch, wall pictures, and the entry desk. I ran my finger over the thick binders laid out for guests to garner inspiration or select from previous designs.

There was no one sitting behind the reception desk, so I took my time looking over the different cards sitting out. There were only two tattoo artists and then the manager of the studio listed.

"Can I help you?" someone asked, poking out from the back. There was a tiny hallway that led to the left and right, with a bathroom right in the middle.

Jamming my thumb over my shoulder, I said, "Sorry, just stopping in to see what you guys had going here. I have a chair in DC and… well, actually, I'm from here, and I was just curious about this place."

My face turned a harsh red as the awkwardness of my sentence caught up with me.

The guy, practically a teenager, had three silver rings in his lip, two in his eyebrow, and one in his nose. He gave me a welcoming smile.

"You're not looking for a job by chance, are you? We have two chairs open, and because of the new owner, we're getting a ton of extra business."

Why was there a tiny ball of excitement spinning inside my chest? Wasn't this what I was talking about before I came here? I mean, in my dream, I wanted to own the shop, but an opening was an opening.

"Uh…" I stepped closer to the desk that separated us, a little shocked, a little nervous. "Do you have an application, or how would I find out more about the position?"

The guy tore off his black latex gloves and minced toward the filing cabinet on the far wall. "I think Alice keeps them in here, but I know it's online as well. Here let me go grab you the card that has the info on it."

The kid thumbed through a few papers, then the door behind me opened with what I assumed was a new client, but I watched as his countenance went slack.

"Mr. Ryan, hi! I mean, hello, sorry." The kids face flushed a bright red, and my own seemed to flush with it, because holy shit, my fucking luck.

I slowly turned to see Wes standing in the doorway with his arms linked over his chest and the purple leash wrapped around his fist. A blunt contrast to how dangerous and handsome he was. His eyes darkened as he assessed me with a new sort of curiosity. Max pulled at the leash to get to me with a little whine, forcing me closer to Wesley's side.

"Sorry, I was coming right back, but I wanted to check this out first."

The kid stepped up right then and rounded the receptionist desk, his eager eyes focused on Wes. "I was just about to give her information on applying here to help cover the extra business we've gotten lately."

I tried to make sense of Wesley's place here, and the kid calling him Mr. Ryan. His name wasn't on the manager card, but perhaps it was outdated.

"I wasn't aware she was staying in Rose Ridge," Wes said to the kid, but he was staring at me.

My slow-ass brain finally connected the dots, and I felt a tiny wince flash across my features.

"You're the new owner?"

The kid was looking between us like he wasn't sure what to do.

The silence stretched, his comment hanging in the air, my question going unanswered.

Finally, the kid coughed. "So should I give her the application info?"

Wes finally looked away from me and gave his attention to his employee.

"No, that won't be necessary."

Hurt wound around my chest and squeezed. It was irrational and stupid, because I wasn't planning to stay in Rose Ridge, regardless, but still, the door I had so excitedly assumed was an opportunity just slammed in my face, and it hurt.

Without saying another word, I exited the tattoo shop and stormed down the street, letting Wes catch up. I was hungry, and I still wanted my grown-up conversation with the man, so I ventured toward the restaurant with the red awnings. While I walked, I worked to fortify my emotions and heart. No more fawning over Wesley's words that kept throwing me for a loop, or his looks, or the way he kept touching me. I wanted a real conversation so I could sell the property, learn what he was hiding, and get the hell out of here.

Skirting the building, I found the front door that had cute lettering outlining the bistro name.

*Clara's.*

The hostess gave me a thin but polite smile while she reached for a menu, then her face broke into something entirely different as she gazed over my shoulder. Her blue eyes lit up, her red lips widened, and her nails raked through her long black hair. I knew without seeing that Wes had just walked in. The way people in this town reacted to him was annoying as fuck.

"Hey, Jules, two please." His voice echoed through the small foyer, and Max whined again, pushing his nose into my side.

Poor guy. It wasn't his fault the idiot had a hold of him, yet I'd ditched him twice already.

I tried to gently tug the leash from Wes, but he only glared at me and held firm.

"Sure, uh…outside, I'm assuming?" Jules asked with a soft laugh, sliding another menu behind the first.

Wes nodded, and we followed her outside. We were seated at a table for two. Max found a bowl of water, where he drank the thing dry then plopped down next to me with a groan.

"Do you want your usual drink, Wes?" Jules asked, leaning over the table. Her cleavage was conveniently on display, and it seemed like she'd popped the top button of her shirt sometime between when I walked in and now.

"Yeah, thanks, and can we have the brisket special, two plates, and an order of onion rings?"

Jules glanced at me briefly, as though she didn't want to bring attention or awareness that I was actually here, then she gave us a quick nod before walking off.

I grabbed the cutlery and began untying the little string. "So, you come here often?"

Wes lifted the glass bottle of water and began pouring us each a cup while he smirked.

"Red, she loves this place. I come here with her and Brooks and whatever date they usually set me up on. They've been trying to get me to be a little more human and a lot less pissed off. They say I work too much and don't have a personal life."

That made me smile. Red and Brooks were adorable, and the image of Wes wedged around one of these small tables with those two and some date while they all awkwardly talked was simply hilarious. You couldn't take Brooks anywhere, and if you added in Red, and an awkward situation, you had pure mayhem.

"What?" Wes asked, smiling at me over the brim of his cup.

"Just picturing that. I bet it was a bit much to have them set you up on dates. Did any of them stick?"

He smiled, and all that sunshine I had been missing suddenly came back, making my heart skip a beat.

"No. Red and Brooks would argue over the dumbest shit in front of the poor girls, and it always made them uncomfortable. They also never got a word in edgewise to ask me any questions. I had one girl ask me for my number afterward, just to see if I wanted to hook up."

It wasn't my business to know how that ended but I still asked.

"Did you say yes?"

His eyes found mine and it felt like a rock had landed in my stomach. I had fucked other people over the span of time we were broken up, it would only make sense that he had as well. Still, the idea of him with anyone else nearly sucked all the air from my lungs.

"Do you really want to know, Callie? I sure as fuck don't want to know a single thing about anyone you've been with. I don't want to know if you have someone waiting for you in DC, or if you got engaged or married. I don't even want to know if you had some stranger kiss you on New Year's."

I sipped my water to help loosen the knot in my throat, letting his words wash over me and help me reassess what I wanted to say next, but it was pointless. My brain and heart were flipping me the bird tonight and saying whatever the fuck they wanted to say.

"Why? If you more than got over me like you said you did, then why would it bother you to hear about any of that?"

Wes leaned in closer, leveling me with a glare.

"Because as far as I'm concerned, they all belonged to me. Every kiss. Every moan. Every touch. Whatever you chose to do over the past seven years was all owed to me. You robbed me of an entire life, Callie. Forgive me if I don't want to hear about some guy named Craig who showed up at your apartment at midnight, only to show up at your doorstep two more nights after that."

*Wait a second…* My spine straightened as goosebumps moved down my arms.

"Or some fucker named Joe who picked you up at a farmers' market and took you to his place, where you stayed until midnight. I certainly don't want to know about some asshole with a cowboy hat who found you at a rodeo and thought he had the right to fuck you in the bed of his truck."

*Oh my God.*

Tears burned the backs of my eyes as my nose flared.

How had he…

"Wes…" My voice cracked right as Jules showed up with our onion rings, breaking the moment. I ducked my face to hide my emotions. The tears were clouding my vision at this point, and his confession had muddied my thoughts.

Once she left, I glared up at him, my jaw tight and my face stern.

"How did you—?" was all I could choke out, but what I wanted to ask was if he'd had me followed, because he'd just recounted—with terrifying accuracy—every single sexual encounter I'd had in the past seven years. It wasn't much, just enough to shatter my self respect and heart. Every time I slept with someone, it was a way to convince myself that I was over Wes, and each time I'd compare them to him. Each time, they came up short, and I'd emotionally disconnect. I wondered if Wes knew about any of the ones who had continued to text me, who wanted more from me, but I just didn't have it in me to give.

Wes glared, and after a few tense seconds he rasped, "The better question is how could *you?*"

I felt like I'd been slapped.

"What do you mean? We were broken up…it had been years, Wes."

His jaw moved like he was chewing glass, and suddenly there was a sheen to his gaze.

"You left me, Callie. You ended things with *me*. I was good to you, never gave you a fucking reason to leave. Yet, you moved on."

Scoffing, I tossed my napkin down on the table.

"And what, Wes? You're so fucking perfect that you never did?" Because fuck that, I knew he had. There was no way he'd become the leader of my father's club without fucking someone at some point. I grew up seeing sex and nudity and learning it was just a part of life, and if anything, nothing to make a huge deal over. It wasn't until Wes that I realized it could mean more.

Suddenly Wes was leaning so far over the table, he was practically nose to nose with me and it made it that much more intense when he ground out, "No."

His gaze slowly moved over my face, landing on my lips as he explained.

"I never could touch anyone after you. You were my first, and fuck, if you ended up being my only…there would never be another after what we had."

My chest was so tight it felt hard to breathe. My breath was a heavy cloud, hanging in my chest, useless and lacking any oxygen.

Tears trailed my face, and suddenly the reason I had clung so tightly to seven years ago for leaving the love of my life just didn't seem very substantial anymore. I missed him. I loved him. It never stopped, yet the distance was a divider in our lives and had tossed us on opposite sides of the world with no way back to one another.

I stared at him, he stared back, and when our food arrived, we ate in complete silence. What could I say to him? He'd not touched another person during our time apart, and I had. Why did that make me want to throw up? Suddenly the food didn't have taste, and I just stared at the plate, pushing the meat around in slow, pathetic strokes.

Not only was I the villain who ended us, but I was the one who moved on, too. I hated myself, and there was no cure for it, but still, the rustling in my heart echoed of betrayal from his lack of action. Why hadn't he come after me? He never tried to reclaim me, and that spoke louder than moving on physically ever would.

Wes paid the check, and then we were on our way back to the property. We hadn't spoken of what I'd read in the library or anything else. I wasn't sure how to bring it up at this point. Wes had admitted why he never wanted to move on physically from me, but I believed with all my heart he'd moved on emotionally.

The sun was below the hills as Wes parked my car off to the side of his house. I wasn't sure why I still assumed he'd take me to the cabin, but he just crawled out of the driver's side and gathered Max up before heading toward the front door.

I couldn't stand it any longer. I needed to know what was happening. "Why am I here?"

Wes examined me from over his shoulder then unlocked his front door. I followed him inside, caging my chest in with my arms. His house was dark, save for the dwindling rays of dusk coming in through his windows.

"Grabbed all your stuff from the cabin already. Got the guest room ready." Wes gestured to the small door under the stairs, off the living room. It was a modest room with a queen-sized bed centered with nightstands on either side. Sheer green curtains hung over closed blinds, falling to the thick carpet on the floor. It was nice, far nicer than the cabin.

"Why am I here, Wes?" I repeated my question, turning to stare at him.

Max had made himself at home in the living room, on the dog bed that had been brought over from the cabin.

Wesley pinned his hands to his hips, glaring at the floor before exhaling, and giving me those whiskey eyes. "There was a picture left inside the mailbox last night."

My brows caved as I worked to process what he was saying.

"There was also activity around the perimeter, by the cabin...so I made a decision to pull you closer."

There was so much he was leaving out, and there was a shuddering in my gut that told me the image had something to do with me, but I didn't want to jump to conclusions.

With a dry mouth, I asked. "What was the picture of?"

Wes continued to stare at the ground for so long I wasn't sure he was going to respond, but finally he looked up.

"Of you, when you were eighteen, after they took you. It's you unconscious in their clubhouse…you and the president."

My breath came out as a sob. "What the fuck does that mean?"

My mind raced, going back to blacked-out memories and terror I had worked so hard to push down. To get rid of.

"They did a rape kit. I wasn't—" I started but Wes abruptly cut me off.

"You were in his lap…he was just holding you."

That silenced me, and had me sliding down the wall. Because fuck, what if they did other things to me that a rape kit didn't catch? It wasn't the first time I had considered it, but every other time the thought would come up, I'd continue on with my life in DC and hide within the new life I had created for myself.

"He wants a war with me, and he knows you're here. It's a way of taunting me, but because they know you're here, we're not taking any chances."

This wasn't happening again. I wasn't going to go back to living my life as a scared little girl, afraid of whoever was pissed off at my dad. I couldn't.

I had no idea when Wes lowered himself to my level, but I felt fingers pull at my hands as they covered my face.

"I won't let anything happen to you, Callie. You have to trust me. But it's partially why I need to read that letter your dad gave you. We're partners now, babe. I need your help just as much as you need mine. They'd follow you back to DC…you know that."

I ran a shaky hand through my hair. He was right, I did know that. And I was sure the chances of me surviving a second disappearance were practically zero, especially without my dad here.

Sadness and grief swept through me at the thought of him not being here to make me feel safe.

I had to figure this out. He wasn't here, but I was still a Stone, and that meant something. I wasn't just going to give up.

"The letter, River."

Heaving a sigh, I crawled to my feet, searching the room for my bags. I saw Laura's things, but mine weren't anywhere.

"Where's my stuff?"

Wes was standing now, running his hand through his hair, gripping the ends.

"Uh...I'll show you."

He walked out of the room and rounded the stairs, taking them one at a time. I had already been in this house, so I knew there was only one bedroom on the top level. Yet, I still trailed him as if I wasn't sure where he was going. Maybe he wanted me to stay in that massive closet of his. Either way, the idea of being in the same space as him both terrified and excited me.

Once we'd made it to his door, he gave me one last look from over his shoulder before pushing inside.

The bed was the same as it was the other day, fluffy with navy blue accent pillows and duvet. There inside the closet were my bags, but they were empty.

I moved further into the closet and then froze. Hanging neatly on the previously empty bar were all my clothes—shirts and jeans, skirts and shorts. My shoes were organized on the shelf, and the small satchel I had with the secret lining where I had tucked away all the letters from my dad was there next to them. There was no use keeping it a secret any longer. I pulled the bag free and unzipped the lining, pulling the letters out. I hadn't built the courage to read the bundle I had originally assumed were from Wes, so while he read the one from the will, I'd be digging into those.

With the notes ready, I spun around to meet Wesley's gaze.

His eyes narrowed on the bundle in my hands.

"Explain to me first why all my stuff has been unpacked and moved in here?" Maybe there was another explanation, and I was jumping to conclusions. Perhaps he was staying inside the club and giving up his personal home for Laura and me to use, and he wouldn't even be here.

Wes let out a sigh before pushing off from the door frame. Then he stripped out of his shirt and shucked his boots.

"I won't risk your safety. This is the best place for me to keep an eye on you."

Heat flushed through me as I considered his response and the way he refused to look at me. He just as easily could have done all this without unpacking any of my things. That was a personal touch that spoke to something deeper.

"Okay." I moved past the awkwardness of the moment and decided to focus on the letters, "I'll let you read that letter, and you're welcome to look through these others too if you want. But I want to know what's going on with the club. I want to know why you don't want to sell this place. The real reason that has you scared."

Wesley's glare hit the ground, and his jaw clenched tight as he considered my request. I stared at his bare chest while I waited for him to agree. His jeans hung low on his hips, revealing the gray band of his boxers. The defined muscles along his abs contracted as he stretched his hands above his head and let out a sigh.

"Fuck. Fine."

He snatched the bundle of letters out of my hand then headed to the bed.

"Well, come on, River, might as well get comfortable."

I walked forward, slipped out of my shoes, and crawled onto his bed.

# FOURTEEN
## WES
### AGE 18

The leather cut felt like a brand, as if I'd inked the laws and vows of the club onto every inch of my skin, so everyone could see that I had finally succumbed to the patch. Even as I rode toward the Death Raiders club under the cover of darkness, I knew the colors and words sewn into this vest would define the next chapter of my life. I only hoped Callie would understand and decide to keep me, regardless of doing the one thing she'd asked me not to.

*If she was alive.*

The thought sobered me and had me pushing the bike faster. No one had told me where to go or confirmed who had done this, but I knew enough to realize this was a tactic from the Death Raiders. They were the only other club that had been battling with the Stone Riders since I had started hanging around the clubhouse and began picking up on conversations. It was how I knew where to drive. The location of the Death Raiders clubhouse was something the Stone Riders joked about frequently.

*Down past Pyle, that old mill would go up in flames within seconds.*

That was something Brooks would bellow when he was drunk. I knew Pyle well enough to have an idea of where to go, which was proved correct as I pulled off a side road leading past the old mill. I slowed my speed, coming to a chain-link fence, and there, about fifty feet down the length of it, were rows of parked bikes. I continued until I saw five members patrolling, likely to keep them safe from sabotage.

I parked alongside theirs and dismounted.

"The fuck?" I heard Giles, one of the newer members yell, as he noticed me.

With a harsh rasp, Hamish limped over to me. "Oh no…no, no, no. What have you done, son?"

I swallowed the lump in my throat. Everyone knew what wearing this leather cut meant. You didn't wear it unless you meant it for life.

"I need to know where she is."

Hamish gave me a sympathetic look that was saturated with pity. It made anger twist my insides uncomfortably.

"Don't fuckin' look at me like that, just tell me."

Hamish let out a resigned sigh, "They're inside, talking to Dirk."

I recognized that name as the president of the Death Raiders. He was a sick man, from what I had heard, which was why Simon was at war with him so frequently. The Stone Riders were careful of what sort of illegal activity they got into—so far it was just running alcohol and cigarettes—but they found out the Death Raiders had started trading harder shit, and there was even a rumor about a woman they had trafficked.

Simon wouldn't stand for that shit close to his home, or his daughter.

It was another reason why my stomach was twisted into a tight knot, the fear of them doing something to her or taking her somewhere…I couldn't even process the thought.

Hamish warned in a low tone. "You head in there, and it might make everything worse." The other members were smoking, talking to each other while eyeing me nervously.

I hated that he might be right, and I could never live with myself if I did make things worse, but I had to get in there.

"There a back entrance to this place?"

Hamish tilted his head, but I already saw the light in his eyes, as if he'd had the same idea.

"Take me to it, and I'll sneak in. You can go back to your post. I'll deal with Simon."

Hamish shook his head but pointed his finger past my face.

"Your bike will be too loud. Walk the perimeter, and after you pass an electrical grid, there will be a two-by-four with white paint on it. To the left there's going to be a keypad, as if you can't get in without using it, but it's a decoy. Squeeze past the fence and keep walking. There will be a door at the bottom of the stairs directly to your left. Knock four times. When it opens, you need to let them know that Hamish sent you."

How did he know how to get in? If he had this sort of access, I didn't understand why they hadn't led with this. Hamish must have read the question on my face because he let out a long exhale and slapped my back.

"There's a kid your age in there, he's the son of one of my friends. We kept our friendship quiet because of our different affiliations, but his son is a good kid. He'll be the one to open the door and lead you to Callie."

I shook my head, confused as fuck as to why this wasn't being used to our benefit.

"Why didn't you just tell Simon to do this to begin with?"

Hamish grabbed for a new cigarette and popped it in his mouth.

"Dirk did this to get Simon's attention. There's a reason he wanted Callie here. I highly doubt he's going to hurt her, but it all depends on what he wants from our club. He's going to barter, but regardless of what they agree on, I want her safe and out of their hands. So go see if you can get our girl while they talk politics."

I didn't wait to be told a second time. I walked the perimeter, keeping my face down and my eyes alert. The cover of darkness helped, especially when I saw a few scouts walking the boundary, smoking. I ducked and waited for them to pass before slowly making my way down the length of the fence. When I approached the electrical grid, I paused, because the setup really did look like it was going to prevent me from entering. There was a camera system, and even an electric fence, from the looks and sounds of it.

On cautious feet, I did as Hamish explained and bypassed the keypad, squeezing through the side fence. I kept going until I came upon the set of stairs he'd mentioned. There I found a rusty steel door at the bottom. Giving one last look around, I knocked four times.

Within seconds, someone was opening the heavy door with a bit of a struggle, as if it took effort to pull on it. My nerves jumped as my fingers itched to grab the gun tucked into the back of my jeans, but I trusted Hamish. He said someone on this side would be trustworthy.

Finally, the door was open, and an old timer poked his head out, slurring his speech. "What the hell you doin' here?"

Fuck. He wasn't supposed to be the one who answered.

I was about to come up with a lie when all the sudden I heard another voice, gaining the old man's attention. Then a person my age replaced the old timer with a set of furrowed brows.

"The fuck are you?"

He had dark hair, almost black, and it fell over his forehead, nearly cutting into his pale blue eyes.

"Hamish sent me," I said in a rush, my fingers loose at my sides. I watched his body language, seeing that he didn't seem tense or like he was wired. As soon as I said the elder member's name, his face relaxed and he moved to the side.

I walked in, keeping watch of where I placed my back.

The door shut behind me, and it took a second to adjust my eyes to the room. It was dim with a single flood light lit up from above.

"Monty, keep up your post, this one is with me." The younger guy nodded in the old timer's direction. He'd reclaimed his seat at a table, nearly falling from his chair. He must be the guard in some capacity, but he was completely trashed, and he looked like he was seconds from falling over.

The guy my age led me away from the storage room and toward a narrow hallway.

"If Hamish sent you, then you must be here for her."

Exhilaration lit up my chest like a fucking Christmas tree. I resisted the urge to grab him so I could shake the information out of him.

Instead, I barely gave a silent nod.

He walked past another storage room, this one with wooden boxes. The kid glanced over his shoulder and said, "I'm Silas."

"Wes," I replied, following him further into the clubhouse. I gathered that this was part of the basement.

"Look, I can take you to her, but you'll have to figure out how to get out of here on your own. They had her up there for a while, just for pictures and shit, but then they moved her down here. I know Simon is trying to negotiate terms, but I have a feeling it's going to take a while."

I was already about to lose it just from the idea of her being here, and what the fuck did he mean by pictures? *Fuck.*

"And what exactly have you been doing with her since she was brought down?"

We slowed at a small set of stairs leading to another landing just off the hallway. Silas turned and met my gaze.

"I have my own fuckin' demons that come out to play, and it's for that reason I'd never touch her. She's been kept safe, but I can't promise how long that will last. Dirk wants something from Simon, something big, and none of us know what it is. We just know that kidnapping his daughter is the boldest move he's ever made against your club and without the leverage would have caused an all-out war."

My eyes kept flicking to the door behind Silas, and while I appreciated what he was saying, there was a fire roaring in my veins to get her and get the fuck out of here.

"If Dirk realizes you've taken his leverage, that war might just happen anyway. If it does, I hope you remember me. I'm not your enemy, and seeing as you're new to the Stone Riders, I hope you'll consider yourself someone I can count on if the time ever comes."

I studied him, curious how he knew, but he only laughed and pulled keys from his pocket, unlocking the door.

"It's your cut. It looks brand new—that, and we've heard of you."

The door opened, and soft lighting flooded my vision. I ignored Silas's last comment and pushed into the room. My eyes skipped over everything else in the room and landed on a long, L- shaped couch, where my girlfriend was tucked under a soft-looking blanket. They sharpened on the woman sitting next to her.

She had dark hair and seemed a bit older than me, but the set of her jaw and harshness of her stare told me she wasn't one to be trifled with. I was almost to Callie when the woman placed a protective hand on her back, glaring up at me.

"Who are you?" Her eyes flicked to my cut, inspecting the patches.

Silas spoke up for me, "Sasha, it's okay—this is the boyfriend, Wesley Ryan."

I gave her a nod. "You look out for her?"

Her chin dipped, her eyes slowly moving to Callie's sleeping form.

"I never thought he'd stoop so low as to kidnap someone's child."

Her gaze returned to mine with tears gleaming.

"Take her and get her as far away from this shit as you possibly can. If you love her at all, you'll get her the fuck out of Virginia."

With that, she stood from her place next to my girlfriend and walked out of the room.

Tears burned at the corner of my eyes as I crouched in front of Callie and gently pushed a strand of hair off her face.

"She's been given a sedative. Nothing harsh. She'll wake up in an hour or two," Silas said softly from behind me.

I continued watching her sleep, her dark lashes dusting the freckled skin above her cheekbones. Her usually plump, pink lips looked cracked, like she hadn't had enough water today, and there was a tiny bruise developing near her temple.

"Who hit her?" I asked, brushing the pad of my finger over the mark.

Silas shifted behind me, clearing his throat. "They call him Poet. He's a big motherfucker. Dirk put him on grabbing her from that parking lot, and he wasn't gentle."

Rage began to gnaw away at my resolve. I wanted to stalk upstairs and find him, but I needed to take her out of here first.

"Thank you, Silas," I muttered before dipping to grab Callie under her legs and back. I brought her to my chest, tucking her under my chin and taking the blanket with me.

"You're welcome…but can you do me a favor?"

Holding her, I turned to see him strapping on a bullet proof vest. "You need to shoot me."

Sasha suddenly reappeared with her arms crossed, standing against the door frame.

"I'll take care of it, Silas, just let him leave."

Silas turned to inspect her with his brows raised. "Mom, I'm not letting you do that."

I looked between them and realized now how similar they seemed.

Sasha stared at her son and then flicked her gaze to me. "Get her out of here."

"Mom, he's going to kill us if you do this."

I had always considered myself a morally decent person. I'd help someone if they needed it, offer money to the homeless, I never stole, never cheated on tests. I considered myself good.

But in that moment, seeing these two people who had helped me possibly face backlash from doing it, I simply didn't care. If I had to choose to help someone, it was going to be Callie.

That may have been the tipping point for me, realizing I'd kill them both myself if it meant I had a way out of there.

Without looking back, I retraced my path through the warehouse. The guard had passed out while watching his show, so I shifted Callie to my shoulder and pulled on the door, slipping out.

My head hung in my hands as I sat across from Callie's hospital bed.

She was hooked up to an IV, and her head wound was treated. But she was still out, and it was making my nerves raw.

Once we'd cleared the Death Raiders club, I took her to a field, where Hamish called a prospect to come and pick us up with a truck. That same prospect would be riding my bike back. I had no idea how the negotiations were going, or what would happen, but I couldn't worry about it.

Nor could I panic over what Simon would say regarding me taking his daughter to the hospital instead of using the club doctor. I had removed my cut prior to walking into the building, so there'd be no connection to the club.

The ER nurse walked back into the small room and checked Callie's vitals. "You should go get some coffee or something. There's not a lot we can do until she wakes up." They weren't admitting her. Yet. The unknown of it all was riding me hard. I knew Callie couldn't fill in the gaps for me, but having her awake was the next best thing. Right as I was about to explain that I was fine, I saw Callie's head lilt to the side then slowly make its way back to the center of her pillow. She was waking up.

I rushed to her side as the nurse began to talk to her.

She was asking a few questions about what happened, but Callie's eyes found mine, and the tears welling in them had me pushing closer. The nurse went silent, finally reading the room, and gave us some privacy by sliding the sheet closed around her bed.

"Hey." I tried to smile, but my lips wobbled too much, forcing a frown.

Callie's voice broke as she grabbed my hand. "Tell me I'm okay."

"You're okay, River. I promise you're okay," I said soothingly while sliding onto the bed with her.

She curled into my chest as a heart wrenching sob escaped her. It broke me in half, rendering me speechless as the reality of how close we came to losing her slammed into me. I clutched her closer as I worked to regain composure and calm the storm brewing in my head.

I wanted to scream. I needed to hit something.

"I got you," I whispered as her fingers grasped hold of my shirt and her sobs increased.

We stayed like that for several minutes, until the nurse gently interrupted and asked to examine Callie.

She gave her statement to the police, which included what she knew.

*Food trucks, hit from behind, everything went black.*

I didn't add anything, knowing I'd have to fill her in once we got home.

"Perform a rape kit," I said with a quaking whisper. I ignored how Callie's eyes swung toward me.

"Why?"

I winced at the panic rising in her tone.

Thankfully the nurse took over, explaining why it would be a good idea, considering she was wounded with no knowledge of who had done it.

It was agony while we waited for all the results to come in. But finally, they cleared her. No concussion. No rape.

Just enough emotional trauma to last the rest of her fucking life.

Not to mention the betrayal she'd soon discover.

I'd hurt her worse than anyone else, and I was terrified of what she'd say when she realized it.

# FIFTEEN
## WES
### PRESENT

THE LETTER DIDN'T TELL ME SHIT.

I'd been waiting on this fucking thing since the day I saw it passed over the lawyers table to Callie, knowing it was meant for me and it was just Simon's way of teasing me. He had told me before he died that if I was doing everything right then I'd have access to that letter because the only way to read his instructions would be to make amends with his daughter.

Fucking meddlesome old man.

Callie was sitting next to me, her eyes moving quickly over the other letters from her dad. I had no idea what Simon had been writing her throughout the years. I assumed it was apologies, and other shit regarding his absence from her life, but I didn't know. I just knew he had handed me one once a month for the past three years and told me to make sure my name was on as the sender, not his.

I didn't know what he was playing at, and sure, there was a part of me that wondered if Callie would open them simply because they were from me, but she hadn't. And it wouldn't have burned as much if I hadn't ever known, so that's one more thing I can thank Simon for.

"You find anything good in there?" I finally asked, giving up on the note in my hand.

He told her to sell.

Why would he tell her to sell the property? It made no fucking sense. If we sold, we'd be out a place to call home and we'd lose our headquarters, which didn't make sense for the club. Where else were we supposed to go? Not to mention all the product Simon had left us in charge of moving from the last big deal he'd set up. If we sold, we'd be fucked, because we had nowhere else to put that much product without landing on someone's radar.

"Nothing but apologies and memories." Callie swiped at her eyes and shoved the letters back into shape, tucking them into an envelope. Her somber expression did something to me. I hated seeing her like this, and considering this was the first time we'd been alone with each other in private, where I wasn't teasing her to shower with me, or pushing her buttons about being here, it was hitting harder than I was comfortable with.

Clearing my throat, I moved from the bed.

"I got shit to do. You know where the shower is, remotes are in the bedside table, and there's food down there if you get hungry. I'll be back later."

Callie moved off the bed, trailing me.

"Wait…where are you going?"

This felt so weird, being back in a domesticated space with her. It was like we'd never left, and yet there was nearly an entire decade between us. She hurt me. Fucking ruined me. So the urge to kiss her, or to soothe her worry, burned the tip of my tongue. All I had to do was think back to her face last night when she realized I had been more than aware of all her encounters over the past seven years, and I'd sober right up.

"I have club matters to handle." I pulled on my boots and leather jacket, which was a replica of my cut. Same patches, same colors, just thicker and more protective when I'm riding.

She stared, her arms crossed over her chest.

"So us being partners now, that was just bullshit?"

I hid my smile by lowering my face, because I liked a riled-up Callie. Used to be my favorite thing to come home to.

"Nope, but there are some things I can't bring you in on. Some shit has nothing to do with the letters, or what's going on with the Raiders."

That was a lie, but like hell did I owe her anything.

Her plump bottom lip was pulled between her teeth as she watched me grab my keys. Her nails dug into her skin, and Max suddenly picked up his head like he knew she was getting pissed.

"What if I have to leave, or go somewhere?"

I grabbed the door handle and pulled, before giving her one last look.

"Don't."

I had to get her hazel eyes out of my head.

I slammed the door behind me without a second thought and hurried over to the club. She'd try to follow; I knew that much. Callie wasn't the type to sit and stay or take orders. It wasn't in her blood, and that used to send a rush to my cock—fuck, still did—but I needed her to listen this time. Thankfully, Killian was pulling up with the blonde-haired friend on the back of his bike.

He parked, and before he could even take off his helmet, she was crawling off the back of his bike. She threw her helmet on the ground then shoved him in the shoulder before stomping up to me. No fear, nothing at all in her eyes but fire.

"Where is Callie?"

Shit, this girl made me want to back up a step. She looked like she was two seconds from throwing a punch, and all five feet two, hundred and twenty pounds of her would try to take me down. She was out of her depth, but she didn't seem to give a single fuck.

I gestured with my head toward my house. "Staying with me. Your stuff is already there too."

Callie was outside seconds later, her face hard and determined. The blonde friend ran over to her, and with one last malevolent glance at me, she put her arm around her friend's shoulder, leading her into my house.

I turned to see almost the entire club watching from the porch. Killian seemed pissed at something; no idea what was going on there, didn't care. I walked inside and headed toward the back, but something inside my chest, squirming uncomfortably, had me yelling to the group of younger members.

"No one touches them. Don't look at them. Don't fucking breathe in their direction, do you understand me?"

There was a rumble of confirmation before I pushed through the church doors.

Brooks, Hamish, Rune, Pops, Killian, and Giles were all staring at me from their place at the table. Church was broadly just a meeting place for us, with one long table and our club's most prized memorabilia up on the walls. This room was a time capsule as much as it was a place of peace and safety. We planned here and set the course of the club right from this room. I thought back to my first time sitting in one of the chairs and watching as Simon went over detailed optics for a run Brooks was making for the Mayhem Riot. I remember being scared shitless but excited too.

That feeling never left me, and I decided it was probably a good idea to always be a little scared, especially in this life.

"You got the letter from the will?" Brooks asked, tapping his weathered finger against the table. They were all in on Simon's joke. If I got back into Callie's good graces, I'd be able to see the last living wish of Simon Stone.

I gave a curt nod, not willing to go into any of the details about Callie. "He wants us to sell."

Just to make sure they knew I wasn't bullshitting them, I passed the letter to Killian so he could read it. He passed it to Rune and so on. Once everyone had a chance to look over it, we sat in silence.

"He can't really mean for us to do that." Giles muttered quietly. The prospect from years ago had transitioned into one of my closest friends, and reliable club members.

Everyone remained quiet while flicking tentative glances at me. It was times like this I wished Killian had been asked to step into this role, but Simon wanted me. Still wasn't sure why, especially when Kill had been the vice president. It took everyone by surprise when Simon told everyone his successor for the club would be me.

"There's something we're not seeing here. There's no way he'd ever want us to sell this place. Not from how many times he'd talk about the future of the club. He's hiding something."

Killian rocked back in his chair before tipping his gaze to the ceiling. "Might be worth a shot to ask his old lady. She was the closest person to him."

Fucking Sasha.

The woman had come into Simon Stone's life a few years ago, but we all knew her from being Dirk's old lady. Something happened over there with the Raiders and suddenly she wasn't his anymore, just club pussy with no way out. Simon took a liking to her. She straddled the line between both clubs, falling for the leader of the Stone Riders while being tied to the Raiders. She was a good person, and I did trust her. Always had, ever since that night she placed her hand on Callie's back, but I trusted her son more.

"Let me meet with Silas first. I need to know how close he is on his end of things. It will help give us a timeline, especially after Dirk sent that photo of Callie."

Killian tapped the table with his fingers, looking contemplative. "You think they're planning on trying to take her again?"

The memory came quick like a rush of adrenaline battering my chest. Callie being taken, finding her in their club. It still felt like just yesterday when I was carrying her out of there.

"Don't know, but we need to be careful."

Pops chose that moment to speak up, effectively putting his foot in his mouth.

"We could always use her as bait."

All eyes snapped to me, and I was already shaking my head.

"She might not wear my property patch anymore, but I made a promise to Simon that she'd stay safe. Offering her as bait isn't an option."

They didn't know it ran deeper than that. It wasn't just a promise keeping her safe. It was me. She'd worn me down in the span of just a few days of being here. I wanted to be unfazed by her presence, and act as though her scent didn't drive me so fucking mad that I wanted to punch something or someone, but property patch or not, she'd always belong to me. Which meant she'd always be mine to keep safe.

"I'll meet up with Silas, and we'll reconvene tomorrow. For now, Hamish, I want you to stay around the club and keep an eye on these younger members to ensure no one bothers the girls."

Hamish nodded, taking a drag of his cigarette.

"Brooks, tell Red to plan a big community barbeque for next week."

Giles gave Killian a confused look right as Brooks sat back in his chair, folding his hands over his large belly.

"What are we doin' throwing a town barbeque at a time like this? That's awful tempting for the Raiders to come crash."

I waved him off, pulling out my cell. "I'm not worried about that; Silas will make sure no one steps foot in Rose Ridge that day."

Brooks glanced quickly at Killian, raising his brow before settling his curious gaze on me again.

These fuckers all looked to him as the second, it should have been him. I had no fucking clue what I was doing wearing the patch of president. It wasn't something I ever wanted, and while the men liked me just fine, they didn't respect me the way they did Killian.

"I'm trying to draw someone out, see if I can pull on a loose thread." I explained, trying to help them without forcing them to ask it. Questioning the president wasn't admired in clubs like ours.

Silas agreed to meet with me, so I waved everyone off. "Try not to die out there, keep Killian appraised of what you're doing."

Everyone filed out of the room except Killian, which is how every meeting ended. Even if he wasn't wearing the patch of president right now, he was still my second in command, and my best friend.

"Laura," Killian muttered, inspecting his nail, digging at some grease on the tip of it.

"What?"

His green eyes landed on me, and like so many of his expressions, it made me uneasy. Killian had this way about him that reminded me of a wolf. In fact, he wore a wolf patch on his cut, like I had the small fox for Callie. Simon was always calling Killian "the wolf." His gaze on me reminded me of his moniker, forcing my spine to stiffen.

"You keep saying, 'the friend, the girls,' I even heard you call her *the blonde one,* once. Her name is Laura."

He had never once corrected me on someone's name. Not ever. Not when I called Natty, the kitchen hand, Nadine, for three months. Not when I called Giles, Garth. Not when I called the mailman Gene when his name was Jason. Killian had been there, hearing me say all these names wrong, because I'm shit with names, but he had never once said a word.

I let out a frustrated groan while sagging back into my chair.

"Kill, you can't fucking fall for her. Please promise me. It will only complicate shit."

He smirked, shaking his head.

"First of all, I'm not fuckin' falling for anyone, but complicate shit for who?" He leaned back, dragging that nail across his shirt.

I glared at my friend, squinting just to see if I could see his facade crack.

Killian remained casual, focusing on his nail.

"They're going back. I'm only keeping her long enough to ensure she won't sell, once she does, which she will, she'll pack those bags, Laura too. Then they'll take that horse and drive back to DC. She was never going to stay here."

My mind flung the image of her in my tattoo shop back at me. She'd seemed eager, excited almost, at the prospect of working there. She was about to accept an application for the seat before I had walked in.

Killian rolled his eyes then let out a sigh.

"You're in quite the mood since she got back, and honestly, I thought maybe it was good because you've been a shell since she left. But this...this depressed, glass half full bullshit is ten times worse."

He was right, and I hated that he was. But what was I supposed to do, just turn off my feelings for her? Forget. Move on...

Fuck. Yeah maybe it was time I did. It would do some irrevocable shit to me to see her go, but there was no question in my mind at all that she would. She didn't want this life, and regardless of how temporary it might be for me, she'd never stick around long enough to find out that I had made my own plans.

"Tell you what. Once I'm done, I'll go on a date that I set up, not Red or Brooks, and I'll actually give the girl a shot."

Killian watched me with a careful tension, as though he was waiting for me to break. There was no doubt that I would break; it was just a matter of time now.

"I have to go meet Silas." I stood from my chair and took two long steps toward the door, but right before I pulled on the handle I paused.

"I'll stay with her until you get back," Killian said softly.

With my back to him, I let out a small sigh of relief and exited the room.

# SIXTEEN
## WES
### AGE 18

I held Callie in my arms as my phone buzzed in my pocket.

Somehow I knew it was Killian calling, regardless that we'd come home without a trace of another member trailing us.

Callie ordered me to explain what happened the second we climbed into the truck and began driving home. So, I did. Slowly, cautiously, and leaving out the part where I joined the club.

Now, we were in the cabin, and she was awake, lying against my chest as the small television on our dresser played some sitcom on Netflix. Neither of us were watching it. Tears kept hitting my bare stomach as she sniffed every so often, wiping at her eyes with the edge of the sheet.

"Did they get the guy who hit me?" she finally whispered after about an hour.

Not fucking yet, but I would.

"Don't know…your dad is handling things," I said instead.

She swiped her finger over one of my abs, and let out a tiny shudder. "Who got me out? I mean, if my dad is still dealing with it, and Kill, then who brought me out? How did you find me?"

*Fuck.*

Hitting pause on the television, I gently pushed the hair off her face and asked her to sit up.

"I need to tell you something. You can get mad…you can hate me." My voice broke as I pushed a lock of hair off her face. "Just don't fucking leave me."

Her hazel gaze searched mine for meaning.

I pushed away the trepidation in my gut and let the confession fall from my lips.

"I got you out. It was me who went in and discovered where you were."

Her brows caved as her head shook with confusion. "But how did you know where I'd be?"

I stroked her jaw as a pained rasp left my chest, "Hamish told me."

She immediately retreated from the bed, and her face twisted with anger. "No, because the only way he would tell you is if you were one of them. That's how it works in the club. You can't know anything at all, even if a life depends on it, unless you're patched in."

She shook her head adamantly, almost as if she were convincing herself.

I slid slowly off the bed, tugging the cut out from under it.

Holding it out to her, I knew right then and there I'd never get the look on her face out of my head, not for as long as I lived. Not the way tears coated her lashes as she gently took the leather from my hands, not the way her lip wobbled as she traced my name, nor the way she sobbed as her nail passed over the fox patch.

My throat grew tight as I worked up a response. "River, I'm so—"

"No!"

She stepped forward and hit my chest, tears streaming down her face.

"You promised me!" Her slaps turned into fists, pounding against my chest.

I walked forward, absorbing the hits, and wrapped my arms around her, sinking to the floor as she cried.

"They can't have you. They can't take you from me."

I rocked her on the floor until she eventually passed out, and even then, I stayed there, terrified of what this would mean for us.

"You wanted to see me?" I asked, approaching Simon while he worked on his bike.

It was dusk and the summer bugs were singing, ushering in the night. Killian had offered to stay with Callie after Simon had sent him in search of me.

After the truth came out about me joining, she wouldn't talk to me. That was two days ago. This was the first time Simon had asked for me since the event, and I wasn't sure how he was going to respond to this news or if it would be any better than the way his daughter had.

Simon stopped what he was doing and stood, abandoning his bike.

He eyed the cut I wore over my dark T-shirt, narrowing his hazel eyes on the patch and the name he'd had sewn in for me. Then in the blink of an eye, he threw his wrench across the garage as hard as he could.

"So, it's fucking true then?"

I backed up a step, only because I had never seen him this angry before.

Simon's eyes blazed with anger as his jaw worked back and forth.

"You interfered."

I grit my teeth, biting back the retort I wanted to make, and instead calmly said, "With all due respect, you were keeping me in the dark and expected me to wait here while you dealt with her being fucking kidnapped. She was taken, Simon. What would you have done?"

He grabbed me by the cut and threw me to the ground with more ease than I was prepared for. I knew he was pissed, so I allowed it.

"I would have fucking waited," he yelled over me, spit flying from his mouth.

I slowly got to my feet, dusting myself off.

Simon's lip curled as he stretched his fingers out.

"You think you love her in a way that would have challenged a father's love for his own child? You think I wouldn't burn the world down for her? She's my blood."

Stepping toe to toe with him, I roared back, "And she's my entire fucking soul. We're bound, her and I. In this life, and even in the next. She will haunt me for eternity, and when the devil tries to pry my soul from her grasp, he'll realize there's nothing to claim because it's hers. All I fucking am, and all I ever could be belongs to her. There is nothing inside me that would have tolerated waiting. You've never once asked if I loved your daughter, and I know it's because you already know. What you don't know is that she's my ending, Simon. She was my first love, there when I just barely started in this world, and she'll be the only thing on my mind when I leave it."

Simon's eyes flicked my way once more before darting around the garage. He paced, while tossing more tools.

"She never wanted this for you. She's going to hate me for it, Wes. She'll blame me."

"I won't let her." At least that was my intention. I hadn't thought through far enough whether this would come back on him. "What do you want me to do? I can take it off, act like it never happened." It wasn't like the entire club had seen me. Hamish and Giles would keep their mouths shut, Killian too.

"They all know, Wes. Because after we'd made a deal for her release, they went to find her and found Dirk's woman instead. She was arguing with him over the kidnapping when her kid spoke up and said it was you who took Callie. Their entire club now knows you stole leverage from Dirk Lenair. You have a target on your back, and because you're with my daughter, she's not safe either."

I scoffed, running my hand through my hair. "She was never safe, Simon. Fuck, she was just kidnapped for being *your* daughter."

Hurt flashed through his eyes before he settled on the stool near his work bench.

"You need our protection. The best option is for you to keep the patch, wear the colors. Ride with us. Callie will eventually accept it, but you'll have to give her time."

I knew he was right, and once I explained all this to her, I hoped she'd understand that we were out of options. Curious about something he'd said, I asked.

"You said you made a deal…"

Simon's face turned up, his hazel eyes shining with something I couldn't place. He stared off somewhere behind me for a while before his gaze met mine again.

"Somethin' like that. I made it before I knew Callie was gone. He went to pull her upstairs, and he'd made it sound like by the time she came up she'd be dead or missing her fingers. I couldn't risk it, so I made the deal. Minutes later, his woman came up, then the kid opened his mouth, spewing shit about you. By then it was too late and the deal had been made. I'll find a way out of it."

The weight of the words felt ambiguous, and the fact that he wasn't elaborating made me nervous.

"You'll report for church every Monday morning at ten. You'll fit within one of the companies owned by the club. Lucky for you, that mechanic shop you're working at does, but you'll transition as the new owner on paper to take heat off the club. We'll begin using that as a place to move weapons. We started trading with the Mayhem Riot from New York. If this goes well, it could be lucrative for us."

Simon finished his sentence with a flick of the cigarette he'd burned through. My stomach flipped at all the information he'd just dumped on me. For one, I had no idea how in depth their illegal activities were, and the shock must have shown on my face.

"What's wrong, little Wes? Didn't realize we dabbled in the dark?"

I cleared my throat and shook my head.

"Just wasn't sure it was—"

He cut me off with a slap to my back as he closed the space between us, "What did you think that one-percent patch meant on the left of your breast?"

Speechless, I just looked down at the white number sewn into my leather cut. I hadn't ever considered it before, or what it would mean for me if I joined.

"Now you get to go explain to my daughter what her future looks like if she chooses to be with a Stone Rider. Good luck, son."

I swallowed the thick lump in my throat, staring down at the new vest he'd placed in my hands.

It was leather, like mine in almost every way except the patches on the front. Instead of a member patch, it had Callie's name with the initials of the club below it, and on the back, instead of the club colors, there were just three words stitched in white.

**Property**
**of**
**Wes**

# SEVENTEEN
## CALLIE

THE LETTERS SAT BUNDLED ON THE TABLE AS LAURA AND I DRANK OUR tumblers of whiskey.

Max ran after the tennis ball I was launching with a ball thrower. The sun had set, and the ice in our glasses nearly melted as we lounged on the back porch. The only reason Killian wasn't harassing us about going inside was that Wesley's yard was secluded, and private from the rest of the club.

Killian had shown up shortly after Laura had settled in, but as soon as she saw him, she decided we needed some fresh air and promptly pulled me outside. He was on the other side of the glass, watching television, glancing our way every so often.

Laura broke the peaceful quiet between us, turning her head to catch my gaze. "There's a bus station about fifteen minutes north of here. Can you drive me to it tomorrow?"

Mine snapped sideways in return.

"What do you mean?"

A long exhale came out of her as she tugged at the fabric of the chair, then squinted as she watched Max. "I just need to get back."

"Did something happen? I thought...I mean, you seemed excited to be here with me."

Her shoulder came up in a small shrug, "I'm still excited to be with you. I just grossly underestimated how intense your upbringing was. This is a lot, and I feel that itch under my skin to get back to work. I'm either going to get a job here and start looking for an apartment, or I need to get back home. My roommates will be expecting a rent check from me soon."

Shit. It wasn't like I had assumed she'd be here forever…I just assumed she'd be here until I was ready to go back. *If I was ever ready to go back.*

"Of course I'll drive you. In fact, if you want, you can take my car back."

Laura shook her head. "No, you'll need it for when you return."

She was right, of course, but there was still that strange sensation thrumming against my chest, like a plucked chord of curiosity where I didn't go back.

I shook those thoughts and dipped my chin to my chest. "Okay, then, I'll drive you."

She looked behind her, where Killian was inside, and frowned.

"We should do one of our infamous girl's nights. Go set up in the guest room, where grumpy motorcycle president threw me, and you can stay with me while we binge watch television shows all night and eat junk food."

I followed where she was looking and tried to piece together what was on her mind, but her focus returned to me, and so had her smile. I gave in and squeezed her hand.

"Let's go raid his pantry."

Max perked up as we eased off the loungers and made our way back inside. He was galloping toward us while I held the slider open for him. Killian's dark brows lifted in silent question as we made our way to the kitchen, but he didn't follow us or ask.

Laura got to work digging through the cabinet while I focused on the freezer. Wes didn't have anything but meat and vodka, plus three microwave dinner meals.

"I'm going to see if he has another freezer in his garage," I said to Laura before taking the side door through the small mud-slash-laundry room, until I was walking into a pristine garage. The humming from the freezer to my left was the only sound in the space, and it was significantly warmer with no air conditioning running, but the sealed floors were cool against my bare feet.

Flipping on the light, I veered toward the stainless-steel fridge, but the far wall of his garage caught my attention. His tools were immaculate, but on the worktable there were a few parts he was obviously in the process of working on. Above the table were pictures pinned to the wall.

At least ten four by six, glossy images were scattered around the space. I walked closer, desperately needing to see who was important enough to Wes to have them pinned to where he worked.

Leaning over the table, my nose was practically against the image of a much younger Wes with his arm hung over my shoulder. In the photo my eyes were closed, my mouth open with a wide smile, and my head was tilted into the crook of his arm.

He was staring down at me with something that looked like devotion. That was the night we'd snuck into a concert to see one of my favorite bands. Neither of us had any money, so Wes would always find some loophole during the summer, when the bands played outdoor venues.

I moved to the next image; it was of us kissing. We were eighteen and living in the cabin. His arm was behind my head to take the photo, as my arms flung around his neck. The next image was of us dancing at sunset. Someone else took this photo, because it was a few feet back from where we swayed under the gold and orange sky. My friend Genny's wedding…that's why I was wearing a dress, and he was dressed in a button-down shirt.

My eyes watered as they moved from memory to memory. Soaking in every picture, branding it to my mind, because when I had left all those years ago, I left this all behind. Every photo, every memento. Anything at all that would remind me of what I had, and here he'd been keeping it all up, as if I'd just walk right back into his life one day.

And here I was.

A sharp inhale cut through me as I swiped at my eyes and moved away from the table. I thought back to the letters I had read earlier, and how angry they'd made me. How his lies had found a new way to tear at the seams of my pride. Wes was salt to every wound I had ever had— every heartache, every hurt. He was the reason I was still hurting, and those stupid letters only proved it. I couldn't believe he'd lied about them. These pictures only worked to enrage me further, proving that Wes was only toying with me.

Stupid Wes probably had cameras in this room, too, and was likely watching me right now. Just to show him I didn't care, I raised both my middle fingers and spun around in a circle. Once I was finished, I walked to his freezer and pulled out two pints of ice cream.

It was late when I heard the murmuring of voices.

Killian had stayed through the night while Laura and I had our own little party in the guest room. We binge-watched romcoms from the nineties while eating our weight in junk food, even going as far as to order food from DoorDash.

Unfortunately, we learned they weren't allowed on the premises, and someone would have to go meet them on the main road. Killian begrudgingly sent a prospect to get our food. He was being suspiciously quiet, even when I bought him his favorite burger and fries. He took his meal and ate it soundlessly on the couch, while I tempted him with an episode of Gilmore Girls. He had shaken his head while giving me the world's most pathetically sad smile.

I worried that maybe I was overstepping my role in his life with my return home, and maybe Killian was still pissed at me. But the way his gaze would linger on Laura had me assuming something else and wondering if maybe I was missing something there. I wanted to ask my best friend, but she had already passed out.

I was about to turn off the television and try to get some sleep when footsteps echoed outside the door. I wasn't ready to see Wes after what I'd read in those letters, or what I saw in his garage so I slammed my eyes shut right as the handle twisted.

I couldn't hear his steps because of the soft carpet, but I could feel his presence drawing closer, until he was right next to me.

I worked so hard to slow my breathing, keep my eyes from fluttering so he wouldn't know I was awake, and maybe it worked because he remained silent. Until suddenly his warm hands slid under me, drawing me to his chest in one quick movement. With long strides, he carried me out of the room.

"I'm headed out, I'll talk to you tomorrow," Killian muttered softly to Wes while it sounded like he shut Laura's door.

We stood still for a moment when I heard another small exchange between the two, but I couldn't make it out.

Then we were on the stairs, obviously headed to his room, and that's when the realization really hit me. I finally dropped the act and stared openly at him.

"I never agreed to sleeping in your bed."

He ignored me, continuing with me flush against his firm chest. It was dark as we passed the small office space and finally entered his bedroom through his open door.

The urge to sneak up here had ridden me all day, just to snoop for more clues about his life, but I remembered he had cameras and stuck to downstairs.

He shut his door with the heel of his boot, and when we were within a foot of his bed, he tossed me. I landed with a bounce, a gasp leaving me.

"Hey—"

It was still dark, but Wes clicked on the bedside lamp, revealing his handsome face, and sculpted frame. Even with a simple T-shirt on, I could see his hard pecs and the way the fabric strained against his well-toned biceps.

With a feral gleam tilting his lips, he grabbed the hem of his shirt and pulled it over his head. I must have sucked in a tiny bit of air, because that grin turned arrogant as he leaned over me, his palms dropping to the mattress.

"And I didn't agree to you ending us. Now strip. When you're in my bed, you're either naked or you're wearing one of my shirts."

I could feel his breath against my face as I stared into his whiskey eyes and felt a tug deep in my belly.

"What happens if I don't?" I whispered.

He framed my head with his strong arms, making me feel both protected and weak at the same time. The smirk fell from his lips as he searched my face, his focus dropping to my mouth.

The tug in my belly tightened, but I couldn't kiss him. I wasn't ready. Not like this.

He lowered his mouth to mine just the same, but at the last second, I turned my face.

His lips landed on my jaw which didn't seem to deter him. His tongue came out, tracing a path down my neck, but he was stopped by my hoodie. I felt his smile against my jaw as my breath hitched.

"I don't think you're ready to find out what I'd do if you don't." He lifted off me, staring down while I returned his gaze.

I should move—strip like he said—but my limbs were frozen. Being in his bed, smelling that familiar intoxicating scent he always carried, was overwhelming me. It had a hint of leather mixed in now, and I wished I hated it, but I didn't.

There was a warning in Wes's eyes as he watched me lie motionless under him. I knew I'd likely regret what happened next, but there was also a small piece of me that wanted to curl into this moment, like a voyeur just watching from a dark spot in my mind. There would always be that little girl who found refuge in his treehouse, and that same girl eventually realized the peace wasn't the space, but the person. Wes calmed all the storms, so if he wanted to raise a little hell then I'd wanted to be on the receiving end.

His lips returned to my skin, marking me in new ways that felt feverish.

"Don't say I didn't warn you, River." His voice was rough against my stomach as he shoved my hoodie up.

His touch was a thing I'd been starved for, and I wanted to indulge, even if I knew it wasn't smart. Even if this would tear at the scar along my heart. Which is why when my leggings were tugged down, I didn't protest.

Hot breath washed over my mound as Wes slipped the silky

underwear down my hips, stopping at my thighs. My sex was completely exposed to him, and with my fists clenching the sheets, I didn't care. I wanted all barriers gone so I could lift my leg, toss it over his shoulder, and grind into him. His hands slid under my ass, pulling me until his nose was hovering over my slit. With those eyes on me, his tongue slowly traced down my center. I was already wet, and as soon as he pried me open, he moaned as if he'd just tasted the proof.

His teeth scraped against my clit, forcing my breathing to become labored, my chest heaving. I needed more, but I knew if I asked, or begged, he'd get exactly what he wanted. This was him delivering a punishment for not obeying him. He knew I wouldn't be able to resist him if he did this, so I kept my fingers out of that thick hair and gripped the sheets instead.

Flattening his tongue, he lapped at my clit in slow strokes, which had my thighs clenching the sides of his face, and a whimper cascading up through my chest. Smiling against my thigh, he repeated the movement, torturing me with the tip of his tongue. He swirled and circled, drawing out gasps and moans from me. I was nearly there when Wes suddenly stopped and removed his mouth from me completely. I opened my eyes to see where he'd gone, but all I caught was sculpted muscle, shadows vying for space along his torso as he stood and stared down at me with a predatory gaze.

I should take the opportunity and stop him, but my tongue was tied with need, nearly about to combust if he didn't finish what he'd started. So, when he grinned wickedly at me and then gripped me roughly by the hips to turn me face down, I didn't object. The roughness of the sheet against my face somehow added to the hollow need aching between my legs. I was desperate for his touch in whatever form it might come.

A light slap landed on my ass, followed by a soothing stroke and a low sound from his throat.

"How are you still so perfect?"

I tried to look over my shoulder, but his hand came out and held my face firm against the mattress.

"Hands above your head, Callie."

I did as he said, too desperate for his touch to argue. My fingers dug into the sheets above me, and then my knees were guided up.

I could only track him in my periphery now that my hands were in front of me, but it must not have been enough for him because he pushed my hoodie down until it was over my arms and covering my face. I could still breathe, but I couldn't see anything. The thrill of not being able to visualize what he was doing shot straight to my core, making my hips move backward.

Another slap landed on my ass as he chided me.

"No moving, just sit there with your ass up. Let me play."

I tried to hold still, but the space between my thighs was wet, my core ached, and I needed him to touch me.

With a firm grip, he spread me wide and made a groaning sound before dragging his finger along the sensitive hole there. Teasing the tightness, he played for moments before slipping lower. I cut out a sharp breath at how intrusive his fingers were, but the friction was divine.

"Soaked, Callie. Fucking soaked," he rasped quietly before pressing a kiss there.

My hips rocked against his mouth, desperate for contact, when his mouth left me again.

"You're not listening very well." Another slap landed, followed by another, certain to turn my ass red. But I was so turned on that all I could do was moan.

He laughed before returning his mouth to my pussy. He was sloppy, licking and sucking, making a mess of my crack while his thumb found a place over my tight hole and three of his fingers sank into my cunt.

"Oh fuck." My voice was muffled by the bed, and out of desperation my hand left the space above me and went to hold my cheek, so he had more room to pleasure me.

But of course, he stopped completely when I did.

Frustrated, I argued, "I'm just trying to help!"

With a slap to my ass, he replied, "I don't need your help. What I need is you to come on my fingers, but since you can't follow instructions, maybe I should just let you stay like this while I go shower, and maybe by the time I'm out, you'll have forgotten about your need for release."

If he didn't make me come, I was going to die. This much, I knew. I was shaking from how badly I needed it.

"Please," I begged, hopelessly.

This dominant side of Wes had always flirted with coming out when we were together, but seeing it in full force was such a rush.

"Let me make you come first."

He paused, but his fingers swiped at my wetness, wiping the mess over the red marks he'd created with his punishing slaps.

"You want to make me come first?" he asked, curiously.

I tried to lift my face, but his hand was there holding me down.

"Yes, I'll make you come first, then you can finish me."

He laughed, tracing a line down my spine.

"Fine, sure, come make me come, Callie."

I hated that it suddenly rubbed me wrong that he wasn't calling me River, but I pushed it down as he adjusted himself, sitting on the edge of the bed. He finally let me up, and I saw that his jeans were down, his cock pulled out.

My mouth went dry as I crawled off the bed and fell to the floor in front of him.

I'd forgotten how massive he was. He wasn't insanely long, but he was thick, *so fucking thick.*

Kneeling in front of him, I wrapped my fist around his base, my fingers barely touching as I leaned forward and took the tip of his smooth head into my mouth. Wes hissed, shoving my hair off my face. I went down far enough that I gagged and then released him, only to lick the head once more.

"Take this off," Wes ordered, tugging on my hood.

I did as he said, pulling the sweatshirt over my head. I was about to go back down on him, but he stopped me again.

"Let me look at you."

I froze, my glistening mouth parted as I sat back on my heels. My underwear had slid down my legs when I got up, so I was just in my tank top, which was skintight and boosted my boobs, so there was ample cleavage.

With a needy whisper, Wes had another demand. "Take it all off."

It was so quiet in his room that part of me wished he'd turn on the television or some music, anything to make it less obvious that this was our first time together since our breakup.

I did as he said, slowly tugging the tank up and freeing my breasts. I sat there while pinching my nipples between my fingers, letting him see me.

Without looking into my eyes, he gripped his shaft and began jerking his wrist, his hand sliding up and down his length. He was touching himself while watching me, and it was a thrill, but I wanted more. I wanted to taste him as he'd tasted me. My hair tickled my heels as I tilted my head back and moaned with pleasure as I rolled my nipples between my fingers.

With something deep rumbling in his chest, he pulled me forward. "Now wrap those lips around me."

I did with a moan, hot from being naked with him and having him hard and already dripping for me. I gripped the sides of his thighs as I bobbed up and down on his hardness, the taste of him coating my mouth but not filling it. I wanted him to combust, lose himself, and more than anything, I needed him to watch as I sucked every drop down. Right as he began to buck his hips, meeting me move for move, he suddenly gripped my jaw, his thumb pushing down on my bottom lip.

"That's enough," he rasped with a heaving chest.

I popped free of him, watching as he clenched his jaw, staring over at his closet, almost as if he couldn't stand to look at me.

I sat with my hands on his thighs, confused.

"But you didn't—"

He abruptly stood, tucking his hard-on back into his jeans, cutting me off.

"Realized I didn't need to after all."

Heat began to creep up my neck. I was naked, on the floor, while my ex literally stopped his blowjob simply because he couldn't stand my mouth on him. Frustration burned under my skin. Why go this far with me, only to reject me at the last minute?

"Is this part of me not liking what you'd do if I didn't obey your rules about sleeping in your bed?"

It didn't feel like that. His threat from earlier felt playful, sexual... this was different.

His eyes still wouldn't return to me as he crossed into his open closet and came back out with a shirt fisted in his hand. Tossing it at me, he passed me, veering for the shower.

"Nope. Just didn't need to finish."

I stood, trailing him while I held onto the shirt. Because I didn't want to be naked in front of him any longer, I pulled the heather gray material over my head.

"You're lying. What the hell just happened?" I should have kept my voice down, and considered Laura below us, but my heart felt like it wanted out of my chest, and I hated that I'd put myself in such a vulnerable position with him.

He reached into his glass shower and turned the chrome handle until a steady spray of water heated the tiles inside. Wes ignored me as he lowered his jeans, and boxers, his cock was still stiff and hard.

I gestured toward it for emphasis. "I'm still fucking wet, you're still hard. Why are you acting like this? Why even start it at all?"

He finally turned toward me and roared back, "Because I'm fucking weak, Callie. Okay? I can't have you in my bed again and pretend like it's not the only place I dreamed of you being for the past seven years. I can't see you naked and not want to touch you."

His whiskey gaze slid down my frame as pain slid into his features.

"Even now, it's killing me not to touch you. You're in my shirt, and I can't put my hands on you, or hold you."

I stepped forward to cut him off, thrusting my hand at my chest. "Then why don't you? I'm standing right here."

Tightness crept into the side of his jaw as he dipped his face, staring at the floor. The silence made my chest ache, and suddenly I wasn't sure if I could handle this truth from him. Before I had a chance to walk away, he didn't give me a choice.

"I can't get them out of my head."

My fingers pushed through my hair as I waited for him to finish, but the weight of his gaze nearly had my knees buckling.

"What can't you get out of your head?"

With sadness in his gaze, he stared at me before shaking his head.

"Every single motherfucker who's had you since you left me. Every person who tasted you, touched you, held you…I can't get them out of my head. With you kneeling in front of me, your mouth on me, all I could think was the others you've tasted. That same position, that sultry look, that perfect way you know to push your tits out, pinch those dusky nipples while making me hard as fuck. How many other guys fell into that, thinking they were the luckiest person on planet earth to have you?"

My mouth parted with a shaky breath as I processed his words.

The guilt tore at me with phantom teeth, and a desperation to soothe his hurt lingered on the tip of my tongue. Right as I opened my mouth to explain myself, he opened the shower door and stepped inside, abruptly ending our conversation.

Tears blurred my vision as I lowered my gaze to the floor and briskly paced my way back to the bed. I wanted to keep going, all the way down to the guest room, but I didn't want to cause a scene if Wes was serious about me sleeping in his bed.

So, I threw the covers back, pulled my underwear on, and turned off the light.

Once the room was dark, and I knew Wes was still in the shower, I let the tears fall. And for five minutes, I allowed myself to break.

It was so easy in my mind, how the past went.

Painful, but clear cut.

I gave Wes a choice, and he didn't choose me.

So, I chose myself, and while I knew Wes did know how many people I had been with since we broke up, not even one of them had ever seen me in that position I'd just been in with him. I hooked up with my clothes on, usually with them just bending me over the couch and getting off, but I'd never once put my mouth on another man. I had never let another man taste me, the way he had.

I had never even orgasmed. I'd made myself sick when I allowed my hurt to draw me into such a toxic place that I agreed to hooking up. If I was over Wes, I wouldn't have beat myself up for it, but with each person, it all came back to him.

The one hookup that lasted three dates was only because it was around my birthday and I was feeling sorry for myself, but I'd never forget how he had lifted my dress and took what he needed from me while I held onto the edge of my kitchen table. Tears ran down my cheeks, and not because he'd entered me bone dry. I cried because that guy had been the third person I had hooked up with, and through the years, I kept thinking the pain of Wes would wane, but it never had. If anything, by that time I'd gotten to the last one, the ache was unbearable.

It proved that a metal casting had been molded around my heart, and only Wes would ever fit it. He was permanently there, and I was doomed to never love again.

I couldn't change the past any more than he could. This was why I didn't want to give in to him because there was too much water under our bridge to navigate any of the waters without incident.

We were broken, and there was no amount of chemistry that would repair what we'd done to each other. I knew where this road would end. Wes was still tied to this club, and I still refused to ever be a part of it.

Based off what just happened, it didn't matter anyway.

Wes didn't want me other than to make a point, and tonight, he'd made it.

I just didn't expect the point to be dagger sharp, or to cut so deep.

# EIGHTEEN
## CALLIE
### AGE 18

My father was in charge of babysitting me today.

It was a rather ridiculous sentiment, but after the past two weeks, I didn't really give a shit. I was beyond caring about who watched over me. Some days it was Killian, others it was Red, and occasionally it was my boyfriend.

I started speaking to him again, but it came in the form of me telling him what to do while he fucked me. We quickly found that to be our quickest and most effective way to get back to normal. I needed him emotionally, but after a while, he was being so supportive that it bugged me, and it felt like I couldn't be angry with him over joining. And I was furious. But after time, I realized there was nothing I could do to change it. So I was either going to accept it, or lose him.

I wasn't really ready for either option, but losing myself to the orgasms he provided so willingly seemed like a good place to start.

I sat on the couch inside the cabin with an oversized hoodie over my body while a sitcom played on the television. My father and I hadn't spoken since it happened.

I was getting better at staying awake and not sleeping through each day, but it was still difficult to put a term to what happened.

*Kidnapped.*

"Callie, I made dinner," my dad said softly from the kitchen.

I peered over my shoulder, making eye contact. "Not hungry."

Hadn't been hungry in a while. Only Wes could get me to squeeze one of those kid Gogurt yogurt packets into my mouth, occasionally a smoothie, but I just wasn't in the mood to eat.

My dad stood there for a while before he clicked his tongue.

"That's enough, get up." He moved to where I was sitting and tugged on my wrists.

"Dad!"

He shook his head. "No, this isn't you. No fucker on this planet gets to dull your shine, baby girl. Let's go."

That was likely the most he'd say on the subject of me being taken, but I wasn't surprised. He had me walking, my feet were bare, but he didn't seem to mind as he pushed his way outside. The sun was setting, dusk was hanging low in the sky, making the ground shadowed. My dad broke away, striding toward the small shed. It was tiny, couldn't even fit an entire body inside. Dad used it for shovels, bug spray and apparently our treasure jars.

"You still have those?" I asked, coming up behind him.

"We haven't made a jar of treasure in a long time. What do you say, should we bury it?"

I laughed, thinking how ridiculous it would be to bury purple sand at the age of eighteen.

"Come on, there's still magic left in there." He pointed at my heart, and for some reason, it made me sniff. Then a tear trailed down my face.

He moved past me, leading us to a patch of dirt, where he kneeled down. His leather cut was still on, and I stared at the president patch as another tear slipped free. He was a powerful man, and the fact that he was out here with me, not just biding his time but spending time with me, turned me into a melted mess.

"Which color should we do, honey? We don't have purple, but we have some red sand. Want to try it, and what if we add some gold flakes?"

I choked on a sob as I laughed. "Where are you seeing gold flecks or red sand? I see an empty jar, without even our usual purple sand inside."

My dad leaned in close, pulling up a palmful of dirt. "You have to use your imagination, sweetie. You used to love to do that when you were little. Just close your eyes and pretend a little."

His shoulder bumped mine, and for whatever reason, I took a deep breath and gently tugged the jar from him. Twisting the cap, my gaze lifted to his, and he poured the dirt from his hand into the jar.

I repeated the same old words we'd used since I was little. "For the magic."

Dad added another handful of dirt, and said, "For the dreams."

We both continued our tradition until the jar was full, and then Dad secured the lid once more and began digging the hole to bury it in.

"You will come back stronger, Callie. You're a Stone. If you aren't sure how to be strong, you look to me and I'll show you."

His lips landed on top of my head as he pulled me into a side hug. I relaxed in his embrace and considered that perhaps there was some magic in those jars, because for the first time in weeks I let free a genuine smile, feeling happy in a way I feared wouldn't happen again.

*Six Months Later*

Wes was late again.

I wasn't surprised. I'd grown up in this life, I knew the schedules, the runs, the way it worked. I had learned how to keep myself busy over the years. I learned how to disappear into the background, dream, create fantasies about living a normal life with normal parents, and one day, be a wife with an adoring husband who had a normal job, who would be home for dinner and bedtimes. He'd be there to read to our kids at night, and to help make breakfast in the mornings.

It was a fool's dream.

Watching the shadows flicker on the wall made me tense up.

Something about the way the movement of the branches outside looked like arms, and hands. All these months later, and still my brain would occasionally reach out, reminding me it was missing pieces of what had happened that night. I had nothing but darkness and a hole in my heart.

Fear rode me, using me like a rag doll. I was always afraid, and while it had already been six months since it happened, nights like these were difficult to shake the feeling in my gut that someone else was coming for me.

Finally, the rumble of an engine cut through the silence, and a pair of headlights flashed on the far wall. I heard his boots on the porch, and then the door unlocking.

Within minutes he was hovering over me.

"Hey, did I wake you?" His lips landed on my forehead, then my nose, and eventually my neck.

I pushed my hands into Wes's hair, loving that he was home. Regardless of how angry I was that he was late again, I was always happy when he returned.

"Where did you have to go tonight, why are you so late?" my voice was raspy with sleep that taunted me but never came.

Wesley's eyes gleamed in the darkness, the lights from outside illuminating enough of his face for me to make out his expression. He was already shutting me out.

"Babe, you know I can't talk about it with you."

He didn't call me babe very often, because I hated it. He called me River.

Why was I suddenly babe?

I let him go and withdrew my hands. "Fine."

Another kiss landed on my chest, this time over my heart.

"Let me shower, and I'll come apologize properly for being late."

I stared at the ceiling as he moved around the room, until I heard the water turn on. Tomorrow was the club picnic, and I already knew what would be expected of me, and I was already dreading it.

I had worn my property patch when I was around the club, but every time I did, there was a slice of my pride that seemed to be cut from me. I never wanted this life. I didn't get to choose the father I had, or the mom. I didn't get to choose my home, or the car we drove, or the way I was picked up from school as a little girl. I didn't get to choose anything about my life, except Wes, it seemed, and now he'd been taken from me too.

Recently, after learning of what Wes had done, and coming to terms with how he'd made his bed, and I was reluctantly going to lie in it with him, I had come to terms with my anger over the situation. Acceptance led to hurt, and a gaping wound where the club was concerned.

I completely detested how happy Wes was with his place in the club.

It was as though he'd found a new family that fit him perfectly, and the connection he had with my dad and Killian was so tight that there was no question he'd become a high-ranking member. Killian was the vice president, but Wes was directly under him and was included in every decision my dad made for the club, which took all of his time. Wesley owned the mechanic shop on paper, but he hadn't set foot inside the garage in six months. Wes had hinted at getting married ever since we were seventeen, and now here we were. I'd just turned nineteen and there wasn't a single conversation we'd had about it since.

In fact, I hardly saw him, and when I did, it was at home.

Tossing the covers off my legs, I sat up and took a calming breath. The shadows continued to flicker along the far wall as the branches swayed outside. The water from the shower turned off, and before Wes could come out, I had to push down these raw emotions. I wanted just one night where we didn't argue about his new role. It's all we seemed to do anymore. I had to focus on the good and assume it would get easier.

# NINETEEN
## CALLIE
### PRESENT

THERE WEREN'T ANY BLACKOUT CURTAINS IN WESLEY'S ROOM, SO AS soon as the sun rose over the hill, I was awake. Honestly, I was grateful, because while Wes looked like a sleeping warrior with that hard jawline and those high cheekbones. I was sure I resembled something that had crawled out of a sewer.

I thought back to how, after his shower last night and our harsh words, he had slid in next to me in bed. I had held my breath, waiting for him to turn away from me, but he shocked me by pulling me to his chest and nuzzling my neck. He didn't say anything, but we both fell asleep like that. Sometime during the night, I escaped his hold so I could reflect on what I was doing and why I was doing it. I needed to focus on getting information and selling the property. Stop fantasizing about tattoo shops and local farmers' markets, and how good Wesley's house would look with mint-colored curtains, or a bench at the end of his bed.

Closing my eyes to erase those domesticated images, I sat up in bed and then walked into the bathroom. Gleaming, white tile stretched below me, cool under my bare feet. The large soaking tub in the corner silently called to me, begging me to feel those jets against my aching back. The glass shower was big enough for a group of people to join inside, although there was only one showerhead. Seemed like a giant waste of space if you didn't have a bench to sit, or a double spout.

Wes had a few masculine shampoos and soaps inside, and there on the small inlet on the back wall were my things; my shampoo, conditioner, and body wash. He'd brought them in after unpacking for me. Even my razor was lying over the top of the shampoo lid. Wes was thoughtful, considerate, and an asshole all at once. It was maddening.

I bit my nail as I slowly turned, finally seeing myself in the mirror. My hair was a mess and looked like I'd been rolling around all night having rough sex. I laughed at the thought and stripped out of Wesley's shirt.

Stepping under the hot spray of water, I took another look around the bathroom and practically lamented over how stunning it was. It was so much nicer than anything I'd had at any point in my life, and while I was happy for Wes, it did leave me feeling a little insecure. Wes had nice things growing up, and I was perpetually poor. Then I grew up to be meager, and while I was confident in who I was, I wasn't assured that I was good enough for someone as accomplished as Wes. He'd gone to college, started his own business, and even had his own TV show. All I had going for me were my skills with ink and the piercing gun.

A few people had tagged me on Instagram, showing off their tattoos and how good of a job I did. I loved reading the comments about how amazing the detail was or how creative the design. I got a few clients that way, and it always made me feel so damn special, like maybe leaving Rose Ridge was worth it. Then the rent would come due, and I'd be right back to wondering what in the hell I was doing.

Wes suddenly walked into the bathroom, making me jump, and breaking me out of my thoughts. His dark boxers molded to his muscular thighs and round ass so perfectly that I had to withhold a groan. With a smirk in my direction, he pulled his morning wood clear of the constraint of his boxers, stroked once, and then shut himself inside the alcove with the toilet.

I quickly rinsed my hair and turned off the water. There were clean towels on a shelf to the left, so I tugged one on, hoping to avoid Wes. Once I darted into his bedroom, I shut myself in his closet and began to change. It was stupid—he'd just seen me naked, and I was literally sucking his cock the night prior—but I was worried if he touched me again, I'd be simpering for him to finish what he'd started last night.

Once I was dressed, I walked downstairs while brushing out my hair. Laura was at the table, sipping a cup of coffee while scrolling through her phone. She wore last night's pajamas, with her knee hiked up, her chin resting on it, her messy hair tied up in a twist on top of her head.

She yawned. "Oh good, you're up."

I smiled and turned for the coffee machine.

"How long have you been awake?"

Right as I opened a cupboard for a mug, the front door opened. Killian walked in, stalling once his stare landed on Laura.

She froze, mid sip, before rolling her eyes and pushing part of her hair off her neck.

"Six," she replied curtly, right as Wes jogged downstairs.

Killian gave him a nod, then took a seat across from Laura. "Six what?"

Laura lifted a dark brow then circled the top of her mug with her finger. "Six, as in the number of men I kissed last night. Do you really want to know the details?"

Killian's jaw went rigid and he leveled a narrowed glare on my best friend. Wes came up behind me, taking the mug from my hand. I grabbed a new one and waited as he poured himself a cup. Opening the fridge, I grabbed the half and half and milk, rotating in time to hand him the milk as he handed me my mug. We both poured a dash of liquid into our mugs, then we traded, repeating with the other beverage. I didn't even realize it was quiet in the room until I looked over my shoulder at Killian and Laura, who were both staring at us.

"What?" I asked.

Killian shrugged, smiling. "Just funny watching you guys, you'd think you've done this a time or two before."

I glanced over my shoulder, seeing Wes already watching me. I broke my gaze and moved away from the counter, the awkwardness of how easily we'd fallen back into our roles trailing me.

"I need to get to the bus station." Laura exhaled, setting her mug aside while standing from the table.

I sipped my coffee while my eyes flicked up to catch Killian's expression. He was staring at Laura, his jaw tight, then he glanced at Wes. For what, I had no idea.

It felt like there were more secrets, and things I didn't know, but I knew my best friend well enough that she wouldn't tell me until she was ready. Maybe if I asked Killian, he'd tell me.

Laura went off to the room to get ready, and a piece of toast with apple butter landed in front of me.

I looked up to find Wesley glaring down at me. "Eat something."

His attention was put on Killian next, where they began talking about different club members and plans that had been made earlier. I bit off pieces of toast while I gleaned what I could.

"Red says she needs more time to plan the barbeque." Killian said, sipping from a glass bottle of orange juice he must have purchased before coming over.

Wes shook his head, staying across the kitchen while munching on his own toast.

"Don't have the time. Just throw some fuckin' hot dogs in there— that's a Costco run. Tell her not to complicate it."

Killian nodded.

"How was your conversation with the Roman?" Killian asked Wes, but his gaze flicked quickly to me.

Who was the Roman? I had never heard that name used before.

Wes stared down at the floor before saying easily, "Fine...there's follow up that I'll need to make. He needs to ask his mother if she'd feed us the intel we asked about."

Fuck, I hated this.

I was dying to know what they were talking about, and it felt rude as hell they were doing this in front of me, but it wasn't anything new. My father had talked in code and half sentences, where bits and pieces were missing, my entire life. Wes still let his gaze linger on me, as if he knew I was curious.

I tilted my head, and he just moved on to a different topic, ignoring me.

About to interrupt them, I opened my mouth right as the guest room door opened and Laura walked out with her bags on her shoulders. I jumped up to help her.

"Make sure she's with you when you come back." Wes told Killian, while pointing at me.

Laura winced, as if she'd run into a glass wall.

"Callie can just drive me in her car, we don't need to be escorted."

Wes stared down at his phone as he replied curtly, "He won't ride with you, just follow."

Laura locked eyes with me. "Seriously?"

I shrugged, blushing a little because it was ridiculous, but things were tense with the Raiders, and I knew better than anyone that it wasn't something to take lightly. Still, that didn't mean I didn't have my own plans to ditch Killian the first chance I got. I wasn't eighteen anymore or walking alone in dark parking lots. I carried mace and a taser now, along with Max… Shoot, I hadn't even checked on him this morning.

"Max?"

There was the jingle of his collar and then I heard him clomping down the stairs.

"Why were you up there?" I asked, stroking his head.

Wes came up next to me and lowered to his haunches with a bowl of dog food. "I put his dog bed in the office. Figured he'd want to be close to you."

Tapering my eyes on the food in the bowl, I realized it wasn't what I had packed for Max. What Wesley gave him was something much fancier, an expensive wet food I couldn't afford because it was more spendy than human food. Ignoring the kind gesture he'd made, I focused on helping Laura.

"Here." Killian stepped up and took one of the bags from me, while we exited the house.

I allowed him to take the brunt of Laura's things, packing them in the back of my car while Laura crammed in the rest. Wes watched from the porch. I took a break from the other two and sauntered over with my hands tucked into my back pockets.

"So, you said yesterday that you'd tell me what you're worried about and why you're afraid of selling. You gonna share, or keep talking in code around me?"

Wesley's lip curled for a half second, almost like he was amused, but he sobered quickly with a quick glare. His phone was tucked into his pocket, and suddenly he was pulling my wrist, tucking us behind the siding obstructing his porch from view.

With his hands on my hips, he drew me close and put his lips to my ear. I closed my eyes because it was so intimate, and I was weak.

"Can you keep a secret, River?"

I nodded, bringing my hand up to grip his arm.

His hot breath washed over my skin as he whispered, "I finished making myself come last night in the shower, picturing you on your knees with those lips all wet from sucking my cock. Then this morning, I woke up hard as stone, still thinking of you, then I saw you in my shower, all wet and soapy, and I fucked my hand to the image and what it would have felt like to have walked in there with you. You make me insane, River, and I don't know if I'm going to be as strong tonight. So do me a favor and don't test me. Just be a good girl and do what I say, so I don't have to teach you any lessons."

Fresh air hit my face as he moved past me, walking down the steps. I swallowed, suddenly needing air and turned to see a smug smile cross his features as he continued toward the clubhouse. Killian was straddling his bike, Laura was in the passenger side of the car, and everyone was waiting on me.

I hustled down the steps and calmed myself enough to drive without revealing how my hands shook. That asshole messed with me on purpose. He knew I was desperate last night, and I had begged him to finish me. I hadn't even slipped my hand in between my thighs last night after everything. I just lived with the ache.

Son of a bitch. Tonight, I was going to pull Max in the bed and put him between us. He thought he was clever, but he had no idea how stubborn I could be.

Laura hugged my neck tight as we watched the large Greyhound bus roll to a stop.

"Are you sure about this?" I asked for the billionth time. I still felt uneasy about her reasons for leaving. I knew her well enough to know she wasn't telling me the entire truth. Something else was going on, and maybe she just wanted to go. That was okay too. I just wished I knew the entire story.

Letting each other go, she took a step back.

"I'm sure. I'll call you as soon as I get back, and if you want I can check on your apartment."

I waved her off. "No need…there's no plants or anything there I need to keep alive."

"What about your mail?" She tilted her head as a few people disembarked from the bus, and others were loading their things into the bottom storage hatch. Killian was placing Laura's bags neatly into one of the slots.

"Actually, it would be amazing if you could get my mail for me."

She smiled and took a step away, "I still have your key from when I last watched Max."

Laura stalled as Killian stood awkwardly, watching everyone bustle around him. Laura focused on him, tentatively tucking her hair behind her ear while going toe to toe with the giant. They were laser focused on each other, silently speaking with their eyes when Killian produced something from his pocket. I couldn't see what it was, but the moment felt private.

I realized this would be my best chance to slip away from Killian without him noticing.

The car was parked behind the partition for the bus platform, so I could drive off without drawing his attention. Hustling into the car, I quickly reversed and watched in my rearview to ensure I wasn't followed. I felt slightly guilty for taking advantage of a situation that seemed delicate between my best friend and pseudo big brother, but I pushed it down.

I needed to get somewhere with Wi-Fi, where I could find a way to contact that blogger. I realized it was a long shot, but there was an entire network of people actively watching every move these clubs were making and would possibly provide unbiased information about what's been happening over the past few years. It may lead nowhere, but with Wesley keeping me in the dark, and now Laura leaving, I didn't have any other ideas.

The bus station was on the outskirts of Rose Ridge, and wherever I went inside the town, someone from the Stone Riders would report back to Wes. Finding somewhere outside the city would be my best option. Navigating to a café along the side of the highway, I pulled in then drove around the side, so it wouldn't be visible from the road. With my tablet in hand, I headed inside and ordered lunch before sliding into a booth.

Connecting to the shop's network, I navigated back to the initial blog I found yesterday. Focusing on the page, I scrolled down to the ambiguous username and clicked on it. There was a connected page for more information, a way to email, and even follow them on social media. I clicked on the Instagram link and scrolled through the images listed. They were of various club members engaging in dangerous or violent behavior. Each post was a call to action to raise awareness regarding some ballot measure to outlaw motorcycle clubs from setting up residence within city limits.

I let out a small laugh because several of these clubs were already operating in illegal activities. A ballot measure wasn't going to do anything; most of the police officers in each county were on the club's payroll. This wasn't the way to get change. If anything, you needed a bigger bully to strike fear into the clubs, but that was asking for a war.

My food came, but I was focused on the comments in each image. Snagging a fry, I clicked onto another person's profile that seemed to be protesting the same agenda as the first blogger. Their images were a little more detailed, with creepy shots of the entrance to different clubhouses. There were even images of kids playing in the yard at one.

"Okay, that's fucked up," I muttered out loud, concentrating on the intrusive images. I was so engrossed, I jumped when I heard someone say my name.

"Callie?"

I looked up and found Sasha smiling down at me. Her dark hair was tucked into a neat bun, while she held her purse to her shoulder. My eyes went to the man behind her. He was tall, with midnight hair and blue eyes, but something about his nose and lips, those were a near replica to Sasha's. As soon as his eyes landed on me, they widened like he'd seen a ghost.

"Sasha, hey." I smiled, but it faltered when the man next to her shifted and I realized the leather cut he was wearing. *Death Raider.*

I froze, but Sasha seemed to register my concern.

She slid in across from me, with a reassuring smile. "This is my son, Silas. You're safe."

That explained the similar features. Silas folded into the seat, pinning me with an unkind glare. He held a sort of dangerous beauty about him, his hair was shaved close on one side of his head, but the top was slicked to one side, similar to something you'd see in the nineteen twenties.

"What the fuck are you doing here?" he asked me brashly.

His terse tone startled me, making me tuck my tablet closer to my chest.

"Silas, stop," Sasha chided.

The waiter came over to ask what they wanted, but Silas glared so hard at the girl she just left without even asking about their order.

Silas focused on the plate in front of me, like he was offended by the mere notion that I needed food. His eyes were pale blue, reminding me of a horse I once rode that my friend had named Moonshine. They were beautiful but unsettling.

"Where the fuck is your protection detail?" Silas repeated. It was quiet but still clipped.

My eyes flicked to Sasha, but her lips smashed together while she stared at the table.

"I don't know what you're talking about," I lied, even knowing that Sasha would likely call me out. She knew that Wes had me followed.

Suddenly Sasha's hand came down over mine sweetly, while Silas lifted his phone and took a photo of me.

"Hey, what the hell?" I blanched, shocked at the intrusion of privacy.

Silas began texting and then his phone rang.

I watched his inky black hair as he ran his hand through it. "Yeah…"

His gaze swung to me. "Right here in front of me." With a mocking tone, he added, "What would you like me to do, Mister President?"

My face flushed as I realized who he was reporting to.

Wes was going to be pissed and was likely just going to have Killian come get me, who would also be angry that I slipped past him.

Silas pressed end on his phone and leaned forward while Sasha elbowed him.

"No, she needs to fucking understand how dangerous this is. I guess getting kidnapped once wasn't enough for the princess."

"Hey!" I slammed my hand down on the table. Fuck this guy and his angry ass attitude, "What the fuck is your problem with me?"

He leaned closer, and a part of me wanted to curl into the corner of my booth to avoid his creepy stare. "Other than almost losing my life because of you, or my mom losing her place in the club," he scoffed, "do you even know the details around how you were rescued, or how your dad made a deal for your release?"

My focus sharpened. *My dad did what?*

Silas seemed to notice my demeanor shift because he sneered while stealing a fry. "I see no one told you about the deal. Not surprised, no one ever asks what Simon Stone sacrificed in order to get you back. Such a shame your overeager boyfriend fucked it all up. Eight years later, and now your dad is dead. Who do you think is responsible for holding up that bargain now that he's gone?"

Fear slid in between my rib cage, forcing my breath to shudder.

Silas smirked and Sasha remained quiet, although her face was about as somber as mine, almost as if we were both getting lectures.

"It's you, princess." He took another fry. "The Death Raiders are after you, because you're the only way Dirk can secure what he's owed."

*No.* This was more information than anyone had given me, but it was all wrong. Like finally seeing behind the curtain, only to realize the secrets all led to my demise. Most of the kidnapping was a blur, but absolutely no one had shared any of these details with me. Not Wes, or my dad…and now I just wanted to scream with frustration.

Silas shook his head, wiping his hands on the extra pile of napkins. My appetite was completely gone, but I worked up the nerve to ask.

"What is it he's owed?"

Sasha tried to stop Silas right as the roar of a bike echoed outside, shaking the thin windows of the café. From the way the gravel crunched outside, I knew Wes was being reckless and about to rip me away from the one and only chance I'd have at answers.

The bell rang over the front door, and I heard Wesley's boots hastily reverberate along the floor. Sasha looked up right as Silas leaned closer and whispered, "Your daddy's club, of course, and every single piece of property it sits on. Your dad traded your inheritance for your freedom, and now it belongs to the Death Raiders."

With a wink, he was sliding out of the booth, following his mother while Wes stopped abruptly next to me. With a severe glare, he stared down at me like I'd just ruined his day. I couldn't even care if I had ruined his plans. My brain grabbed hold of the information Silas had just leaked and tried to process what it all meant. Why would my dad leave me something in his will that was owed to someone else?

"River." Wes regarded me coldly then grabbed my elbow, forcing me out of the booth.

"Ow, Wes, that hurts," I snapped but he kept walking, dragging me along with him. Sasha and Silas were forgotten as Wes rounded the side of the café. He finally let me go as he fished for his key, gliding next to his bike.

I searched the lot, the sun partially blinding me as I held my hand up for cover, but my car was nowhere to be found.

"I had a prospect take it," Wes clipped out, apparently picking up on my silent question. I didn't appreciate him manhandling me or being a dick, so I scowled at him while he straddled his bike.

"You made a copy of my car key?"

Wes shook his head, laughing acerbically while pulling on his sunglasses. "No, River, we fucking hotwired it. Now get your ass on the bike. We've already been here too fucking long."

I was so upset I couldn't even speak, but I did as he said because I wasn't eager for trouble to show up in the form of a rival club realizing the president was here, alone. I climbed on behind him, not wasting time with space. My hands hooked over his stomach and I rested my face against his back.

With a twist of his hand, his engine roared to life and Wes brashly sped off, uncaring how gentle he was. The wind was a solid wall against my face, making it impossible to cry, which I was grateful for because I was tired of crying. Tired of feeling weak and emotional regarding this entire situation. I had felt gratitude when my father left me the property, but it was a ploy.

Somehow, deep down, I knew it. This was all a strategy, and I was two steps behind everyone else, and I was sick and tired of feeling like a fool because of it.

The sign for Rose Ridge flew past us as we entered the city limits. My hair blew behind me free and unbound, and Wes sped up, passing cars illegally as the turn for my old street came up. Before long, the dirt from the road was kicking up behind us as Wes raced down the path, coming to a quick stop in front of his house. He was clearly upset, but I was too, and I wasn't going to apologize for trying to get information about the club. He wasn't telling me shit.

As soon as his engine cut, I quickly crawled off his bike, shoving at his shoulder a little too hard. Wes secured the bike, but I wasn't waiting by his locked front door like an idiot. I kept walking, until I was clearing the clubhouse door.

There were a few members playing cards, prospects were working on hanging something, and Natty, the girl from the kitchen I had seen helping Red, was on her hands and knees, scrubbing the floors. She looked up at me as I passed her.

"They don't use Swiffer mops in this place?"

Natty's face flushed pink. "Uh…I prefer this to those things."

"So you're a house mouse?" I watched the door for Wes. I knew he wanted to fight, but we had an audience in here, so maybe he'd choose to cool down instead.

Natty continued to scrub. "Not exactly. I don't belong to anyone, but I work for my room and board. I have my own room with a kitchen and living space up on the second floor. People leave me alone, I help Red in the kitchen, and I clean the club. It's a good deal for me."

That was good to hear. I knew this was common, especially with girls who'd been liberated from stripping, or sex work. In some scenarios, we had women who loved the life; stripping was good if you could do it in a safe environment and you kept the majority of your tips, same with sex work. It was good, if it was safe, and was a benefit. Unfortunately, with these clubs, men took advantage of women more often than not, and the cost outweighed the benefits.

"I think you're in trouble," Natty whispered up to me, her big green eyes stared in shock as Wes barreled through the door. She must have seen him passing by one of the windows. I crossed my arms, standing off to the side as though I couldn't be bothered by Wesley, regardless that I was slightly terrified. Not that he'd hurt me, but this was a new Wes, and I wasn't sure what he was capable of.

His gaze caught mine. He flexed his fingers, stretching them out before stalking directly for me. "Get your ass in my house, River."

He reached for me, but I moved, putting the sofa between us. His head tilted to the side, as if he couldn't understand why I was evading him.

"You need to calm down first."

He laughed, and then grabbed the sofa and flipped it backward, advancing toward me.

*Holy shit.*

"Calm down? You ditched your detail and snuck off, unprotected, in rival territory. You literally put yourself in harm's way *again*."

Okay, the *again* comment hurt like hell. I didn't mean to get fucking kidnapped when I was eighteen. There were things I wish I had done differently, but I had no idea they'd be willing to ever go that far. On quick feet, I moved again, this time around the poker game.

"Better move fast, Prez, she's already eyeing the stairs." Hamish grumbled around his cigarette.

Wes cut off the path that would have allowed me to escape, and then as I turned my back to put the pool table between us, his arms came around me.

The old timers all cheered as Wes held me to his chest, walking us backward.

"Now, are you going to act like an adult, or do you want to keep playing games?" Wes asked, his lips warm against my ear.

My chest was heaving for some reason, but I relaxed in his arms.

"Fine."

Wes walked us backward, "I'm going to let go, and you're not going to run away."

I nodded while eyeing the exit. I could run to the cabin, or even the treehouse, and have the upper hand.

Closer to my ear, Wes said, "If you do, I will punish you later tonight. That ass looks good streaked with my handprints."

I stilled completely, and when he released his arms, I didn't run. He relaxed, glaring at me while pinning his hands to his hips.

"What the fuck were you thinking?"

I wasn't about to argue about this or be talked to like a child in front of everyone, so I bolted for the door.

"Son of a bitch!" Wes yelled, but seconds later he was behind me.

I ran for his house, hoping he'd unlocked his door because every second was precious. Twisting the knob, I practically cried with relief when it turned. Since I wasn't petty, and it wouldn't be any use, I didn't bother locking it. I just ran upstairs and locked myself in his bedroom.

Max was already lounging on Wesley's bed, so with the door locked, I shucked my boots, and slid under the covers next to Max. He made a chuffing sound while relaxing his head against me and I curled further into him, like he could save me from Wesley's wrath.

I heard Wes yell from the level below, but it was muffled. Something broke, and then his boots hit the stairs. Seconds ticked by and then he twisted his doorknob.

"Open the door, River."

"No! I don't need another lecture from you. I'm so sick of you and your stupid ego, and your stupid mean streak, and your stupid control during sex, and I'm mad about last night. I know I fucked up. I know I ruined everything when I got taken." My voice began shaking as I continued. "Please just leave me alone."

He went quiet, and I relaxed. He'd listen, and let me process this afternoon before—

The sound of something smashing had me quickly sitting up in bed just in time to see wood splintering around Wesley's boot as he kicked the door in. Max jumped up, barking at the intrusion.

I watched every step it took for him to get to me, and all my fire had finally fizzled out. His eyes blazed as he stared, and then he shocked me by bending at the waist, gripping my chin and pressing his lips to mine in a hard, punishing kiss.

I was confused, but also completely enraptured.

Opening my mouth to him, his tongue slipped inside, and I melted under him as he advanced, claiming more than just my mouth. His strong hand cradled my jaw, perfectly positioning my face so he had better access, while my hands went limp at my sides. He knew this was what would render me completely frozen and unable to fight him.

I kissed him back, molding my lips to his, and then he stopped with a rush of air against my mouth.

"Don't ever do that to me again. Promise me, River. Never again."

I stared, confused at the shudder in his tone, but I nodded.

"I promise."

He straightened and without a look back, he was gone, out of my space. I heard him on the stairs and then the front door slammed shut.

I eventually fell asleep curled around Max, and when I woke up Wes was gone and the remnants of the broken door had been cleaned up. The memory of his kiss played through my mind, making me trace my lips with the tip of my finger.

His kiss was just as memorable as it had ever been. It was moonlit paths at night, starlit skies and first kisses in the dark. He was still just as overwhelming as ever, and my lips seemed to remember how his kisses used to linger. I remembered when I was seventeen, daydreaming at work while tracing my lips because of how he'd kiss me.

Now, I was in his bed, hiding from having to face the consequences of my actions.

Giving out a dramatic sigh, I got out of bed and went searching for Wes. I scaled the stairs, seeing that sunset was bleeding through the blinds along the back wall, casting a glow over the hardwood floors. Rubbing at my cheek, I pulled on the freezer to see if I could find any food. A knock at the door had me shutting the appliance door while I looked around, as if Wes would materialize.

Seeing there was a small security camera feed set up next to his landline, I was able to see who was on the stoop. Curiosity and insecurity bled through my actions as I tugged on the door.

"Oh hey." Natty, the girl from earlier, smiled at me, holding onto her foil-covered dish.

I slid out of the door a bit more and gave another look around, "Uh, hi. Wes isn't here, if you were looking for him."

Had Wes lied to me?

Maybe he hadn't had sex with anyone, but did he have dinner with Natty, or other women from the club? Maybe he had companionship, which in my book, was a thousand times worse than a hookup.

Natty ducked her head, laughing. "No, I was looking for you."

*Oh.*

"Well, come inside." I moved so she could walk in.

"Sorry…I know this is awkward, but I felt bad for you after today. I know the stories about you and the president, but you seemed frustrated."

Right, because I had made a complete fool of myself running from a man I was still in love with and knew would never hurt me.

Trying to brush it off, I took the casserole dish from her and set it on the counter.

"Wes would never hurt me, but I hate when he gets his way. That was just my way of fighting back…it was sort of stupid."

Natty slipped onto one of the stools, "I didn't think so. I thought it was sort of cute. If my love story doesn't have flirtatious evasive maneuvers in it to avoid conversations, then I don't want it."

That had me laughing, while turning to grab a serving spoon.

"Well, I appreciate that, and this…did you make me spaghetti?"

Natty perked up. "Sort of…it's called million-dollar spaghetti…I hope you don't have a dairy allergy. Nowadays most people do, I should have asked."

I shook my head, "I don't…and this smells delicious. Do you want to join me? I think Wes has some beer. Probably not any wine around here, though."

"There's not. I tried to get Red to buy some, but she said——"

"Wine creates whiners," we both said in unison.

I broke into a laugh, so did Natty.

"So you've been here for a while then?" I asked, grabbing two plates and dishing a portion on to each one.

Natty accepted hers and answered while I took a bite.

"Two years…Simon made a deal for me during a weapons run. Dirk had been abusing me… Uh, he——" Natty trailed off, pulling her sleeves down to cover her wrists.

"You don't have to tell me," I rushed to assure her.

She shook her head, blinking. "You know this life…you know there are good clubs, and bad ones. Death Raiders, well, they're one of the bad ones, but there are some good people inside it. You met Sasha—she talked to Simon on my behalf, and he traded a bunch of weapons for me. It was the nicest thing anyone has ever done for me."

Emotion clogged my throat at thinking over my dad doing something so sweet. He had his good moments, that was for sure. And at his core he was a good man. This world was a lesser place without him.

"I was sorry when he passed, but the other men in this club are good like him. Wes and Killian, Giles and Rune…they're all good guys. I'm happy I'm here, and well, I don't know if you're sticking around, but I wanted to introduce myself and hopefully make you feel welcome. I heard you grew up here, but it can be tricky finding your place again."

I was so moved by her thoughtful gesture that I skirted the counter and pulled her into a hug.

"Thank you, Natty. That is so sweet."

She patted my shoulder, and then Max made his way downstairs, barking at the new person in the house.

"I better get back. Red usually asks me to help with the extra members on game nights."

"Do you know if Wes usually plays poker with the guys?"

Natty stood but scrunched her nose.

"Not usually. He used to back when I got here, but for the past few months he hasn't. If I had to take a guess at where he was, I'd say out on a run, or meeting with someone from another club, but I'm not technically supposed to know anything."

I walked her to the door and hugged her again. "Well, thank you, and don't be a stranger."

Giving me a little wave, she ran down the steps and darted back over to the club. I locked up again and decided to have a relaxing night. It wasn't very often I had such luxury at my fingertips.

I was on the hunt for a candle, which led me to snooping through the boxes in the top of Wesley's closet. I had already checked all the obvious places, but surely, he had an emergency kit in his closet or something. I tugged one down, finding his childhood memorabilia inside. I remembered it from back when we'd lived together.

Sliding it to the side, I started on the secondary box, prying it open. My fingers froze and my breathing tightened in my chest.

It was my box.

Everything I left behind, including…I gently touched the leather and traced the words as my eyes misted. Candles, nail polish, books… everything was here, and he'd kept them for nearly a decade.

Suddenly, I couldn't breathe around the tightness in my throat. I couldn't think of the implications around him keeping it all, so I closed the box and shoved it back where I found it.

A soak without candlelight would be fine because suddenly the desire to relax, or even be alone, was gone.

# TWENTY
## CALLIE
### AGE 20

Dusk had claimed the sky, and with it a chill cut through the air, making me wrap my arms tightly across my chest. The winter months were supposed to be slower for the club, seeing as everyone put their bikes away and drove their trucks. There was usually less travel, which meant less partying, and fewer nights where the music was blaring loud enough to be heard from the main road.

However, it was October, and here I was, feeling like a little girl again trying to outrun another loud party. Except instead of running away, I was slowly walking toward it because my boyfriend was somewhere inside. We were supposed to look at a house today, but Wes never showed. He hadn't even texted, or called—not even a DM. I just stood there with the realtor, looking like an idiot while he tried to show me the house, all while knowing I wouldn't make a decision without my partner.

I needed to cool off, so I drove around for a while, and it seemed as though my boyfriend had finally remembered me, by sending me a text roughly an hour ago, asking me to come down to the gathering. I hated the part of me that resented him so much, because he knew how badly I hated these parties. He knew because he used to be the boy who saved me from them. Now he was the one delivering me right into the mayhem.

I had been in denial about our relationship for a while, but the house thing today severed a piece of my hope for us getting back to normal. I assumed if we could move off the property and get some distance from the club, it would make things easier, but now that dream was gone, just like all the others we had. Summer vacation, camping trips, date nights, a trip to Wyoming to see my aunt and cousins. A trip to see his mom and sisters. None of it happened, and while I was showing up as a receptionist at a dental office, day in and day out, doodling art for tattoo ideas, more and more of myself was starting to disappear.

I loved Wesley, but not more than I loved myself. I was about to turn twenty years old, and I already felt like I was locked into a life I never wanted. As a child, I couldn't change it, but as an adult, I owed it to myself to at least try.

The party was strewn out on the lawn, with a large bonfire and people drinking themselves stupid. I pushed in through the back door, moving out of the way for a couple making out. There was another pair fucking against the wall. I was pathetically used to it, so I kept going, completely unfazed. There in the main room were so many men and women it was hard to make anyone out, especially with all of them wearing similar cuts.

I wasn't wearing mine that indicated I was property of Wes. Frankly, I thought it was bullshit. I never wanted to be someone's fucking property, and the man I loved knew that. Yet, he still asked me to wear it when I attended these things. Tonight, I wouldn't, and I didn't give a single fuck about it.

Red was behind the bar, serving drinks and blowing kisses. She didn't have to serve, but she liked to keep an eye on how much liquor the girls were giving away. One time a sweetbutt took a whole bottle of vodka upstairs with her to seduce someone. Red nearly lost her mind.

Brooks wasn't too far from the bar as he played pool with Hamish. Killian had a girl in his lap as he smoked a blunt. I hated how distant his gaze was as the girl kissed his neck. I wanted him to be happy and find a real relationship, something with meaning like Red and Brooks, but his taste was always with the girls who just got to their knees and disappeared the next day.

My eyes kept moving looking for Wesley when someone grabbed my ass.

"You are the best-looking thing in here," the guy rasped into my ear, pulling me by the hip with his free hand.

I pushed at him as panic seized my limbs, making them feel heavy and frozen. I knew logically that he'd feel stupid and terrible as soon as he realized I was Simon's daughter. In the past, the panic would relent, but my brain and body seemed at odds as anxiety robbed me of breath and fear prodded at my lungs, worsening as his grip tightened.

"Get off me." I attempted to push him, but his lips landed on my neck as more of his long arm wrapped around me.

"I like fighters."

Tears were building in my eyes as I continued to push at him with no avail, and then in an instant, he was gone.

Wesley was there, and he looked furious. His beer bottle was tossed to the ground, and then his fist landed in the guy's face.

"Fuck!" The jerk doubled over, holding his face.

Wes's eyes were wide, gleaming with malice as he grabbed the guy by the vest to stand him up, then he punched him again. This time I heard a crack.

"I didn't touch nothing that was yours, Ryan. What the fuck?!" the guy screamed, spitting a glob of blood on the floor.

That's when Wes finally looked at me and must have realized I wasn't wearing my property patch, because that angry glare was now aimed at me. With a clench of his strong jaw, he grabbed me by the arm and hauled me past all the craziness until we were pushing into the cold night air. Once he let me go, I started walking away.

Fuck this.

Fuck him.

"Callie, wait," Wes said at my back, but I kept walking.

He kept pace with me. "You can't come here without your cut, you know that. Guys don't know you're spoken for. They don't know you're mine."

I laughed, because fuck this guy.

Spinning on my heel, I shoved his chest.

"You forget that I grew up in this fucking bullshit, Wes? I know exactly how this works, and not wearing a fucking piece of leather shouldn't ever give a free pass to grope someone. I'm a goddamn person, Wes. Not a piece of property. You used to be able to see the difference."

I spun away, continuing to walk. I hadn't even touched on how afraid that encounter had just made me, or how frightened I was being in a massive group of bikers after being taken. Rival club or not, on nights where extra members arrived, I turned into a terrified nine-year-old again.

He matched my pace, walking right next to me.

"Where are you going?"

Tears were in my eyes as I shook my head. "The only place I ever felt safe from this life. The only place that used to make me feel like I could actually be free from it."

Wes pulled my wrist to stop me.

"The tree house is a mile down that road, Callie. It's freezing. Just stop."

His leather cut suddenly enveloped me as he slid it over my shoulders and then he wrapped me in his arms.

"Let's just go home, baby. I'm sorry."

My heart swelled with the need to make him understand that I couldn't keep doing this.

There was an itch under my skin that was desperate to leave this place.

"Wes, I can't do this anymore." My voice came out as a whisper, then a sob, as my throat tightened. I had been holding those words back for so long it felt painful to finally let them free.

In the dark, it was difficult to read his expression, but his arms tightened around me.

"Is this about the house? I had a surprise for you. I planned on telling you tonight. Your dad gave me permission to build a house on the property, it's over there on the edge, where the canal is."

*No.*

I had to get out. I had to leave. I couldn't do this. *I wouldn't.*

"I can't be here anymore, Wes. I love you, but I don't want the club."

Wesley's silence stretched, becoming louder like a screaming echo. I kept expecting him to say something, but he didn't. It was when his arms loosened around me that I realized what was happening.

"I can't leave, Callie. You know that better than anyone. I can't just quit."

My hands slid up his chest, cradling his jaw. "I can ask my dad. He'll make an exception. I know he will. Please, Wes. Please just let me try."

Wes held my hand to his face and closed his eyes.

"It can't be undone."

He was wrong. There had to be a way I could undo this. For us, for me.

There had to be some benefit to being the president's daughter.

With tears staining my face, I decided for the night I would drop it. I let Wes take me home, and when he slid inside me that night and held me to his chest, I knew it was him saying goodbye. I knew because he fucked me five times before the sun broke into the valley, as if he was afraid of losing me. As if he knew I was already gone.

I found my father in his office.

When I was a child, I found it so strange to see him sitting at a desk with a pair of black rimmed reading glasses while he read over paperwork and made phone calls. It was the only time he seemed like a normal person, and I used to pretend he was just a regular dad, who did taxes for people or something else that required him to work from home, but seeing it now as an adult felt strange. Like I'd outgrown this place.

"Knock, knock," I said, leaning against the frame of his open office door.

His gaze lifted from the papers, his mouth spreading into a smile.

"Hey, I was wondering when I'd see you. Feel like you have been absent around here."

Ignoring that comment, I pushed in, setting the coffee and donut on the table, then I slumped into one of the chairs facing his desk. The office was small, his desk an old rusty blue, with old filing cabinets on the far wall and paint stains on the cement floor. It wasn't much, but considering our house was a piece of shit, it wasn't a shock.

"What brings you in today?" My dad lifted the coffee to his lips, smiling over the brim. "You always pick the best places to go for this stuff. No one can ever get my order just right."

Toying with the edge of my shirt, I smiled at him, taking in his hazel eyes that matched mine and the dark hair he had tied at the nape of his neck. A few strands of his hair fell free along the sides of his face, and I realized then that my father was sort of beautiful. In a hauntingly dangerous sort of way, he was a piece of artwork. Suddenly I felt like a little girl again, desperate for him to bury a glass jar full of treasure with me.

"It's the splash of cream and spritz of sugar." I smiled, lowering my chin.

I let out a tiny breath I'd been holding and met my father's gaze.

"Dad, I want to leave."

His countenance didn't change much. I suspected it was his ability to mask his emotions. After years of being the harsh president of a dangerous club, he knew better than to reveal his true feelings.

"Leave where?" His eyes dropped to the donut on the table. He took a generous bite while I considered my words carefully.

"I called about an apartment in DC. I just..." I trailed off, trying to sort through my thoughts. "This life, the club. I need space from it."

My dad nodded, taking another sip of his coffee.

"You think about college at all? That could be good for you; I can help with the money."

Shaking my head, I sat forward in my chair. "I don't know, maybe down the road, but for now, I'm just getting a job and an apartment."

"I'm happy for you honey. I think it'll be good for you to spread your wings a little bit."

He wasn't getting it, and I was starting to get annoyed.

"Dad, I want Wesley to come with me. I want you to let him leave the club."

His demeanor changed then. His jaw clenched as he studied me, almost as if I had just transitioned from being his daughter to becoming one of his enemies.

"Have you asked Wes if he wants to leave?"

Biting back the smart response I craved to give him, instead I decided to stay calm.

"Wes said he can't leave because this"—I spread my hands wide, looking around— "can't be undone."

My dad focused on the table, chewing the remaining donut before finishing off his coffee.

"He's right. It can't."

My stomach dropped out.

"But you could decide it, you could let him," I argued, sitting on the edge of my seat as I tried to make him see why this could work if he just allowed it.

He shook his head. "Wes knew what he was getting into when he put on the patch. He has a role here, a job. This is part of his life now."

Pointing at my chest, my voice rose as I cried, "I'm part of his life."

"Then stay."

Fuck, I just wanted to scream.

"Dad, please. I'm begging you. See past this stupid club, please. Just let him go, let us go, live our lives. Let us start over in DC, together."

A knot had formed in my throat as my dad leaned back in his chair, his hazel eyes taking on that familiar gleam that he gave to the people who needed something from him, and he held the power. He sat there like a Roman emperor, holding my fate in the palm of his hands, and somehow I knew he was going to crush me.

It was like all the times I asked him not to throw big parties, or not to invite out-of-town members, or if I could sleep in his room because I was scared, and he'd tell me no. It was always no with him, and there was a fucking crater inside my chest that was filling with spite.

With a whisper, I asked him once more. "Please, I'm begging you. Just let us go."

My dad's expression crumbled the smallest bit before he stood.

"I got shit to do, Callie. If you're leaving, then go. I love you. Wes can't. You'll have to choose."

With a long stride, he turned his back and left his office, leaving me numb and utterly heartbroken.

Stupidly, I tried one more time with Wes.

All my things were packed, and my stomach was fluttering with nerves as I waited for him to come home. I had texted that I needed to talk to him, that it was important. He had replied saying he'd be home by lunch.

I went out of my way and made his favorite meal. Teriyaki chicken bowl with rice, but the sauce was a special recipe that required a lot of work, and usually he loved it. Especially if I paired it with his favorite beer. Lunch came, and went, with no Wes. Eventually, I caved and ate my bowl of food, then washed all the dishes, put them away. Another hour passed, and I put his food into Tupperware, feeling stupid, and that cavern in my chest grew.

Another hour passed, and that's when I cracked.

I found the property patch and laid it on the table with a note.

*Wes,*

*I was going to ask if you'd come with me today over lunch. I made your favorite...it's in the fridge if you decide to have it later. I would have explained it all to you, told you all the reasons why I can't live this life anymore, then I realized you already know them all. You've been my protector and friend since I was nine years old, Wes. I've loved you my entire life, but I also love me, and when I was little, all I ever dreamed of was getting out and starting a fresh life away from the club. So that's what I'm doing.*

*I'm headed to DC. I'm not changing my number, if you want to call me or reach out. I love you, and I hope this isn't goodbye forever.*

*-Callie*

# TWENTY-ONE
## CALLIE

WES HAD RETURNED SOMETIME DURING THE NIGHT.

I felt his lips on my forehead, his fingers tangle in my hair, and then I remembered him snapping his fingers and whisper-yelling at Max to get off the bed. Considering Maxwell's face was currently in my armpit, and his large body was in the middle of the bed, it seemed Wesley's efforts were unsuccessful.

Sitting up, I peered over my behemoth dog and bit back a laugh at how tiny the slice of space Wesley's side of the bed had. He was practically falling off because Max laid diagonally. Feeling marginally bad about that, I decided to get up and make him some breakfast. My behavior from the day prior had caught up to me. I knew I'd fucked up. I just didn't want everyone else in the world to know too.

It took me a long time to accept that the kidnapping wasn't my fault, so when it had been implied that it was, it triggered me. My efforts in going off alone weren't to get hurt. I just wanted answers, and I was still angry over feeling like I was all alone in my efforts to obtain those answers. Maybe a nice breakfast would encourage Wes to open his mouth and spill some secrets.

The breakfast of scrambled eggs, toast, and bacon, with a side of fruit, was plated right as Wes came downstairs. He looked sleepy but somehow still radiated sex appeal with his disheveled hair, bare chest, and the smattering of tattoos covering his sun-kissed skin. My mind immediately went back to how good his lips felt against mine. I turned from him as my face flushed.

"So, you were out late last night," I commented, as more of a conversation starter than actually caring where he was. Wes led a motorcycle club and had already explained that he'd never touched another woman during our time apart. I wasn't worried about him being with someone, I just wanted answers from him about the club.

Wes bit into his bacon, watching me with exhaustion lingering in his gaze.

"Had to drive over to Grundy last night."

I paused mid coffee pour. "Grundy is like three hours away… that's a really long round trip."

He nodded, reaching for the cup. "Usually I'd stay overnight, but I wanted to get back."

My stomach swooped, assuming he just wanted to get back to me.

I needed a reality check.

Taking a bit of my egg and hoping to avoid the awkwardness I knew was evident in my tone, I said, "Well, I'm glad you made it back."

"I see you didn't starve. Saw that massive casserole in the fridge."

Smiling at the reminder of my new friend, I nodded. "Natty brought it over last night."

Wes grunted, finishing off his food.

I was about to ask what he wanted to do today, but he beat me to it.

"Uh…" He cleared his throat. "I wanted to take you somewhere today. You ready for the day or need more time?"

I hesitated, a little confused. "Yeah, I mean, I just want to clean up breakfast and get someone to watch Max."

Wes moved away from the bar stool. "I'll ask Red. You get ready."

For what? Were we hiking, or going somewhere nice…a movie? *Fuck.*

· · ·

Thirty minutes later, I was on the back of his bike, wearing jean shorts, my boots, and a cropped shirt. My hair was down, and a bucket helmet sat on my head.

Wes slowed his bike enough that when I peeled my face away from his back, I could see branches overhead and a thick canopy covering us. The bike slowly traveled down a grassy slope and then came to stop on a familiar riverbank.

He'd taken us to the place I'd brought him after he beat up that jackass in school. That was the first time I realized the crush I had on the boy next door was reciprocated. I'd never forget the way he'd stormed over and started hitting Logan, the crazed look in his eye telling me he never planned to stop. I had already fallen for Wes by then, but that day cemented my obsession with him.

From then on it was all secret kisses, notes being left behind, and secret meetups. I hadn't been back here since I was in high school, when I just needed to see Wes. I had come out here and waited for him, then we spent the whole day making out on the riverbank, dipping into the river and dreaming up a life together.

"Why are we here?"

Wes lowered the kickstand and helped me off the bike.

The air was cooler here thanks to the considerable amount of shade. The birds chirped, flitting around in the top of the trees, creating a beautiful melody to go along with the sound of the gentle river.

Wes gave me a soft smile before removing his leather cut and placing it carefully over the seat of the bike, then he walked toward the water. His shirt came off next, then his boots, until he was in just his boxers.

"What are you doing?" I asked, glancing around to ensure no one was watching us. I shouldn't have worried, with how dense the foliage was.

Without sparing me a glance or an answer, he slowly made his way into the cold water.

"Shiiiit, that's cold," he hissed; his arms hovered above the water while his torso went rigid. I was still standing on the bank, staring down at him, perplexed and confused.

"Come on, River, get in here with me."

I laughed. "No thanks."

His hand shot out along the surface, splashing water up at me. It hit me in the chest in a cold rush, making me sputter.

"Wes!"

He laughed, running his wet hands over his hair and face.

"Get in here before I come get you. If I get you, I'll toss you in."

That sounded miserable. This water was frigid, even in the summer, so I briskly began stripping out of my layers until I was in just my bra and underwear.

Ice cold water met me as I gingerly stepped in, my feet slipping on the rounded stones at the bottom as I tried to find my balance.

"I don't remember it being this hard when we used to come out here." I flung my arms wide, trying to adjust to the temperature while not falling on my face.

Wes was there a second later, taking my hands in his.

"It's not that bad. You just have to find a way to relax and let the water do the work."

I watched as he led me deeper into the river, until it went to our chests, and we were floating. After a few minutes the cold started to ebb, and the heat from the thick summer air was enough to ward off the chill. Soon enough it was refreshing. I tipped my head back, getting my hair wet and smiling up at the stark blue sky. With the water soaking my back, I twisted my hair into a bun and pulled it into a knot on top of my head.

I hadn't realized my back was to Wes, but when I heard his intake of breath, I knew he'd seen the tattoo I'd gotten on my neck, usually hidden by my hair.

He cut through the water, and then his cold finger was trailing over the design that I had Axel, one of my friends, tattoo for me back when we were both in training together. He added shading so the key looked three dimensional, like it was real.

"You once said if you could tattoo it onto your skin as a way to make it happen, you would," Wes muttered, almost in awe as he stroked the replica of the key he'd given me. It was the same exact design with the stars and everything. My frustration from the day before began to dissipate as he brought up what I'd said that time he realized I carried the key around with me. I turned around, coming nose to nose with him while keeping myself afloat in the water.

"What did you do with it?" I'd been wondering since I found that empty spot behind the picture in the cabin. I assumed it'd been lost over time, or maybe he chucked it, but when Wes gave me a sad smile and pulled me closer, I wasn't prepared for his answer.

"You said it was a good luck charm. After you left, I considered maybe it wasn't, but I put it above my mantel at home just the same. I guess I'm superstitious." He shrugged, looking so much like the boy I once knew it made an ache in my chest bloom to life.

"Guess I'm foolish for still wanting to keep it, but I can't seem to let it go."

Wesley's lashes were coated with water as he stared at me, confessing these truths. Pushing closer to him, I placed my hands on his shoulders. He anchored at my hips, holding me in place while we floated. I stared at him, and for the first time in years, I felt like I really saw him.

With a whisper, I began confessions of my own. "I guess I'm stupid for making it last forever on my skin. Even after I left you, I couldn't let go of you." His gaze searched mine. "I loved you…I begged my dad to free you of the club so you could leave with me. I left so I'd have a chance to chase my own dreams, free of the club and all the trauma from it, but my biggest dream was always being yours. I was so young…and I made the biggest mistake of my life."

Wesley's thumb came up, tracing a tear that had fallen unbidden from my lashes. There was so much happening inside me, like that casting over my heart was being pried open, melted, and reformed.

"I just didn't know what to do, River. I went insane when you went missing. They couldn't tell me anything, and I was expected to just sit back and wait. I couldn't. It's not in me to sit and wait, so I made a choice. I would have left, but Death Raiders knew what I had done, so they put a hit on me. Your dad wouldn't let me leave with you because that hit would put you in danger."

"How come no one ever told me?" A broken plea left me, hating the secrets of the club. Hating this stupid wedge that had divided us far from one another.

Wes pulled me closer, pressing a kiss to my nose, then my jaw. Softly, slowly.

"Couldn't, River. I wanted to, but I also wanted you to live your life and do it safely. Your dad had a long talk with me about not coming after you…about how love sacrifices and does what's best for the other person."

My hands moved through his hair, clinging to his neck as he held me.

"I was young and stupid." His hands moved to cradle the sides of my face, pulling me closer. "So fucking stupid to ever risk losing you."

With a shaky breath between us, he kissed me.

Warm lips moved over mine, and my hands curled into his hair as I deepened it, opening for him and welcoming his tongue to tangle with mine. The storage locker of my heart was broken open, freed, and renovated to make room for whatever was happening right now. Something new and deep…something raw.

I moaned as he pulled me closer, his left hand sliding against my ass, pulling me against his hardening length. Our mouths moved in sloppy, open-mouthed kisses, our tongues tracing lips, our moans increasing as my legs wrapped around his waist and I attempted to claim the friction my body needed.

We both were breathing hard when I felt some of the water recede around us, and I realized Wes was carrying us toward his bike. Water pebbled along my skin as I continued to kiss along his neck, and he kissed mine.

It wasn't until we reached the bike that Wes shifted me in his arms. I was guided back, until my head was lying between the handlebars of his bike, my back was against the gas tank, and my ass on the warm leather. My legs went to either side of the bike, straddling it in a way that exposed me to any bystander who might ride by on a mountain bike or stroll through a nearby trail.

"These need to dry," Wes rumbled, while tugging my wet panties down my legs. I smirked as his mouth gaped. The warm air hit my sex, and it was soothing against my silky slit. Tracing the

WHERE WE STARTED    227

naked skin with my fingers, I watched as Wes looked on like a man starved.

I lifted up, unclasping my bra and freeing my breasts. "This does too."

Wes laid it with my underwear over the back of his bike, then slid his boxers down. I didn't have to care if someone came upon us. If Wesley was this bold with his nudity, it likely meant this trail and place was hardly ever visited.

"You look so fucking beautiful, River," Wesley murmured, slowly stroking down my rib cage, cupping my breasts. With one hand he was pinching my nipple and with the other he was prying open my pussy. I gasped at the way his calloused finger felt along my smooth entrance.

Stroking inside me, my eyes fluttered closed as he curled his finger and then used his thumb to rub my clit.

"Yes." I reached behind me and held onto the handlebars as Wes played with me, and when he brought his mouth down over my peaked nipple, I held him there by burying my hand into his hair.

"So fucking good," Wes rasped against my breast.

I ached for more, so I slid my free hand down my body, pushing his fingers further into me, then my hips lifted with a gentle rock, and I was riding his hand.

"There you are, my perfect girl," he whispered in awe before pressing a kiss to my chest. "Keep going. Fuck my hand, River."

My mouth parted as I increased the movement of my hips, but I could see his thick erection bobbing against the seat as I moved, and that was going to feel so much better inside of me than his fingers.

Releasing him, I sat up and pulled him closer.

"Fuck me, Wes. Right here, on the back of your bike."

He made a rumbling sound of approval as he reached for his leather cut, then lifted my back so I was sitting up. I knew it was to help cover me if anyone found us, so I slid my arms through and then he pulled his jeans on, leaving his zipper and button undone enough that his cock could easily jut upward. Once his boots were on, he stabilized the bike between his thighs, and guided my leg over his hip.

The angle allowed me some height, so I could easily sink down onto him. Holding onto his shoulder, and with his hand at my waist, he helped me adjust.

"Fuck," I breathed as his fat cock pried me open in ways my poor vagina hadn't been used since he last entered me. The girth of this man was unlike anyone I'd ever been with. We didn't speak for what felt like two entire minutes as he grunted, the muscles in his forehead straining as he continued to pull me down, spearing me with his length.

Once he was fully seated inside me, we both froze, adjusting and allowing the swelling of his cock to acclimate to the tightness of my pussy. I inhaled a sharp breath before his hand went up my back, stroking along my spine and pulling me forward.

"I'm not going to last long"—he kissed my shoulder—"but move those hips, River. Fuck me until you're dripping down my cock. I want you to make a mess of my seat as soon as I pull out of you."

Pent-up need unleashed at his words, and I did exactly as he said, rotating my hips forward and back, sliding up and down his dick while gripping his shoulders. He lowered his face, taking one of my nipples into his mouth while I ground harder against him. The friction of his jeans and the zipper against my sensitive center just increased my pleasure, drawing out a moan from me. The water babbled in the background, birds chirped, and we fucked under a canopy of trees, adding our own soundtrack to the world around us.

I could tell Wes was holding back, probably to keep his bike from falling over, but I rode him hard, circling my hips into a figure eight, tethering my hands at the base of his neck, and then he gripped my ass cheek and squeezed while dragging me against him.

"So fucking insatiable, River. You really haven't been stretched or taken care of since you were last with me, have you?" he reverberated while tucking loose hair behind my ear.

I shook my head, gasping for air as my climax slowly took hold of me.

"You poor thing, your cunt is squeezing my cock so hard, it's milking every fucking drop from me—" It was his turn to gasp, and then I was seeing stars.

"Wes!" My head tipped back as I moaned his name. My hips

shuddered forward as my orgasm ripped me open and robbed me of breath.

Wes held my ass in place as he rocked forward once, twice, and then he was groaning into my shoulder, finding his own release. Our chests heaved as we both went limp in each other's arms, and when Wes helped me up, and off his shaft, there was indeed a mess that followed. On instinct, I closed my thighs, but Wes held them open, staring up at me with that feral grin.

"Keep em' open, River. I told you, that mess is mine, and it belongs here."

Flushing the smallest bit, I let him handle me, while he leaned back, watching as his release dripped down my slit onto the seat. With a groan, his finger slid back inside me, dragging the remnants of our joint release from my cunt until it was smearing his seat. "Every piece of you belongs with me when I ride, especially what's drawn from that body after we fuck."

*God fucking damn. This man and his mouth.*

I was already rocking my hips again, because he hadn't lied, it had been too long since I'd been taken care of, and Wes knew my body intricately.

With a small chuckle, Wes helped me up until I was standing barefoot in the dirt, wearing his cut and nothing else. His eyes blazed as they trailed down my body. The breeze was making my nipples pucker, and the wetness between my thighs had me clenching them together.

"I don't ever want anyone else on this planet to see you like this. I'm an obsessed motherfucker, too zealous for my own good, but fuck, you've ruined me."

I was back in front of him within seconds, pulling his mouth to mine in another kiss. I wasn't sure what we'd just done, or if this was a way of hitting reset for us, but I wasn't brave enough to ask, and I wasn't strong enough to hope.

Guilt rode me hard as I listened to Killian get his ass chewed by Wes.

I had assumed this little conversation would have taken place yesterday, but I was wrong.

Kill was on the back porch, sipping a cold beer when Wes lit into him about being focused on his own shit and losing focus of what's on the line. Apparently, it was my life that was on the line, and after talking to Silas, I realized now more than ever how dangerous leaving on my own was.

Once Wes was finished with Killian, both men walked back inside. Max didn't even lift his head from my lap or move from taking up half the couch. I locked gazes with Killian, seeing his eyes narrow on me in a glare as he passed. I mouthed, "Sorry," but he ignored me, storming out of the house and slamming the door shut.

"That seemed pretty bad," I mused, slipping off the couch.

Wes locked the door after Killian left, and then took off his cut and boots.

"He'll get over it."

In just his T-shirt and jeans, Wes returned to the living room and tugged my hand into his, encouraging me to follow him upstairs.

"You don't like hanging out in your living room?" I asked as Wes shut his door then slid the small dresser in front of it because the lock had busted when he kicked it open.

Max had followed us inside, plopping down on a what looked like a brand-new dog bed. It was bigger and plusher than the one I'd brought.

Wes stripped out of his shirt, tilting his head. "Easier to get shot down there."

That was a sobering thought. It made me curious how many times Wes had been shot at during his time with this MC. But also, it would have been nice to know when I was all alone here last night.

"I chewed Killian's ass for losing you, but we need to talk about what happened yesterday."

I silently nodded, watching Wes slowly strip out of his clothes.

"Are we bathing first?"

He smirked. "We are."

I jumped up, running into his bathroom excitedly.

"I freaking love this tub."

Wes laughed as he bent over and started the stream of water, ensuring the tub was properly plugged.

I still had my body wash next to the spigot because Wes had no bubble bath. Pumping in a few handfuls of soap, I moved the water around, letting the bubbles froth up. Once the tub was halfway full, I stripped and settled inside, then made room for Wes. He adjusted us so I was in front of him, leaning against his chest, while he caged me in with his legs. Once the tub was full, I turned off the faucet with my toe.

The quiet settled around us, and it was peaceful, comfortable. I shut my eyes and relaxed in the firm chest at my back, relishing when his strong arms came around me.

"You met Silas," Wes rumbled into my neck, and my eyes popped open.

Stroking down his arm, I asked, "Is it true that he was there that night?"

"He and Sasha are the reason no one touched you. They protected you, without even knowing you. When I broke in, they helped me get you out. Not all Death Raiders agree with the direction Dirk has taken things."

I tried to piece together a new story based off what Wes was saying, painting Silas in a light that didn't have his brash words or rude tone, but it wasn't easy.

"I know I owe them my life, but Silas was a bit of an asshole to me."

Wes laughed, and I loved the way it felt against my back, but to teach him a lesson, I yanked on his leg hair.

"You can't laugh at him being an asshole to me."

"Owwww! Shit, River." He laughed even harder, pulling me tighter against him. Then with a gentle kiss to my ear, he softly said, "You can't go places alone. I know this is temporary for you, but I promised your dad I'd keep you safe."

I stared up into the clouded window above the tub, seeing strokes of gold and orange infuse the glass. The sun was setting, and it created a dreamy glow inside the room, but as much as I wanted to sink into the moment, Wesley's words gave me pause.

I pushed off his chest and turned on my ass, needing to see his expression.

"Is it really just about keeping a promise to my dad?"

His gaze slid over my features, and when I assumed he'd break, he seemed to fortify instead. His jaw set and his hands left the water, going to the sides of the tub. Somehow the move made him seem distant and cold, and instantly had me reconsidering our moment out at the river.

"You're leaving, and I refuse to get used to you being here. Or the idea of keeping you. It's not personal for me, it's physical. I mean, fuck, this is all I've wanted for seven years, but it can't be more than that."

Fuck that hurt.

Even though I was apprehensive about that being his answer, I still didn't expect it to come out of his mouth. Not after what I read in those letters, and seeing our past pinned up in his garage, not after the way he held me this afternoon. There was more, and he was just a chicken shit.

"So you don't have feelings for me?" I slid to the opposite side of the bath, annoyed at how sensitive I still was—sore. He had the audacity to say this to me after we'd literally just fucked on the back of his bike?

Wes tilted his head, clenching his jaw, "Why argue about it when you're leaving the second you sell? It doesn't matter."

It absolutely mattered.

Without thinking, I blurted, "What if I didn't leave, what if I stayed?"

He scoffed, "I'd say, for how long? You'll stay for a year, or until the club gets under your skin again. Then you'll leave. This is a waste of time. I want to enjoy what we can have while you're here, and when it comes time to let you go, I will."

I pushed loose strands of hair off my face with a shaky hand, belatedly realizing this conversation was frustrating me on multiple levels. Why was he being so stubborn? Why wasn't he acting like the old Wes who would tell me we could make this work? I wasn't sure I was ready to stay, but I had done a lot of growing in the past seven years, and with each new day I was in Rose Ridge, I realized I missed home. I could have a life here and still be free of the club.

I was mad, and all I wanted to do was lash out and hurt him, so I did.

"Should have probably mentioned I'm not on birth control at the moment, so that might ruin your little, 'fuck her and let her go' plan." Without another word, I stood and sloshed water all over the place while exiting the tub.

I didn't even get a towel as I walked into his room and headed for the satchel I'd put those letters in. I wasn't ovulating, so there was little chance I'd even get pregnant. Still, it was shitty of him not to ask, and wrong of me not to offer. Reckless on both our parts.

I dripped all over the floor, and it was messy and wet, so I grabbed a random robe, tying it off before stomping back out into the room.

"You said you didn't send these"—I held up the bundle of letters my father had sent— "that they weren't from you…but they were, just like the one you sent two weeks after I left."

Wes tied a white towel around his waist. He looked subdued, and reflective, almost like a small piece of hope had floated through him and now he wasn't sure how to get rid of it.

"What are you talking about? I didn't send you a letter after we broke up."

It was my turn to scoff, because that letter was a fucking doozy.

"Let me summarize it—*Dear Callie, I think you did the right thing by leaving. You always were the brave one of the two of us. I think now that I've had time to clear my head, I realized what we had wasn't love, it was pity. From the start, all I did was pity you, Callie. So, I hope you find it in your heart to love again, and you move on with someone who loves you in ways I never could—* sound familiar?"

Anger radiated from Wes. With jerky movements, he tore the towel off his hips and pulled on a pair of clean boxers. It wasn't until he paced the edge of the bed a few times that he finally said something.

"When did that letter arrive?" His voice was hard as a rough stone, grating against my nerves as I wondered at his reaction. He was acting like he'd never heard the words in the letter, and something inside me both sank and rose with hope.

With an unsure voice, I tugged at the terrycloth of the robe. "I told you…exactly two weeks after we broke up. It was your handwriting, Wes. The return address was from you."

That's why I believed it was from him. It was his handwriting.

"Fuck!" he screamed, throwing a water glass that was on his bedside table against the wall. It shattered on impact making me jump and Max bark.

"I never sent that. I'd never say those words to you, Callie. In what universe would I ask you to move on?" He pointed aggressively at his chest, seething in anger. "In what world would I tell you our love wasn't real?"

My nose burned, because I didn't want to believe it was him who sent it. I was in denial for so long, rereading it every night, trying to find the lie within the lines of text. But the more I questioned it, the more I realized it had to be him. But if it wasn't, then…

"Never once did you call, or text…or anything, Wes. It left me no choice but to believe that letter."

"Because I couldn't have you until I was sure I could offer you a life you didn't want to leave," he screamed, making me recoil.

Striding forward, he gently rubbed my shoulders. "I'm sorry. Fuck. I'm sorry I yelled; I just don't understand what the fuck is going on." It wasn't him yelling that had made me recoil. It was his desperation to get me back.

"Me either…I mean, why would my dad leave me a piece of property that was owed to a rival club, knowing it would put a target on my back?"

If I thought Wes was angry before, it was nothing compared to the storm brewing in his dark gaze now. With a harsh whisper, he asked, "What did you just say?"

I gripped his forearms, not wanting him to leave. "Silas told me. It was the bargain my father made when I was kidnapped. The property, once my dad passed on…he gave away my inheritance to Dirk, and he said now that my dad is gone, the debt falls to me."

Wes searched my face, like he couldn't process what I'd just told him. He stepped back once, twice, and then fell to the edge of the bed. He cut a path through his hair with his hand, while he concentrated on the floor.

"Where are the letters you said I sent you…the ones from over the past few years?"

I was still holding them, but he seemed too lost in thought to register that I was. I brought them forward, lifting them until Wes was carefully taking them from me.

He crinkled his brows, inspecting the outer note left by my dad.

*Dear Callie,*

*Forgive an old man for meddling, but I have a lot to apologize for…a lot of regrets, and what role I played between you two is one of them. These are letters I found shoved in the bottom drawer of Wesley's rolling tool bin, something he never intended for you to see. But I think you should. Love, Dad*

Wesley's face paled as his grip tightened on the letter.

"Do you know what he's talking about?" I asked, unsure at his odd reaction.

Wes merely glanced up at me before flipping the page over, reading it out loud.

"I moved out of the cabin today. Packed up all our stuff and took a room in the clubhouse. I'm next to Giles, and he's not so bad…just always talks and he's always with someone at night. I think that's the loneliest part, River. Everybody has someone, but you've been my person since we were nine. My best friend. My only one. How am I supposed to just turn that off?"

His face flushed as he lowered the page to his knee.

I stood, biting my nail, nervous that he was about to say that wasn't from him either, but he swallowed, and glanced up at me shyly.

"This one is from me."

Before I could react, he flipped to the second letter, voraciously pulling it open, reading the note from my dad first.

*"Callie, hope you're well, I've been feeling a little under the weather. Things are pyling up here, my hands are shit, my eyes are going to hell, but I can't shake this feeling yyyou need to see Wes. has to say to you."*

"The spelling errors in those are weird. If he didn't know he was sick until six months ago, then that letter would have been three years ago. The timeline is strange," I mused, as Wesley bunched his brows as he reread the page.

Wes clenched his jaw, reading the portion he wrote out loud.

"River, you started an apprenticeship to become a tattoo artist. I'm both excited and nervous, and a little jealous. How did I never know you wanted this? You're so talented. I wish you'd design me a tattoo. I wish your hands would draw it permanently onto my skin. More than anything, I wish I could live there, under yours."

I sunk to the seat next to him, tiring from standing and watching. He read letter after letter. Confessions of him watching me from afar, tiny truths that he'd never really left me. He'd been there the whole time, waiting and watching. The notes from my dad became more and more poorly written. The last one I received was almost indecipherable.

. . .

*"Callie, this mghtyyy be the lst one tht I wryyyte but I luv u- myyy grl, I myyyss yyyou. Pleeese gyyyve him a secnd chnce."*

Wes stared at the note, then sifted back through the others. While he wasn't touching any of the letters he'd sent, he was laser focused on the loose notes that my dad had jotted his thoughts on. So much so, he suddenly jumped up and ran toward the bedroom door, freeing it of the dresser. I followed him, his big robe weighing me down as I watched him pull out a pen and click on the lamp over his desk.

He smoothed out the notes from my father, circling different words in each one.

"What is it?" I asked, trying to see what he was seeing.

He wrote the letter y three times, then circled it. Then he found another word, and another, while sifting through the notes.

"Son of a bitch!" Wes finally declared, straightening his spine.

"What?"

Wes spun around, his eyes searching my face frantically.

"I think he's trying to tell us something."

My brows dipped. "Tell us what?"

Wes stormed back into his room, grabbing a pair of jeans and tugging them on.

"There's only one way to find out. If you want to come, you need dark clothes, and you can't be afraid to get dirt on them."

Puzzled, I walked into my side of the closet and began looking through my stuff.

"Why?"

Wes turned me until I was facing him, then he kissed me. His tongue pried my lips open, tasting me as he deepened the kiss. Within seconds we were panting, then he released me.

"Because we're digging up a grave."

# TWENTY-TWO
# WES

WHAT THE FUCK WAS SIMON THINKING?

The question ran on repeat through my mind as we drove one of the trucks from the club to the edge of town. It had no traceable plates, so it was perfect for what we were planning. Inside, wearing skull gaiter masks, along with black ball caps, were Killian, Giles, Rune, Callie, and myself. Callie was on my lap in the back next to Killian because I still didn't want any of the fuckers from the club around her, and the other two were up front. The guys didn't even blink when I told them we had something to do, and no one questioned why Callie was with us.

In general, women didn't go on runs, or get to know about our business. I had no idea why it was such a big rule, but after being in the club all these years, I knew Red was still clued into the secrets, and so were the other old ladies—they just never talked about it. Callie was the most essential piece of this fucked-up puzzle and it was time we started using that to our advantage, instead of leaving her in the dark. Besides, she'd just run and do her own thing if we did.

My heart was still recovering from when Silas sent me that photo of her sitting there in a café bordering rival territory. The girl was going to be the death of me, which was why I decided it was time to start including her in this shit. She deserved to know, and I deserved a break from stressing out over her safety.

Once we pulled up to the cemetery, we all quietly exited the truck. Callie found my hand in the dark, while Giles, Rune and Killian grabbed shovels.

"You realize how traumatizing this is going to be for her if Simon is, in fact, inside that coffin?" Giles whispered from the back of our group.

Killian laughed, while Rune grunted his agreement.

Yeah, I realized it would be a shock to her, which was why she wouldn't be looking inside when we pried it open. We walked silently, while Giles veered off, heading toward the small office where Gunther, the night groundskeeper, worked. We'd either pay him off, or knock him out. Either way, he'd be handled.

We found Simon's grave, and with the way Callie slowed, I knew it was already hitting her. He was like a dad to Killian, and even me in different ways, but no one had the same memories with him that Callie did. Dead or alive, this would hit on a thousand different levels for her.

I pulled her aside, away from everyone else, and tugged the fabric around her nose down, doing the same with mine.

"Hey, find a spot a few graves over. You don't need to watch us do this."

Her hazel gaze glittered under the moonlight as she shook her head.

"He tried to tell me something in those letters…if there's even a chance he's not dead, I want to be there when you find out."

Shit, I was worried she'd say that. I wanted to protect her from the hurt this was going to cause, while also letting her be included. No one ever explained that love was going to feel like you were losing your goddamn mind and heart all at the same time.

I pulled her in and kissed her. I was a coward, and I owed her the truth about how I felt, but my pride wouldn't allow it. Deep down, I knew she'd leave me again. She didn't want this life, and there was nothing I could do to make her stay. Even if she was pregnant, even if there was the slightest chance we'd created a life. She'd still go.

With that somber feeling thrumming through me, I turned around and headed back to the grave. The guys had already started, so I jumped in to help. Callie crouched down next to the headstone, handing us waters as we needed them, and after a few hours, when Giles tossed his shovel, she picked it up, jumping into the hole to dig too. She didn't miss a beat, tying her hair back, throwing her shoulders into it, as she shoved the tip of the tool into the earth. Swiping at the sweat on my forehead, I let her get in a few scoops before I grabbed her by the hips and lifted her up.

Killian gripped her wrists and pulled her out.

"I want to help!" she whisper-yelled.

I let out a sigh and continued digging, and she grumbled a few other things to Killian before he jumped in to take her place.

Finally, as the first light of dawn touched the sky, the tip of my shovel hit something hard. Everyone froze, except for Callie. She scrambled to the edge of the grave, peering down.

"Get her back, I don't want her to see if he's in here."

Giles moved to guide her away from the opening, but Callie pushed at him.

"It's *my* father, my fucking blood. I want to see, and if you push me again, I'm jumping down there with you."

Fuck.

"Fine," I called up, bending over the coffin to dust off the top. My nerves were raw as I shook out my hands. This was the craziest fucking thing I'd ever done, but I had to be sure that I was seeing what I thought I was in those notes he left Callie. Simon had always been a calculated man, and while I didn't appreciate the fact that he was likely the one who sent Callie that initial letter, telling her to move on, I understood why he continued to use her to communicate through and why he kept pushing for me to be the president after he died.

When he got sick, he told the entire club who would precede him. There was no vote, no general election held with a majority decision. Simon chose me, and no one argued, not even Killian, but now I understood why he'd done it.

It was all because of Callie, the one person on this planet he could trust that wouldn't be touched by club politics, or swayed by a rival decision, or money. And the only person who would ever have a way to her, on this intimate of a level, was me.

"Want me to do it, Prez?" Killian called down, and I knew why he offered it and I appreciated his respect in adding my title so it didn't seem like he was questioning whether I *could* do it. He just didn't want me to be the one to *have* to do it.

I pulled the crowbar out that I'd brought with me into the grave and shoved the end into the side of the casket, breaking the seal. Once it was cracked, I wrapped my hand around the edge, and pulled. Dirt slid through the opening, and I was going to feel really shitty about this if the remains of our beloved president were in fact inside, but as I pulled it back, I heard Callie gasp first.

"Son of a fucking bitch!" Giles yelled next, and then Rune let out some sort of curse.

I finally saw inside, and my mouth went slack.

Empty, save for a single note and a few sandbags, which likely was the reason his coffin seemed heavy enough as we carried him from the hearse to the grave site.

I tucked the note into my pocket, too angry to read it. Slamming the lid of the coffin down, I crawled out of the grave, and instantly glanced away from Killian's curious gaze.

"Let's get this shit cleaned up before the sun comes out. It's only been about a week, so no one's going to notice once we bury it all again."

Killian moved first, and then Rune. Giles was still shaking his head, while Callie sat with her hands shoved into her hair, her back against the backside of her father's tombstone.

I was shaking, but I wasn't going to show anyone. The fucker actually made me believe he'd died. I mourned him. I cried for him.

Killian locked eyes with me, then glanced down at Callie. We did this a lot, where he didn't want to undermine me, or make it seem like I needed his instruction, so instead we learned how to communicate silently. He was telling me to get her the fuck out of here.

I bent down, grabbed her by the elbow and pulled her up.

"Not a fucking word about this to anyone. No one can know about this until we figure out what it means." I snapped at the guys and tossed the keys to Killian.

I'd call a prospect to come and get us, but a part of me knew she needed to walk. Just like I knew what she needed yesterday. I was tired, thinking back to how much time had passed since I brought Callie home with me, and how insane I'd been going over being close to her. Holding her hand now felt so right, but it also felt strange. Like we'd stepped out of the past into a future that was all wrong for us. She was supposed to be my wife, at home sleeping. Safe and sound, and not wondering if her father was alive or not.

We were a mile down the road before she finally pulled away from me and tore off down a random trail.

I went after her but gave her space. She was speed walking, kicking up dust as she walked, but she was already filthy from the grave, so it made no difference against her black clothes. Fuck, I must look like I just exhumed a grave as well, which meant we needed to stay off the main road.

Catching up to her, I pulled on the back of her sweatshirt to get her to slow down. "Talk to me."

She spun, eyes rimmed with tears, her beautiful face streaked with dirt. She still had her hat on, and her mask around her neck.

"And say what?" She threw her hands out. "That my dad lied to me, that he manipulated us? Did Sasha know? Was this why she didn't go to his funeral, why she couldn't bring herself to take anything of his down, because she knew?"

I shook my head, trying to pull her closer. "I don't assume she did…Sasha is a Death Raider. She's been straddling life and death by dating Simon Stone for five years. There's no way she would have been allowed to show her face at that funeral. You don't think we were being watched that day? That Dirk didn't drive down to see for himself that his greatest rival had died?"

He wasn't the only one.

The leader of Mayhem Riot was on the fringes, so was Jameson from the Chaos Kings, and Alec, from Sons of Speed. They all waited to see Simon lowered into that hole, and to see who would take his place. I had a target on my back every second during that funeral; it was partially why I didn't go to Callie when I saw her leaving that day. I wanted to—fuck, I was angry with her, but not enough to stay away from her—but I wouldn't while it was dangerous for her.

"So he tricked everyone? Why would he do that?"

I shook my head, kicking at a rock. "I think it had to do with the deal he made with Dirk, but I'm not sure. He left some hints as to where we can find him, in those letters. I want to take it into church to have the guys see if they know for sure or not."

Callie wet her cracked lips, nodding.

I pulled her closer, pressing a kiss to her neck. "We'll figure it out, okay?"

Her hands wound up my back and sunk into my hair.

"Okay."

Once we turned back toward the road, Callie tucked her hand into mine and asked, "What will you do once we find him? He obviously planned all this, which means he's still the president. When he comes back, will you just go back to being the vice president?"

Watching the dirt at our feet, and the way the early rays of sun streaked across it, my mind took me back to when Callie was leaving my treehouse. After we'd turned sixteen, I'd walk her back home every morning and kiss her goodbye. We'd always been inseparable after that day in the river. Our crush became an obsession, which quickly turned to dependency. She was my everything, and I remember staring at the dirt like this while we walked back, thinking up ways I could explain all that to her. Even now, the words I wanted to say were stuck behind my teeth, rattling in my lungs to be freed. But my fucking pride held on to them, shoving them down until they were nothing but air.

"Same shit, I guess," I rumbled in response. What good would it do to tell her I wanted out, that I wanted a regular life? Even if I accomplished it, I wasn't leaving Rose Ridge, and some piece of me would still be a part of the club. They'd become my family, and with all this shit going on with Simon, the property, and the Death Raiders, I wasn't going to leave them high and dry.

Callie kept her face down as we walked, and the silence stretched uncomfortably.

"What about you, now that you know he's alive and selling is off the table? You going back to DC?"

Fuck, I wanted her to say no. I needed her to, but why would she stay? I'd given her no reason to.

She remained quiet for a long time, and then released my hand, itching at the palm that had been inside of mine.

"Guess I'll go back too. I considered moving back here, getting my own spot at a tattoo shop, but that seems kind of dumb now. I feel like this has all been just one giant mistake."

I was glad she couldn't see my face because it was reflecting how badly it hurt to hear her say that. Still, I wanted her to come home if she wanted to, and I knew a big reason why she wouldn't, was if she didn't feel like she was wanted, which pissed me off. So much so that I stopped and turned toward her.

"If you want to move here, then why don't you? Who cares about the club, or the past, or even me? Do what's good for you, Callie. You've lived in DC for seven years; how come you never went anywhere else? You never moved to Montana, like you talked about when we were younger, or Wyoming. You never went anywhere. You just worked shitty job after shitty job, stuck to your shitty apartment and kept your head down. It was like you were waiting for your past to clear up, come back, and tell you it still wanted you."

Anger twisted her features as her arms crossed in front of her.

"I followed a dream. I became a tattoo artist, and part of figuring out where you want to go takes time, and money. Something I haven't exactly been flush with. It's not like people are offering me Netflix specials."

A scoff left my chest as I shook my head.

"A dream I never once heard you talk about. Suddenly you woke up and decided to ink designs into people's skin? You could have gone to school, Callie; you could have done anything you wanted."

"I did do what I wanted!" she yelled back, stepping closer. "In the real world, Wes, people don't get to just do whatever they want. Rent is due, bills are due, most people have to work, and they survive paycheck to paycheck, just happy they have a roof over their heads for one more month. I don't live in some imaginary world where I have a car reliable enough to drive a thousand miles across the country, or unlimited funds for gas and food. I grew up poor, Wes. I left here with nothing. I have worked my ass off for those meager things you're now pointing out as failures. Tattooing was something I discovered I loved when I lost you."

That landed too hard, and in the wrong place.

"You did not lose me, River. You *left* me."

Stomping past me, she yelled back, "This is impossible. I *did* lose you. And long before I left. You weren't coming home, Wes. You were late every night, you seemed to forget that I didn't want to belong to the club or be forced to go to parties. You forgot that I used to run away from those parties, Wes. I'd run to you, and all the sudden you weren't there for me. You were the one dragging me into them. You were my safe place, and then everything changed. I did lose you, you're just too enamored with your new life to see it."

My chest felt like she'd just slammed a brick into it. I grabbed her wrist and pulled her back to my chest, breathing heavily.

"What are you saying?"

Her hazel gaze searched mine, like she was trying to figure out why I couldn't see what she was trying to communicate.

"I'm saying I didn't leave because of the club. I left because *you* left me. After I was kidnapped, I was alone, Wes. All by myself most nights. You wouldn't tell me anything, so even when you did come back, there was nothing but fucking between us. There was no more emotional intimacy, and I missed you."

I swallowed thickly, about to open my mouth but—

Hunter, one of the newer prospects, suddenly pulled up next to us, rolling down his window. "You need to get back to the clubhouse. The Roman just showed up and said he's looking for you."

I clenched my back teeth together, grabbed Callie's hand, and pulled her behind me. Callie crawled into the backseat, but I slid in right next to her and held her hand in mine while the prospect drove us back.

We pulled up in time to see that Killian and the others had returned. Red walked out of the main house with Max on her heels. We'd asked last night if she and Brooks would watch over him before we left, and it seemed the beast did fine. His nose immediately went to Callie's stomach as soon as we exited the truck, and Callie smiled down at him, stroking his neck. I liked seeing her with him; I couldn't figure out why except that he took care of her. I could tell. When she was sad, he seemed to catch on and go to her, and he was as tall as a small horse, so he kept people away from her. I sort of felt like if she didn't have me, I was glad she had Max.

Red put her arm around Callie, steering her back toward the kitchen, talking her ear off.

People were saying my name, others were headed into church, but I went after the women and pulled on Callie's wrist, stopping her.

"You're with me."

Red's eyes rounded, and so did Callie's, but Callie recovered quickly, putting her hand in mine as we walked toward the church doors. Members watched on, staring at us as I broke one of the fundamental rules of the club. *No women in church.*

But fuck tradition.

The men were already assembled around the table, and there wasn't a single empty chair save for mine at the head. I slid it out, taking a seat, pulling Callie into my lap.

"What's going on, Silas?"

My friend glared at Callie, clenching his jaw before clearing his throat.

"You sure you want her here for this?"

I gripped Callie's waist, pulling her closer to my chest, while catching the eye of every man at the table.

"Right now, it's the rest of these fuckers I'm not sure about. But River stays, from here on out. As long as I'm president, she's welcome in these meetings."

There was a grunt of approval around the table, and I relaxed when Callie's fingers rested on my thigh, under the table, her back pressed into my chest, and then Silas opened his mouth, and everything went to hell.

"Dirk sent me here to kill you, Wes."

# TWENTY-THREE
## CALLIE

I really freaking hated Silas.

My glare was severe enough that he realized this, that or my death grip on the edge of the table gave it away. While I knew I wasn't supposed to speak up in this meeting, I couldn't help the angry whisper that left my chest.

"What the fuck did you just say?"

Silas scowled back, those pale blue eyes brutal as he set his jaw.

Wes gripped my waist, trying to pull me back against him, but like fuck was I going to sit here and listen to some Death Raider discuss the semantics of his murder. Maybe I was on edge because of my father, and maybe I was just over all this club bullshit. Didn't really make a difference in my mood either way. I was on edge, and the deeper this hole seemed to go, the angrier I became.

Silas finally let out a small laugh, looking around the room. "Relax. He wouldn't be sitting here alive if I had any intention of following through with the threat." His blank inspection returned to me. "You, on the other hand, I haven't decided about yet."

Wes went rigid behind me.

"Start explaining, Roman, or we're just going to make an executive decision. Any threat to Little Fox is a threat to the club," Killian warned, bringing his hands together in front of him.

Wes had a death grip on me, which was the only indication that he was barely in control of his temper.

I looked over at Silas with a new understanding as I considered what Kill had just called him. This was the Roman they kept talking about. Stupid nickname, if you asked me, but maybe I was biased and just hated his guts.

Leaning back, unfazed, Silas stared at the wall across from me. With a malicious smirk, he shook his head, which had my eyes scanning the space he kept drifting to. There on the wall, among other memorabilia, was a Death Raider cut with a railroad spike pinning it to the wall. Dried blood covered the leather, including most of the white lettering that revealed the name: *Poet.*

Whoever the man was had obviously died, maybe that was angering the other Death Raider in the room?

Finally Silas let out a sigh, lounging back in his chair. "Dirk wants Callie. He's been looking for a new old lady, says he wants her, and said he's willing to renegotiate terms of the property."

My belly filled with dread, while my skin felt like someone had just splattered it with mud. I didn't remember Dirk; I'd never been close enough to see him while conscious, but I didn't have to remember him to know I never wanted to be in the same room as him. *And apparently I had, at some point.*

I turned my face to take in Wesley's expression, but he gave nothing away. He was all walled off, brick and stone so that nothing showed. There was a tiny part of me that was curious if Wes would prefer this, so I was out of his hair and his precious club was free and clear of the threat of being taken. I realized no one had spoken, and all eyes were on me, as though they were waiting on my decision, all except Wes.

The tightness of his fingers screamed that he was about to lose it.

"What do you say, Wes? Think your precious *River* can take one for the team by being the new queen of Raider territory? It'd make her untouchable…might be the safest place for her."

My lips parted when he used my nickname. No one else had ever used that nickname but Wes. It was his endearment for me, and only his.

"Ah, fuck," Killian sighed, scooting back in his chair.

I had no warning before Wes briskly stood, depositing me in his chair.

It all happened within a single breath. Killian lifted Silas by the arms, holding him still while Wes stepped up and punched the Roman in the nose with a sickening crunch. Then he threw another hit, and another. I winced each time I heard his fist connect.

"You think this is funny? Think you can come in here and say *that* fucking name?"

Another punch landed in Silas's stomach, but Killian held him up, so Wes continued to have a clear shot, but he didn't need anymore. A silver-plated revolver was pulled out and was now pointed directly at the Raiders forehead. The room went silent.

Silas didn't say a word to defend himself, nothing at all.

"Wes," I whispered, as the hammer was pulled back and the gun was prepped to shoot.

Wesley's fist was red as he stared Silas down, pointing the gun directly at his face.

The room watched on, and I noticed all the other members had their guns drawn, down and out of sight. The only sound was Silas's heavy breathing and Wesley's boots as he stepped closer to the bleeding man.

Wes gripped Silas by the hair and tipped his face back, placing the gun to his cheek. "She is not a commodity in this club. She is not a piece of property to be traded or discussed. You don't look at her. You don't speak to her. She is mine, and only mine. Do you understand me?"

The deadly quiet in Wesley's words slid into my chest, cracking something open. It was like smashing a mirror and being able to step through it, into a different time. My mind flashed back to feeling left out, forgotten, and alone, and it all reeled into this one moment, right here where Wes had just boldly chosen me. Not the club, not something that would benefit them, but me.

Silas smiled, showing his bloodied mouth, and the idiot stared at me from his awkward position.

I realized then that he had a death wish, an actual desire to die.

"Fine, Ryan. She's safe from club politics. I'll let you keep what Simon stole from you. But mark my words"—he tipped his head, his broken nose gushing blood as he caught Wesley's gaze—"what I did here was a kindness to you. I expect it to be repaid when I'm president of the Death Raiders. Your club took something that belongs to me, and when the time is right, I'm coming back for it. Understand?"

Chills swept down my arms, knowing there was something deeper going on here. Silas knew something or had made his own plans. I wanted to speak up, try to calm things down, but I knew I'd only make them worse, so I sat there and bit my lip so hard I could taste blood.

"You don't get to just come in here and pick a Stone Rider to keep, like a puppy," Killian joked, strengthening his hold on the hostage in front of him.

Silas continued to stare at Wesley as though they were silently communicating.

"When that time comes, you won't have a choice, and I never said anything about them being a member." That sinister gaze fell once again on me, making my insides recoil. What was he talking about? The only nonmembers in a club were… *women.*

Wes finally stepped back, and Killian let go. Silas roughly shook his arms once, then someone handed him a rag for his face.

"You're going to need to set that," Pops commented, gesturing to the Raiders broken nose. "Want me to do it?"

Silas glared. "Fuck off, old man."

Wes moved behind me, crossing his arms over his chest while the remaining members sat quietly around the table, waiting for the meeting to pick back up.

"What's your play if you were supposed to kill him?" I suddenly blurted, as I saw Silas retreating toward the exit.

He paused, lifted his chin to Wes, then glanced back at me.

"My plan was to go back with you. Dirk would let me live if I at least had something. Since I don't, I won't go back, at least not until

I'm sure I can kill him. Once I do, I'll become president. When that happens, I'll be back for what's mine."

He gave one last look to Wes before pushing through the doors and leaving the club.

My entire body felt wired with adrenaline. Someone was brutally beaten and almost shot in front of me, and while I had been exposed to a lot growing up here, I was never around the violence. Dad was always sure I was kept clear of any real danger, as often as he could. I saw tiny drunken skirmishes, but nothing like what had just taken place. No one else seemed thrown by it. Wes placed a hand on my shoulder, then played with my hair as the rest of the meeting seemed to move on.

Addressing the table, Wes spilled the news about my dad.

"The grave of Simon Stone is empty."

A shock rippled through the room as members broke out from around the table, all speaking at once. All except Killian, Giles, and Rune. They flicked a quick gaze my way before Wes took hold of the room again.

"We suspect he's alive, based off some letters he sent Callie."

The folded pile of papers landed in front of me, and the room quieted once more. Wes explained the pattern he'd seen in the notes from my father: the extra usage of the letter y, the misspelling of a word to make it look like the town of Pyle and a few other things Wes had picked up on. The notes were passed around the table, from member to member, until they all returned. The room was somber, contemplative for several minutes until Brooks finally spoke up.

"It's gotta be the Triple Y ranch on the edge of Pyle. That's near where his old lady lives. There's no chance she's in the dark on this."

Giles nodded, adding in his two cents. "She might have been before, but I doubt she still is."

"She stopped showing up at the clubhouse with the Death Raiders. It's partially why her son is so on edge. He's worried about her," Hamish offered.

My heart softened, thinking about Sasha. It complicated my feelings for Silas in a strange way. I didn't like him, but I could understand his rage if he was afraid for his mother's safety. It didn't seem like he was too pleased that his mom had been dating my dad, or the danger it put her in.

Wes spoke up from behind me, bringing my thoughts back. "So we head out this afternoon, see what we can find. If Simon is there, we need to figure out what his plan is, and bring us up to fucking speed."

The men all grumbled their agreement, but it was Killian who spoke up and asked, "What's the plan with Dirk? He's obviously going to be organizing a war if he thinks Callie will supplement what's owed to him and Silas never returns."

Wesley returned his fingers to my hair, gently stroking a few pieces while he explained, "We're facing war regardless. I had hoped Silas would have already taken the club, but if he's not ready then we must plan to fight. If Simon is alive, he'll have a better chance at reaching out to the other clubs."

Giles lifted his hand to signal Wes. "I have a connection in Chaos Kings."

Killian turned in his chair, lifting his chin toward Giles.

"What sort of connection do you have? Aren't you from California or Denver, some fucking place like that?"

The room broke into laughter, including Giles. But he put a stop to it when he said, "Yeah, yeah...I grew up in Nevada, you fucker. But my cousin grew up here."

"And who's your cousin?" Pops asked sarcastically.

Giles stretched out in his chair like a king as he said, "Jameson, the leader. Fuckers."

The room went silent. Blood relations were rare in rival clubs, but when they were found, they were tighter than even the club connection, unless Giles and his cousin were at odds or hated each other, but he wouldn't have suggested him if that were the case. Made me curious as to why he chose Stone Riders over his cousin's club, which was only about two hours west from here.

"Okay, well, reach out to your cousin, see if he'd accept a meeting from me and Killian," Wes ordered, and the room broke out into commotion like they all knew when Wes was finished speaking. I felt like I was trying to play catch up. I spun in my seat and found Wes staring down at me with a curious expression.

"You wanna grab some breakfast with me, River?"

My belly swooped as I smiled up at him.

I stood, allowing him to grab my hand and pull me out. The club filed in around the kitchen bar, and Red began instructing the other girls on dishing up breakfast. I assumed we'd be taking a seat as well when I saw Killian pull Natty aside.

They exited through the side door, right as Wes pulled my hand, so we were following. I glanced quickly to find my dog lying inside the kitchen, taking up a massive chunk of the floor while Red worked around him. I slapped my leg and called for him as we moved. "Max, come."

His head lifted, and within seconds he was trailing us as we walked.

The sun was still clearing the valley, washing over the manicured yard, when we caught up to the two. Natty gave me a worried look while holding her elbow. Her thin frame was hidden by a large black zip-up hoodie, but I didn't miss the pink lace dress that went to her calves, or the cute boots. I tried to remember what day it was, and realized it was Sunday, and she looked like she was already ready for church. She was stunning, while I had seen her before, out here, under the sunshine, it was like she was a different person. With her long gold hair and her green eyes that resembled gems. She had a small nose that was perfectly set inside a heart shaped face, with high cheekbones and a wide mouth. I'd seen her smile when she'd brought me the casserole, and for some reason her face seemed so empty without that warming grin gracing her lips.

"What's wrong?" she asked, her voice slightly shaking. I wanted to reassure her, but I had no idea what was going on either.

Killian glanced at Wes before explaining.

"Nothing at all, we just wanted to ask you somethin' real quick."

Natty searched both their faces, curiosity and confusion evident in her drawn in brows and narrow eyes.

Wes placed his hand on my hip, shifting on his feet. Max poked his head between our bodies, standing directly next to me. His eyes kept bouncing around from person to person like he wasn't sure what we were doing.

"Simon arranged for you to be here from the Death Raiders a few years ago, right?"

"Yeah, two years ago," Natty said.

Wes flicked his gaze to Killian, who focused on Natty.

"You don't have to expand, or share anything you don't want to, but would there be any reason for Silas Silva to be upset over you or anyone else being here?"

Natty's eyes narrowed but it was too quick, which caught my attention.

"No, not at all. Silas wasn't around during my time there, think he was traveling or something. Why?"

Wes and Killian glared silently at one another for a long moment before Wes let out a sigh. Max chose that moment to let out a chuff and plop to the ground, throwing his body weight against me.

"He mentioned coming to claim someone. Just trying to figure out who he might be talking about."

Natty lifted her chin toward Killian. "My bet would be your vice president. Killian was talked about over there a lot. The men want to fight him, recruit him, or kill him. The women all want to fuck him."

Killian tipped his head back and laughed.

Wes smothered a smirk, but I tilted my head, inspecting her lie. She was covering something up, and I had no idea why, but something told me to let it go. Besides, we hadn't mentioned the tip Silas had given about the person not being an official member.

"Okay, thanks, Natty. You can head back in."

She turned on her heel to leave, but then stopped, spinning toward us again.

"Just out of curiosity…rival clubs can't just show up and claim people, right? We're safe here?"

Wes nodded, solemn and firm. "Of course, you are. The only way someone could come and claim one of their previous members is if there was a rule broken, or a deal made where all parties agree on it… or war. In some scenarios, in order to end a club war, we'll look at all our possible options and take the route of least resistance if no harm will come to the other party."

Natty's face paled as if she'd seen a ghost.

Wes and Killian stalked away from her. Max took a second longer to get to his feet, which allowed me an extra moment to squeeze her hand.

"Don't worry about anything, it has nothing to do with you."

She gave me a polite smile then rushed back toward the club, but there was something about it that set me on edge. Natty wasn't telling us the entire truth, and while that was her prerogative, I worried about her safety. I wanted her to know she had nothing to worry about here. I'd have to find her later and see if I could dig a bit deeper into that.

Killian veered for his bike, while Wes led the way to his house. Max already knew what to do as he pushed his nose to the door, waiting for Wes to unlock it. The laugh vibrating Wesley's chest while he patted my dogs head melted every fucking part of me. So much so, I was practically vibrating to kiss him the second he unlocked the door.

Once we pushed through, Max ran to his water and food bowl. Wes tossed his keys, then locked up behind us. The feeling of normalcy settled over me, taking me back to when we lived together. Although, he never used to lock the house the second he'd walk through it.

"I'm sensing this is a habit now that you're the president?"

Moving toward the fridge, I pulled it open and searched for food.

Wes came up behind me and stuck his nose in my neck. "It's a habit now that I have you here. I won't risk you getting hurt."

I spun in his arms, looping my arms around his neck.

I wanted to call him out on the no-feelings thing. I knew he was lying. I knew he was just protecting himself, but something had me holding back. I didn't want to argue right now. Not after everything.

Gently tugging his hand up, I examined his knuckles.

"Same old Wes." I clicked my tongue, turning around to grab ice, but he stopped me by pulling on my belt loop.

"We're covered in dirt, River. Let's go shower."

Horrified, I looked down at my clothes and realized I just sat through that entire meeting with dirt caked to my face, clothes, and hands.

"Oh my gosh, I can't believe you let me just sit there like this. No wonder poor Natty looked like she was worried we were going to hurt her."

Wes laughed low in his throat then planted a kiss to my jaw.

"You look perfect. Even covered in dirt, even exhausted, even with Max's drool all over your jeans."

"What? Oh my gosh." I pulled away to check, but he held me against him.

His lips moved down the column of my throat, where he tugged the gaiter free, and then unzipped my hoodie. Fabric dropped to the ground as he lifted my tank, continued to kiss, and then unclasped my bra.

I lifted his shirt, relishing the way his abs stretched, and I traced each hard muscle. His fingers wrestled with the button of my jeans as mine did the same with his, and suddenly we were in a race to see who could get the other naked first.

Wes won, and he claimed his victory by carrying me to the table.

"I need to be inside you," he grumbled in between kisses.

My back hit the wood, and calloused hands slid down my thighs, spreading them as Wes pulled me to the edge and stood between my open legs.

I stared up at him, catching his golden gaze and finding it impossible not to smile. Pride surged in my chest like a beacon, bright and warm.

*He grew up to be everything I hoped he'd be.*

Holding my breasts together, I bit down on my lip as he stared down at himself.

His gaze heated as he spit onto his length, then coated himself by rubbing up and down his shaft. It was the hottest thing I'd ever seen him do. I wanted him to do it again, and more. I wanted everything. Every dark thought, every corrupt idea, I needed it all.

Aligning himself with my center, he pushed inside, grunting as he encountered the tight fit. His chest fell forward as he pushed my left leg up closer to my face so he had better access.

"Yes," I hissed as he withdrew and slammed back into me. The jolt had his grip leaving my leg and moving to my waist, circling my hips as he watched his heavy cock slide in and out of me.

I was panting, desperate to move my hips to meet his thrusts, but he held them firm as he fucked me with deep strokes.

"River, there's so much I want to do with you, so many different ways I want to defile you." He slammed into me, making my tits bounce and our skin slap together in a loud echo. "So many ways I want to mark your perfect skin and hear you gasping in pleasure."

He leaned over me until his mouth landed on my nipple. His thrusts slowed but continued.

"Do it. Do all of it. I want it all, Wes," I gasped, lifting to fuck him the way I needed. His harsh grip remained on my hips as he returned to fucking me ruthlessly fast. My orgasm came without warning, and while I was slack jawed, moaning my release, Wes suddenly pulled out of me.

Gripping his length, he pulled me down the length of the table by the back of the thigh. It happened so fast, I didn't have time to even register that he was holding me up while half my ass was off the table. My face, however, was in the perfect position to catch Wesley's release. He'd never finished on my face before, not anywhere on my body except inside me, but maybe this was because I'd mentioned I wasn't on birth control, and he wanted to be careful.

*Why did disappointment churn in my chest at the thought of that?*

I blinked, opening my mouth to catch the milky release as it jutted from his cock. It was all over my face and sticky, but it didn't stop Wes from taking a bit by my cheek and spreading it to my lips and tongue.

"So fucking beautiful. I like seeing you like this, covered in the aftermath of what you do to me. You've deprived me for seven years, River. You have a lot to make up for. Let's go get in the shower, because I already need you again."

Sure enough, his semi hard cock was fully erect again. I smiled, spreading some of his release from my face to my nipple, and he groaned in response. Lifting me from the table, my legs went around his hips, and he smiled at me while he took the stairs two at a time.

The shower was refreshing, and while Wes did pin my chest against the tile as he fucked me from behind, when he finished, he pulled out again, and this time he spread his release into my open mouth. Frustration prickled under my skin. This was my fault, and it wasn't like it was fair to not use protection, in hopes that something might happen that he wouldn't welcome.

This was his life too, and we were in the middle of a messy, dangerous situation that wouldn't warrant a surprise baby anyway. Why on earth was I so annoyed that Wes didn't want to finish inside me?

After the shower I tried to brush it off.

"Do we have time to relax a little? I thought we had to do the Triple Y ranch?"

Wes pulled on a pair of boxer briefs and loose jeans, while looking over at me. "Did you see what was inside the casket?"

I shook my head, because obviously it was empty.

Once he buttoned his jeans, he took my hand and led me downstairs, where he began making breakfast.

"There was a note inside."

How did I miss that?

I hopped, sliding my butt onto the counter. Watching as Wes moved around his kitchen with ease, he grabbed eggs, cracking them one by one then starting on the bacon.

"I haven't read it yet, but I also didn't volunteer it during church."

Taking a blueberry from a container he'd pulled out, I swung my legs and asked, "Why didn't you just toss it in with the other and let the club figure it out?"

Wesley's somber gaze collided with mine.

"Because something tells me that note is meant for me, or for you…just like the others were."

I wanted to say that didn't stop him from sharing my personal letters with the entire freaking club, but it wouldn't matter. He was right. My dad was calculated, and if he'd led us far enough to discover he'd faked his own death, then he'd want us to read that note in private.

"So, what are you waiting for?"

Wes focused on the pans of sizzling food, the aroma of bacon filled the room and I remembered I hadn't even had coffee yet this morning. Jumping down, I moved around him to start the pot when he suddenly caged me in.

"Can I read it first? I just have this weird feeling. He knew I'd be the one to break the seal and pop it open, he knew I'd find it first. I just want a second with it, whatever it is."

Pressing a kiss to his chest, I smiled up at him. "Of course you can," I turned away from him and made my way toward the living room. "Will you make me some coffee while I go check on my boy?"

Wes lightly smacked my ass and laughed. "Your boy is a *beast*, River. But yes, go relax, I'll bring you some food then we'll go take a nap."

I did as he said, finding Max in the living room, resting by the fireplace. Bending down, I kissed his nose and patted his face while assuring him that he was still my number one boy. When I stood up again, I realized I was standing directly in front of the mantel, above which was a framed photo of a picture someone had taken of some mountain in Oregon. It was stunning, but it was what lay behind the picture that had me staring. I wasn't sure it would be there, or if Wes had already moved it, but I moved the frame to peek.

The purple key, streaked with stars, rested there on the nail, making my belly swoop with hope. He was telling the truth—he'd kept it.

A fierce sense of need and ownership came over me, so much so that I slipped the key off the nail, quickly glancing toward the kitchen to ensure Wes wasn't watching. The key was a gift when I was just fifteen, and a part of me wanted the magic back that it had always provided. A sense of wonder and hope, that one day I might find my happy ever after. I knew what Wes had said, but he was right, now that selling wasn't an option and my dad was alive, it changed everything.

Technically, I could leave…and maybe there were reasons why I should, but I wasn't entertaining any of them. I was going to tuck the key back into my purse and hold on to it until Wes held up his end of our deal from all those years ago. He promised me it would go to a house of our own one day, and I was going to stick around and see that happen.

Warmth invaded my chest as I made a decision.

I was staying in Rose Ridge, and I was going to be here until Wesley Ryan fell in love with me again, and then I was going to make him marry me, regardless of the club, or the things that broke us before. We came back to each other, and I wasn't going to take it for granted.

Just so I didn't go back on what I decided, I pulled my cell out and shot a text to Laura.

> Me: I'm staying here. There's a lot going on, and it's all a bit of a shit show but I'm officially staying. I'll call when things settle, but I wanted to let you know first

She replied almost immediately.

> Laura: I'm the first to know…that means you haven't told Mr. President then?

I checked to see if Wes was coming.

> Me: not yet…I just realized it, and wanted someone to hold me accountable.

> Laura: Then it should be him. Tell him how you feel, Callie. You two deserve to be happy. Seeing you together it sort of sent me into this deep dark spiral of reconsidering all my life choices and whether or not I'm wasting my own life here. Maybe I should find someone that looks at me the way Wes looks at you.

My mind instantly went to what I saw in Killian's gaze when the two of them were saying goodbye that day, but I didn't text that. Instead, I told her the truth.

> Me: You should, and maybe you should try and do it here. I might need a roommate if Wes doesn't want to live together right away.

> Laura: I just spit my water because you're so ridiculous. That man wouldn't let you walk five feet away from him, much less live across town. I have to run back on shift, but I love you.

> Me: Love you too

Right as I dropped the cell, Wes walked in, holding a tray. "Let's eat in bed."

I smiled, following him, positive I'd just made the best decision of my life.

Now I just had to get the courage to tell him.

# TWENTY-FOUR

## WES

CALLIE'S DARK HAIR FANNED ACROSS THE PILLOW AS SHE SLEPT. SHE was curled into my side as I sat up against the headboard. For some reason the image of our bare feet tangled in the sheets of my bed was so fucking domesticated that it was making my chest hurt and clouding my brain.

I wanted her to stay.

I needed her to.

But what could I offer her now that she would have accepted back then?

Everything was the same. She still hated this life, and it's the only thing I knew as an adult. I'd taken the very roots that had strangled her and wrapped them around my chest cavity, using my heart as the seed. For seven years this life was all I needed, and now here she was again, in my arms, and she was going to leave me just like she did last time.

Swallowing the thick ball of tension in my throat, I let out a sigh and dug the note from the bedside table, realizing now would be the best time to read it.

Killian had already texted me, explaining that he'd wait to have the guys move on the Triple Y ranch until later. He knew about the note, but he was respecting the fact that I hadn't discussed it with him yet.

Unfolding the lined paper, I scanned the black ink and my insides filled with dread.

The only thing written on the note was an address.

One I was particularly familiar with, because it was *my* address.

Over the past three years, I had been slowly building a house, and while I didn't live in it now, I was still planning to at some point, at least once I figured out how to hand this shit over to Killian and wasn't needed here as often. Except, no one else knew about my property. I had hired an out-of-town construction crew to build it, with nearly every facet in it being custom built, and the location was at the top of the ridge that looked down into the valley. You could see the entire town from the living room.

Why would Simon Stone write the location down and then leave it in his casket?

Callie moved next to me, and I quickly crumpled the note in my fist. I couldn't exactly explain it to her, considering I wasn't planning on showing her the house any time soon, or ever—if she was going to leave. It would be the equivalent of peeling back the skin over my heart, cracking my rib cage, and handing her a paring knife. I hadn't poured my heart into that house; it was my hope that laced those walls, and it was the only thing that kept me going day to day without her.

Callie settled back into my side, relaxing enough that her breathing evened out. It was getting later now, past lunch time, so we would need to leave soon. I had a bad feeling that once we did, things would change between us.

It made a panicked energy pulse under my skin, making me crave her. I wanted her in my arms again. I wanted to be inside her, to push all this fear out of my head. When I had Callie on the table downstairs, she'd accepted this new ravenous appetite of mine so well, even begging for more from me. I wanted more, and I was a greedy motherfucker, selfish too, so I was going to take what I needed. I was going to have what I wanted.

Even if that meant I filled her so full of my seed that she got pregnant. If she was worried about protection, she would have scolded me about fucking her bareback in the shower. No, I knew this was a way of testing the waters with us. She was being just as reckless as I was, tempting fate to do something to seal us together. She had no idea what that did to me, the idea of trying to fuck a child into existence. God damn, it was so fucking enticing.

I moved down the bed, allowing one of my darker thoughts to take form. She'd welcomed it, told me she wanted whatever I had in mind...whatever I could think up.

I'd marked her in ways I'd only dreamed of, but now...

Now I wanted to claim her.

She was wearing one of my shirts, and under it, I nearly groaned as I discovered she wasn't wearing anything else. I was in just a pair of boxer briefs, but while on my stomach, I slid them down, freeing my cock. It was already semi hard, while I stared down at Callie's silky-smooth skin, and equally smooth slit. I craved tasting her, but this time I needed something different while she slept.

Gently pulling on the back of her knee, I adjusted her enough that when I knelt in between her opened legs, I was notched perfectly at her entrance. Holding my shaft in my fist, I lined directly up with her slit and watched her face as I slowly entered her. She was so fucking tight. Shockingly so, which made me wonder at her experiences, since me. The fuckers who'd had her, didn't actually have her, not like I ever did. Just thinking of her with someone else made my grip on her hips tighten, not in anger at her, but possessiveness. Even then, she belonged to me, and a part of her knew it, which is why she didn't allow them to stretch her, or please her. I knew what it took to get her off, which meant there was a good chance she hadn't even done that.

She needed this. *She needed me.*

I pulled out, letting out a shaky breath before plunging back in. It was rough enough that Callie's eyes snapped open.

"Wes!" she gasped, but it was followed by a deep moan as her leg came up, dropping to the side so I had better access.

Roughly gripping her ass, I pulled her onto my cock as I thrust. Her jaw dropped on a silent gasp as her fingers grabbed hold of the sheets.

"Fuck, River," I rasped between clenched teeth, repeating the motion of sliding out and pulling her down against me. It wasn't deep enough of a connection for me, so I moved my hand from her ass to her back and lifted her, so she was straddling me, her knees going wide on either side of my hips. She stared down at me, cradling my jaw as I controlled how hard we fucked by circling her waist.

She swiveled her hips at a brisk pace, keeping her gaze locked with mine. The way our skin slid against one another drove my need for her higher. Her hands came to my shoulders as I roughly shoved the shirt up over her head. I needed her breasts pushed up against me as I fucked her. Chests heaving, her pebbled nipples pressed into my chest as we slowed, and on my knees, I moved us until her back was pinned against the headboard. With a growl, I began forcing my cock into her tightness at a reckless pace.

"Fuckkkk. Wes. Shit. Shit!" Callie screamed as her orgasm took hold of her. Her knees compressed my waist, her pussy clenching tight against my dick, but I pulled her ass hard against my cock, coming with a choked rasp.

"You think you scared me with that bullshit about birth control, River? You think I'm afraid of marking you over and over, filling you up to the brim with my cum, until you give me a baby?" My thumb pressed against her pulse while I continued to fuck her. Her heavy-lidded eyes stayed on my face as our bodies moved.

"You think I'm afraid to play the same game as you, tempting fate to tie us together in some sort of toxic, fucked-up way? Putting a baby inside of you isn't going to scare me off, River. For as long as I have you, consider us in a game of Russian roulette with fate. Each time we fuck, we're going to see if that's the one that'll ruin us. Because I know you're going to leave me, and even with a baby, but it'll still tie you to me, River. You won't be able to walk away without being marked by me."

Our foreheads stayed pinned together as I continued to hold her against me, finishing my own orgasm with a heaving chest.

She sagged against me, her lips finding mine in a fevered kiss.

With both our breaths mingling, she tipped my jaw back and caught my eye.

"Do you want me to stay?"

The question pierced through me, tearing at an already gaping hole. It was too big of a request, and if I told her yes, and she left anyway…fuck.

I looked away, lightly kissing her shoulder. "Would it make a difference?"

She stayed quiet for a stretch of time, slowly stroking my hair before eventually trying to crawl off me, but I held her firm.

"Would it?"

Her hazel eyes turned on me, sharp and focused. Her pink lips parted like she wasn't expecting me to turn this on her, then finally she answered, and I was glad I hadn't exposed my heart because she'd just fucking ripped through it.

"No. It wouldn't."

I assumed as much. Giving her one last squeeze, I let her crawl off me. I didn't follow her as she cleaned up or as she dressed. She knew what would come after this. We'd find her dad, and then she'd pack her things, and she'd leave my life again.

This time I was at least grateful I had kept some of my heart tucked under my sleeve, never allowing her to see it for what it was. She owned all of it, the entire fucking thing. If only she wanted to keep it.

The cab of the truck was quiet as we drove up to the house.

I was nervous to see her reaction, even with her not knowing it was mine. It made her acceptance or disappointment even more important. We didn't talk about what happened at the house or what either of us said. Our relationship was fucked up. I knew it, and she knew it. We loved each other, in our own strange ways, enough that we were literally trying to create life, or at least not doing anything at all to prevent it. I considered it a challenge, and she wasn't shying away from it, while also not confronting any of it.

It was better to just move past it.

Which was what I had been doing while moving through the motions of finding someone to watch Max and talking to the guys about heading to the Triple Y ranch. I wanted them busy while Callie and I headed up the bluff.

Now, winding through the roads that led to the top of the ridge, I wished she would say something. I wanted her to yell at me, or fight with me. Fuck, I wanted her to ask about the note that I promised to let her read. She hadn't. I eventually offered the information and ended up just saying all that was on the note was an address. She merely nodded and got into the truck.

I hated this.

But it was going to happen no matter how badly I didn't want it to. From the start, this is where we were going to end. Best to just let it unfold.

"Oh wow." Callie sat up, peering over the dashboard as the house came into view.

My fucking stomach twisted with eagerness. She unbuckled, so she could see more from the edge of her seat. Her eyes were wide as she stared in awe.

"Whose house is this?"

Once I parked, I saw no other bikes or parked vehicles, so I focused on her.

She jumped out of the truck and raced to the edge of what would one day be my yard. Once I moved in, there'd be grass where she was standing, for now it was all dirt. She held her chest as she stared down into the gorge, viewing the entire town.

"You like it?" I asked, coming to stand next to her.

Tears lined her eyes as she continued to stare at the scenery, then she turned toward me with a tight voice, "Would it matter?"

I regarded her, letting the wind rustle my hair and blow her shirt up as we stared at one another and with a low murmur, I answered, "Yes."

She searched my face, about to say something when we heard a door open and close from behind us.

"Well, you made it. Guess that means you got back into the good graces of my daughter and dug up my grave, you son of a bitch."

Callie spun around, paling.

I turned in time to see her dad do the same. Simon looked the same as I last saw him. Dark hair with streaks of silver, tied back at the nape of his neck. Hazel eyes that matched his daughter's and a jaw made of stone that rarely spread into a smile.

"Simon, want to explain what the fuck we're doing here?" I asked, moving up the hill with Callie on my heel.

His stare stayed on his daughter.

Before I could repeat my question or push my irritation on him, Callie launched up the steps and ran into his arms, throwing herself at him. He caught her in a tight embrace as she cried, and he kept his eyes on the sky above, his face stern.

I could hear her crying things about missing him, regret, and having to bury him.

He muttered a few things I couldn't hear, while stroking down the length of her hair. I hung back to give them a moment, remembering this was their first reunion in seven years. For whatever reasons they had, they'd both stayed apart that entire time, without so much as a phone call between them. Perhaps that was why Simon's eyes were rimmed red now, or why his throat kept bobbing as he tried to control his voice.

Once he let her down and she swiped at her face, I decided to step closer.

"So, you two are back together. Seems I fixed what I had a hand in breaking." Simon assumed, while we entered the house. Neither of us corrected him that this was just temporary.

I hadn't set foot in the house in over a month, so it felt strange to be back inside. The main floor was all open concept with a substantial living room facing the valley, with floor-to-ceiling windows. The balconies from the second and third floors were visible from here as well, each one with this view.

Callie's face was turned up, taking it all in.

She wandered until her feet carried her across the hardwood floors, and she was running her fingers over the chrome appliances in the kitchen.

"Seriously, who lives here?" she asked curiously, while opening the wine fridge.

Simon's face turned in my direction, as if he was waiting for my reply. I didn't give him a reaction, or any indication whatsoever that it was my house.

He cleared his throat and finally decided to explain what the fuck we were doing here.

"I'm sorry I faked my death. It was shitty, and I know everyone is pissed about it."

I laughed, shaking my head. "Pissed?"

Simon glared, then focused on his daughter. "But if it took my death to get you back here, then maybe it was worth it."

"Were you even ever sick?" Callie let out a tiny scoff, in response, fresh tears lining her eyes.

Simon swallowed and ducked his head. "Yes, I'm still sick, just haven't kicked the bucket yet."

Callie stalked off toward the living room, tucking her arms in tight against her chest and shaking her head. This had to be so much to deal with. His funeral, the grief, dealing with our past, and now this twist. Fuck, I wanted to just hit pause and give her five seconds to catch up.

"Look, I have a reason for everything I did, and part of it, you already know."

"The deal you made, right?" Callie interrupted him, the heels of her boots clicking over the hardwood as she made her way back to the kitchen, where we were standing.

"Yes. I made a deal eight years ago with Dirk, the deal being once I died, the property of the club would fall to him. Not you." Simon lifted his chin.

"Then why put me through this? Why make us sit down in that lawyer's office and go through all this bullshit if it was never mine to begin with?"

Simon shifted on his feet, looking down at the ground.

"Because if you sold it before Dirk could get his hands on it, then there was nothing he could do to get it."

I shook my head, confused. "Then either way, you would have

fucked the club over. We would have had to regroup somewhere else."

Simon sneered, glaring over at me. "Mighty fine concern of yours, Wesley, when you've got more money than God. Why do you care what happens to the club? You're leaving it, right?"

Callie's gaze swung in my direction.

"What?"

I clenched my jaw, trying to bite back my response. No one knew I was leaving. I hadn't told a fucking soul.

"Why would you assume that?"

Another voice suddenly cut into our conversation, echoing from one of the levels above us. "Well, why else did you build such an ostentatious house, Mr. President, if you didn't plan on leaving?"

Dirk Lenair, leader of the Death Raiders, stepped down from the stairwell, clapping his hands together. The man was a brute, at more than six feet and well over three hundred pounds. He had tattoos over nearly every inch of his skin, all down his fingers and hands, all along the side of his face. He was all muscle, and his eyes were so dark they almost looked black.

"Surprised to see me?"

Callie backed up until she was behind me. I found it telling that she chose me to protect her. Even with her dad right there, it was still me she trusted when shit hit the fan. Funny, because at this point, I felt like she was the only person I could trust too.

I cut a glare back to Simon, only to find his face closed off, revealing nothing.

"What are you doing here?" I asked, glancing at both men.

Simon stepped up, laying his hands out.

"Well, see, here's the thing. Since I'm not dead, Dirk can't have his property, but he's still owed something."

Dirk laughed, cracking his knuckles. "You stole from me eight years ago, Wes. I'm here to collect."

I laughed, because fuck them both.

"You stole from *me*, you fucking prick, and if you think there's even a chance that you're going to touch Callie, you're insane. I'd die before you even breathed in her direction."

Dirk smirked, peering at something behind me.

"That can be arranged."

I turned in time to see Silas but failed to see the bat.

"River, ru—"

The hit came with a sickening crunch, paired with a sound that echoed off the walls that practically tore the skin from my bones, and it wasn't my scream. It was hers, and that hollowed, painful sound would follow me straight to hell, and like the selfish fucker I was, I'd be grateful for it. Because in the end, that kind of pain could only mean one thing.

River loved me, and perhaps she never stopped.

# TWENTY-FIVE
## CALLIE

"WES!"

I was still screaming, as if I could wake him up.

My voice had gone hoarse, and two of the men in the room had already yelled at me to shut the fuck up, but I wouldn't.

There was so much blood. There was no way he was alive. I needed to get closer to him to see if his chest was rising, or if there was a pulse. The cracking sound was still rattling around inside my head, making me relive that moment when his eyes rolled into the back of his head, and he fell over.

My dad had continued to pull me away, and my legs were kicking at thin air but there wasn't anything else I could say. Nothing else I wanted to say. It was just Wesley's name on my tongue, crying until he answered me back.

"All right, Dirk, let's talk terms," my dad said over my screaming.

Dirk gave me a salacious smile, all teeth and venom. "Marriage, and a truce."

I spat on the ground, my voice a wobbly whisper. "I'm not fucking marrying you."

Silas was silent as he hung in the background, but I wanted to hit him. I wanted to take that bat and bash his disloyal brains in.

"Wait, I changed my mind." Dirk suddenly snapped his meaty fingers together. "Let me burn his house down, while she watches, and I won't need to marry her. Afterall, I still want the freedom to fuck whoever I want without worrying about defiling the marital bed."

Seething angry, I reached for something, anything to keep them from torching this place while Wesley was unconscious inside it. *Please just be unconscious.*

"This isn't even his house, so it's a waste of your time, and I saw cameras. The owners have already seen you."

Silas and Dirk laughed at me, and not for the first time, I felt foolish and like I was the butt of the joke.

Dirk jumped, sliding his butt on the counter, looking like an oversized toddler. "Stone, don't you have a way of provin' it to her?"

My dad relaxed his hold the smallest bit and cleared his throat. "Honey, you still have that key you used to carry around everywhere with you? When I asked all those years ago, you said it was for the house Wes was going to get for you one day."

I felt sick.

He didn't. Wes would have told me. He would have brought me up here and shown me and asked me to marry him.

*Would it make a difference?*

He'd asked me that when I asked if he wanted me to stay.

Silas poured the contents of my purse on the ground, adding to the reasons why I wanted to murder him.

"Here it is."

He plucked it up and walked to the front door.

"How did his little promise go?" Silas asked my dad, giving me a mocking smile.

"Shoot, they were so young, I think if it unlocks the front door, then that means this is the house he wanted for them to live in when they were ready to settle down."

They laughed, and when Silas locked himself out on the front porch then used the key to open the door, they both teased with a sigh.

I couldn't breathe.

"So fucking sweet, and how fitting he'll burn alive in the home he had built for you."

No, it wouldn't end like this. It couldn't. We didn't get this far to have it end like this.

"Dad, why are you doing this?" Tears burned my nose, clouding my vision.

I heard him laugh, and while Silas and Dirk joked to one another, he whispered in my ear, "just trust me, honey."

Louder, he explained.

"That day I made a deal for you, I also made a deal for Sasha. If I back out on this now, I lose her. Dirk will kill all three of you. This is war, honey, and sometimes there's hard choices in war so people stay alive."

My gaze moved to Silas, and my mind reeled as I watched him begin to pull pieces together as well.

"Where's Sasha now?" I asked, keeping my gaze on her son.

My gut told me he needed to know, and maybe that was why he was here. If my dad was playing an angle, perhaps Silas was too. It gave me a modicum of hope. Maybe that hit wasn't as bad as I imagined. Or maybe I was already delusional, and this was just me grasping at straws.

"My favorite place, blossom." Dirk drew closer to me, casually caressing my face.

I wrestled with my dad's hold on me. "The beef shack?"

Not even a real place, but Dirk laughed the same.

"No, baby. It's your new place of employment. Strip club in Pyle called Strings. Sasha works the pole there when I tell her to. I have someone making sure she doesn't leave until we get this sorted out. Don't be jealous. She hasn't warmed my bed in a long time. I don't like sharing, which is why Wesley here is going to have to die. I can't run the risk that you'll go back to him."

I had to keep them here and talking and give Wes time to wake up. Because he had to wake up. He had to. There was so much I still had to say to him, and still so much I had to do. I couldn't lose him.

My dad finally released me, and I dove for Wes on the floor, but Dirk grabbed my wrist and roughly pulled me away.

"The terms, Dirk. Two years. You can't hurt her, and she doesn't work the pole if she doesn't want to. She's an ink slinger; let her work at one of your tattoo shops."

Dirk let out a sigh, inspecting me from head to toe.

"How long ago you fuck him? I can't risk you being pregnant."

"We've been fucking like bunnies since I came back, barely stopped to drive up here." I spat at his feet, resulting in a slap to my cheek.

"Hey!" my dad yelled, pulling me back from Dirk, but the leader pulled a gun out, holding it to my dad's face.

"I want her for ten years, and if she is pregnant, she gets rid of it. No argument."

My dad faltered with his hands up, and my chest felt like a fire had been lit inside it. I was hyperventilating. My dad couldn't make a trade. I didn't belong to him to trade.

Dirk tilted his head, and with his firearm swaying to the side as if he were inspecting the house, he said, "Fires take too long. Why don't I just put a bullet—"

A gun went off, and my eyes slammed shut. The echo from the shot was still ringing in my ears as I slowly blinked, realizing it wasn't Dirk's gun that had fired.

Something wet landed on my face and arm, but I didn't want to look down to see the color. Dirk's body slumped to the floor a moment later. Silas stood there with his arm outstretched, glaring down at the body.

"That was taking too long."

My dad moved first. "Help me get Wes up. He needs ice. You hit him the way we talked about, right?"

Silas ran over, crouching to help assess Wesley's injury.

"Of course. I used the set kit from the drama club at the high school. I hit him in the back, knocking the wind out of him. I think when he fell, it may have knocked him out, but he should be fine."

I searched Wesley's chest and head, trying to piece together what Silas was saying.

"There's so much blood." My voice wobbled, along with my lip, from trying to hold in a sob.

Silas held up a plastic bag. "All part of the set—I think it's corn syrup and red food dye."

Relief swelled in my chest as I moved, pulling Wes's head into my lap, stroking along his hairline. I was a mess now, but I didn't care.

"Wes?" I said, lightly slapping his cheek.

"I'll help them, and I'll make sure they get out of here, just go get my mom." Silas locked his eyes with my dad, who seemed torn on what to do.

"Callie, I'm so sorry about this, honey. You were never going to go with him, but I know you were scared. I can explain everything, I just —"

I was too angry to even hear him speak. "Just go get Sasha."

With one more pause, and a streak of remorse in his gaze, he ran outside. The sound of his bike reverberated through the house before dying off down the road.

It was just Silas and me with an unconscious Wes.

"If we can carry him to the truck, I'll drive him down and I'll take him to the emergency room."

Silas grunted, slapping at Wesley's face.

"He should wake up here in a few."

The silence in the room stretched and then Silas let out a heavy sigh.

"Look, before he wakes up, I need you to promise me something."

I examined him, seeing how tired he looked, with his pale blue eyes rimmed with red and bags under his sooty lashes.

"Why would I help you?"

His jaw clenched before letting his head hang forward.

"I deserve that. I have my own reason for being upset with your father and his club. But I shouldn't have taken them out on you. I don't know what Wes is planning, but I know after this, he's going to step down. I know where he lives, and where he plans to raise his family. If he considers me an enemy, he'll wage war on me, and as of right now, he'll have the backing of the club to do it. I need time, and I need an ally."

"So why not just explain this to him?" I asked, adjusting Wes in my lap. His eyes were still closed, his breathing even.

Silas stared down at him. "It won't matter. I put you in danger. If it were me, and someone did this to my woman, I'd kill first and ask questions later."

My mind went to Natty, for some reason, still curious if there was more to their connection.

"So you want me to speak on your behalf?"

Silas nodded slowly.

"I'm about to become the president of the Death Raiders. I need Killian to see me as an ally."

I opened my mouth to ask how he knew it would be Killian who took over when he beat me to it.

"Your dad is going to disappear with my mom. He doesn't have a lot of time left—that part was true about his little act. They want to get away from all of this while they can. Once the other clubs realize Dirk is dead, they'll start circling. I need allies. I know Wes is getting out, but I also know he loves Killian like a brother and so do you. You guys will stick close enough to the club to help him transition."

I considered my words carefully as I traced a line down Wesley's forehead.

"Assuming he wakes up and everything is okay, then you have my word. But"—I made sure I had his attention before saying—"only if you swear not to ever hurt her."

Silas dropped his brows into a shelf, shaking his head.

"Who are you—"

"Whoever it is you're coming for. We all heard your claim. I don't know your reasons, or your past, but I have to know you won't hurt her."

His jaw worked back and forth as he waited to respond, and I felt Wes move the slightest bit under me. My eyes darted down to inspect him, but he was still asleep.

"I don't know who you're talking about, but whoever I decide to claim, no harm would come to them. Not ever. The entire purpose of claiming them would be to protect them."

That was good enough for me. I nodded, and he grunted and then stood.

"I'll have cleaners come out here, but I need to leave before Wes wakes up. Until next time, *River*." Silas gave me a half salute, along with a flirtatious smirk, and then darted out the back door.

I lightly slapped Wesley's face again, because I wasn't keen on being alone in a room with a dead body while the love of my life lay unconscious in my lap.

This time he blinked. My heart soared, when I was able to see those whiskey eyes once more.

"Wes."

His hand came up, pushing a strand of hair off my face. "River. We in heaven?"

A tear slipped free, and so did a sob. "No, baby, we're in our house. There's a dead body on the other side of the island. Silas is going to have someone come clean it."

Wes started to move. "No. No one else can know where we live."

I helped him up, but he was unstable, gripping the counter for support.

"Jesus, what the fuck happened?"

"I'll explain it later, but you better call Silas if you don't want more Raiders here to clean this up."

Wes pulled out his cell from the front pocket of his leather jacket and blinked at it.

"Call Killian. He needs to be here; he'll know what to do."

I took his phone and did exactly that.

"Where the fuck are you? The ranch was a bust," Killian launched in right away. I cleared my throat and explained.

"Kill, we need you. We found Dad, and it's a long story but the——" Wes gently took the phone from me and took over. "Kill, I need my house cleaned. No…" Wesley's gaze landed on me. "Not that house. Head up the butte, but only bring Giles, Brooks and Rune. No one else."

Wes hung up then handed me his phone.

"Pull up the Roman and dial."

I hesitated for a second. "Before you do, you should know that Silas was only playing a part. He killed Dirk. Saved me. He wants an alliance."

Wes laughed, holding his head. "Fuck that guy."

"I promised him, Wes."

Gold-brown eyes landed on me, hard and unyielding. "You promised him?"

I nodded. "He knows Kill will take over; he's stepping in to take Dirk's place. He knows you want him dead because he has this location and if you ask Killian to go to war on your behalf, he would. He doesn't want a war, Wes. He just wants peace."

A scoff left Wesley's chest, while he started to pace around the kitchen, slow but steady.

"He wants time to strategize, nothing more. For now, I'll honor it, only for you, but if he ever gives me reason to question his loyalty again, I'll put a bullet in his brain."

I clicked on his contact and shot a text explaining to stay away, we had our own cleaners.

Silas replied with a thumbs up.

"Let's get out of here, Wes. I can't even enjoy this house you made me, with that dead body in here."

Wes froze, staring down at all the contents of my purse poured on the ground. My key was still in the front door. Kneeling, I began to gather it all and tuck it back into my purse.

"You used the key?"

Lifting my shoulder, I explained. "They did, to prove you'd built it for me. They wanted to burn it."

Wes moved, taking one small step at a time until we'd cleared the door and I pulled the key out, tucking it back into my purse.

"And what did you think when you saw the key unlock that door?"

Telling him what I thought wouldn't make a difference when he needed to understand what I meant.

"Earlier, when I asked if you wanted me to stay, and you asked if it would matter. I said no because I'd already made up my mind, Wes."

His eyes found mine, his fingers tracing the palm of my hand as I led him to the truck, and we got inside. Covered in fake blood and bruises, we stared at one another as the sun began to set, and the purple streaking across the sky reflected across the windshield.

"What did you make up your mind about, River?" Wes groaned, shifting to take pressure off his back.

Turning toward him, I smiled. "I'm staying. So, no, it wouldn't matter if you wanted me to or not. I've already made up my mind."

Wesley's face snapped from the view in front of us to my face. "What?"

I reached for his hand and pulled his knuckles to my lips.

"I'm staying, and if you want to take it slow because you think I'll leave again, then fine. We can. But I'm not expecting anything, Wes. I know the club is a part of you, and it's a part of me too. Silas said my dad really is short on time, and as angry as I am with him, I want to spend what time he has left near him. I want to wake up every day with you, and I want babies."

He moved, leaning over the console until he was cradling my jaw. His lips moved over mine, then a whisper.

"I want forever. You agree to stay, to be mine, you need to understand it's for good. I stalked you when you went to DC. You were never really free of me; this time I won't even let you leave."

I laughed, stroking his hair. "Then you've got my future, Wes. Either way, I think our story deserves another chapter."

He smiled against my lips.

"Fuck yeah, it does."

*One Week Later*

The cabin was immersed in streaks of gold as the sun gently filled the valley.

Shielding my eyes, I looked up to the hill above the ridge line and smiled. Wes and I had plans to move into the new house starting next week, and I couldn't be more excited. Killian had the entire place cleaned, and when Wes and I went back three days later, there wasn't even a trace that someone had been killed there days prior. It gave me a chance to explore the whole house properly.

Wes had built us a three-story dream house. Each floor was magnificent with small touches, like the colors he picked out, and the style of the handles and faucets. They were all things I'd dreamed of having one day, back when I'd lay in bed with my Pinterest app open, visualizing a life with Wes.

The property sat on five acres, and while the house sat at the top of the butte, the yard expanding behind it was flat, with verdant foliage and tall trees. It would be the perfect place to raise a family. While I still had no ring on my finger, it wasn't needed. Forever was stamped on my heart, etched into eternity. As long as I drew breath, Wes would be mine.

The sound of tires crunching drew my gaze behind me to the older pickup truck rolling to a stop.

I tugged my sweater tighter as I closed the gap and watched as Sasha rounded the vehicle to help my dad out of the passenger side. His face was pale today, and his frame looked gaunt. Pain hit me in the sternum as I realized I'd have to go through losing him all over again. We had no idea how long he had. The doctors had said it could be six months or three years, but people had beaten those odds before with pancreatic cancer and lived longer. Just depended on the body.

My dad smiled as he saw me approach, and his arm came around me in a tight hug.

We'd decided we needed a redo. A fresh start, where he saw me, and we reconnected, without club politics, or using me as bait to draw out Dirk. So, we settled on having breakfast in the cabin every Saturday morning. Eventually, once we moved into the new house and Wes approved, we'd do Sunday dinner up there. I had plans to even include Silas, since my dad had informed us that he was marrying Sasha in the town chapel next week.

The two of them had plans to move into a house about an hour outside of Pyle, on a ranch where Sasha could grow her garden and Dad could live out the rest of his life, married and happy.

With his arm around me, we ventured for the front door, but my dad stopped short.

"You ever wonder about those glass jars we used to bury out here?" His gaze spread slowly over the property behind the cabin.

I nodded, following his gaze.

"I tried to find them when I stayed here at first...I thought I'd remember when we were last out here."

He started for the side of the house, making a humming sound.

"I'm going to start breakfast, okay?" Sasha called before opening the door to the cabin.

Dad and I walked together as he bent low under one of the smaller trees. With the toe of his boot, he dug at the softer soil there.

"Here. I made sure it followed this line here. See the trees, how they form a U shape around the yard?"

Following the line of trees, I realized he was right. It wasn't a perfect shape, but it loosely formed a horseshoe. Kneeling down in the dirt, I pushed my fingers into the dirt and began digging, unsure if we needed a shovel or not.

My dad just stood patiently as I dug for the treasure. I was about to give up when my fingernail touched something hard. I looked up at him with a wide smile on my face. He sunk to the ground next to me and began helping me unearth the jar. Once it was freed, I held it between us, inspecting the clouded glass of the mason jar.

I tried to untwist the cap but couldn't get it to loosen.

"Here, let me try." My dad took it and gave it a good twist, and we both smiled when we heard the pop of the seal.

I felt like a little girl again as he began to pour the purple sand out. I held my hands up as he emptied it over my fingers, and I felt a few tears begin to well within my eyes.

"Remember what you used to wish for?" he asked, staring down at me with a gentleness I wasn't used to seeing again.

Clearing my throat, I nodded. "When I was really little, I'd wish for a horse. I wanted one to ride and to take me on adventures. After I turned nine, I would wish for Peter Pan."

My dad laughed, likely not understanding but my heart warmed at the memory.

"Wes used to tell me stories when I'd crawl into his treehouse. My favorite was always Peter Pan and Wendy's story, and that first fall, after all the extra members went back and you took me out here to camp, I wished for my very own lost boy who'd take me to an island, away from everything I'd ever known."

My dad's gentle voice wove between us as he sat in the dirt with me, staring at the purple sand I used to call treasure. "But Peter Pan wasn't about Peter and Wendy. It was about the Lost Boys, and Captain Hook."

"It was to me," I inclined my head, "I focused on the adventure it must have been for Peter to finally have a Wendy in his life, someone to share different things about his island. The mermaids, and even the crocodile. She was a new adventure for him. The kind he'd never had before or ever again, the kind only a first love can give you." I smiled through a clogged throat.

My dad studied me while I dusted the last remaining specks of treasure from my hands.

"You know, I never had anything to give you. I was a poor, single dad with a club to my name, and that was my only means at really making any money. I wanted to leave you something, give you something more than purple sand and imaginary fairy dust. I thought by letting you go, and cutting your ties from this place, I'd given you a gift. I only brought you back because I had the chance to leave you this place."

His eyes misted, the hazel turning gold as the sun invaded our little shady spot. His chin lifted as he continued. "I messed up so much of our relationship, honey. I know I don't deserve you, but do you think you could give an old man a second chance?"

A sob escaped through a laugh as I got to my knees and threw my arms around my dad.

"I'm already planning family dinners in my mind, Dad. I love you."

Once he drew back and I helped him up, we made our way back to the cabin, and he muttered softly, "Maybe now that we're clear of the club, you can finally have that life you dreamed of with Wes."

Smiling, we rounded the side of the cabin, clearing the front, and I saw a new bike parked next to the truck. My stomach dipped with excitement, knowing Wes was waiting inside.

"I have a feeling we'll still be linked to it for a while. Besides, Wes helped me realize these roots aren't all bad."

A kiss landed on my forehead as he pulled on the screen door.

"It's good to have you back, sweetheart."

"It's good to be back, Dad."

And for the first time in my life, I meant it.

# TWENTY-SIX
# WES

KILLIAN WAS WAITING FOR ME WHEN I PULLED UP TO THE HOUSE.

He was helping me lay down sod before the sun got too high and it was too hot. Callie and I were moving into the new house in a few days, and I wanted to surprise her by having the yard finished. Kill offered to help me—well, several of the guys did, but I wanted to talk to him alone first.

"You eat already?" I asked, lifting the bag of donuts I'd grabbed from The Drip before driving up.

Killian's arms were folded while he nodded.

I could tell he was pissed by the way he tossed off his cut and started aggressively raking the dirt to get it even.

"Look, I know you're pissed," I started.

"You don't know shit!" Killian yelled, swinging his wild gaze my way. "No, I'm not pissed, Wes. I'm fucking hurt. You sent me on a wild goose chase, and you almost died because of it. You almost got Callie killed. She's my family, Wes, as much as you are. You should have told me!"

He threw the rake across the yard.

Kilian's chest heaved as he pinned his hands to his hips. "I tried to stay quiet and respectful for weeks, Wes, but fuck this. I can't believe you did that. I can't honestly even process how close you both came to dying. Now Callie made some sort of alliance with Silas, the new leader of the Death Raiders, and you're stepping down? Just fuck all this."

He started walking back toward his bike, belatedly remembering his cut.

I followed him, keeping calm so he could get out all his anger.

"What am I supposed to do now? Simon is gone, half the club won't even get to know he's still alive. But I'll know. This is too much change for our club at one time. I need you to stay on for a while, Wes. I can't do this—" he trailed off, clenching his jaw tightly before leveling me with a hard glare. "I feel like I just lost my entire family in one day. I need you around for a while."

I was close enough now that I pulled him into a hug. Like fuck did we do this in front of other members, but Killian was my brother, and I felt like shit for making him feel this way.

"I'm not going anywhere. Callie's here, too...stepping down doesn't mean leaving."

We separated, and Killian ran his hand over his head.

"Pretty sure Callie is going to have something to say about that... she left because of the club."

The sky was turning a darker blue. The sun was getting higher, and we were going to have to lay this grass in the hot as fuck afternoon. I bent down to grab a new rake and started scraping over the gravel and dirt to level it out.

"Callie didn't leave because of the club. She left because of me. I was keeping her out of the loop and ignoring her. We were young, and I had no idea how to balance the role I had taken on, not to mention that I wanted to do right by Simon. But Callie feels at home here."

Killian smiled, letting out a laugh as he started joining me with leveling the yard.

"You locking that down then?"

I scoffed. "Fuck yes, I am. I want it to be as inconvenient as possible for her if she ever tries to leave again. I plan on proposing as soon as we move in, and I keep trying to put a baby inside her."

Killian laughed, shaking his head. "Fuck, stop. She's like my little sister."

We worked while talking shop for the next several hours, until all the sod had been laid and the irrigation had been set up to keep it alive. By the time we made our way back to the club, it was close to dinner, and all I wanted was to eat and then practice getting Callie pregnant. But as we pulled up to the clubhouse, we were met with chaos.

At least a hundred bikes were parked around the garage, spilling into the front yard and taking up the bonfire space. The doors were wide open, with members drinking, dancing, and partying. We hadn't thrown a party like this in months due to the president's sickness, and transition of power to me. It was poor taste to celebrate when your president was dying.

Parking the truck, Killian and I both piled out with confused expressions.

I didn't think Callie would be mixed up in the madness inside, but I heard Max bark and then he was galloping, cutting through people, whipping them with his tail while he made his way to me.

I bent down to greet him with a pat to the stomach and chest.

"Where's your mama?" I asked, walking inside with him on my heels.

Callie wouldn't have left him inside unless she was here to make sure he was safe.

Searching the space, I found several members who only came around for special occasions and a lot of out of towners, some retired. Sweetbutts, new and old, were sitting in laps and serving beer. A few people were hanging out without a cut or patch but I just moved past them. I needed to find Callie.

I was searching over by the kitchen area when all the sudden the overhead music lowered and everyone huddled around me seemed to make a path by moving to the side. Max stood next to me, alert, with his head up, but then he darted forward as soon as I saw her.

Wearing her hair up high in a ponytail, Callie's hazel eyes were lined with black, her dark lashes framing them. Her lips were plump and pink, glossed over with her favorite lip color. She wore those cute as fuck heeled boots, and a pair of shorts that barely covered her ass. Her shirt was trimmed in lace, cupping her breasts so tight it pushed them up, and there over her bare shoulders was a familiar leather cut.

My breathing hitched as I processed what she'd found.

Callie Stone just walked in wearing my property patch, looking like she was ready to fuck the devil, and I was completely at a loss for words. She looked like she just stepped out of one of my wet dreams.

"Mister President," she flirted, tilting her head to the side.

A few people around us clapped, and a few seemed to be smothering smiles.

I stared into her hazel eyes, desperate to touch her. As soon as I reached out, she stepped back with a smirk.

"I have a question for you, sir."

Smiling like a love-struck idiot, I laughed. "Whatever it is, the answer is yes."

Perking up, she took two steps forward, allowing me to pull her into my arms.

"Great! Then it's settled. I'll marry you."

Everyone let out a chorus of shouts and cheers as the party resumed, the music blaring and Max barking.

"Did you just propose to me?"

Tucking her face into my shoulder, she pressed a kiss to my neck before replying.

"Technically you agreed to *me* marrying *you*, but either way, we're engaged."

I made a pleased humming sound while holding her to me.

"So this is our engagement party then?"

Tipping her head back, those pink lips spread in a smile. "I guess it is."

"Well, then, I want my own celebration."

With her lips at my ear, she whispered, "What did you have in mind?"

The sounds from the party could still be heard in our room next door, but I didn't care. Tonight, Callie was all mine, and this time I was taking her, knowing she was here to stay.

I'd given her instructions on what to wear, and now as I walked in from the bathroom, I could see she obeyed.

"You have a thing for it?" She lifted the edge of her property patch and smirked.

Rubbing my cock through my boxers, I returned the smile.

"I do when you're naked underneath it."

"Whatever you say, Mister President. I'm here to please you."

Her pretending to be here for my pleasure was definitely sending the blood rushing straight to my cock. She'd reapplied her lip gloss, and kept her hair high, and all I wanted to do was wrap my fist around it and fuck her from behind while I stared down at the words on the back of that patch.

"Is that right?"

Crawling on her hands and knees, she moved to the edge of the bed, showing me her swaying ass as she went.

"Yes, I'm your dirty slut tonight. Use me however you want."

Ah, fuck. I was granite, painfully so, and the bulk, with my weeping tip, was too much to be contained in my boxers, so I pulled them down and gripped my shaft.

"First, I have one thing I need you to put on for me."

Callie sat back on her heels, spreading her thighs, and I nearly choked from how sexy she looked. Focusing, I reached into my top drawer and pulled out the ring box, then cracked it open.

"River, you sort of stole my thunder, but I don't really care, as long as you say yes in the end." I held up the diamond ring in front of her.

Those pink lips parted on a gasp.

"Oh my God!"

I wouldn't tell her I'd had that purchased for years, or that I'd added to it, just hoping one day she'd come back into my life and wear it. Sliding it onto her finger, she stared down at it with tears brimming in her eyes.

"You were really going to propose?"

"Of course I was. The day we moved into our new house."

She jumped from the bed, leaping into my arms. "I love you."

Pulling her back, so I could kiss her, I traced her lips and moved my mouth slowly against hers. "I love you too."

After a few more sweet kisses and with the engagement ring on her finger, I tossed her back on the bed with a smirk.

"Now get on all fours again so I can teach you what it means to wear that patch."

*Callie*

I was drinking tea, to soothe my throat after our zealous round of sex. I had taken a bath and came down to make some dinner. Wes ate, and pretty much passed out.

I couldn't stop staring at my ring.

Nor could I ignore that the ring looked awfully similar to something I had picked out nine years ago while we were walking through a jewelry department. There were extra bands of diamonds added to it, but the center diamond was the same modest princess cut that I had found when I was just seventeen years old and in love with the boy next door.

Peering over at Wes, and seeing him in his gray sweats, bare chest, half cuddling my dog, it was that sunshine in my soul feeling, chasing all the darkness that had hung around me for the past seven years. All the struggling through rent, living paycheck to paycheck. Meaningless connections and friendships until I met Laura.

*Laura.*

Alarm shot through me as I pulled up my phone to send her a text.

> Me: So I have news…. sort of big news.

The dots on her end started moving but stopped. My brows caved as the dots repeated the process a few times, and then there was a soft knock on the door. Wes didn't stir, so I tiptoed off the couch and peeked at his security camera.

Seeing who was there, I quickly unlocked and pulled the door open. Searching the porch, I curiously asked, "What are you doing here?"

It was dark out, and the club was still going, but it had died down quite a bit. There was a bonfire burning in the front, offering a bit of light to Wesley's porch.

Laura was pulled in, and I locked everything up once more.

"Hey, sorry for randomly showing up like this."

"No, are you kidding me? I'm so happy to see you."

She fell into my arms for a hug, but I could sense something was off with her.

I heard the movie pause and peeked over to see Wes standing from the couch, rubbing his eyes.

"Hey, Laura, nice to see you. Guest room's open if you need it."

Placing a kiss on the side of my head, he headed upstairs with Max on his heels.

I took the opportunity to pull Laura by the wrist and settle into the couch. The cubby in the middle section had a few snacks I'd stashed, so I pulled it open and handed her a rope of red licorice.

"Why are there moving boxes everywhere?" Laura lightly nudged one by her foot.

I looked around, realizing things were a little crazy. I hadn't really noticed before, with the engagement and orgasmic bliss from earlier.

"Wes built me a house. Three years ago. I just found out. We're also engaged." I held up my hand, and Laura tipped her head back in laughter.

"God, I missed you. Of course you're engaged and the love of your life built you a house. So you're moving in soon then?"

I shrugged, biting off a piece of licorice. "A few days."

"Well, Wesley isn't renting this place out by chance, is he?"

Wide-eyed, I turned toward her. "Are you saying what I think you're saying?"

"The rental car I drove down here is packed, and when you texted me that you were staying, I abused my key privileges and loaded your stuff too."

I was going to cry.

"Laura…are you for real moving here?"

I was having a hard time grasping the concept, because she grew up in a small town and had wanted the bigger city life for as long as I had known her. Why would she suddenly want tiny Rose Ridge, Virginia?

"I think this place grew on me. Also, I miss you, and living in DC is boring without you there. I'm also utterly dependent on you for more tattoos. I don't trust anyone else."

Leaning over to pull her into a hug, I let out a happy sigh as I addressed her earlier question.

"From what I understand, this place will go to the next president. Wes is acting president for a while, but the person in charge will be Killian, and I haven't heard if he wants this place for when he's here, or not. But I can ask for you."

"Uh, I can just look for some place in town. If you're not going to be here, then it might be weird for me to be."

Her eyes dropped to her lap.

"Well, stay with us for as long as you want—in the new house I mean."

Tipping her chin up, she smiled. "Okay, as long as Wes doesn't mind."

I waved her off. "He would never."

At least I hoped not. Didn't matter. My best friend was living in Rose Ridge with me; there was absolutely no downside to this situation.

# TWENTY-SEVEN
# WES

*Two Weeks Later*

THE THING NO ONE TELLS YOU ABOUT OPEN CONCEPT HOMES IS HOW badly it echoes when there's too many people inside.

Shoving my hands into my pockets, I stared out the living room windows, enjoying the view of the town when I heard Laura crack another joke, which resulted in Callie laughing so hard she snorted. Usually, I'd love the sound, but after living with both women for two weeks, it was starting to get old.

I wanted to be the one that made my fiancée laugh, and our sex life had practically disappeared the second her best friend showed up. I didn't mind Laura, but I was ready for her to move out. So much so that I was about to do something that was going to piss off *my* best friend.

Speaking of Killian, I watched his bike as it cleared the hill and he parked alongside my truck. I'd put my bike away for the winter because I had a passenger every time I went anywhere now. I knew the threat of Dirk and the Death Raiders was over, but I had a hard time accepting there'd be no backlash, and the other clubs had been concerningly quiet about the loss.

Using the excuse to leave the house, I exited and met my friend halfway up the porch steps.

"I need to talk to you about something."

Killian flicked his gaze to the house once before following me down the stairs and into the garage. I'd had it custom built for special projects; it could fit six cars if I needed it to. Currently it held my bike, a work in progress, and my tools. The waxed floors gleamed as I sauntered to the fridge and pulled out two beers. Turning to hand one to Killian, I paused as he fussed with the sleeve of his shirt. He wore a navy button-down shirt under his leather cut, and his dark denim pants looked new. Even his boots looked fresh.

"You dress up or somethin'?"

Killian gave me that deadpan expression before taking a drag of his beer.

"That what you brought me in here to talk about?"

Touché, asshole.

"I wanted to ask how church was going?"

He'd been leading them for the past two weeks after I'd told the club that I was having Killian take on more of a role as I moved. It was a great way to start getting them used to him giving orders and handing out jobs.

Killian shifted on his feet, tucking his free hand into his pocket.

"Fine…there's some meetings coming up. Giles' cousin agreed to a meeting. Even if we're not going to war right now, it'd be good to establish a connection with him. You'd need to be there for that."

I nodded, because I had anticipated as much.

Killian took a long pull of his drink before jumping to the next topic. "There's been talk about Simon…"

Having not told Killian what Sunday dinners entailed, he had no idea his previous president would be in attendance within the hour.

"We'll ask him how he wants that handled. He'll be here soon."

Kilian's verdant gaze clashed with mine in surprise.

"You fuckin' jokin'?"

Shaking my head, I took another swig of my drink. "Sunday dinners. Family only."

He had no idea that included Silas, too.

"Look, I need to know what you plan to do with the apartment? It's yours to use as needed once you're president, and you know I won't give a fuck if you use it now or in six months. I also know you already have your own place, but Laura is driving me insane, and I need her to move out."

Glancing off to the side quickly, he tossed his empty bottle in the glass recycle bucket.

"Seems like you made up your mind already."

"You're never there... I was thinking if you could talk to her and see if it would bother her if you did need to crash there, that way you'd have somewhat of a roommate situation."

Killian laughed, with a shake of his head.

"You think that woman wants to be my roommate?"

Shifting on my feet, I crossed my arms, automatically sliding into president role. Something I needed to learn to stop doing.

"Frankly, I don't care. You're both adults, if she's uncomfortable then she can find an apartment in town, but what I need is for there to be a gap in time where she's not in my house every day. Callie told her to cuddle with her while they watched Twilight the other day."

Killian shrugged. "So?"

"They were in our fucking bed. I ended up sleeping with Max on the couch. I want to be able to fuck my fiancée in our bed when I want. Or on the kitchen counter, or the table. I had big plans for this house when we moved in."

Pinching the bridge of his nose, Killian let out a heavy sigh. "Fuck, Wes. I told you not to talk to me about fucking Callie. She is very seriously like my little sister, you asshole."

"Then consider this your motivation speech to play nice and stay scarce so Laura can have the rental to herself."

With a wave of his hand, he gave in while walking toward the exit.

"Fine, but if I have to crash there, I'm not worrying about offending her. If I take a sweetbutt back there, and we fuck, I don't want to hear any shit from you or her. Or Callie!"

I'd let him think whatever he wanted to as long as it meant Laura was moving out.

Feeling happier about finally having the house and my fiancée to myself, I walked back inside and when I saw Silas leaning against the living room wall, dodging the sun like a fucking vampire, I didn't even make a snide comment or try to hit him. Callie had called a truce with the moody fucker, but he was still on my shit list.

It made me uneasy that he knew where we lived, and one day when Callie got pregnant and we started having kids, he'd know where my children lived. I had to play nice, until I moved at least, and he had no way to get to us. Didn't mean I hadn't reinforced the fuck out of our property.

"Yay, family dinner," Killian said under his breath, passing Silas with a glare.

Seems it wasn't just my shit list that Silas had landed on.

It was dark as Callie and I walked down the stone path to our backyard. The night sky stretched above us, looking like a piece of velvet that'd been poked too many times with a needle, revealing white stars. I'd placed a string of lights to illuminate the path from the house to the small fire pit with Adirondack chairs, then another hung from the pit to the large sycamore off to the side of the yard.

"Today was fun." Callie sighed happily while leaning into my shoulder.

I grabbed her hand to keep her steady and smiled.

"Even though Laura left?"

"We were both ready for that." She laughed, but because she was slightly tipsy, a cute snort followed up the tail end.

"But you seemed so happy to have her here."

Rounding the fire pit, she was about to settle into one of the chairs when I pressed into the small of her back to continue down the path.

"Of course I was happy, but two weeks is a long time and I wanted to enjoy our new house without roommates."

"Fuck, I'm glad to hear you say that."

We walked down the stone path leading to the sycamore, and I didn't suspect that Callie even realized what we were doing.

"Besides, she wanted that apartment. It's nicer than anything she'd find in Rose Ridge that she could afford. She needs to find a job."

I needed to close the Laura subject, so I offered, "I'll get her something with the club. One of the businesses."

Pulling her close and making sure she was in the perfect spot, I took out my bandanna and placed it over her eyes.

"Trust me?"

"Yes, honey. I think we're past that."

Gripping her hand, I led her forward until her hand was on the wood plank.

"Okay, put your foot here and then stand up." She did as I said, and I stayed hovering behind her, making sure she made it up the rest of the way.

"Why am I climbing a ladder? I'm sort of drunk. This feels dangerous."

Focusing on the wood and limited visibility, I hefted my shoulder into the door and lifted it.

"Okay, place your hands here and just crawl onto the platform."

She was in a long sundress, so it was harder than I anticipated, but eventually she climbed all the way inside and I crawled in right behind her.

"Okay, take this off." I helped to untie the blindfold.

She blinked and pushed a few pieces of hair off her forehead as she looked around.

There was a tiny glow lamp on the little table I'd built, but otherwise it was dark.

"Is this…" Callie turned her head, inspecting the space. "A treehouse?"

I smiled, bending my knee while staring at her.

"It's our treehouse."

Callie's face snapped back, examining me with shock.

Placing my hand on one of the boards near the back, I dusted my fingers over the writing.

She moved on her knees, crawling closer so she could see it.

"Peter loves Wendy." Her gasp was cut short as she spun back to me. "I wrote that while you were sleeping when we were ten. It was always about us, but I was too shy to ever admit it."

I smiled. "I fell in love with you that first night you popped through that wood hatch. I couldn't stop thinking about you all year."

Callie swiped at her eyes letting out a tiny laugh. "I sort of had an idea when you brought two sleeping bags and enough food to feed five people, that next summer."

Ducking my head, I toyed with the edge of her dress. "I just wanted you to be okay."

"You pitied me?"

Scooting closer, I tucked a curl behind her ear and answered honestly.

"I did at first, but it was more than that. If it was just pity, I would have been able to stop thinking of you, right? I think I was obsessed, River. You were a little thief, sneaking in and taking my heart, staking a claim to my entire future."

Warm lips landed on my jaw as Callie tucked her head into my shoulder.

"So you took it down and rebuilt it here for our kids?"

I smirked, stroking her hair.

"I tore it down and rebuilt it here for us, because it's where we started. It's our origin story, and if our kids want to play in it one day, then they will."

Another kiss landed against my throat.

"I love you, Wes."

Wrapping my arms around her, I whispered back.

"I've always loved you, River."

# EPILOGUE

## THREE MONTHS LATER

Callie

THE GUN BUZZED STEADILY IN MY HAND AS I MOVED IT IN A STRAIGHT line down the arm of the man in my chair. He was getting a new skull with roses blooming from the skull, with the MC labeled across the bottom of the image. I'd been working at Dead Roses for roughly two months now, and while it was an amazing job and a thousand times better than what I had in DC, I had a lurker.

Taking a quick break, I swiped over the line I'd just drawn and sat up in my chair, heaving a sigh.

"Are you going to sit there the whole time?"

Wes lowered his cell phone but kept his boot up on the edge of the shelving system.

"I'm the owner, it's my job to be here."

My coworkers all smothered laughs around me. I had overheard one of them saying they didn't like me working here because they always felt like Wes was literally staring over their shoulder while they worked. It was tense, and no one ever felt like they could relax as long as the boss was around.

"Babe." I tore my gloves off, placing a piece of plastic over the work I'd done and glaring at my husband. "You can't come with me to work every day."

Moving his phone, he smirked.

"Actually, I can. You only work part-time; it's perfectly timed with my schedule."

There were more smothered laughs and throats being cleared.

Frustrated, I stood and pulled him into the break room, but before I could open my mouth, he was placing his finger over my lips to stop me.

"You're married to the president of a motorcycle club. Until Killian officially takes over, I have to worry about your safety, and I'm not taking any risks. Especially now that you're pregnant."

The fight fled from me. I knew he was right, and I wouldn't do anything to put the baby at risk, so I considered a compromise.

"Okay, fine, but you can't be back there while I work. It's not fair to everyone else."

Wes pulled me closer by the loop of my jeans, until his mouth was practically at my forehead.

"Fine, but you have to wear your property patch when you ink club members. I don't need them thinking just because you're touching them that they can touch you."

Pressing a quick kiss to his throat, I smiled.

"Fine."

Tipping my head back, Wes captured my mouth in a lingering kiss.

"Fine."

I left my husband in the break room as I returned to my client and finished his tattoo. By the time I was done, I was ready to head home. I was planning something with Sasha and Laura for a big Christmas-themed party.

For three months, I lived in a bubble with the man I loved, the club I finally warmed to, and my best friend, who was integrating with the club as best as she possibly could. She worked as Red's new assistant, which I wasn't even sure was a thing, but the books needed a new set of eyes, and Laura had a good sense for numbers.

She'd been living in the apartment Wes and I vacated, which as far as I knew was going well. She'd even befriended Natty, which was nice for me because it meant more girls' nights, which meant I probably should include her in the party plans. I grabbed my phone to jot down a note when all the sudden the bell rang over the front door, making my head pop up.

I heard the receptionist speaking to someone, and then Wesley's booming voice was cutting in. I set my things inside my purse and made my way out into the front, stopping when I saw a familiar man.

I'd seen his picture somewhere...

He was thin framed, wearing a button-down shirt and khakis, carrying a recorder and tablet.

"Mr. Ryan, I received your email. Thank you for agreeing to meet me in person, one on one. As I said a few months ago, a public barbeque wouldn't have felt safe to me," the man said, gripping the shoulder strap to his leather bag.

Wes smirked, ignoring me as I walked up. He did it because he wouldn't reveal his weakness, and I knew that but still stuck around, being nosey.

"You're the blogger, right? The one posting all the ballot measure stuff about the clubs?"

It finally clicked in my head. That's why he was familiar to me, his picture had been in one of the Instagram images. Not on his profile, but the secondary one I found that invaded clubs' personal lives and privacy.

The blogger swallowed, making his Adam's apple bob. "Yes."

Wes stepped forward and stuck out his hand. "Wesley Ryan. Owner of Dead Roses and President of The Stone Riders Motorcycle Club."

The man nervously slid his hand into my husbands. "Jeff Hynes."

"Great, Jeff. I've been wanting to talk to you about this group you've got going on."

Jeff narrowed his focus on me for some reason, maybe because I was just standing there doing nothing.

"I'm not sure what we'd have to discuss, Mr. Ryan. You stand for everything I'm fighting against. I'm pushing to get your clubs shut down, and there's nothing you can do to stop me. I know you think you're so strong, but the cops and the mayor are on our side. They're sick of the violence too. There was a random shooting here just a few months ago, and it was completely covered up. There are internal investigations that are starting, and we're not going to stop making noise until they hear us. We're done having you here in Rose Ridge."

Whoa. The guy was brave, I'd give him that.

I flicked my gaze up to catch Wesley's golden stare and couldn't help but smile. He was so sure of himself, this boy who once went to church camp and now controlled one of the most powerful clubs in Virginia. I never thought I'd be proud of him in this role, but I was.

Really fucking proud.

"Well I won't stop you from pushing your agenda, but you should know we won't stop pushing ours either."

Jeff glanced at me again, making me feel slightly uncomfortable.

"Is that a threat?"

Wes laughed, tipping his head back.

"No, little man, you'll know when I threaten you. For example, look one more time at my wife, and I'm going to shove that pen through one of your eye sockets."

Jeff's face flushed red, but I noticed his eyes didn't budge from directly in front of Wesley now.

Adjusting his strap once more, he inclined his head. "Rumor has it you're stepping down as president. You don't scare me. Without the club, you're not as intimidating as you think you are."

Wesley's gaze fell to the floor, but that smile on his face only increased in size.

"You know what, Jeff, you're right. I am stepping down soon, but guess what? You think I'm intimidating? You won't like the wolf who's coming after me."

Jeff scoffed.

"That supposed to scare me, or something? Let me guess, he's bigger and more terrifying than you?"

Wes lifted his head, gesturing toward the street through the glass window.

My hand came up, covering my mouth as I watched Jeff's expression catch on to what the man near his car was doing. Wearing his Stone Riders cut, Killian smiled while pouring gasoline all over the small blue Prius. I assumed it belonged to Jeff.

"Make your own decision about how scary he is, but there he is now. I guess he didn't like the way you were staring at his sister. Good luck shaking his fangs from your neck now. You want to wage a war on my club, it's him you're going up against."

Killian gave a little wave through the glass window then brought out a metal zippo from his jeans and flicked open the lid.

Jeff screamed, running for the door right as Killian threw the lighter on the car.

It went up in flames, and Killian disappeared as a truck came and then zoomed off.

Wes grabbed my elbow and pulled me in the back while Jeff ran toward the front, yelling for people to help him.

I grabbed my things and followed my husband out through the back entrance and got into the truck, hating myself for the smile I couldn't shake. This life was crazy, but it was mine, and I was embracing every single messed-up, sordid detail that made up who I was raised to be. The wife of the most powerful man in Rose Ridge, and even when that title shifted, I'd be the sister to the wolf of Rose Ridge.

This was going to be insane.

But I wasn't missing it for anything.

# ALSO BY ASHLEY MUÑOZ

The Wrong Boy

Vicious Vet

# ACKNOWLEDGMENTS

There are always so many people to thank for these books, and while I am usually dragging my family through five layers of hell to meet a daunting deadline, I didn't this time. I finished early, and without having to disappear into a dark void where no one heard from me for days on end. Yay for progress!

This book really was made possible because of a few key people, and I hope I do justice in thanking them all appropriately.

Amanda Anderson, during opening your own bookstore you still made sure I had your attention and help. Your dedication to helping me grow my brand has been absolutely essential in where I am today and the progress I've made since January.

Melissa McGovern, my girl. I will never forget how you saved me from naming Laura something deplorable. You never stop holding up the standard and reminding me of how far my writing can and should go. You never let me accept less, and I really can't explain how grateful I am for you. This book wouldn't exist without you. To my beta readers, Kelly, Amy and Casey. My ride or dies, thank you much for always pulling through, and for helping me craft this story into something worthy of celebrating and being proud of. Tara Finnell, thank you for reading this early and making sure I got all the MC details just right, and lets not forget that insane situation where you had to help me handle a real life MC scenario that nearly made me pee my pants with our own personal one percent club where we live.

Secondly, to my personal, virtual assistant- Tiffany. Thank you so much for standing in my corner for as long as you have, you never give up on me. We've seen the lows and experienced the highs, but through it all, you're always there. I couldn't do this without your attention to detail and constant encouragement.

To my Book Beauties, thank you all for your love and support for this book and all my others, I love you all and am so grateful for you.

To Beck, thank you for being my biggest supporter. You are the only person alive who only has compliments pouring out of you the second you see me. It makes me feel like the luckiest person alive, you loving the cover and premise for this book meant so much.

Lastly, but certainly not least- Thanks to God for creating this gift within me, and for loving me through all the dreams I constantly lay hold of.

# ABOUT THE AUTHOR

Ashley is an Amazon Top 50 bestselling romance author who is best known for her small-town, second-chance romances. She resides in the Pacific Northwest, where she lives with her four children and her husband. She loves coffee, reading fantasy, and writing about people who kiss and cuss.

Follow her at www.ashleymunozbooks.com

Printed in Great Britain
by Amazon

40015422R00179